Missing the Ark

Missing the Ark

a novel by

Catherine Kidd

conundrum press / Montreal

© Catherine Kidd, 2007
except all chapter headings © the respective creators or estates

Cover photographs by Catherine Kidd
            taken at Paul Spicer's cabin on Milbury Lake
Author photo by Pierre Arsenault
Edited by Andy Brown
Copyedited by Liane Keightley

Library and Archives Canada Cataloguing in Publication

Kidd, Catherine, 1967-
        Missing the ark / Catherine Kidd.

ISBN 978-1-894994-21-7

        I. Title.
PS8571.I34M57 2007   C813'.6   C2007-900777-5

Dépot Legal, Bibliothèque nationale du Québec

Printed and bound in Canada on 100% recycled, ancient rainforest friendly paper.

Distributed by Litdistco: 1-800-591-6250

First Edition

conundrum press
PO Box 55003, CSP Fairmount, Montreal, Quebec, H2T 3E2, Canada
conpress@ican.net
www.conundrumpress.com

conundrum press acknowledges the financial assistance of the Canada Council for the Arts toward our publishing program as well as the Department of Canadian Heritage through their internship program.

Dedicated to my mother, Carole Joyce Kidd
and to the memory of my father, Peter Lister Kidd

CHAPTERS

Book I

1. Green-eyed beans... 13
2. Lost quays... 22
3. Swing set... 32
4. Blueberry buckle... 36
5. Tympanic membrane... 45
6. Macula lutea... 53
7. Mummy bandages... 57
8. Tissue samples... 64

Book II

9. Pink narcissus... 73
10. Bestial rooms... 86
11. Saint Joan... 97
12. Simian crease... 106
13. The back of Mackenzie King's head... 111
14. Hide and seek... 121
15. Cephalopod... 132
16. Inn of the three monkeys... 136
17. To a field mouse... 147
18. How to skin a squirrel... 152
19. Mastodons... 157
20. A big fat hen... 163
21. The headless bride... 168
22. The camel's back... 179

23. Metaphormosis I: Ammonite... 192
24. Aeroplane bones... 198
25. Covenant... 206
26. A hollow leg... 213
27. Lunar unicycle... 221
28. Isis Millipede... 227
29. Metaphormosis II: Sea peach... 235
30. The Tower... 241
31. Zoose... 246
32. Das blaue licht... 252
33. Red delicious... 258
34. Hole in the middle... 264

Book III

35. Global warming... 275
36. Shades of yellow... 281
37. Bruxism... 287
38. Happy the ghost boy... 293
39. White elephant... 298
40. Arachne... 302
41. Ecdysis... 313
42. Hen's teeth... 319
43. Metaphormosis IV: Ant heap... 326
44. Biscuit tin... 331
45. Pin cushion... 339
46. Animal husbandry... 345
47. Bridal Veil Falls... 347
48. Crossing guard... 355
49. Horse mother... 357
50. Milk... 366

Missing the Ark

Book I

1

GREEN-EYED BEANS

> This question of answering when and where an event took place becomes more complicated, according to the theory of special relativity, because rods can change their lengths, and clocks change their rhythms, depending on the speed at which they operate when they are in motion. Therefore, we must answer the questions when and where an event took place in terms of a definitely moving system, or in terms of the relationships between two moving systems.
>
> —from *World Book Encyclopedia* entry for Theory of Relativity

The groom from the campus riding stable sends red roses to my mother. I never see the little gift cards but there must be some, somewhere. According to stubborn faith in things unseen, the cards are hidden in a kitchen cupboard behind all her baking ingredients, or upstairs among her mysterious bottles and jars.

I don't snoop through my mother's things anymore. After a certain point with people the case is simply closed and sealed with wax, you stop trying to figure them out. You just let them be there in the room like a lamp that's turned on, or one that's turned off.

Just now I see her. She is a cool queen sitting out there on the lawn, a chess piece near the sun-bleached yellow circle where the plastic turtle-pool used to be. Not a pool for turtles, but a pool of molded plastic in the *shape* of a turtle, with a small slide extending down the turtle's neck and into its shell. The shell of the turtle had been concave, inverted and green like a coloured contact lens.

The other day, one of the daughters of the cedar-haired woman slid down the slide and broke the turtle's neck. A bit of her leg flesh got caught in the snapping crevice, bruising her badly. How she screamed and screamed. The pool was taken away the same day, by the groom from the riding stable, who was always cheerful about doing things in the yard next to my mother's.

Just now my mother is snapping string beans. When I watch her through the kitchen curtains, the flowers on the table blur and bleed. Roses and baby's breath, corpuscles inside her house. If I focus instead on the dozen red roses right here on the table, then it is my mother, and the lawn, and the pile of beans she's snapping, which mesh together like cells, sunlit yellow-green. The cellulose fibres of a plant.

Baby's breath. The smell of it, recalling nausea. Two pudgy lobes hang on either side of Rose's face, those are her cheeks, with such tiny red lips between. A cyclopean nipple. A cupid's bow, eructing. Rose is my little girl. I love her best when four fingers and her thumb are curled about a strand of my hair, or held fast to one of my own fingers, which unlike hers are bony and yellow. Rose is less than one. I have loved her best when her pastry-cheeks, her tiny restless lips, were fastened to my breast, suspending for a moment the crisis of being, or provoking it. But now I've been prescribed pills, so Rose and I have had to stop this communion. From now on she'll be fed on formula from bottles which have to be sterilized. At times I hate the weight of her.

"You're hungry." My mother says this. I step over the threshold of sliding glass doors onto the small concrete patio, hot to my feet, then cool onto the lawn, and this is the first thing she says to me. She seems to say it every time she sees me looking at the baby, whose crib has been set out here on the patio like a cake, with a gauzy yellow cake cover to keep mosquitoes away from her blood. Sweetly, it seduces them.

I am both sulky and hungry today, apparently, yet I step out and turn a cartwheel on the grass, not gracefully. But for an instant, my hands are feathered green, and my legs are spread wide open to the sky. I feel the oily sun-heat slide between them, and think of mermaids in green bathing caps with sequins. Turning and turning, their feet turning to fins.

"I'm not hungry at *all*," I say to my mother as I slouch down like a walrus beside the growing mound of string beans. "I ate all those oysters," I tell her. "I ate the whole *tin*."

In fact, I'd even licked out the tin, unable to shake off the image of a feverish cat cutting her tongue on a jagged lid, licking oyster juices from a can. God knows where these images come from. The desire for symmetry perhaps, or resolution, the probable resolution of jagged metal against skin. Sometimes your mind just has to make the jump, when all the evidence is right there in front of you. In my mind, any television army doctor, hurrying toward a helicopter with supplies, will always be decapitated by the spinning blades, just as my mother will always lose her fingers in the soup she purées in the blender, in my mind. It seems inevitable, aesthetically. I will always cut my legs in the shower, even if the razor sits untouched on the edge of the bathtub. The image seems to leap up at its own possibility.

Looking at a surface of skin inevitably recalls the fluids coursing beneath it. It is incredible to me that people manage to remain discrete and self-contained at all, without somehow rupturing and flowing together, like a broken yolk or the piebald waters of the Fraser River. Some people are tougher than butternuts to crack, and are in no danger of this loss of identity. My mother would be one of these people. Some people carry their own containers, like the one I used to carry my retainer around in. They do not open unless pried.

But I do remember the silky rush of water down my legs, in a warm wash, and wondering what its ingredients were. Whether silvery particles of memory could be lost along with it, like the bath water with the baby. This is the only explanation which makes any sense to me right now. Sometimes when I look at Rose, I find myself believing that she must have absorbed in utero whatever it is I can't remember. As though amnesia were a liquid environment from which other things were born.

Salmon Court. This is the name of the cluster of student housing units where Rose and I live with my mother, and sometimes Dr. Spektor, when he is not home with his wife. The housing units are arranged in a big circle, with a breech for cars to drive in and park in the centre, marbles in a chalk circle. All the front doors of the cluster open onto the parking lot and courtyard, at the centre of which is a concrete-bordered island with a single tree. It is a large oak tree. These housing units were built in 1967, but the tree must have already been there, judging from its magnitude. Which is strange, to build a circular cluster of housing units around a single tree, as though it were the tree's idea. I imagine the roots of it underground, pale as larvae fingering the soil, spreading out their shadow-branches like a phreatic brain.

Around the outer circumference of Salmon Court, all the patios glint their sliding glass doors like the grooves round the edge of a quarter. On the day side of the circle, where my mother sits snapping string beans, the lawn slopes down to the highway which eventually runs along the coast. On the night side, which seldom gets much light, there's a deep ravine. I imagine that, from the air, Salmon Court must look like a big green eyeball. The highway is a high concrete brow, lashed with the mindless ocean beyond, and the deep crease beneath it is the ravine. A single tree is growing out of its pupil. Since I've been forbidden to stimulate my brain with books, for the time being I amuse myself with this sort of aerial nonsense. It's really not that hard to imagine seeing things from above.

Out here on the lawn is a metal swing set, and one of those carousels you sit on while someone pulls you round and round until you're sick. It's a cheap one and it wobbles. The campus housing unit was built for married students with children, which theoretically would be my mother and I, respectively, though I'm not particularly a child and she doesn't particularly act like she's married. At her most sentimental, she reminds me, *You know you'll always be my little girl.* But it is only in this sense that I am one, and it's only been since the birth of Rose that I ever remember hearing her say it. Babies make people soft in the head.

But I outgrew swing sets and carousels at least ten years ago, and Rose won't be old enough to play on them for another few years at least. So my daughter and I don't really fit in here. The other mothers who live in the housing unit have children who are two or five, or seven or ten. Some people in the unit seem to assume that Rose is my mother's daughter, because whenever we are outdoors it is generally my mother who dotes on her. The other people in the unit must wonder what I am doing here.

I see the swing set and the carousel every single day and I think I hate them. Most playground toys are essentially vehicles which don't go anywhere. You can go up and down, or back and forth, or round and round, but you can't *get* anywhere in particular. There must've been a time when I just wanted to *move* and didn't really care if there was no point to it. It's probably good for children to do that. They can worry about destinations later as long as they don't wait too long.

My little brother Gavin had learned quite young how to leap from a swing in mid-air, his sneaker-feet landing in the sand like paratroopers, before tearing off in some other direction, toward some other destination. He'd been quite good at this, which is probably why he isn't living here anymore. But it had always made more sense to me to simply stop pumping, rather than leap. Then wait for the swing to come to a natural halt, or at least slow down enough to jump without risking injury. Some people would say this was sensible. But it's not very courageous, and it takes much longer than jumping off in mid-air.

My brother Gavin is in the army now, stationed somewhere along the eastern border of Turkey. It's difficult to pick him out in the photos he sometimes sends home to my mother, it's been so long since anyone's seen him. I admire the multiple anonymity of uniforms, and how his voice tends to fluctuate between crackling static and the deep tones of a full-grown man neither of us really knows, when he phones home at Christmas time, if he phones.

The swing set and the carousel in the yard are painted shiny stripes of red, blue, and yellow. Primary colours. It's eerie how they sometimes look more real than anything else here. If these days were a movie, the scene would keep cutting back to the swing set and the carousel, but especially the swing set, as though it represented the most primal object on the landscape. The most uncomplicated or uncontaminated one. There must be a type of purity in motion for the sheer sake of moving. Which is why so many sentimental love scenes show couples dancing, and everyone gets choked up, trying to remember the last time they did something for the sheer kinesis of it.

"Take from the unsnapped pile, kitten, not the bowl," says my mother. "That pile is the heads." I keep eating all her raw string beans, heads, tails, spines, and all. My appetite keeps changing, even now. Sometimes I'm still eating for two, or three or four, or even less than one, though my mother says these things should have long stabilized by now. I think she used the word *cemented* or *crystallized*, rather than *stabilized*; some word associated with her work as a dental hygienist at Dr. Spektor's clinic. My mother thinks that my maternal habits should have become as routine as flossing by now, but I have to wonder how she's never noticed that she herself is the only person ever in the history of the family to floss routinely.

Rose stares at the sky through the yellow netting of her crib. Her face does a twist and seems to recoil into itself, scrunching her eyes and trying to swallow her lips both at once, her fingers opening and curling shut like sea anemone.

"It would be nice to have a few pictures of Rosie-Posie where she isn't scowling like that," says my mother. "Honestly, the two of you are quite a pair. Like a couple of old women."

Every time my mother catches my daughter not-scowling, she runs for the camera. But I think maybe Rose scowls because she can see things the rest of us can't, like through walls or underneath skin. Babies are supposedly unable to distinguish between themselves and other objects in their landscape. When Rose is looking at something, supposedly, she assumes that thing is part of herself. But I do wish that whatever it is she sees didn't make her scowl all the time. It seems a bad reflection on *something*.

The groom from the campus riding stable comes up the hill toward us, with a red plastic pail. It surprises me again that he is so young. I know from the water sloshing over the side of the pail that there are koi inside, my mother having offered to assist a man named Troy in the design of an ornamental pond for the new Japanese pavilion across campus. My mother knows nothing about designing ponds, but endeavours to wear outfits resembling the outfits of women who look like they might. Her wardrobe reminds me of loungewear worn by Diana Rigg on The Avengers. The groom from the riding stable also knows this man Troy, who is sort of his boss, but neither one knows that they both know my mother quite minutely. Sometimes the groom from the stable comes up the hill with miniature trees to show her, or a model bridge to straddle ornamental streams. It doesn't appear she's explained to him yet that it's actually a certain architect she's recently become interested in, and not a certain architecture. She tells the young groom that his koi are *beautiful, beautiful,* over and over again.

"Yeah, they're beauties, eh?" he says, chewing his cheek, while my mother's lips make fish bubbles, saying *beautiful, beautiful* over and over again. There is material evidence in the pucker of my mother's lips, an emphasis on *ooh* and *oh* sounds. A fish-bubble kissy-lip phenomenon which only appears when she speaks to men who are probably her lovers, or prospective ones. More haphazard versions of these *oohs* and *ohs* were extended to men in general, but with certain ones became more pronounced. Suddenly she'd choose to speak of ladies' shoes, the rolling blues of noon in June, her collection of ornamental spoons, and certain beautiful tunes to which she couldn't seem to remember the lyrics. She'd tilt her head and hum a few bars, hoping the young man would join in with the words.

But the groom shakes his head and has no clue. The tune must've been before his time, he says, daftly. He lifts his trouser leg slightly at the knee, then squats down beside my mother. They talk instead about how greatly appearances are improved by the addition of flowering plants. The groom squats with his brown trousers bunched up, while my mother smoothes her yellow sun-suit quietly over her thighs. Then she seems to remember that Rose and I are sitting right there practically next to her, and that we've never been formally introduced to the groom.

"This is my daughter, Agnes, and this is baby Rosie, my daughter's daughter." My mother and the groom turn immediately to gurgle at Rose.

"Look at her, will you? Have you ever seen such a lovely little girl? Rose is such a good baby, such a quiet baby. She never gives us any trouble at all, does she, no-oo-oh.... Agnes on the other hand was born face-first, imagine!"

She means to be casually witty, or something. But it surprises me greatly that she's been telling near-strangers the face-first thing for as long as I can remember. My mother's thighs spread open very wide, with my startled red face in between them. Why would she want to go handing people this picture? Sometimes she even reaches out and frames my face in her labial hands when she tells the story, pressing against my temples, reddening my cheeks. I can't fathom why she'd want to conjure up this image to near-perfect strangers, let alone to her lover who is scarcely older than I am.

I don't mind her telling the story, so much, if it's taken to mean I'd been born full of curiosity, just wanting to take a good look at the world, from the very moment I was pushed into it. But she might add the detail that I'd tried to brace myself back with my elbows, as though I'd taken one peek and decided I was better off where I was, which is why they had to resort to extracting me like a tooth.

"Wasn't really my fault," I tell the crouching groom, who doesn't seem to want to know any of this.

"I didn't retreat back inside," I say. "I was pulled back and out some other way. It's not like I was planning things that way."

"Well, that's sounds like you all over," says my mother, who believes I've been evasive about rites of passage since the day I was born. "Not saying a body shouldn't do things in her own time, and on her own legs, kitten," my mother says, "once she's located them, that is."

Sitting out there on the lawn, my mother looks as though she has no legs at all. Her yolk-yellow sun-suit is tucked under her knees like a pedestal, a sunnier yellow than my fingers holding back the kitchen curtain. I have retreated back inside the housing unit, my mother having embarrassed all of us with the story of my birth. I wait in the kitchen until the groom goes away again, taking his red bucket of koi with him. My mother and the groom don't kiss each other this time, as they predictably might, maybe because they think I am watching, which I am.

Now she sits cool as an egg on the lawn, as though waiting for something else to happen. Some other rupture to her serenity. The sound of the telephone ringing, or Rose crying, or dusk descending like freon gas. She doesn't keep her eyes on the beans she's snapping, not always, but lets them wander like sheep over the lawn, gathering wool. Sometimes she gazes across the yard, to the communal driveway where a hanging sign says *Salmon Court* in painted orange letters on brown wood. The sign is suspended from an L-shaped wooden gallows, like in a ghost town, swaying when it's windy and soaking up rain, getting bloated then drying out again, and weathering, weathering. The driveway leads up and around the centre of the courtyard in a loop, then doubles back in a running knot, trailing off to the road.

Listen. Lately I've been making some plans. I've been planning to write a very long letter to Rose, who will be one year old soon. Or sort of a letter but more like a zoological garden of things past. It seems the right time to do it, to put things in writing, though it's plain that once creatures of memory are penned, their behaviour changes irrevocably. Like creatures in zoos, the memories become aware of being watched, and have more limited options how to respond to the watchers' eyes. But seeing as there's this current concern regarding my inability to remember things properly, I must backtrack. I must follow tracks backward, and retread them. Once I catch up to myself in the present, I'll be ready to find some way of jumping off the swing. Though it remains to be seen what that might mean.

When my mother finally comes inside, she sets down her big bowl of green beans and touches a certain place on her throat with her hand, the place she always touches. She rubs it with her fingers as though invisible stitches were itching her. She comments out loud how little she notices the mountains here, despite how huge they are, looming green and purple like cabbages at dusk.

2

LOST QUAYS

Rose. Today on the grass by the swing set, the cedar-haired woman from next door tells me you are too quiet. She truly is apple-cheeked like the blue-gingham girl in the ad, forever biting into white bread paved with bright yellow butter. Cheek flesh round and shiny red, sun-speckled, beautiful. The woman has a child on her lap, too. Her son, Happy, is about four, crowned with his mother's curly cedar shavings, happily humming meandering tunes to himself. Encircling the crown of his head is a paper tiara with three-pronged construction-paper tulips glued to it, and the words *Happy Birthday, Happy!* in purple felt pen.

The woman has two other children, who are five and six. The older girl, Megan, is sitting at a distance, balancing a plastic cow on the roof of her plastic barn, while Regan, the younger one, is closer by, ripping up handfuls of grass and trying to stick them to her chin.

"My goodness, your Rose is so quiet," the woman says. "I hope her little ears are working all right," she says, earnestly, searching my face without guile. I'm generally unnerved by such a look. My brother used to give me that look sometimes but not since he was maybe five. A look of innocent non-comprehension, as though I've just sprouted horns. Sometimes a person can't return a look of innocence with the same kind of look, it just can't happen, in the sense of mirrors reversing things. As soon as a person starts noticing looks of innocence, it is likely that person has already drifted *away* from it, looking at it from the other side. The cedar-haired woman bounces her humming son and looks at me like that but I can't respond in kind. I am not able.

"I do hope her little ears are working all right," she says, searching. I look down at the top of your head, Rose, at the chestnut rosette where your hairs whorl toward a centre like the design on a thumb print. *Whose thumb, anyhow, this pressure from above?* In truth, I'm just as much in the dark as she is as to why you're so quiet. It seems to me you *can* hear things pretty well, most of the time. I haven't dared to think you *can't*. It has felt imperative to write everything down before it's too late, before something happens and something else is lost forever, but I've always assumed the thing in danger of being lost was my ability to *tell* the stories, not your ability to *hear* them. Wouldn't it be terrible, Rose, if I'd chosen to recite everything into a tape recorder instead of writing it down, a tape recorder which only plays things *once* then eats the cassette so nothing can be transcribed? Then it turns out you're unable to hear? Then the entire Lower Mainland falls into the Pacific because we're sitting on a fault line? Wouldn't it be symmetrical, according to some pattern set in motion by God knows who? Wouldn't it be stupid?

Baby seeks and maintains visual contact. This was listed as a good sign in one of the books my mother gave me about infant health, so I report it to her immediately.

"I know she does, those big brown eyes of hers," my mother says, replacing my face with her face in that space two feet in front of your face. Which is about as far as you can see, as far as I could tell from books. Your eyes do not refuse to meet mine, nor do they stare vacantly into space. They do seem to fix on objects with a certain impartiality, as though any cat or colourful plastic ring or human face were equally perplexing, fascinating, jubilant, terrible.

Imprinting. This refers to the projection of a mother-image by a creature of one species onto a creature of another species who is not its biological mother. Goslings do this readily, and chickens, and some mammals, too. A gosling who's taken from its mother may fix upon the first pig or dog or human it sees, and follow that individual everywhere. This looks pretty funny even though it's quite sad, because a pig or a dog or a human is not properly equipped to teach a gosling how to be a goose or a gander.

"What a quiet, good-natured baby," a peering woman said to me in the park, shortly after you were born. "She doesn't cry at all, does she?" I was just barely accustomed to lifting up my shirt in public and still hoped there'd be a sort of immunity nursing mothers had, which prevented strangers from coming up and speaking to them. Anyway it isn't true that you don't cry at all, but you do it with peculiar discretion. It is not usually your cries which wake me up at night, but a fussy, impatient sound you make with your feet, thumping against the plasticized mattress.

Either that or you wake me up telepathically. I can't prove this, any more than I can prove that my father was able to bend spoons with his mind. But as water is drawn to water there is a magnetism we fall into, you and I, for certain. It hasn't been a lack of connection that's been the problem, as I could easily explain to any doctor. More often I feel *too* connected to you, Rose, this person who was born older than she's supposed to have been, whose eyes look one age while her body appears to be another. I feel I've known you all my life and can't imagine you not being here. Anyhow I couldn't change things now even if I wanted to.

When my mother becomes tired of the chesterfield, she haggles a new length of cloth and changes the pattern. *If you don't like a pattern, change the pattern.* When a garland of popcorn and cranberries is long enough to run three times round the tree, she bites off the thread with her teeth and ties a knot. *If you're through with a pattern, break the pattern.* What laws decide who'll be able to change patterns and who will be broken down by them? It seems that certain people are able to readapt their living spaces to the periphery without ever addressing the unspoken things in the centre. With certain people, there seems to be a giant hole in the middle of things, which a body has to fill up with some surrogate.

Parthenogenesis. Since your birth time has remained pregnant, as though something still hasn't been born. Many times a day it occurs to me, *Shouldn't I be doing something?* But I've been forbidden to do much of anything for the time being, even anything much to do with you, until I cease to manifest symptoms of what essentially appears to be boredom. But looking inside, I'm doing millions of tiny invisible things, imperceptible changes at a cellular level which must eventually yield some *thing*. The splitting of parts into new and independent entities, which form more of themselves, without conscious effort. Sometimes choice is conceived by a nudge from the outside, some penetration of the personal by the extra-personal. But other times it seems to begin inside and of itself. I am surprised to consider that perhaps choices are meant to be gentle.

So I've been secretly planning these letters to you, Rose, in case I'm not allowed to keep you or you become unable to hear, or in case anything else bad happens, though not only for these reasons. And I've been discovering that just about any housecat or gumboot is able to mate with the private cells of a person who is writing, and conceive something. Which is exhausting, to be so vulnerable to fertilization by every single thing one sees. When every sense is a voluptuous organ drawing the world inside. It seems I'd been pregnant for years, in some sense or another, but didn't get the metaphor until it came too literally.

I remember my Great Aunt Hilda teaching me how to blow eggs, the pin-prick apertures she made in both big and little ends, so that the contents could be expelled like scrambled jazz from a saxophone. I must have conceived of myself as a human egg ever since. There seemed to be some fragile fault line which I always thought would rupture, if I didn't learn to hold things very cautiously inside.

Or perhaps the world was just set up that way for little girls. In such a way that one's sense of self-containment becomes either too gelatinous or too brittle; it either cracks from lack of flexibility or is too porous, allowing a million willful little things to wriggle in and alter the way a girl conceives of herself. She may learn very early in life that self-containment is something too easily ruptured from without, as though the whole big sky were a phantom lover who flies through the night, ravishing dreams. Dreams which survive build up over time like gathering cells, and finally something must come from them. Something must be brought to issue, after what seems like a lifetime of gathering material for the task.

But even if it's true that dreams are there to tell me something, it's still up to me to interpret them, and often I'm dead wrong. I suspect this is true of memory, as well. There's the sphere of what-actually-happened, which is unrecordable because of its myriad possible interpretations, and so it becomes fictional. And then there is the other sphere, the fictional one, which is meant to stand in for what-actually-happened, which fiction then becomes real. What memory selects becomes what is real, even when it contains only a few scraps of the original story from a skewed perspective. You can look at most any history book for proof of this. *What-actually-happened* is a primordial swamp of possible stories. Natural selection favours certain memories which then evolve and grow legs, creep from the primordial ooze, adapt themselves to the demands of survival in their habitat. Memory decides which parts of itself will be threaded with the evolving story, and which parts will remain buried as fossil fuel.

So what will I learn, by writing these letters to you, Rose? Whatever it is seems to stick like peanut butter to the roof of my mouth, not digested yet, not sunk to the visceral level where any nourishment can be gained from it. Things newly reckoned ride about on high horses in the head for a time, before they finally descend to the level where learning becomes sense, and becomes of the senses. Perhaps by that point there's nothing more to say of them.

Clinking bits of memory often come when I'm standing at a sink. This may have something to do with reaching into warm water, feeling around for knives and cups at the bottom. I'm washing dishes at night in the half-light of lamps from adjoining rooms, with the kitchen lights off, and there's only the feeling of warm water on hands, the dull gleam of stainless steel, the hollow noise of china objects in a sink. You get me out of bed four or fives times a night, until eventually I just stay up like blue fuzz on the television. Washing dishes becomes a substitute for dreaming. Among these interrupted dreams are a few disturbing ones about breasts projecting metal spikes. Stumbling from those dreams to you in your crib I hold you all the more closely, whispering *Rose, little Rose* in your ear, with every faith you can hear.

Lately, Troy the architect has been bringing blueprints and buckets of kittens to show my mother, while to another woman on the west side of the housing unit he brings horsemeat for her hyperactive Irish setter. I come out and sit on the grass with my mother and Troy as though we were a friendly party of three, my mother, her potential new lover, and me. It does seem perfectly natural, even the tension. A gravitational pull is exerted by my mother's attachment to these various men, and I feel myself drawn into their frame of reference.

The big orange cat who often comes round has just had kittens, so Troy the architect brings over a few to show my mother. The kittens look like cartoon mice with giant heads, ratty little tails, and eyes gummed shut like molluscs. My mother peers into the bucket and points at each fuzzy face as she counts them.

"Five!" she announces. "Imagine five of those little things all wanting a piece of you, poor mama!"

I reach into the pail and touch one of the little cats on the forehead, watch its side moving up and down, slowly. It isn't moving much. At last it pushes its head against my finger and gums at me, flagging the toes of a forepaw. It kneads its paws against thin air, pushing and sucking at nothing. Troy picks up the kitten by the scruff of the neck, so its face pulls back narrow as a Balinese shadow puppet. One of the forepaws is gimpy. It curves inward like a lacrosse stick, and is much shorter than the other ones. Also, there's a rounded bald patch on its belly which sticks out like a pink velvet egg. Other than that, it appears to be a fine little cat.

"Poor little thing!" my mother exclaims. She half-covers her mouth and stares at the kitten, while I can't take my eyes from it.

"It's okay, it's okay," I keep saying, meaning maybe we should put the little cat back in the pail now. I feel uncomfortable seeing it hanging there with us all staring like it's a rabbit from a hat. The kitten has no choice but to grin and grimace at us, with its skin pulled back so tight against its skull, it has no choice about much of anything. *It's okay,*

I keep saying, waving my hands downward at the pail as though this could bring the kitten back down to solid ground.

The litter had been born under a backhoe only a few days earlier, Troy explains, and this one had remained pretty much in the same position since birth as before it. Curled up like a shrimp, scarcely moving except to suck at nothing or knead the air with its gimpy foot. This one had been born last, like a muttered afterthought or an idea not quite formed. Maybe its mother had thought she was already done, reclining exhausted, contentedly licking clean the rest of her brood. Then suddenly this little one.

"Its brothers and sisters wouldn't even let it up to the bar," Troy tells us, "which probably saved it, seeing as it's usually the freaks which a mother cat'll turn on." His voice slows to the pace of a person reporting demonic possession as he tells a story about another cat who'd gone mad, killing two of her litter and eating them. I tell him it's not that unusual for a mother cat to eat some of her young, it wasn't like she was some kind of vampire. He says he *knows* that, he'd probably seen more litters of kittens than I'd ever see. So I tell him about mother hawks who lay only two eggs, then let the twin siblings battle it out between themselves. The larger sibling usually pushes the smaller one out of the nest, or pecks it to death, probably because there won't be enough food for both of them to eat, or because one of them wasn't healthy enough to live very long anyway.

"That's a hell of a thing for a young mother like you to be thinking about," says Troy.

"I don't know, pet," my mother agrees. "You'd have a hard time convincing me that it's natural for a mother to eat her young. *Imagine!* I've always tended to think there was something of the devil in a cat."

It strikes me as strange that my mother does not like cats. Also, that she calls all cats *she*, except the various prowling un-neutered males of the neighbourhood, for whom she seems to have a certain degree of respect. Most of the domesticated cats who live around the housing unit make her suspicious, they're partly the reason she's set up that lacy yellow net over the crib. She believes that cats are able to inhale the souls of babies, mouth against mouth, and run away with them. I don't know what a cat would want with baby souls but your grandmother insists the superstition is based in fact, that cats are seduced by the milky smell of the baby's breath and will coil themselves up on the sleeping faces of babies, smothering them to death. My mother swears to God she saw this happen once to a little boy, when she was just a very little girl. After a glass or two, she swears she *saw* this once, but she won't say where or when, or even who the little boy was.

Nit-picking. Anyone who has ever seen a mother monkey searching for, and plucking out, small parasites from her baby's skin knows that nit-picking is not something done without love. "You know you'll always be my little girl," my mother says, but then she also picks and scrapes my teeth with metal instruments, at least once every six months, and pesters me with pamphlets from the mental health department. If it isn't tooth decay, it's the decay of some other faculty. She finally has me almost convinced. So this afternoon, when she asks if I'd like her to make the phone call on my behalf, for your sake Rose, as well as my own, I say, *Yeah, okay, you might as well.*

She's sitting in her old mustard armchair, the armchair which used to be mustard, which has been recently recovered with a peach and navy floral print trimmed from old drapes. She's painting perfect white beach pebbles with clear nail polish so they'll stay shiny.

"Why not just put them in a glass of water?" I ask her. "They'll stay just as shiny."

"Because they'd grow slime on them, kitten," she says, keeping skillful eyes on her brush work. On the coffee table in front of her are several beer bottle caps, with pebbles set in them to dry. "I had to soak them in bleach all night to get the slime *off* them to begin with." So this is why the living room smells of bleach.

Yeah, okay, you might as well. I said it, and now sit anxiously in the hanging basket chair while my mother explains on the phone that the appointment would not be for *herself* but for her *daughter*. She doesn't refer to herself as your grandmother, but refers to you as her daughter's daughter. When she addresses you directly, she is Mum-Mum while I'm referred to as Mum. I am just one mum, while she is two mums. *Mine and yours, Rose.* She's been taking care of us both. She's arranging, on our behalf, the appointment which might help me see that a possible separation, presumably short-term, would definitely be the best thing for both of us, in the long run.

"She just needs a little breather," my mother explains to the receiver. "Oh, *really?*" she says after an interval, then makes an extremely disappointed noise which seems to correspond to the length of the waiting list.

Meanwhile on the radio, a woman in Toronto is talking about baby Wilma, who is an orphan. Wilma was found with long scars all over her large white body, like those slashes across a raw baguette before it's put in the oven. The scars were from the propellers of motor boats. Imagine an enormous white rabbit with no ears. Imagine the face of a baby beluga whale, its soft alert eyes full of simple questions with difficult answers. Now imagine the shape of a boat as seen from beneath the surface of the water, from the perspective of a baby beluga whale. A shimmering tapering shape, with whirling activity where the tail ought to be.

The woman on the radio says that Wilma has been seeking out these shapes and approaching them, following them around, imitating their sounds in an apparent attempt to speak their language. The stuttering, blubbering chatter of motor boats like the noises my brother Gavin used to imitate in the bathtub, pushing his toy tugs and sailboats from one end of the beluga-shaped tub to the other. *Brr-brrr-rrr.*

I'm hanging here in the basket chair waiting for my mother to get off the phone, wondering what Wilma thought she was *saying* to the boats. What she thought was being said to *her*, or whether she was only imitating. Whether Wilma thought the boat was a mother beluga or thought of herself as a baby boat. *Now imagine the shock.* Imagine the flip of the baby beluga mind, when this stuttering maternal shape turns round with a tail-full of razors, scarring her for life.

The woman on the radio says it happened more than once. Wilma had variously applied for adoption by motorboats, sailboats, personal water crafts, canoes, and kayaks. There'd been one potential mother, a canoe, whom she'd taken by surprise and entirely capsized. Its passengers were sent toppling into the chilly water, until a team of researchers came to haul them out and brought them to shore. Wilma herself retrieved the canoe, guiding its body through the water with her nose, and gently returned it to the humans she had accidentally dunked.

Yeah, okay, you might as well, I said. Because my mother was at the end of her rope as to how to help me. She'd watched me grow more and more despondent and even a bit paranoid. It seemed to her that it'd be better for both of us if I had some time to readjust to the changes in my life, without the added stress of caring for a baby. It would seem to make sense. The way the idea was introduced, slowly and over several weeks, I could only assume my mother was seeing something I hadn't dared to see. There was a fear hanging in the air that somebody's child would come to harm, unless somebody else took care of her for a while. So tonight I sit up with you, Rose, in the hanging basket chair in the dark, all night. The spider plant casts shadows of calligraphic bamboo on the opposite wall and I hum to you like an instrument with only one string. At two o'clock I hear my mother tip-toe down the stairs to go meet Troy the architect after Dr. Spektor has gone home to his wife. At last you and I are the only ones here, Rose, and you reach out your hands to touch my mouth, my hair, and my eyes, and you laugh when I do.

3

Swing set

Last summer before you were born, I had no problem wearing cut-offs with a yellow happy-face patch on the right-brained thigh, and a turquoise, short-sleeved sweater from one of my mother's old twin sets. Berenice kept all her twin sets, the salmon-pink one, the avocado-green, the mustard-yellow one, colours of melamine dinnerware. She wore the mustard sweater set and a brown skirt once for a photo, looking like a wasp with hardly any waist at all. There she was with my father, leaning over the railing of the *Queen of Squamish*, her lips so red like a gash and my father's hair blowing out of place.

But this summer I have you, Rose, and all my clothes are black and shapeless, which your Mum-Mum says makes me look like a widow or a depressed person. She wants to know if I am either of these, and would I tell her if I were. I tell her I'm a black fish, the name of salmon after spawning, leaving her to ponder the potential harm in filling my head with the spawning habits of salmon.

In the mirror I lift my breasts in my hands and let them fall, the weight of them. When I climb the stairs to my bedroom, I feel pins and needles inserted at my heels by invisible imps, and the empty heaviness of my belly. You are too young to really know what I look like, that I haven't been feeling too pretty these days. Or really that I don't have much clue what I look like anymore, outside of what I gather from my mother. In dreams I seem to resemble a plant.

The colours of the swing set and carousel in the yard are waxy primary colours, unadulterated colours, red and blue and yellow. I can't stop looking at them. Most days they make the grey sky flatten into two dimensions, so everything else looks like wet newsprint. Nothing but the swing set and the carousel assert themselves out there on the rainy lawn, even the grass looks grey today. Perhaps those colours are meant to jolt the mind back to the garden of our first world, when things were simple and uncontaminated by hyphenated colours with too many crayon box names. Sarasota Sunset. Midnight Teal. Burnt Umber.

But I prefer these, the mongrel colours. It's difficult to accept that there really are only three colours in the world, and all the others are their bastards. Whoever came up with that idea? Probably someone who also had romantic ideas about childhood and purity and how everything could be traced back to simple formulas or groupings of three. There's nothing necessarily wrong with that, but what if it turns out that there are *five* primary colours? If there are only something like a hundred pure substances in the world and everything else is made up of them, then almost everything in the world is a bastard mongrel, or else becomes one. The actual paint which painted those primary colours is, itself, a mongrel of minerals, a bastard of molecules. There can't be anything so bad about being one.

When I was five or six, I took a handful of oil pastels and left them in the sun in a salmon tin until they melted together. I thought I'd end up with the most beautiful colour in the world but that's not what I got. I got a muddy greasy hockey puck, which made muddy greasy marks of fish guts pinkish-grey. I still have the disc in a box somewhere, to prove this experiment was conducted with this result, but have never been able to draw any formal conclusions from it. Only that the term *pure substance* seems to have very limited application.

But earlier today I saw Regan swinging very high on the swing set. Her legs pumping up and up, then hanging down like two white rabbits on the descent, her lilac dress fluttering, with no breasts at all. I saw a thin pale strip of her little thigh, which made me so angry I wanted to slap her, couldn't tell you why. The worst names came to me, the names I almost wanted to call her. I hardly noticed her face and only vaguely noticed the shapes of her yellow hair in sunny baubles all over her head. She was all pale legs and fluttering and breastlessness.

I watched as the two front hooves of the swing set lifted up slightly and thumped down, leaving the ground, then pounding down again, with her swinging and swinging from the red and yellow beam, toward me, and away, and toward me harder. The hooves thumping, lifting higher, horse-mad with every pump of her little white legs, pumping and pumping. I could see that the swing set was going to topple over, I could see so clearly what was just about to happen.

Suddenly the two front hooves of the swing set reared up all the way, only the two back hooves still planted on the ground, the girl suspended in hang-time like a gazelle. The great blue-red-yellow arch falling back like a broken jaw, the crossbeam missing the girl's head by only a narrow stretch of sky. Then the whole swing set toppled over, with the little girl standing there screaming and screaming but otherwise unhurt in the middle of it all, the jaws of the swing set fallen open around her, the chains dangling slack in her hands. The only resolution of swinging too high was toppling over, I could see it all so clearly. Which is why I started yelling at the girl to be more goddamn careful with herself. She jumped off the swing and ran away crying. Then I had no idea why I was yelling at her.

Later I have to wash my Darth Vader duvet cover after the gimpy-foot kitten pees on it again, like kittens do, especially when there's a new presence in a house. The tiny cat goes into a hobbling chaos, chewing at things and peeing on things, mostly my things. As though I'm the one responsible for chaos in the house. But surely the chaos must have partly to do with Troy and Dr. Spektor and the groom from the riding stable. They're the ones currently upsetting the balance of things between you and my mother and me. Sometimes I think the only reason Dr. Spektor still comes around is that he knows he's competing with somebody else, each sniffing the scent of the other and adding his own. They are like me, mongrel colours to taint the primary three, whose units are relative and shifting. My mother would be yellow. She lightens things up for better or for worse, like a new coat of paint in the kitchen. My father would've probably been red, like the groom from the riding stable is red, because there's something inversely penitent about red, the B-side of ecclesiasticism. Red is what religions are built upon and try to contain. Blood, wine. Which leaves me with blue.

Who knows, the groom from the riding stable could be the best thing that ever happened to my mother. It could be that he's breaking a bubble which has kept us stewing in our own juices for way too long. Could be he's relieving some of the pressure building up in the housing unit ever since I came here. The young groom could be relieving stress, the way a four-legged table is more stable than a three-legged table. The more legs, theoretically, the less stress on each of them.

But I'm not sure the groom from the riding stable is absorbing his share of the stress. He's in and he's out of here, and doesn't leave much of himself behind. He only leaves a bouquet of roses and baby's breath, and once I found a pair of his suspenders by the kitchen sink. Which means the extra stress must've been absorbed back into the house, like a quantity of dark matter, invisible and unspoken about. Rose must breathe it in, the net over her crib couldn't filter out something like that. I must absorb it, too. Who knows, maybe the excess pressure starts to affect the internal wiring of a house, muffling sound waves, sending surges through cables, causing a build-up of ice in the deep freeze.

I do realize that none of this is the fault of the groom from the riding stable in any direct way. He's more like the guy who accidentally backs into a lever and starts up an infernal machine which has been rusting for years. Despite that horse grooming involves bridling things, breaking their wildness and taming them to domestic use, he's had the opposite effect on the wildlife of the house. There have been so many secrets, so many things left unspoken, that the addition of one more could easily break things wide open just when everyone hoped they were settling down. I almost wished my father would come home after all these years, maybe catch her with the groom. But you know, I wouldn't be surprised if even that failed to provoke a crisis. Some species have a terrifying ability to adapt themselves to just about anything.

4

BLUEBERRY BUCKLE

Thimbles of Eucharist juice to oblivion, in such a tiny crystal glass, a doll's slipper, only the fairest in the land would fit it.

— Carved underneath an East Van church pew and signed *L.U.*

When my mother drank I could easily love her, almost anybody could, there was something of redemption in finding her favour. It was not easily found, like a region of the body only a soulful lover could open up. The frills on the sleeves of her blue dressing gown are frosty regalia. My mother Berenice, the polar opposite of those sad bitch dogs who used to limp around Great Aunt Hilda's barn, always whelping, always whining, dining on leavings no one else would touch. My mother is always waxing incredulous that she'd somehow got herself to be a grandmother already.

But she's my *mother*. I cannot remember my face between her breasts, they are different objects to me now. Remote, controlled. She could pour them from a dress like cream, never quite so much that anyone could say they tasted it. She wore lilac perfume which rolled up from a tube like lipstick, the colour of dental wax. Lilacs, blooming only for a very short time. She gave off the scent of something you'd better pick right now if you're going to, else the opportunity be forever lost.

Yet her edges became softer, like towels from the dryer, when she drank. Dust specks from her old mustard armchair would fly about her head in lamplight like sprites, and I'd wonder again if she were the Fairy Queen after all. The one who steals the human child and hides her in the rushes, replacing one with another. Replacing one with an other, then *another* other.

"I am frankly *exhausted*," my mother exhales, "of selecting men in whom I have *precisely* no interest at *all*, thinking this would afford at least partial immunity, then falling for the poor bastards anyhow."

Gutterballs. This is my mother's phrase for men of a certain type, or rather men of a certain type of relationship to my mother. Men whose minds, she says, are in the gutter, or their balls are in the gutter, or their minds are in their balls which are in the gutter. "I *know* what they are thinking," she'd say, nodding her head like a wobbly spice rack, sage and thyme. But if she did know what they were thinking, she never told me, to any satisfaction.

"You know very well the sort I *mean*, Agnes," she says, wagging a finger in the air. "The ones who never really hit the kingpin head on, but sort of shuttle off into inconsequentiality. You'd best beware of those ones."

In this model, my mother oddly saw herself as the kingpin, who never got touched in quite the right way, never enough to bowl her over completely. Only to stand in wobbly expectation, until some bigger machine swept away the whole mess. But if the lovers were the bowling balls, this meant they had to do most of the moving around. It didn't astonish, then, that so many of them would start out well, but suddenly veer off in favour of lower ground; a more prescribed path or a narrower one, a previous relationship or back to the legal one, a more discreet *exit*. The only other option was to bang straight into my mother, face-to-face. And no one I have ever known has done this willingly if they knew what they were doing at all.

Rather than pay her phone bill regularly, my mother rents a space in a storage freezer, to store a fox fur a man once gave her, because she cannot bear having the thing inside the house, but she can't bear to give it away either. It's a cloak of three stitched together foxes, probably the fanciest thing she owns. It was a gift from a visiting dental surgeon from Japan, who had taken her to dinner, spinning slow atop the rotating restaurant downtown. The dental surgeon ordered veal, while she had chosen shrimp, with a tiny Neptunean trident to worry them out of their shells. The big box of foxes was sent to her at Dr. Spektor's dental clinic the next day, with a card reading, *To my Hot Red Fox.*

"Well, it was awfully gracious of him," my mother says, "but a bit like sending a lifetime supply of frozen veal to a cow."

"It says in one of my books that termite larvae are more delicious than shrimp," I tell her, "both of them are arthropods. Shrimp are like grubs of the sea. If you imagine them brown, instead of pink, they look just like big bugs."

"Ugh," says my mother, pulling her whole face away and tucking it under her collarbone in a manner resembling snails.

"Well thanks so much for the information," she says. "Not to change the subject, pet, but what I've been thinking lately, is that I'm not sure how much all this reading about bugs is particularly useful to you, right now. I mean looking toward the bigger picture. I'm not sure you should be filling your head with creepy-crawlies and their nasty little habits when, frankly, you've got a baby to take care of, not to mention an equally runny state of mind. Only to be kind, pet. We should just pack all those buggy books away in a box somewhere for a while, until things start to gel with your situation, if you see what I'm saying."

Perhaps there is a type of human permafrost, caused by the freezing of blood in the veins. Blood being mostly water, the molecules would change their shape, become pointed and crystalline, beautiful and remote, meltable upon the tongue, if only you could manage to catch one as it falls. A type of freezer-burn may occur, when the heart is frozen and thawed, and refrozen again. The biggest challenge of looking over one's shoulder, backward toward the past, is to survive whatever bitterness the mouth of history may breathe back at us, freezing our faces to salt.

My mother stands at the bathroom sink, applying lipstick as though her mouth is a face she is shaving. Her method looks as though she is trying to scrape something off, rather than put something on. The tube jerks upward in chisel strokes, downward like a trowel, while her blue vinyl flight case of cosmetics sits close by. The tool kit of that sculptor who liberates the true face hidden in the stone.

"It's not about covering up," she says, "it's about enhancing."

My mother's face is magnificently enhanced, which is not to say it isn't beautiful. Chartres Cathedral is beautiful, and Ukrainian Easter eggs are, too.

She claims to be perpetually misinterpreted. When my mother Berenice speaks to people, especially to men, her hands are pregnant moths, anxious to alight and lay on their arms, the backs of their hands, their shoulders. She moves her splashy mouth as goldfish do, hungrily or simply breathing. Colour rises to her face like grenadine. She only needs a paper umbrella, a slice of piña in her hair, to become the very receptacle of thirsting. But she claims to be perpetually misinterpreted, for all it gets her. There is apparently something she *wants* but it's seldom what she gets.

When my mother conducts her rendez-vous here at Salmon Court, they're either upstairs in her bedroom or in the bathroom with the shower going full blast. Or if I am upstairs, downstairs at the kitchen sink with the vacuum cleaner turned on. I have the impression she thinks they're being very quiet, but they are not. I hear scoldings for naughtiness, instructions how to move, suggestions where and how to brace limbs. I envision her knuckles against the steel frame of the kitchen sink, above which there's a small window, and wonder whether she looks outside, or whether he does. They would see the tree at the centre of the courtyard, the single tree which grows like a fancy toothpick in a slice of rye bread. Or maybe they keep their eyes closed, completely transported.

She doesn't think that I don't know about the groom from the riding stable, she only thinks I won't say anything about it to Dr. Spektor, and she's right. Why would I? I haven't really behaved any more responsibly than she has, in that sense. The sense of delivering too much of oneself into other hands. So now I must take care of you, Rose, and get out of my mother's place as soon as I possibly can. Out of these stifling rooms where silence is driven like a knuckle into the mouth, and bitten down upon. To muffle moaning or weeping or the rush of quick excited laughter.

I've started taking you with me out to cafés on Commercial Drive, or to the noodle shop on Princess Street, or the accommodating limbs of driftwood at Spanish Banks. Mostly I do this to facilitate my mother's meetings with the groom from the riding stable, or with Troy the architect, or with Dr. Spektor, when he's actually here, or whoever else. She can make as much noise as she likes, then.

Sometimes my mother and the groom go out to the campus riding stable together. I am envious of this. Imagine, in a stable full of *horses*, their swinging manes and tails, the quivering limbs of them, their glossy and muscular rumps. I don't begrudge her any of this, I honestly don't, but it makes me miss Buffalo man fiercely, the thick warm animal smell of him. It also makes me hope my mother never meets him, who is closer to her age than mine and can be as dumb as a bull with a ring in his nose in the face of flattery, the choreographed revealing of charms. That must sound terrible, to insinuate that my mother would make a pass at the father of her own grandchild.

My ear is pressed to the wall because I am alone in this bed, and it doesn't help to hide my head under the pillow. If you can't beat them, join them, I think, and press this auditory orifice to the wall.

Aural sex. Sex behind a wall, heard from an adjoining room. The sounds people make when they think they're not being heard. The discretion of noises and the discretion of speech seem entirely different matters, if one is a bit unmeasured then the other may be utterly precise. In most other situations, my mother never made a sound she did not intend, if she could help it. Was the groom one of those with whom she could not help it, or did she mean me to hear?

Tonight, with the moon framed in my window, it is me and the moon and the lover whose face I can't see, or won't know until I see it. That makes three. And the banging and me is also a party of three, the banger and the bangee and me. It takes two objects to make a banging sound, at least one of which is moving. Then there is the one who has to lie there and listen to it.

I pull my Darth Vader comforter up around my ears, and delete the possibility that they do not know they can be heard. Once, in a prayer, a false prayer of disgust and half-sleep, I prayed to God that you didn't have to listen as well, as though you would have cared, or even understood the sounds as anything distinct from the barking of dogs in the yard.

❧

After the groom from the riding stable has left, my mother hums little tunes, like a chickadee about the housing unit. She becomes temporarily cheerful. She barges in on my tooth brushing, stands behind me in the bathroom mirror, and suggests that I try wearing my hair up, *like this*, for a change. Suddenly the cool coil of her fingers in my hair, pulling back at the temples and attempting to affix a butterfly clip. But the butterfly clip will not stay, it falls and clatters into the sink.

Her fingers tremble with irritation as she retrieves her skinny cigarette from the side of the porcelain, where the countertop is golden brown in patches, like a roasted marshmallow from previous cigarettes. I stand too-conscious of her other hand, still tangled in my hair. The same fingers which had just been combing up the back of a young man, his blind and naked back. Her long and tapered fingers, the brush of a stable groom, combing whorls in the rumps of horses.

It seems to depress my mother that nothing can be done with my hair. She drinks another half-bottle of holy wine, and rubs the remains of her pancake make-up deeper into her skin like a salve instead of taking it off. Next, she becomes positively possessed by the desire to bake a blueberry buckle. Which she does, alone in the kitchen at four in the morning, banging pots and pans like gathering artillery.

You and I remain upstairs, wide awake under a blanket, with your yellow stuffed giraffe. You don't flinch at the racket of banging pots, but look up at my face, my wincing eyes and tragic mouth. You watch amazed, and your face tries to copy. You scrunch up your brows, and for the first time I see the crease between them, which is exactly like mine, which again is exactly like my father's was. Noticing this is both warming and chilling at once. Your eyes are darkly baffled like mine, the colour of potting soil or bitter chocolate. But more like potting soil, receptive and porous, taking things in. You search my face for a sign that whatever is happening is funny, so I puff my cheeks to make you laugh.

I open a chocolate box on the night table and retrieve a hidden book on neurological development. My mother would never object to me eating a whole box of Purdy's creams, but there was this other matter of being forbidden to over-stimulate my brain with too many books. So I hide my biology books in purple chocolate boxes. I stuff myself with anatomy and zoology in private. There's a certain page I keep returning to, with triptych images of neural webbing in a newborn brain, a six-year-old brain, and an eleven-year-old brain. The newborn human brain has only one or two little neural tadpoles swimming around in there, that's about it. Then suddenly, the six-year-old brain is a dense bramble of secret passageways, branches and channels as wild as ivy, everything being connected to everything else in the jungle of the six-year-old mind.

But then by the age of eleven, the branches are much more sparse again, much of the underbrush has been clear cut away. It's more like a birch forest now, rather than a jungle. The book explains that this is because, by about the age of eleven, the brain decides which of its various connections and patterns have been proven useful to the survival of the organism, and which patterns, never having been positively reinforced, must be quietly weeded away. What sort of information tended to get weeded away, and in favour of what, and according to whose list of priorities?

Even from upstairs, I can hear my mother discussing blueberries and the young groom's recent visit with her spoons and mixing bowls, a slurring membranous voice buoyed by vowels. Recipes in her old cookbooks have names like *Oven Smothered Lamb* and *Battered Shrimp*. There is a tiny CHANGE sticker on the side of her refrigerator, reminding her when to buy a new filter for the water purifier.

Finally I hear the hot oven door exhaling, and a loafish object being set down on a metal cooling rack. Then my mother goes to bed, of course, thickly climbing the stairs and closing her door. She had no intention of eating a blueberry buckle, only of constructing one. I am the one who is expected to eat it, to creep downstairs and eat the whole buckle, on the dark patio in the moonlight. Rose, you will sit with me, wrapped up in a blanket with your yellow giraffe. Even the trees out there will be stained the purple of blueberry buckle, like my mouth and my tongue and my fingers, when I feed both of us with your blue baby spoon, with the ducky on the handle.

I have no idea why I'm the one who is supposed to do this, eat the whole buckle and whatever other perishables, nor even why this baked fruit-porridge thing is called a *buckle*. Buckles are also metal clamps which hold up trousers. That sort may be more pertinent to all concerned, those belts which hang on the back of a bedroom door from a hook, like an eel, or slung doubled over the knob.

Buffalo man had worn a belt buckle with an American bison cast in pewter. This was only an artificial coincidence, since I bought him the buckle myself, and I'm the only person who ever called him Buffalo man. The buffalo belt buckle was like a Saint Christopher worn by somebody who only subsequently changed his name to Christopher. This rumination was the real reason I felt obliged to eat all those buckles my mother baked, I was bound to do it, padding down the stairs like a woman sleepwalking.

I had given Buffalo man the buckle on his birthday, which was only a few days before I dropped the bomb about the pregnancy. He made a joke about it being too late to worry about keeping his pants pulled up. So it was always the buckle I watched, when he stood beside the bed and pulled aside the strap to slip the metal tooth out of the hole. I would watch the metal head of the buffalo falling unclasped, hanging from his belt loop like a heavy bag of nickels. But I have not seen Buffalo man since you were born, and he has never seen you at all. We never made a decision on whether we were going to see each other again, though it felt inevitable that eventually we would.

Now, bursting with buckle, I sit in the rattan cocoon chair and read to you about spiders. I have arrived at the topic of spiders, after learning from the neurology book that the translucent casement covering the brain is called the *arachnoid membrane*. I point to pictures of spiders and tell you the names of their parts, their spinnerets and their pedipods, then read you a long description of their digestive habits. Spiders are able to inject enzymes into their prey to pre-digest them by liquidating their contents. In this way, they are able to relocate the messy task of digestion *outside* their own bodies, by snaring some other body to house the whole process. Then all they have to do is drink up the essence, once it's done.

5

Tympanic membrance

There are three things which are
stately in their march, Even four
which are stately when they walk:
The lion which is mighty among beasts
And does not retreat before any,
The strutting cock, the male goat also,
And a king when his army is with him.

— Proverbs 30: 29-31

The locked room of the old house on Dormier Street was tucked beneath the basement stairs like a small gland, oyster-like, self-contained. No one held a key to it except my father.

Just as I knew the words to certain hymns without remembering how and when I had learned them, I knew that there was a mat inside the room, and many stacks of paper things, notebooks and magazines and binders and books. I must have been inside the room at least once, unless a person can inherit knowledge of a room she's never seen, the way young cuckoos inherit the song of the genetic parents they've never met.

I knew there was a rowing machine in the room. Not the kind which plugged into the wall and had a digital screen to monitor how many strokes and how quickly, but an older type, with only a seat on an aluminum rack, and a set of handlebars. Under the seat were four grooved wheels, which rolled back and forth along the parallel bars of the rack, like a boxcar. The handle came at the end of a long lever, which was held in tension by two thick springs. The machine creaked when in use, back and forth, back and forth like a swing set in a playground. *Pull, release. Pull, release.* Until I found out what the machine was and what it was used for, I had imagined the source of the sound to be a torture device, or some other unspeakable thing which only grown-ups could use, behind locked doors.

The basement room was where my father went instead of going fishing or out to pubs, instead of working in a parish or an office or a factory, instead of sitting in an armchair in front of the fireplace and cleaning his pipe or his rifle or his boots. Sometimes he would stay down there for days, surfacing only for meals, which he would spoon into margarine containers and take back downstairs with him.

"What is Dad doing down there?" my brother would ask. And my mother would say, "Why don't you ask him yourself?" because she knew that neither of us was going to do that. We knew that my father didn't want to be asked, without knowing the reasons why not. I became accustomed to envisioning him as the sound of creaking wheels running back and forth along a track, red hands with white knuckles curled round a set of handlebars, like the hands of my friend Effie's father on the handlebars of his motorcycles, only different since the rowing machine didn't go anywhere.

My father seemed only to appear in shifting parts. It was impossible ever to see him fully and accurately, as though to do so would have been unbearable. Sometimes he would come upstairs half-dressed in knee-shorts and an undershirt, like a man sleepwalking, but I would see only the elastic brace on his knee or the hair under his arms. Other times I would steal a glance at his face, and could tell by his cheeks whether or not he had his teeth in. Or I'd notice only his hair, floating in dark wild wisps about his head, like a blizzard of gnats.

I drew a dark room in my mind and tried to place him inside it. Which was a fair task, not being certain what the space around him looked like, not knowing how much I had to shade in to be left with an accurate profile of him. If I didn't shade in enough, then I would envision him larger than he actually was. If I shaded in too much, his image would be too small, like the time I'd tried to draw a white crescent moon by colouring in the sky around it with black felt pen. The black had flowed so easily from the pen that I had gone too far with it, until there was not enough blank page left even to make a moon.

I envisioned the rowing machine. Once I had seen the seat of it without the rack, when my father had brought the seat out of the locked room, to fasten a square cushion of yellow foam to it with silver duct tape. I could envision the buttocks described by the two concave hemispheres of the seat, and extrapolate from there. My father's back would be bent, reaching forward to grasp the handles at the end of the lever. His head would be bowed, maybe his face would be scrunched like the faces of Olympic rowers or the galley slaves in *Ben Hur*.

I had seen his face like that at least once before. It was on an aeroplane, when we went to Winnipeg. As the pilot's voice announced that we were beginning our descent, the stewardess came down the aisle with a tray of hard candies. She said the candies would help stop the earache I was getting from the change of air pressure, and were a safer method of achieving this than plugging my nose and blowing until my ears popped, as I had been doing. The stewardess had winked at me, with pale green eye-shadow. I liked her.

"You go ahead and take a couple, sweetheart, if it's okay with your mom," she said.

"Well, they're *your* teeth," said my mother the dental hygienist. The stewardess laughed and I took two red candies.

My brother had the window seat and my mother was sitting beside him, in the middle, with me on the aisle. My father's seat was next to mine across the aisle. I was sucking one of the red candies, which turned out not to be cherry, only red-flavoured, but still it seemed to help. I sucked and swallowed and sucked and swallowed as the stewardess had told me to, then looked across the aisle to ask my father which colour he had chosen and whether it had a flavour, and whether it was helping. It seemed not to be helping. My father was bent-backed and red-faced, doubled over with his head practically between his knees. His large red hands were held over his ears as though holding the plates of his skull together.

My mother said that this was the reason we so seldom went on trips. My father found landings extremely painful, because of the punctured eardrum in his right ear. It was the hole in his eardrum which was responsible for his canine habit of tilting his head to one side like the RCA dog in order to hear things clearly. The hole also meant that sucking hard candies was not enough to counter the pressure pushing in on his unprotected ear canal. I imagined the air pressure needling into his skull, wheezing around in there and creating bubbles of air inside his head, air pockets holding the scent of aeroplane food and aeroplane carpets and the swirling blue chemicals of aeroplane toilets.

There wasn't anything I could do. I couldn't even pretend I hadn't seen him, bent over like that, though I wished with all my heart that I had not. The *Please fasten your seatbelts* sign had been lit up so I couldn't escape to the bathroom, and it was forbidden to go sit someplace else. The only other options were the exit doors indicated in red, located two at the front and two at the rear of the aircraft. And airlines tended not to consult people my age as to what constituted an emergency. The emergency of witnessing one's father unable to take pressure does not formally constitute an emergency, although damaging side effects have been shown.

A picture absorbed by the eyes is a strong intoxicant. It can remain in the blood stream for years, changing its composition in trace but significant ways. It must be common knowledge that pictures can have this effect, or television stations wouldn't bother warning grown-ups that certain programming might be inappropriate for family viewing. But no PG warning ever appears in the upper left corner of a retinal screen, to protect people my age from things they might not want to see their parents doing. And anyway the whole suggestion of parental guidance becomes moot in this case.

It is for good reason that the unmasking of heroes often occurs without forewarning, the impact of unmasking somewhat dependent upon not being prepared to see it happen. Masks have been snatched away by curious lovers, virtuous rebels, riotous rivals. Sometimes they are vindicated, seeing what they see, other times they're devastated just as easily. There are risks involved in the desire to unmask things. I'm telling you this, Rose, on the off chance that you may need to know it someday, if you're ever faced with a choice to know or not know something. I shouldn't call it advice because advice should only be given out by the very wise, but it has seemed to me that some illusions are vital.

Without them a person's head may explode, or implode. Illusions are a membrane between pressure without and pressure within.

Also, there's a difference between not needing to *know*, and needing *not* to know. I didn't need to know about my mother's latest lover, for example. Probably because on some level I already knew about him, his necessity, his inevitability. But I had needed *not* to know of the bowed slope of a spine, the puncture of an eardrum, the possibility that emperors may have their clothes stolen while they're splashing around in the bathtub. I had needed *not* to know of the soft pale face of Darth Vader, beneath the mask. I had needed not to know that in the final reel, *my God*, the mask and cloak would fall away to reveal nothing more than a face like any other, only paler, softer, more vulnerable than most to the tiny violences of invisible rays. In the dark theatre, my eyes had sought longingly the red exit signs to the left and right of the screen, but there was no point in leaving my seat, it was too late to un-see what I had seen.

There is no way of repairing disillusionment, despite that so much depends upon illusions. The illusion of time travelling in a straight line is one of these necessary fictions, and the illusion of humans being effectively smarter than dogs or cats, in terms of observable behaviour. The meanings of things in general is probably an illusion, but people do insist that things have meaning, for simple reasons of faith. If there had been any way of un-seeing my father bent over like that I would have done it, I would have followed it out onto the narrowest ledge of faith, and severed completely the suspension bridge of disbelief. So that there was no way of crossing back.

The air pressure in this cabin is controlled for your comfort. Perhaps this is what should have been written above the door to the locked room. It seemed that my father had to be very careful of outside pressure. It seemed that the pressure of things went directly into his brain and gave him headaches, and made him unable to do much of anything. Perhaps his ears were too open, just as my eyes were too open. They took in more than they were able to contain. Perhaps it was right that he learn to cover his ears, just as I had to learn to cover my eyes.

There had to be a balance between what pushed *in* from the outside and what pushed *out* from inside. Either there was not enough pressure in my father's head to counteract the weight of the world, or there was too much. I had hoped that it was the latter. I had hoped that there was so much force inside my father's skull, that the world was simply too thin and insubstantial for him. "Sometimes I think my head is so big because it's so full of thoughts," the Elephant Man was reported to have said. "What happens when thoughts can't get out?"

I had hoped that it was this way with my father, rather than the other way round. That his head might explode implied a certain degree of inner strength, force, even a certain amount of dignity. Explosions are things difficult to contain. But that it might implode was unbearable to consider, as though his head were a shrinking balloon, a Styrofoam cup in the oven. If my father had been more like Darth Vader, the *real* Darth Vader, before the unmasking, he might have worn a black helmet to hold the plates of his skull intact, to balance the pressure within and without. To hold himself together. Instead he locked himself in a basement room and rowed back and forth, back and forth. Perhaps in the faith that simple exertion would strengthen the force inside his body, the force pushing back when the world pushed in.

What is Daddy doing down there? my brother would ask, and I would tell him that our dad was only protecting us from the enormous weight and force of his brain. That our father's brain could lift a body into the air by sheer force of will, without even touching the person. That his thoughts alone could fill a room and swallow the air like a black hole, and so he had to hide them. I wasn't sure anymore that this was true, but thought we should do everything we could to believe it.

Other times I told Gavin that our father locked himself up for the same reason that a compassionate werewolf might chain up his human body during the day, so that at night his lupine form couldn't cause regrettable harm to other humans he cared about. He was only protecting us from the powerful creature he sometimes became. It didn't occur to me that this could have any negative effect on my brother's perception of our father, since most children were more impressed by Mr. Hyde than by Dr. Jekyll anyway, and would eagerly trade all their Luke Skywalker bubblegum cards for even a single Darth Vader one.

My, what a big strong man my daddy is, I said once. *What a big strong man.* It had been at a Greyhound bus station, several years earlier, when Gavin still had to be carried about in a backpack like an overdue library book. Bus stations and airports are like distilleries where years of words spoken or left unspoken are condensed into a few parting phrases or words of greeting, or oblique general reminders on how to go about having a safe journey. *Don't take any wooden nickels,* my father would say. *Keep your neck covered and don't catch any bad germs,* would be my mother's advice. This particular occasion was one of those trips to my Great Aunt Hilda's place, which was less of a visit and more of an attempted escape from the invisible elephant in the house. My father would stay at home to battle it alone, while the rest of us got out of the way for a couple of weeks.

Neither of my parents spoke during the whole drive to the Greyhound station. As soon as the green Torino pulled into the parking lot, my father got out and hauled both big suitcases out of the trunk, then went striding over the blacktop like a colossus. It looked that way to me, at least. All he was doing was carrying our bags into the station, to deposit them there, before driving back the same way he came and arriving home to an empty house, outside my vision. I was only about three, and couldn't have lifted even one suitcase. One of my father's footsteps covered more ground than three of mine, his legs longer than ski poles compared to the chunky limbs toddling breathlessly after him. Striding over the blacktop like that, he looked like a man who was going somewhere.

My mother had got out of the car more gradually, like a woman determined to take her time. She pulled endless green chiffon scarves from her purse, carefully draped one over her head and tied it under her chin. She watched herself calmly in the rearview before splashing out into the bright brisk air. The scarf was to hold her jaw closed, I thought. She sometimes reminded me to hold my jaw to prevent the speaking of things which weren't prudent to say.

Now she was pacing coolly across the blacktop several yards behind my father with my brother screaming and struggling in her arms. My stumpy legs in pink tights hurried as quickly as they could after him, then doubled back to catch my mother by her camel coattails, to help move things along. *My, what a big strong man my daddy is*, I babbled breathlessly, receiving in response a sharp cuff to the ear from my mother which rang hot like the hum of a space heater for quite a while afterward. I wasn't sure at the time what I'd done wrong, or wasn't sure *why* it was wrong.

It had been very chilly in Winnipeg. During the flight home I created as many distractions for myself as possible to avoid noticing my father. Luckily it was my turn to sit by the window while my brother had to sit across the aisle from him, but I thought it best to borrow my mother's blue gelatinous eyemask which obscured peripheral vision entirely. I took five red candies from the tray this time, and put them all in my mouth at once. This covered the possibility of speech. I kept my headset on even after the in-flight audio entertainment went dead to muffle my hearing as much as possible. From my mother's perspective I was making a scene, when a different stewardess than the first one came to collect the headsets and I wouldn't let go of mine.

"I suppose it would be too much to ask you to wait until we got *home* before you started making *scenes*," she whispered shortly. But what I was doing was trying to prevent a scene rather than make one. It would have been a scene to see my father curl up in a ball again like something unborn, it would have been a bad scene. Seeing it twice might have exceeded the limit of pressure my own skull could withstand, and I might have exploded, or imploded. Everyone had things which they preferred not to see, surely my mother of all people would have to appreciate that.

6

Macula lutea

One of the anatomy textbooks I'm currently forbidden to read defines *macula lutea* as the yellow spot at the exact centre of the retina where vision is most acute. This is the central area of the visual field, the spot which sees whatever is being directly looked at.

The book goes on to describe a sort of blindness, where what is looked at *directly* is exactly what the eye is unable to see. In this condition, the point of fixation is blacked out by a *scotoma*, or island-like gap, in the centre of the visual field. The subject is still able to see objects on the periphery, but as soon as she fixes her vision on any of them directly, they disappear. The point of visual fixation becomes a permanent black hole, described by the visible objects surrounding it.

To be a patient suffering from this condition would be very frustrating, if the thing you are most drawn to seeing is precisely what you are unable to see. In order to catch even an indistinct glimpse of it, you would have to focus your attention elsewhere. Only then might the desired object slip into peripheral view, like a blurry phantom who vanishes as soon as you turn your head again, no matter how quickly you learn to turn your head.

Perhaps it would be possible to rig up a trick with mirrors attached to your head, like the rearview mirrors on a motor scooter, adjusting them so that they might catch the reflection of the object in the blind spot. But you'd only be able to glance at the mirrors side-long, catching only an oblique and probably distorted reflection of the thing itself, not a reliable report of its particulars. Possibly your picture of what-you-can't-see would be no more accurate than if you locked yourself in your room, to weave speculative tapestries of what the object might have looked like, from the best and worst possible angles.

The locked room in the basement, where my father spent most of his time, had been a bit like this. If there were a movie about the old house on Dormier Street, the eye of the camera would keep shifting to the locked door of the room, and everyone would feel the prickling suspense of wanting to know what was behind it. Then, in the end, the door would swing open, and someone or something would be either devastated or vindicated.

It would be a strange little movie, Rose, don't you think? All about the environment surrounding certain mysterious interiors which would be absent or missing from the landscape. Maybe things are like this with all families; there's always *something* or other which a family conspires not to see. But the difference between a movie and this life, is that in movies you usually get to find out what the hidden thing looks like in the end. The whole trajectory of the story is aimed at that revelation. Whereas in this dimension, people carry secrets to the grave, which is how skeletons in the closet are made. Through the mutual merging of secrets between consenting adults.

I hope that you will be able to recognize this phenomena if it continues to happen in your own life, Rose. Perhaps you will also feel as though someone has cut out a central piece of the picture, and buried it in a box beneath the floorboards, sealed it up behind a brick wall, drawn a thick velvet curtain over it. The collage of memory or history you end up with is stitched together from peripheral scraps. You try to fit them together like a puzzle. Eventually, they begin to describe the shape of the missing piece, as an empty space. They name it as such, an *empty space*. The whole purpose of this historical quilting project would be to describe the environment surrounding an empty space. As opposed to throwing open a door and exposing the bones of emptiness. But there's no movie, and to this day I don't know why my eyes keep returning to the points of fixation which were traditionally blind, with dim rough shapes slouching along the periphery of the house.

Sometimes, before my father disappeared from Dormier Street, I used to creep round the side of the house where he had stacked up the various things he had found and dragged home. There was a rusty shopping cart with one wheel missing, and a knobbly glass shower door with the frosty silhouette of a voluptuous mermaid, and a roll of chicken wire the size of a canoe. There was also an avocado green porcelain toilet, a tractor tire, and a concrete pylon which someone had covered with a million Moosehead beer bottle caps.

Behind all these things was the window of the locked room, covered over with a piece of stained cardboard and a faded curtain in brown gingham. It wasn't possible to see inside the room, but it was possible to tell whether or not the light was on by the presence of a yellow glow fingering the cracks around the cardboard. Sometimes I would crouch down on the roll of chicken wire, put my ear up close to the cracks, watching the gust of my breath turn to ragged little ghosts on the pane. I would listen so carefully. Sometimes I could hear my father speaking to himself, only I was never able to make out the words. Probably it was his own stories he was reading out loud, the bible stories he used to write but never showed to anyone.

He might have called it *transcribing*. He was able to recite the stories simultaneously with receiving them, recording himself on a small hand held tape recorder, then writing them down later on. He didn't believe the stories came from within himself, but from somewhere *outside*. Those same forces might have been responsible for his punctured ear drum, an extraneous hole in the ear canal for the purpose of special correspondence. Some documentation must exist because he wrote the stories down, but it is hopeless to ask my mother about it. I have looked and looked for his binders but haven't ever found them.

The imagination is a crazy witch, but it is better to be for her than against her. I'm sure there have been times when that sort of thing must have been rather a comfort, hearing voices. To be guided by a disembodied but pretty little voice must be better than following no voice at all. It would have been soothing to listen, even if no one else could hear, and even if the words arrived all scrambled, which they sometimes did. Once I'd found a few of those little doll-sized audio cassettes with my father's voice recorded on them, speaking in a passionate but incomprehensible tongue.

There are men who grow black beards, like thick forests to conceal themselves within, in the hope of being mistaken for wolves. But some are the reflection of wolves, the image of wolves in negative film, the after-image of a wolf after all mythology has been ruminated. My father was not a wolf in sheep's clothing, but the other, the inversion of this. To shear his beard and cast his nightly colour off, he might have been exposed, as gentle, woolly, meek, and mild. It had taken all my strength not to believe it so, had even required his assistance. He had secretly conspired with us, leaving the house when he did to keep our private sense of symmetry intact. But even after he left I could hear him, I could see his shadow in the negative space he left behind.

7

Mummy bandages

> Under three things the earth quakes,
> And under four, it cannot bear up:
> Under a slave when he becomes a king,
> And a fool when he is satisfied with food,
> Under an unloved woman when she gets a husband,
> And a maidservant when she supplants her mistress.
>
> —Proverbs 30: 21-23

Sometimes a woman who looked almost exactly like my mother would leave the old house on Dormier Street all dressed up for the evening, without telling anybody where she was going. Those nights I might notice a sparkling rhinestone choker fastened round her neck, and know it concealed the sutures where my mother's head had been removed, and replaced by the head of her beautiful monster twin. I would never choose those evenings to snoop through the hat boxes in her closet.

Mum's the word. It was my father's habit to spell the word *mum* with a *u*, as in, *Give my love to your mum, sincerely, your dad*, written later in sparse notes left on the kitchen table. Most of the teachers at my school said it was customary to spell it with an *o* in this country. So I always used the whole word *mother* instead, avoiding the short forms and any other spellings of the things of which we weren't to speak.

My little brother used my father's *u* and called her *mummy*, like those ancient bodies preserved in scented salves and bandages, whose internal organs were packed away in jars with animal-headed lids, whose brains were removed through the nasal cavity with a hook. Those bodies had been known to reanimate. We had seen it on TV.

So Gavin and I invented a game called *mummy, mummy* to play in the basement those evenings Berenice went out without her real head on. First we would wind me round with a sheet of white gauze fabric, which my brother had found wrapped up in plastic in the storage closet. I sat tangled in my costume of cobwebs, on the tan vinyl Laz-Y-Boy which was draped with mosquito netting and missing a foot. First I'd sit smiling and calling to Gavin in cooing tones, *Come to mummy* with outstretched arms, promising lemon drops or plastic soldiers.

Eventually Gavin would creep from behind the stray zebra mattress propped against the wall, or from under an overturned washbasin. He'd be jangly-nerved and laughing, his cheeks shining like copper coins. When he drew near enough to touch, I'd place one veiled hand on his scruffy copper head and let him climb onto my lap, as though he were a fawn or a basket of knitting. He was still small and trusting enough to curl up quite happily, as though we hadn't already played the game a dozen times before. He must have known at any moment the mummy's face would change, but was able to suspend his disbelief and leave it hanging there, like the rubber Godzilla above his bedroom door. Gavin was a cowboy of reckless trust, as though each day were a set of silver spurs with not a speck of tarnish from the day before.

It was then the change would begin to occur. The flip from one mummy to the other. It would begin in my fingers. If they had been lovingly combing his hair, now they'd curl like spider legs about his scalp, they'd lift a swath of mosquito net and smooth it over his face and neck. Again I'd whisper *mummy* in chillier tones than before, like a creature in my gut dragging itself from sleep, my little brother screeching and scrambling from me. He would flail his arms and kick until he struggled free, then he'd *run*.

But I knew he'd never get away. There was no escape, upstairs was off-limits. *Muh-m-my*, I would murmur, stiffly lifting my body from the chair, stalking him across the basement floor with outstretched arms, brittle where they'd been soft only a moment before. He'd shriek and laugh hysterically when I caught him, when I pinned him to the floor beneath my knees, when I smothered his face with gauze and gently bit him. Then when I let him go again he would spring up immediately like a broom with arms. Then he'd become the sorcerer and I the apprentice. He became the spider and I the fly.

I was to play the roles of both mummies for the time being. The experiment I was concealing from my brother had to do with finding the precise demarcation line when the one mummy became the other, like mapping a lunar eclipse, charting the precise point when shadow and moon were fused in the eye of the viewer. Or like the rejoining of previously separated conjoined twins. I had to play the metamorphosis as fluidly as possible, to blend the two faces as invisibly as she was able to do.

Gavin was less precise in portraying the meiosis of mummies, his mummies shifted back and forth amid giggles and squeaks. One moment he'd be kissing my cheek with his small wet mouth, the next he'd be screeching in my ear and pinching my arms with his tiny blunted nails. To him, the game was basically unified, the two mummies were more like different facial expressions than separate identities. Their opposition was like writing your name with your left hand as opposed to writing it with your right. One version looked tidier than the other, but both were still under the command of a single body, which was his own.

What was important to Gavin was that things were there for his use. I knew this from watching him eat. While I divided items on my plate into discrete little islands, he wouldn't take a bite until everything was mashed together into one homogeneous paste. When no grown-ups were at the table, the mashing would be accompanied by mouth-made sound-effects, the crashing of buildings and toppling of telephone lines, the crushing of passenger buses beneath the tines of his fork. Tokyo could be populated with plastic soldiers or boiled carrots, all that mattered to Gavin was that he was much bigger than they were. He could chew them up and swallow them if he wanted. But if my mother came in to see what all the fracas was about, the crashing would suddenly stop and my brother would turn small again. As though he were only a four-year-old boy instead of the fifty-foot reptile he knew himself to be.

There were other monsters in the basement as well. I may as well admit the house on Dormier Street was haunted. Everybody in the family had a monster-double prowling around down there. My father and his monster-double were estranged from one another. His monster disliked him intensely, and was probably responsible for keeping my father locked away in his secret room, as though the survival of one depended on the virtual absence of the other. Yet I clearly sensed the presence of my father's shadow in all things dark and intangible, and loved him to distraction. He was the gallant villain in movies and books, the man who tapped out my heartbeat with the soles of his shoes, the masked man whose black cloak was vaulted space. But in whatever form he appeared, he seemed to dislike my father, and did all he could to trip him up and hold him down. In this way they were shackled together like convicts, each depending upon the other.

My mother's monster-double was more difficult to detect because it could assume many faces, which it was able to graft imperceptibly onto the face of my mother. The shadow-twin could weave a tangled nest beneath my mother's hair, peering out through the eyes at the back of her head. Her twin was a plastic surgeon, blending with a sponge so the two skins couldn't be told apart. You'd have to catch my mother on a very bad day to even trace the demarcation line at her throat, where the one face was molded over the other. Most days it was impossible to tell them apart, but at the end of the day my mother was the stronger of the two. It was she who decided when the twin was permitted to speak, when she was to hold her tongue.

Mum's the word. The phrase unearthed the tongue of my mother's monster-double, the part between the pursed and painted lips which sealed her in. This was why my mother's silence was never empty, why her terrible withdrawal of speech spoke more sharply than shrieking ospreys. When the glass bell of silence descended and steeled her, it was the tongue of her twin my mother withheld, like a woman screaming underwater. We felt her captivity echoing through the house even though we couldn't hear a sound.

My own monster-double lived in exile, a parallel universe only visible through certain secret windows, of which there were three in the basement. Hanging on the wall over my father's workbench was an old medicine cabinet he'd found in the trash, made of white painted metal with scabs of rust at the joints. The door of it was a mirror, with two more mirrors hinged like wings to the right and left sides.

My twin was deranged, inverted, she rewrote my diaries and spelt all the words backwards. If I wrote *star* she wrote *rats*, if I wrote *lived* she wrote *devil*. If I let the wings of the mirror lie flush with the body of the cabinet, there was only one of her behind the glass, like the transparent barrier dividing a person in prison from the one who comes to visit her. The twin was left-handed while I was right-handed, the left hemisphere of her brain was the right hemisphere of mine. But if I looked into her eyes she stared directly back.

She had no voice but could mimic me like a ventriloquist, mouthing the words simultaneously with my speaking them. Often I believed it was the other way around, that she was the speaker and I only the mouthpiece, that the words came originally from her while I could only amplify sound. Without her I'd have been invisible. Yet if my father ever emerged from his locked room while I happened to be sitting up on the workbench, she disappeared just as quickly as I did. My twin could reproduce herself indefinitely, the way cells do. If I tilted the wings of the mirror inward a little, there were three of her: one full-faced, one in right and one in left profile. If I turned my back to her and closed the wings about my head in a triangular box, there were thousands of her, all talking at once, or else silent.

I believed that all little girls had an almost infinite number of twins, which was why dolls were invented. Unlike my friend Effie, I didn't believe that dolls were the babies we were all going to have some day. Effie's Barbies didn't look much like babies anyway. Dolls were invented to represent the shadow-twins of little girls, who were all shapeshifters and could take on many forms. Little girls were different entities to different people, and were able to change their personalities accordingly, because they were made that way. As opposed to being born that way.

But sitting there with my round head in the triangular box, I couldn't help but be reminded that I still had one more twin, the neglected twin, the one who was excluded from the infinite group of us. *Infinity plus one.* She was the twin outside the box, the headless girl-body, who sat quietly waiting among the other tools on the workbench until I opened the cabinet wings again and rejoined her. She was the one who was always getting in the way, always under foot, always treading on everybody else's toes.

Headless bodies and bodiless heads. Movies and storybooks were full of them. Invisible girls, headless girls, bodiless girls, beautiful girls with no arms and legs, girls without faces, girls without tongues, girls who appeared as a series of dismembered parts buried below floorboards. Girls who could hear but couldn't speak, girls who were lovely to look at but couldn't see. Beautiful girls who appeared to be dead but were actually living, and beautiful dolls who could speak and move like living girls. Girls whose hands would creep away like white rabbits while they slept, girls whose feet could turn into fins, girls who appeared to be girls but were actually ocelots or vampire bats or foxes or geese. Girls who were under the spell of a wicked queen or a tyrant king, girls who spent their days weaving beautiful tapestries no one would ever see. Girls locked up in a dungeon or an attic or a basement to die of a beautiful disease, or chained to a rock to be devoured by sea monsters.

I was realizing several things about mirror images. That losing and finding oneself in this way was not much different from touching oneself in that way little girls should never talk about, if they did it at all. Some things about this realization felt just fine, while other things felt unwholesome. I wouldn't have wanted to get caught doing either one, my circular head in the triangular box, or my hands circling angles of myself, angling circles. Doing these things felt partly shameless, because alone, and partly shameful, because lonesome.

So later when I was sitting with my head in the triangle-mirror-box, and I heard footsteps coming down the basement stairs, I tore my head out of there so fast that the left wing of the cabinet swung back and smashed against the forked tongue of a crowbar on the shelf behind me. An infinite corridor of possible twins scattered over the workbench and onto the floor, like jagged broken teeth, not one of them cutting me. I was instructed not to leave the basement until I'd gathered up every single splinter of myself and safely disposed of them.

Collecting up the pieces from the concrete floor, I caught glimpses of my twin doing the same thing underground, a reaching shoulder or a hanging tassel of hair, the bending crook of a knee. I hid all these parts under the orange shag in the spare room, where my brother and I played *mummy, mummy*. So now there was another monster in the basement, who had her head and her body and all her parts, but hadn't reassembled them properly yet. She was *my* monster-double.

In dreams, I stitched her together with dental floss and a darning needle, but she always looked disproportionate. There were either too many parts or too few, and they were all of different sizes. The creature I was left with looked as though she'd been made up of spare parts.

Then one day, when I was brushing my teeth, my mother came in and looked my mirror-twin right in the face and said, "Damnit, you definitely have your father's eyes." It sounded like an accusation.

I was concerned that backward-girl would be expected to return the eyes to their rightful owner which I didn't want her to do. I relied on her to look back at me whenever I looked at her and would have hated to stare into empty holes. Probably I wouldn't be able to see her at all, if she gave up our eyes; I'd have to give mine up as well. That was the emerging cosmology, anyway, that anything that happened in *this* dimension had an equal and opposing consequence in the world behind the mirror.

8

Tissue samples

Our skins are so elastic. The largest organ, the largest elastic. Skin is pinched and springs back, for years of pinching it will still spring back, up until a certain point, when you pinch or are pinched and the pinch mark stays. If you keep saying the same thing over and over again, eventually somebody writes it down. Memory nests along the lines where elasticity is lost. The lines around her eyes a twin haiku of bird prints in the snow.

— Luther Underhill on a White Spot napkin somewhere in the Interior

The secrecy at the centre of the family, when I was growing up in the house on Dormier Street, was an invisible elephant which roamed from room to room. Even those of us who were unaware of its particulars could still sense the space it took up, the air it displaced. We all learned to suck in our guts, and breathe more shallowly, creeping along with our backs to the walls like spies. The elephant got bigger every day, feeding upon every single word we did not say. It became parasitic to the family, following us wherever we went. I did not know how old it was, but knew that elephants can live a very long time and have excellent memories.

My father had avoided the elephant by disappearing to his oyster-like room below the basement stairs, with his notebooks and his cassette recordings of God-mumblings, and his rowing machine which didn't go anywhere. My mother did it by making sure that all tarnishable surfaces were kept as shiny and white as possible, from teeth to kitchen chrome. There would be no elephant hairs found clogging the drains, no large round footprints plodding up the basement stairs.

My brother's method was to stage phony wars, to build kingdoms out of his mashed potatoes and peas, then plow down their segregated communities with his fork. I simply moved upstairs to the attic of my brain, where family ghosts allowed themselves to be plainly seen but not heard and not spoken about, as though the girl in my head were one of those Japanese cartoon cats who have enormous eyes but hardly any mouth to speak of, or with.

Many of these elephants exist. There may be one in every family, becoming a sort of family familiar, born of secrecy, breeding secrecy. I used to imagine ways of exposing the elephant, setting up drums of paint above all the doorjambs, making booby-traps out of white flour and a mop bucket. There ought to have been some foolproof way of detecting the opening and closing of doors, the comings and goings of secrets. It seemed inevitable that some sort of bomb would fall, eventually, like a blizzard of fingerprint powder. Then once the dust had settled I could point and say, *There, you see? There is our elephant, coated in dust.*

But these days my own memory betrays me, and I find only blank tapes of dead air where surely I thought I'd find evidence, eventually proof. At the moment there is nothing I can point to without looking like a lunatic, pointing and sputtering at nothing. My mother says I tend to over-react to things, making mountains out of mole hills. But someone has written of the analogy of a trout flipping and thrashing about in a pond, looking as though it has lost even the simple mind which trout are thought to possess. From a distance it appears that the trout has gone quite mad, until a closer view reveals a nylon line just barely detectable, and traceable to a hidden figure on the shore who holds a rod.

Perhaps the analogy ceases to be useful here. The secrets of a family are rarely so simple as to be traced to a single figure with his rod in his hands; the fisherman flatters himself who thinks so. Yet when the slippery flipping and thrashing continues, there comes a time when somebody must pick up a thread and follow it through to some sort of resolution. And if lately I have felt the task falling to me, I suppose it's because of you, Rose.

Sometimes I wake up in the middle of the night to feed you formula, then suddenly start hauling out boxes, looking for some object I'm convinced I have lost.

Because of the way people's stories tend to bleed and blend together over time, inanimate objects are sometimes the only way of proving that a memory you have is your own, that you didn't make the whole thing up. If I find whatever-object-it-is I'm looking for, I will record it in a notebook, with a detailed description under the heading *Observations*, along with anything else I can remember about where the object came from, and sometimes a diagram. I will develop hypotheses of origin, and observe how these are borne out by source exploration. These are some of the ways in which I plan to retrieve the memory which certain people believe I have lost. I would like to pin pages up on the wall, until they begin to make a picture, but must be more secretive than that.

Once I have compiled an inventory of everything I'm able to find, I plan to give the notebooks to you. They will comprise a sort of bestiary, one of those paper zoos of fabulous beasts who may no longer exist in reality but who lurk the corridors of memory regardless, vanishing in the mist of grey matter when you turn to look at them directly. The wide eyes of children see them everywhere, these fantastical beasts who may be grotesque, beautiful, familiar, and strange. They lie coiled in childish objects, trying to become the dreams and nightmares of grown-ups, who then have to decide whether to let them be or chuck them out. The reason parents are so grateful when you take out the garbage is that the task is analogous to growing up. Being a grown-up means finally learning how to chuck stuff out, and what stuff to chuck.

A few months after you were born I resumed a certain habit. It used to be that a wad of Kleenex was perpetually kept balled up in my left hand, for no other reason than to be holding something, an excusable something, a thing which no one would question reasons for holding onto, like a wallet or a child. Kleenexes were like this, too. People simply assumed you had the flu, which used to be basically excusable. Kleenexes were clean, yet in the plural contained the word *sex* backwards. Clean sex, inverted, absorbing any variety of errant fluids, bleached and recycled to absorb more of the same.

So for years I kept two or three Kleenexes bunched up in the palm of my left hand, at all times, even when I slept. Some people wear dental appliances when they sleep, to prevent them from grinding their teeth, to loosen the tight muscles of their jaws. A person might hold Kleenexes for similar reasons, to prevent the clenching of fists during dreams, the grinding of nails, the traces of crescent lunar stigmata on their palms in the morning. A wad of Kleenexes might be like one of those padded plugs or stoppers, which a doctor inserts in the mouth of a person in danger of biting off her own tongue. Such people might include clinical idiots, epileptics, and persons undergoing electro-convulsive therapy. Kleenexes offered a milder alternative for functional idiots like me.

But when you were born I had *you* to hold onto, rather than the Kleenexes, and you held onto me. Slowly you began to teach me other ways of holding things. I did not dig my nails into your arm, I would never do that. A baby is not to be held for the same reasons as a Kleenex. Not an absorber of tensions, a stopper to prevent the gnashing of teeth, a rag-end of desperation. When you were born I began to learn a different way. There was nothing else but to do it, to break a habit and make a new one, a newer habitation.

Then when my mother started her my-daughter-is-one-crazy-mother campaign I picked up the Kleenex habit again. Or sometimes it was one of your animals, the yellow giraffe, or the two plush mice like fuzzy dice in pink and blue. I'd carry them around all day, clutch them to my breast like lilies when I slept, since more and more your crib is moved to my mother's room at night. This is meant to be temporary. *Be patient, be patient,* the mantra seeming to answer all questions, assuaging all fears. But I must be cautious now, that some psychic hiccup doesn't strap me down to the bed for years, *be a patient, be a patient.*

So my mother may be right, that since your birth I've been unwell. That I worry about things which don't really exist or matter, in the real world. Certainly I've been preoccupied. My mother may be right, that moving here to Salmon Court with her was the best thing for me to do, for the time being. That I should rest and let myself be taken care of, after a fashion. She wouldn't be too happy about these letters I've been writing to you, though. They're only meant to be little stories, they don't seem to do me any harm, though she might worry what they actually *mean*. But it seems more important to keep the mind warm and active, than let it chill and congeal like a horrid jellied salad.

The other day I discretely rinsed kitten piss out of my Darth Vader duvet cover and left it hanging on the line overnight like a wet pelt in the dark. That night I slept under the white down comforter without the cover, which was less than comforting because of a pointless aversion to white things. My mother calls this aversion precious and irrational. Maybe so, but it's her job to polish people's teeth to keep them as white as possible. She also polishes kitchen appliances to keep them as white as possible. She bleaches her fingernails and her legs and her bed sheets to keep them as white as possible. But nothing remains purely white, without leakage of blood, expulsion of fluids, smears of streaky mascara and tears. Stained sheets are examined as evidence in several contexts, all turning on life and animation or the cessation of these.

White has several shades: winter, eggshell, milk. If primary colours are a holy three, then white is the absence even of these, isn't it, the unmanifest beyond the colours of the manifest. *White*, nothing, the absence of anything, or the presence of everything on which to tether faith. *White*, the most desolate Arctic place, sublime, hostile, silent. A surface absorbing no visible rays, deflecting everything, retaining nothing. *White noise, white light*, the absence of contrast, of differentiation. *White hope*, failing to attain the anticipated. The point where metal almost sublimates itself, *white heat*. The whites of eggs, the whites of eyes, of wedding dresses. Frothy peripheral environments to the stuff of life, where vision is not focused.

Rose. Today I stood looking at the smooth pale skin of your back in the mirror, swaying you to and fro. Even beneath the lacy yellow net of your stroller, the fresh outdoor air reaches you and gives you some colour. I see you are looking healthier. Beneath your skin I see all your purple veins, like beautiful subaquatic ferns. You are so small.

In time, I will give you a pair of shiny new boots, and a full empty field of snow to run in, laughing and leaving your mad little boot prints wherever you like. It should be just after a new snow, before anybody else has walked there. It should be new, and you should be able to mark it with your own two feet however you like. But there are a few things I must do before that time. Truthfully, my first desire when I look at these blank sheets of white paper, is to pick up a fountain pen of black ink and scribble things all over them. *Any* things. Even one word changes the whole composition of the page, it becomes a point of fixation, like an eyeball, a place from which to begin to see.

Book II

Book II

9

Pink narcissus

It's now my eighteenth birthday and I am sitting on a craggy rock at Burrard Inlet like the *Girl in Wetsuit*, a statue marooned on a tiny island offshore, which people mistook for a clone of the Copenhagen mermaid. Because of passing resemblance, and because the mermaid was more famous. Objects which look alike do not necessarily resemble each other reciprocally.

I am trying to look past the pitted skin of the water at whatever pulses beneath it. I've brought my biology notebook to take note of those things, and make presumptuous diagrams of them, for my course on invertabrates at the university. As though a still-virgin biology student in a red kangaroo jacket could have any understanding of water creatures. As though a surface-dweller could decode the habits of deep-sea inhabitants, or accurately figure them as they might figure themselves.

And I am a copy of a copy. Copying the pose of the *Girl in Wetsuit*, re-posing as *Biology Undergrad in Jeans and Red Velour Kangaroo Jacket*. The criss-cross laces of the kangaroo hang open like a discarded shoe, and salt mist condenses between my breasts as though the wet air were a lecherous god rubbing himself against my throat and perspiring. No body's face is mirroring mine, the sky is overcast today, the surface of the water churns and turns, chopping itself into glassy bits. No face can be reflected there unless dashed to pieces, like flour and lard under a pastry knife. I'm not really looking for faces today which is difficult not to do. You tend to read faces everywhere if you've got one.

Burrard Inlet, September 17th
Only still water offers up the reflection of a peering face. Only water which is unmoving, is able to reassemble the parts of a face and mirror them back like two statues in love with one another. Love is as impossible as sustaining the same pose for many hours, which some people can do. Artists' models, for instance, and mimes.

But it is essentially impossible, to be reflected in stasis that way. Someone is bound to drop a stone in the water and fracture the bottom-face into fragments. Or the top-face might fall in, dragging its body with it, in a desperate embrace of the face who is little but a shade of the seer.

They're both comprised mostly of water, anyway, which conforms to the shape of whatever receptacle will receive it. They are drawn to each other in this, the one falling into the other. So the beloved disappears in shards of water, and the lover is all wet. Feels foolish, wishes not to be seen. Or wishes to be rescued lest she drown, chasing shades in water too deep to be fathomed.

Eventually I do see them. *They open and close once every three beats of my wrist pulse, opening slowly, hovering like that before closing quickly in a spasm.*

Contrary to my diagrams, they often don't look round at all, but are harried-looking about the edges, like the flounce on a vanity table. *They are as graceful and elegant as any animal I've ever seen, they, having no brain, having no use for vanity tables.* I find there are tears stupidly streaming down my face, unchecked and unpremeditated. And these from what, from nothing. From watching the mindless binary spasms of jellyfish.

I draw a four-petalled floral shape in the centre of the diagram, and colour it powdery pink.

This pink flower is the sex of the jellyfish, who is either male or female according to our classifications. Unlike the marine leech, who is both, unless neither. Sometimes language is like those knick-knacks on the window sill of Great Aunt Hilda's porch. Both language and my Great Aunt Hilda consign to purgatory things which can't be reconciled, things which are neither here nor there but simply other, like marine leeches are other. This is supposed to mean that they're both male and female at the same time, as though the creature embodied a paradox. But surely a marine leech is no contradiction to itself. It's simply another order of creature entirely, not a hybrid of two things.

Being both one thing and its own opposite is a logical impossibility. Hermaphroditic creatures such as marine leeches are logical impossibilities, even though they seem perfectly coherent in themselves, and they don't appear to give a damn about my diagrams. Logical impossibility is the diagnosis of an observer, the agnosis of an observer.

I don't give a damn about my diagrams either, once they're done. Drawing them is like confessing your heart to a lover, who turns out to be sleeping when you thought he or she was listening intently. This may have been why I so stupidly wept when I drew jellyfish or leeches or polar bears at the zoo, or maybe it was a memory.

Once I came here with my father, to this very beach, when I was seven or eight. I waded out through liquid glass until the cold edge of it slid between my legs and slooshed the cotton gusset of my leopard two-piece, a sharp intake of breath, abdominal muscles folding neatly into themselves like a magnolia at night. I imagined genitalia as a sea anemone, sheer and smooth, opening and closing in labial spasms like the lips of a goldfish.

"My Agnes feels perfectly at home in the water," my father was telling a woman in a yellow sun hat, who had set down her tartan blanket right beside his. *Perfectly at home.* I couldn't hear him say it, I was out among the waves, but I knew he'd be saying something like that. My father's mouth appeared to be moving in tempo with the nodding of the woman's head and I knew he was talking about me the way a dog can hear her own name, can tell when she's being spoken about. I'd come to rely on it, as he relied on my conventional faith in his awesome mind which could bend truths without even touching them.

So I was obliging him, doing tricks and back-flips for the woman in the yellow sun hat. I had even recited Bible verses to strangers at his request, thinking them silly for being so impressed. It wasn't like I wrote the words myself nor even fully understood them.

The woman held down her yellow sun hat with one hand, and turned her head to watch me flip bottom-up like a leopard-skin duck to walk my hands along the ocean floor. I'd been briefly at peace then, frantic peace, hearing nothing but the footsteps of the Walking man thudding in my eardrums. He was with me even here, underwater, even upside-down with my legs kicking at the sky like pink slippery shrimp.

The soles of my feet fell back and struck the surface, as I flipped and came up streaming, the aeroplane pressure in my ears at the sudden change of elements. I could hear nothing but *pulse*.

The Walking man had been an object of desire for as long as there was breath, he had simply always been there. Even Darth Vader, my later obsession, was derivative of him. Or Vader was the voice and hands of him, who had no voice, no hands, no form in *space* except the sound of his footsteps which was incessant. But like breath in meditation, his steps were only noticeable when focused upon, and then became all-consuming, unbearable, huge like death. Minute and desolate, like death. And so I only noticed it sometimes, the muffled sound of his steps through dead leaves, usually at night just as I was falling asleep. Even if I buried my head beneath a pillow I couldn't smother the sound, once it had arrested me; it only amplified itself. Like the lover on the Grecian urn, the Walking man was never to be reached, would never reach me, only pursue me forever walking.

Sometimes the sound would feed upon itself. The footsteps of the Walking man would quicken by the very act of my listening to them. I would break into a sweat and plead with him to stop his steps, but this would only make him walk more *quickly*, the sound rushing in my ears, quickening my pulse. The warmer I became, the more quickly he walked. He excited me. I desired him. I wished that he would come to me and crush me at last, or quit me once and for all, quit his walking once and for all and leave me to rest in peace.

I felt compelled to give him form, in my mind's eye. He was tall, and dressed in a black cloak which sloped about his ankles, obscuring his feet, which did not appear to touch the ground at all. It was amazing to me that he could make a sound, he whose feet seemed not to strike the earth, but only struck a barrier of some sort, and broke it clean, creating sound.

It was several years before I realized his true identity. And so I find the first man I desired was nothing but a little girl, myself, reading her *own pulse* as a pursuer, a suitor. A man relying on the beating of her dislocated heart to move his steps, just as she relied on his pursuit to stir her pulse. And so the barest sustenance is implicated with desire, to be an object of the Walking man's desire, to be a little girl who figures her own pulse as exiled, aged, and other. Was it *this*, self-love, self-loathing, which clocked the workings of the heart from the beginning?

I waded out further toward the shimmering latitude slicing the scenery in two, cellophane-blue above, glass-green below, and I transgressing the border between them. Then suddenly from somewhere inside my belly, somewhere behind that bare section of skin between the top and the bottom of my leopard two-piece, came a hot stinging sensation which burned like leaking chemicals. It was beginning *inside* and burning *outward*, eating through the fibres of my stomach to get out like I was birthing a meteor through my navel. I yelled and clawed at the thing, only making it sting more sharply, then tried to run back to shore through water thick as tar. Stumbling-tumbling until at last, a damp clambering thing, I gained the beach and stood screaming at my father and the woman in the sun hat, who both came running as though they were my parents.

"You have a jellyfish burn, sweetheart, *that's* all," said the woman, crouching before me like an archeologist, reading rose-tinted hieroglyphs on my belly. I was incensed. If any subaquatic creature had touched me, I would have known it. I'd have felt it glide against my skin, the slither of incendiary mucous. I would have been able to tell what was happening.

"No, you're *wrong*," I insisted, "it came from *inside*. There's something inside, and it's going to eat a hole right *through* me. It *is*."

The hat woman just smiled maturely at my father, as grown-ups do when they think they know better. As grown-ups had done another time, when I reported that Tufty the cat had sprouted six pink pox along her tummy, and that we had to get her to a hospital. *They're not pox, pet,* my mother had said, though she couldn't seem to tell me what they were.

꧁

I pull the laces of my red kangaroo tight to my throat and close my notebook, that paper closet where creatures of my fancy were hanging suspended in two dimensions without depth. I had failed again to animate them, had only figured them as vanity tables, shapes of no relevance to any species but my own. My human feet crush the bones of crustaceans and cephalopods as I quit the beach, the crunching of my footfall like a pulse, or the presumption of explorers who believe themselves the only sentient beings for miles around.

Soon I turn incidental again, among others of my troubled species. A troop of Brownies are gathered at Lumberman's Arch to compete with each other in friendly contests of physical agility. The young girls are tethered to each other in pairs, joined at the hip with the boneless legs of discarded pantyhose, tied once at the ankles and once at the knees. They are running a three-legged race. Pixies and faeries and elves laughing at their own clumsiness, their foolishness, these mortals. Their bundled pedestrian limbs, the unaccustomed effort of co-ordination which they usually took for granted. The most graceful among them have devised little songs to orchestrate their steps, leading with the central composite leg and letting the other two follow. Others do not laugh at all, to find themselves suddenly sharing limbs with creatures fatter or thinner, taller or shorter than they. I might have been one of these. I might have panicked to find myself drawn into such a contest, such a monstrous fusion of bodies, at that age. I might've chewed through my leg to escape.

"You should have more *friends*," my mother was fond of telling me. I was never sure whether it was a practical suggestion or a measurement against some ideal. She was right, I should've had more friends, that would have been fabulous. But for whatever reason, I wasn't growing up to be that kind of girl. Such as it was, most of my friends were objects that could be set on a window sill and communed with in silence. I had collected to myself an inert menagerie of such friends. A tiny slipper made of amber glass. A litter of cats, black and white, from bottles of Gato Negro and Gato Blanco. Nine ladies dancing, porcelain maidens from packets of Red Rose tea. A set of wooden blocks with letters and numbers, and pictures of animals or objects whose names began with the letters depicted. D for duck. A for apple. M for mouse. The objects of my affection were still objects quite literally, I seemed to identify with things which did not speak. I also hated them for their silence, their lack of animation, their passive ability to be stuck in a pocket and carried from place to place by somebody else. Also I envied them this.

༺

I wished that there'd been some of those miniature circus tents, crisp green and white-striped, standing in dispersed caravans up and down the beach, as in old movies of discreet Victorian couples enjoying afternoon picnics by the sea. The women would disappear inside the tents and rustle around in there, then re-emerge wearing humourous bathing costumes, carrying parasols, with their hair tucked up in puckered bonnets resembling jellyfish. When my Great Aunt Hilda was young, no one ever used to see naked ladies. Possibly ladies were never naked entirely, in the popular mind. Possibly their innermost undergarments were permanently attached as with paper dolls, sexless and painted on their skin since they were first pushed from their perforations.

It was the day of the jellyfish burn. I was eight years old, or seven. My father had packed up the tartan blanket and my sand pail, while the woman in the yellow sun hat examined the reddish markings on my belly, arranged in a circle like a bite. My skin was bumpy and shivering like plucked chicken parts rolled in grainy bread crumbs, the sand and bits of barnacles stuck to my feet. Salty strands of hair wept cold on my shoulders and strayed into my mouth. The tips of my fingers were wrinkly and numb like cod tongues.

I wished that there'd been one of those changing-room circus tents, but there'd been none. The nearest changing room was half a mile down the beach, attached to the french fry pavilion. That changing room was dark inside, with gritty concrete floors which stank of pee and foot baths, with metal grids on the windows like a mental hospital. The toilet paper dispensers in the stalls were always empty and locked with a padlock, as though they didn't want anyone to break in and replace the roll. You had to bring your own.

"I don't think there's much to *do* with a jellyfish burn," said the woman in the yellow sun hat, "but they may have some *spray* at the nurses' station to take down the sting a wee bit." She had an accent like my father's, which explained why they'd wound up sitting beside each other on the beach and striking up a conversation. Scottish people have special radar for each other.

"You'd best wriggle out of tha' *suit* so we can get you off to the nurses' station," said the woman in the yellow sun hat. "You're shivering like a *leaf.*"

I stood there uncomprehending. Perfect strangers did not request you to take off your clothes and surely if they did you were not supposed to listen. I looked to my father. *He'd* know the right thing to do, in this case. He, who knew *nothing at all* if not how to go about *hiding* oneself. But, "Go on, then. Do as the lady says," was all my father said, "before you catch your death," as though death were an old boot in the pond.

The woman took an extra beach towel from her bag, done up like a store bought jelly roll, and handed it to my father to make a curtain. He held up the corners and snapped it open expertly like a table cloth, raising his eyebrows at me as though performing a magic trick. I hated that. He made me think of clowns who visit hospitals, performing unfunny tricks for sick children. As though the kid was supposed to forget the tube in her nose or the other one down *there*. I set my teeth at him but he'd already looked the other way. He was holding up the towel to shield me, staring off down the beach in the other direction, while the woman in the sun hat was kneeling down on the intimate side of the curtain, pretending to help me with my wet swim suit.

"I can do it *myself*..." I said.

"All right then, Snippy," she said. I turned away from her, toward the towel-curtain, where there was a terry cloth print of a thin woman in a grass skirt with scallop shells stuck to her boobs. *How did they stay put? Maybe suction cups, or little clamps.* I crouched down and pulled the top of my leopard two-piece over my head, scraping sand up my armpits, then reached up to drape the top over the edge of the towel.

The towel sagged, and my father started to turn his head.

"Done? Oop, sorry."

"Stop *looking* at me!"

"*My word*!" laughed the woman in the sun hat. "Whatever makes you think anyone's interested in looking at *you*?"

Now my ears were burning like the burn on my belly. My teeth were clamped together so hard I thought they'd crumble. Still crouching, I tried to peel down the bottoms of my two-piece, attempting to step out of the leg holes without standing up. First balancing on one foot like a pelican, then the other foot. Then I felt a hand on my bum. The woman with the yellow sun hat was brushing off sand. *Pat, pat, pat.* Her soft little fingertips on my bum going *pat, pat, pat,* the grainy scritch of her nails.

It wasn't my fault. I just scooped up a little handful of sand and chucked it over my shoulder. I wasn't aiming. But the woman started sputtering like a goose, and my father dropped the towel, and suddenly I was crouching naked under the sun. Which was glorious for a moment, until I realized that I was crouching *naked* under the sun. Then all sense of personal space fell away like the sides of a magician's crate. My space, her space, his space, all merged together with no separate containers.

The woman was holding the top of her bathing suit open like an apron, and was bouncing up and down, her red breasts bouncing up and down like gathered apples, sand jumping out like live fleas from between. She was spitting out bits of sand and making Queen-of-Hearts noises of scandalized surprise.

"Well, *fancy!* You're nothing but the *cheekiest* wee monkey I've ever met in my life!" Then her tears came, in supplication to my father. "I was only trying to help, you know, I never dreamed she'd…"

"You *touched* me," I growled.

"Your skinny bottom was covered in *sand*, you cheeky wee thing," she said, "you'd have got yourself a *rash* and I should've let you!"

My father's face was lifted in the silliest grin, he didn't seem to know what to do. He raised his palms and patted an invisible beast like he was trying to calm it. *There, there. Whoa, Nelly.* Too many untamed things were confronting him, things he'd rather push away for as long as he could. Two angry females. A pair of bouncing breasts. His naked daughter. The gathering eyes and whispers of passersby. My father gathered up the beach towel and brushed it off.

"You'd best cover yourself, Agnes," he said quietly.

"That's *my* towel," the hat-woman wailed, snatching it from him. So my father unbuttoned his short-sleeved shirt and handed it to me. *Here then, take this.* Now he was shirtless, curly-haired and pale, except for the reddened triangle at his throat and red arms from the elbows down. I put on the shirt and did up all the buttons. My father's shirt came down to my knees and smelled like him. Coconut oil and perspiration and dander, like a sweaty macaroon. I wrung out my sandy bottoms and put them back on, then my flip-flops with the rainbow straps. My belly was still burning as I stood by, while my father mumbled apologies to the woman, then allowed her to take down our phone number for some odd reason. *Just so I can check in*, she said. Then my father and I trudged up the beach together, in silence like soldiers.

Ho Ho. Red neon letters blinked above a giant rice bowl with crossed chopsticks, straight ahead on the port side. *Jolly, Roger.* My father helped me make a pirate's hat with a sheet of Cantonese newspaper, which had come wrapped around the chicken's foot I made him buy me for forty-nine cents at a Chinatown butcher's shop. The smell of newsprint and raw chicken on my head. We had both seen the tray of chicken's feet in the window of the butcher's shop, tangles of claws and segmented joints, pale raw skin. When my father said they were for making soup I thought he was fooling, so I begged two quarters then went inside and bought one chicken foot. Now I was walking around gesticulating with it, observing how people would turn around and stare. Testing how long I could continue making a spectacle of myself before my father would react. I held the foot up in the air like a cutlass, slashing it left and right.

Arr, I'll slash 'er ear to ear, I growled, *Keel haul 'er, that's what I'll do.* I was thinking of the woman in the yellow sun hat who patted my bum. My sense was that, for the rest of the day, my father would do whatever was necessary to restore things. I had already made him walk shirtless all the way from the beach to Chinatown, and I'd keep him walking all the way home if he didn't stop me. There was the shadow of an awkward grin still on his face, and it felt like I could push my luck as long as the grin persisted.

"I'm going to be a *Vam-pirate*," I hollered. "Agnes the Vam-pirate Bat keel hauls all of 'em, I'll get 'em *all*!"

"Do you even *know* what keel hauling is?" my father mumbled out of the side of his mouth as we walked along. He wasn't looking at me, he was busy smiling and nodding at the elderly Chinese couple who were giving us the widest possible berth on the sidewalk. The man frowned and clicked his tongue. I knew my father *hated* that, just as much as I usually hated disapproval, only today it didn't matter. Today it didn't seem to be *me* that people were disapproving of, but some *other* wicked little girl who was currently occupying my body. But more accurately, disapproving of her *father*. I marvelled at this. If I tried a similar stunt with my mother, it would be *me* who got the disapproving looks, while my mother would get sympathetic smiles and remarks of condolence from other women. Why was *that*? There seemed to be a certain vibe or pheromone which my mother possessed and my father lacked, which made people less disposed to sympathize with him. Until the people got to know them both a bit better, when things tended to reverse.

I remember quite clearly becoming aware that I was a wicked little girl, and that there was nothing I could *do* about it. At least not until I got to be a grown-up. The woman in the yellow sun hat *had known*. She had seen right through me, like my mother could when she squinted up at my grey dental X-rays. But my father didn't seem to see what a terrible little girl I was, and this surprised me. Pirate hats and chicken feet, I learned, could be obtained from him like candy from a blind baby with no sense of smell.

"No, I don't know what keel hauling is," I sniffed. *"Does it matter?"* I didn't suppose there was only one way of doing it. You *keeled* something then you hauled it around, like a cat hauling around a bird, just to torment it a little.

My father stopped suddenly at a quarter on the sidewalk. I picked up the quarter and stuck it in my eye, holding it there like a monocle. *Arr, maties.* I squinted up at him one-eyed. But now my father's eyes were cloudy blue so I couldn't see beneath the surface to the thousand living things beneath. *Were they poisonous? Did they love me?* Could he keep them quiet like my mother could, or was he more like me?

"Why are we stopping?" I asked him.

Then my father took me by the shoulder and ushered me over to a bench. I slouched away and sat on the ground instead. He sat on the bench. If I had been with my mother, I'd already have fallen through the ice, I'd have already gone way too far. Blue, numb, and floating, with my feet not touching the ground. But this was a new sensation, treading thin ice with my father. I'd pushed my luck a little bit to see how far it would go, and so far there seemed to be no boundaries. I couldn't quite tell where he stopped and I began.

"Listen," my father said slowly, *"keel hauling* is an extremely unpleasant thing to do to a person. It's when you take someone and drag them under a ship, you take a cable and run it under the keel of a ship, which is its underside, then you drag the person underwater against the sides of the ship, and up the other side." His voice was calm and instructive, as though he were saying, "Those ones there are rabbit tracks," or, "The nearest post office is that way, on the left." He was smiling as though I were a stranger, but I could see the beads of sweat standing out on his brow. He was still shirtless, and I was still wearing his cotton short-sleeved shirt like a smock with my leopard bottoms beneath. His words came sharply, through his teeth, which were false. It was the only time in memory that my father looked so directly into my eyes.

"Do you understand, Agnes? The person is dragged against the underside of the ship. And if you're not dead the first time, then they do it again. You come out with your skin shredded from barnacles and most of your bones broken. Can you imagine that, Agnes? Is that really what you'd like to do to the lady in the yellow sun hat? Hm?" He tilted his head politely and waited for my answer.

"Well, *is it*?"

Now my head was full of images of the woman in the yellow sun hat all bloody and shredded and dragged onto the deck like a mass of red seaweed. I really hadn't wanted that. I wished there was a wad of folded toilet paper in my pocket, to stuff in my ears and sop up all my wicked thoughts. I scratched at the ground with the chicken foot, like a hungry chicken does when it tries to find edible grains among the gravel.

10

Bestial rooms

Among smells of popcorn and pipe tobacco, sweet-stagnant water, fish and feces, I find a vacant bench near the Stanley Park Zoo. Black cast-iron arabesque, with wooden slats painted turquoise, like the subconscious of a swimming pool. The shrill lilt of peacocks reaches my ears from somewhere in the bushes behind me. *Ee-yeu, Ee-yeu*, like some taunting accusation, as though the excellent birds have caught me at an indiscretion.

Which it seems they have, as presently a chimpanzee dressed like a Davie Street hooker is soliciting me, knuckle-strolling back and forth past the park bench. She is decked out in a tattered gown of teal satin trimmed with peacock feathers and wilted lace, tawdry like a colourized photograph. The chimp wears hibiscus-red lipstick, and is carrying a tin box with a slotted lid, which she rattles to indicate the coins inside it. She thrusts the box at me and screeches, then grins all teeth. I resist. She curls back her liverish lips and waggles her head to and fro, so that the green plastic baubles affixed to her earlobes shake audibly. Still I resist, unsure of what service my coins would buy, or into whose hands they'd ultimately fall. I scan the crowd but see no one who looks as though they might be in the business of pimping a chimp.

She continues to bare her teeth, which only resembles a smile from a distance, since they generally have to scare the chimps to train them to do that. It doesn't seem to be a matter of choice with her, not a matter of *if* I pay her but simply *when*. She'd probably been trained to expect payment as inevitable, like tolls for road construction, or death. Trained by some human who believed that the end of persistence was having one's way, no two ways about it. Who was I to argue? I reach into the front pocket of my jeans and withdraw a silvery quarter with a picture of a lynx. I slip the coin into the slot. The chimpanzee curtsies graciously for me, but I strangely feel like I've been had. Even though I'm the buyer, I still feel that I've been bought, and now have nothing but lint in my pockets like Kleenexes under my pillow when I am sick.

The sharp report of a referee's whistle slits the air suddenly, and at once the chimpanzee turns and scuttles away, trailing her skirts through pools of orange soda and the ashen castings of geese. A bearded man in aviator sunglasses and a grizzled great-coat appears from behind a postcard booth and scoops up the chimp in his arms, hurrying off without turning around, disappearing into the scrum. In a moment I leave the bench in search of polar bears.

Polar bear. It is believed that the hue of a room has a substantial effect on the mental state of its inhabitants. Which is why lunatics are put away in white rooms or pink, to pacify, to mollify them. The polar bear pit has been painted pale turquoise like a swimming pool. And like the worst of swimming pools it smells, unwholesome, of astringent chemicals and waterlogged organic matter. It must have been deliberate to paint the pit this colour, this turquoise-green, rather than snowy white, to which the bear would've been accustomed. It must have been part of an experiment into the psychic adaptability of polar bears.

Perhaps it had been necessary to make the polar bear believe that he had died and gone to hell. First, he had been shot in the rump with a slug of drugs, in facsimile of his death. Then, he was relocated, and allowed to reawaken to this reeking scene of lurid green, where there had once been snow. This, predictably, would have a substantial effect on the self-concept of the polar bear. According to his previous experience, such environments as the green underground pit were more the habitat of his food than himself. They were home to those silvery comestibles to be scooped up in the claws and eaten. Thus the predator finds himself in an environment simulating that of his previous prey: the polar bear brain is inverted, flipped on its back like a crab, exposing vulnerable underparts to those who would prey upon him.

Around the pit are gathered groups of humans, like doctors in the gallery above an operating theatre, to observe the drama of unwholesomeness unfolding before their eyes. It seems the polar bear has gone *mad*. He paces back and forth, back and forth, swinging his head like a pendulum down there in the pit, his pink and grey succulent tongue lolling like a pepper steak from his mouth. But the remarkable thing, the thing which we should remark, mark you, is that the bear is walking *backwards*.

As polar bears tend *not* to walk backwards in their natural habitat, having no reason to, we are to take this behaviour as symptomatic of a mental split. The bear's gone bipolar, that's all there is to it. Just as the desire to move *forward* is indicative of mental health, compulsive *backward* movement betrays perversity of mind. It appears that the bear no longer cares where he is *going*, but is considerably more interested in where he has *been*. And so he walks backwards, retracing his steps, as though trying to decipher how he got from where he *was* to where he is *now*. Or perhaps, in effect, the bear is trying to move backward in time, leading with his rump in the delusional hope that some benevolent sniper will shoot him again, and that he will reawaken in the snowy pristine place from which he was initially abducted. But clearly, in accordance with our diagnosis, this hope is *delusional*.

If I were shot in the rump with a dart and relocated to a clean crisp room of pristine white with no mirrors no pens no notebooks no snacks no any-other-object in which to locate myself, I am sure I would do nothing but stare at my hands, which are yellowed and thin, like the fur of the polar bear now appears yellowed and thin. Neither I nor the bear would be able to camouflage ourselves among ice caps, we'd no longer blend and fit in with our surroundings.

When I turn from the polar bear pit, the eyes of the bearded man in the grizzled great-coat flash like a camera from behind mirrored aviator sunglasses. He is there for a moment, then he is gone, taking something with him. In pursuit of the invisible lost thing which I believe is mine, I follow him, in the direction of this most recent sighting. It leads me to an aviary of hawks.

The plastic plaque engraved white-on-black reads *Red-tailed Hawk*.

How dare you? reads the fury in her eye. She perches indignant, on a small wooden platform attached to the stump of a tree shorn of limbs. The tree resembles a scratching post, one of those inanimate whipping-boys built for the amusement of domesticated cats, those cats who still bear their claws but are trained against using them to their purpose. A prosthetic limb, standing in surrogate to the defenseless legs of tables or the bare ankles of human masters. The bark of the tree is shredded and scarred, with pustules of sap gathering like sores over its trunk.

Her sleek glossy head is framed in a diamond, one of the windows of space between the twistings of the chain-link fence. This is all that separates her hawk eyes from the eyes of onlookers, the unprotected eyes that could so easily be plucked out by her talons, or marred blind by her sharp curving beak. The hawk's beak is held open, soundlessly, as though her shriek were pitched so high that only gods could hear it. Her thin reptilian leg is jessed with a shiny metal shackle, bearing something like a serial number on the crimp.

The ceremony of innocence is lost. I didn't recall its ever having been there, I must have missed that part. Like being sent to buy popcorn, just as the planet Alderon is about to be detonated into billions of fragments, *Billions of voices suddenly crying out and being silenced.* Then returning to your seat and noticing the silence, the empty space, but not knowing how it got there. What conspicuous absence it was covering up.

What did I miss? you whisper, and receive in answer only a hiss.

Sshhhh... d'you want to miss the next part as well?

This was how it had been growing up. Time had passed strangely, somehow my brain had been sent for popcorn when it should have been watching the action. I always had the sense that something had been lost, that I had slept through something, and woke up older than I was supposed to be. And so I learned to fill the empty space with surrogates, replacing the moon with the Death Star for instance, and found that it functioned just as well. I'd seen the destruction of Alderon so many times that I knew what I'd missed, what was missing. I knew that merely missing a history did not necessarily prevent it from repeating itself. It would come again, it only needed to be rewound.

Turning and turning the widening history of my mother over in my mind, I would have thought she'd draw closer to me, close enough to hold at least in the cold embrace of memory, but she only flew further away. I'd begun to accept that it would always be like this, two magnets repelling each other. It might have been my appetite, so much more like my father's, which appalled her, or else my earth-bound need for her descent and return to my arm.

How dare you? scry the eyes of the raptor. *How dare you ask for more after all I've sacrificed?*

It might have been different had I been less artless, less without armour. I might have been more hearkened to if I'd worn a thick leather gauntlet on my arm, and been impervious to the changeable tides of her lunar nails which dug into my arm under the dinner table. I might have been more desirable to her that way. But it was not me who fastened a hood to her beautiful falcon head at the end of the day, to calm her, to silence her, to sever her connection to the world. She was perfectly capable of doing this herself. She would lie back in her big mustard armchair with a cool blue gelatinous mask placed over her eyes, like goggles of antifreeze. She'd lie there perfectly still and cool and detached.

"Listen, pet," she would say, "could you simmer down please. Your mother is resting her eyes." As though my mother and her eyes were entities separate from the speaker, and all three of them were worlds away from me. There were things she simply preferred not to see. And so it was no surprise that my affinity was with my father, his clumsiness, his failing sense of humour, his well-meaning interference with her life. It was no surprise that I identified with him, and sought out his likeness in men, recognizing in them his hunger, and my own.

The Petting Zoo. Within a circular enclosure of wooden fences they keep the animals from storybooks. Woolly lambs, floppy-eared kids, awkward calves with knobbly knees had gamboled about in books, before I ever knew them to exist as flesh and bone. Before they became understood as edible, they *spoke*, wore red woolen scarves knitted by their nannies, and were able to communicate with human children, frogs, trolls, and rocks.

Once upon a time they had shell-pink ears, over-sized heads and blinking eyes like limpid pools, brushed with long curly lashes. They had tiny black hooves like the shiny patent shoes I'd worn to Sunday School, trotting through storybooks, *trip-trapping* over footbridges. Or straying lost from the flock, only so that they might be found again. And they were always found again. At the end of the day, they'd curl up with their mothers, and tell of their adventures in plain and simple English. And their mothers would listen, and feed them tea and cakes before putting them to bed, beneath a smiling crescent moon with a night cap on.

The gate of the petting zoo is latched but not locked. The latch is like a parrot's beak clamping down over a metal finger. There is a small maze of fences just inside the gate, which you need to walk through in a short zig-zag to get into the yard. The sign over the gate reads *Petting Zoo*. It is the only sign I've seen which does not say what the animals are, but rather what you are supposed to *do* to them. The animals inside the enclosure are named that way, as the recipients of touch.

Sometimes the petting zoo is called the *Children's Zoo*. Children are those creatures who want to pet things, who understand things in terms of petting, who believe that if you touch something then it becomes yours. Their mothers go with them through the little zig-zag maze and into the yard, while their fathers stand outside the fence like uneasy lifeguards, wearing peculiar grins or shuffling their feet. Some of them smoke cigarettes, as though they are waiting to hear of the birth of one more, and whether it would be a boy or a girl. Sometimes the children would call to some of the men, *Look Daddy, this goat has an earring on*, or, *Watch me feed him, Daddy*, and the fathers would watch and nod, or stub out their cigarettes, or call things back. *Thatta girl, sweetheart. Atta boy, son*, or, *Don't let 'er bite off your finger.*

In one corner of the yard, standing spindly by itself like a small straight-backed chair, is a tiny grey kid. It blinks and hobbles in the sunlight, the half-sunlight, its shivering hindquarters straddling the border of light and shadow. Someone has built artificial troughs and mangers as well, and painted haystacks, even painted in a few artificial livestock in the stalls. All around are the trappings of storybook barnyards, as though to make the living flesh and bones of sheep and goats appear as fictional as possible. The small goat wobbles its head from side to side, shakes its floppy ears, then takes two baby steps forward, as in the game Mother, May I? It stops, blinks again, and bleats mechanically twice. *Mehh. Mehh.*

Scattered crouching on the sawdust-ground like chickens and hens are children and mothers, of which I am neither. Not a mother yet, not a child anymore, but some creature sketched onto the scenery as a practical joke, like a person in a chicken suit. I am awaiting erasure, a hand from the sky to reach down the pink rubber butt of its pencil and carefully scuff me away. The grey goat looks like this as well, tentative, two-dimensional, unsupported by anything of depth. Its shivering coat is grey, the barn is red, the shadows and sunlight slice through everything. *All things drawn and quartered.* Suddenly it seems that so much depends on touching the goat, recalling the compulsion of children to touch things. I have no child of my own yet, and no quarter in my pocket to purchase a handful of feed from one of the red-metal dispensers, attached like parking meters to the fence.

Then from outside the frame a crumpled wad of greasy paper comes tumbling, pushed along by a low gust of wind, stopping when it hits my shoe. *Soon the winds would change.* I turn to see the bearded man in the grizzled coat pop the tail end of a hot dog into his mouth and lick his fingers. His tongue looks unusually long, he is probably one of those individuals who can touch the tip of his nose with it. He wipes his mouth with the back of his hand, and lumbers away as though we haven't even been watching each other. I leave the petting zoo without even touching the goat, and follow the arrows to the buffalo pen.

Buffalo.

His body is commanding and indifferent, like an ode by a poet two hundred years dead. The mount of his shoulders and slope of his back follow a familiar pattern: ascent to a climax, a more gradual descent of events like diminishing vertebrae continuing to the end of the tail. The humourous irony of the hairy tuft at the very tip, wiry tendrils foreshadowed by the muzzle, branching out in ambiguous directions. Even now, I know that most animal attachments terminate this way, unruly and fraying, but with some nod to conventions of symmetry. The bodies of buffalo are inevitable, like stories.

The impossible premise is the head. That head alone would fill a bed and topple it, it is monstrously large, elephantine. Like the head of the Elephant Man, who tried to rest his huge misshapen skull on a pillow, and allegedly suffocated under the weight of it. They say he built a model church of paper with his one good arm, his slender and feminine arm, unlike the other which hung from his shoulder like a sacrificial lamb. The church is still on display, they say, in the London museum, where I've never been.

I always wondered why, while other girls were cultivating crushes on those actors best known for their portrayal of the Hardy Boys, I was haunted by strange erotic dreams of Darth Vader and the Elephant Man. Neither ever touched me, but spilled his mind like thick fog into my ears, stroking my brain. That each of them wore a mask, and that beneath the mask they were not known to be handsome, perversely, I think it was this.

And now am I similarly drawn to these massive beasts who once made the endangered list and came back. Unfit for survival not through natural selection, but through the schemes of men in their attempts to collect and commodify, unless this is also natural selection. Even the smell of buffalo seems a commodity, recalling some unremembered history of bear grease and beeswax candles, tack leather and lanolin and lamp oil, pemmican and woolen stockings, the boiling sap of maples, Hudson's Bay blankets, reddish curls of chiselled cedar, perhaps the very skins of them stretched taut across the wooden frames of snow shoes. Perhaps the buffalo remembered it all, the way history repeats itself, and does not bear repeating.

I touch the forelock of a buffalo. His coarse hair, oily and matted, swallows my hands to the knuckles, I can feel his hard and massive skull beneath. I can see the labial folds of skin around his eyes, and again at his stifle, his pendulous foreskin, the clefts between his hooves encrusted with manure. And over all this the mountainous shoulders arch up, descending his back to the end of his tail, his breath clinging in quivering beads to the hair of his beard.

I sense that I am not alone, that the bearded man is there again. His presence was prescient in the ponderous tread of buffalo, in the heavy imprint of their ruminant hooves like seeds split in half, hemispheres divided. I am distracted by him, cloven in my mind between wanting to run and wanting to wait. I want to see what will happen, or rather *how*, the only apparent variation being in the details. The arc of desire seems conventional, inevitable. It feels impossible to retrace my steps once I've entered into it.

Over my head comes a heavy pulse like a mechanical heart, or the angry breathing of a bull before the gate is released and its hooves pound the dust of the coliseum. I look up to see the jointed carriages of the toy train rattling against the sky and *he* is there again, hunched over the railings of the caboose and looking down at me. He sets his smoking pipe between his teeth and holds it there, then reaches into the inner breast pocket of his coat to retrieve an instrument. He raises the sight to his eye and shoots, *a flash*, and I am caught, blinded by his after-image as the toy train clicks away, to leave me standing like a stunned rabbit in the arc of head lamps. My voice alone tears after him, unbidden, "Who are you?"

But the train is gone. I stand with the buffalo for a still, suspended time. Still, but not unmoving, the way the centre of a spinning wheel appears still but is not. My head spins, my thoughts spin out in blurry spokes away from me. *I feel I am a vehicle for something.* There are thoughtless actions unbridled by presence of mind, which yet are familiar, having come before, played out by other actors or other characters of the self. Desire sometimes feels that way, like a sort of nostalgia. Not an invitation to move forward into something new, but a force drawing *backward*.

Desire is a drawing room in the back of my mind. Being drawn there, I might recognize it as a place of previous tenancy, the furniture and wall hangings having changed, but still I know that I've been here before. The object of desire has been here before also, in some form or another. I can creep among the ruins and recognize that person by scent. I'd be willing to bet that there is at least one in every crowd, the ones we're drawn to irresistibly for no reason we're able to admit. These people might just as easily become nemeses as lovers. They carry a certain charge which may either attract or repel, but which cannot diminish until some other force breaks it.

I feel a tremor up my spine, like a flash of dark wings on the periphery of vision. I turn to look over my shoulder and once more he is there, standing just a stone's throw away and slightly behind, exhaling vanilla smoke like an engine from another time. I am not surprised to find him waiting at the heart of this maze of bestial rooms, at last, like the seeds at the centre of an apple, or the worm which noses in blindly then eats its way back out. His lips, set in the bramble of his beard, are full and mobile, sensuous lips which don't seem to close completely, but hang slightly open and moist. The shoulders of his great-coat are hirsute and barbarous, holding dust like a carpet. Holding scent, the sleek musky oil of his hair and the heady incense of vanilla pipe tobacco. His nose is large and bumped, as though it has been broken. As though he'd been using it for years to push his way through revolving doors.

I can't see his eyes. Instead I see myself, reflected twice, moon-faced and sallow in the mirrored lenses of his sunglasses. His hands are remarkably large, unbuttoning his coat and reaching inside to take out his camera again. There is a yellow sunflower, bright and artificial, pinned to his lapel.

"I thought I should offer you this," he says, making as if to unlatch the lock of his camera and pull out its celluloid entrails. "I didn't mean to snap at you like that, I was actually aiming for the buffalo. A man needs to be sensitive about these things, these days. I'll hand over the negatives if you like, just say the word."

His fingers click open the lock, keeping the camera pressed shut, waiting, but I'm not willing to speak to him just yet. He will speak once more before swinging open his camera and exposing his film to the light, I am willing to bet, and willing to wait. I want to hear his voice again anyway, and so I say nothing.

"Here I stand," he says wryly, "on the very brink of exposing myself to a young lady I haven't even met yet, and she hasn't the courtesy to stop me from doing it." His voice bears as many textures as trees, a soft fluttering in the upper registers, a coarser cadence below, the coagulate thickness of its resin. The smoothness of those places where the bark is stripped away.

"Your call," I say. I want to know if he'll actually do it. How well he can read me, how easily I can be read, or not. I want to know whether or not he'll pull out the film like doves from a hat, send it spiralling to the ground in golden curls. But instead he flicks the closure with his thumb, back into locked position.

"Then I'll keep it," he says, "since ours is not a culture which believes that souls are captured in the blink of a shutter."

"Since it may not be a culture which believes in souls at all," I say, unsure whether or not I still do.

11

SAINT JOAN

When I was in grade two, my mother cut my hair terribly short and enrolled me in an after-school care program. It was like a grade two holding-tank for children who couldn't be trusted with their own set of keys. Also for those kids with no dads whose mothers worked all day, and those with no mums whose fathers worked all day. And for the kids whose parents both worked late, and for the kids whose mums wanted to watch The Oprah Winfrey Show undistracted by their own home-game version. I was none of these. My father was home all day, every day, while my mother was at work helping Dr. Spektor drill holes in people's teeth. After the broken-mirror incident in the basement, my mother decided it might be better for everyone involved if I simply stayed at school, until somebody could come get me, instead of going home and snooping around the house and pestering my father, or whatever it was I did between the hours of three and five-thirty.

My grade two haircut seemed deliberately hideous. Very short bangs and white walls over the ears like boys in black and white TV shows, making my face look wide and moony. After-school care was a kind of special class. When the last bell rang at three o'clock, I would follow the rest of the leftover kids down hundreds of stairs, deep into the dungeon of the school. Through the boiler room, with its monstrous dragon of pipes, and into a large unbreathable place called the *Open Area* which smelled like a cheese only grown-ups would eat. The Open Area had only two windows, with bars on them, way up high against the ceiling where none of us could climb out.

The two staff guys were both named Steve; they had long hair and they basically let us do whatever we wanted until somebody came to cart us away. Usually this would be my mother, on her breathless flight back from Dr. Spektor's clinic in the green Torino, with flying scarves and wet naps to wipe away whatever was stuck to my face.

The Open Area was as big as a parking lot, with squat concrete pillars planted here and there, like sparse trees. The pillars were the colour of oatmeal, acting as speed bumps during games of tag, when we'd speed and bump into them. Above our heads branched an Etch-a-Sketch network of pipes, turning and disappearing through the ceiling and wall into the boiler room, where the Steves said they cooked rats to put in kids' lunches.

In one corner of the Open Area was a thick blue stack of exercise mats, and a gymnastic pommel horse. One of those headless horses with four wooden legs and a stuffed leather body. It was not from falling off the pommel horse that I would lose my two front teeth, I wish it had been that. Then I could say, *I lotht my teeth falling off a horthe.* People said the easiest things in the world were like *falling off a horse* but when you think about it, it's no small accomplishment to even get up on one.

My friend Effie was not enrolled in after-school care. Her mother was always there waiting for her in front of the school, at exactly three o'clock, with a healthy snack and some pink sequined tights in a bag. Effie's hair was long enough to make braids now, which she wore curled up in lemon danishes on either side of her head like Princess Leia. Boys renamed her, and girls did too. Many names, many of them not very nice. As I watched her mother reach across to unlock the passenger door, I thought that Effie would grow up to be someone whose name would change several times in her life, and that she would have very little to do with it.

The Steves had hair almost as long as Effie's, and one of them wore a chunky silver ring with a turquoise stone, like Effie's dad. Steve and Steve usually spent most of their time sitting in a musty green truck in the parking lot. If any of us wanted to ask them a question or tell on somebody, we had to go out and knock on the window of the truck. Then one of the Steves would roll down the window, and a lot of grey smoke would curl out smelling like moldy pumpkin.

Occasionally, Steve and Steve would pile us all into the back of the pale green truck, and take us for a ride along the serrated blade of trees cutting the road from the ocean. They drove so fast we thought we'd break the sound barrier and enter an asteroid belt. Whichever Steve was at the wheel would have to swerve back and forth like a space-fish to avoid colliding with the asteroids.

"Watch out, Steve One," Luigi would shout, "there's an asteroid heading right for us on the port side. Disengage missiles." Then Steve One would drag the steering wheel in tight circles, making shooting sounds with his mouth, along with the screeching of the tires, the smell of musty pumpkin and the bumping of our bodies, shrieking and laughing and falling about like real space travellers.

On clear days, when the mountains suddenly appeared out of nowhere and it was warm enough for the Steves to take their shirts off, they would march us down to Trout Lake for a game of Red Rover. We'd be divided into two teams, given either green pinnies or orange ones. "Carrots on that side, Peas on the other," called the Steves, reminding me of those baby plates with dividers to separate the different vegetables from each other. Then the Peas held hands with the Peas, the Carrots joined with the Carrots, in two rows facing each other across the field, and someone would yell, *Red Rover Red Rover, we call Tillie over*. The littlest kid always got called first. Then the poor little kid would have to run at the line of clasped hands, aiming for whatever looked like the weakest link. If she managed to break through, then she could capture somebody to take back to her side. If she didn't, which she wouldn't, she was captured by the enemy and had to join their team, even though they didn't particularly want her there.

But usually Steve and Steve just stayed in the truck. After a few weeks we all realized that the Steves didn't much care if Luigi said a bad word, or if Garth made Tillie eat a bug. "Better notify the family of the bug," was all the Steves would say. Eventually we stopped knocking on the window altogether, and just did whatever we wanted.

In one corner of the Open Area, on the floor, was a record player whose playing arm ended in a three-fingered hand with a white glove. The needle was hidden on the underside of the glove, like a diamond hidden in the hand. The needle arm resembled the hour hand of a Mickey Mouse watch, but much bigger, connected to an eerily exuberant mouse face on the inner lid of the record player. But unlike an hour hand, which spun around a *face* which stayed basically *still*, the arm of the record player stayed basically *still* while the *face* spun round and round. This was big news. I ran out to the parking lot and knocked on the window, to ask the Steves about it.

"Is time actually in the *face*, or is it in the *arm*?" I hollered at the Steves until they rolled down the window. "I mean, is it measured by the part which is *moving* or the part which stays *still*?"

"Time doesn't move at *all*, kid," said Steve Two. "It's *us* who are moving. Time just, like, hangs around. Breathing."

"Don't listen to him," said Steve One. "Time creeps in its pretty pace, you know, and we're just swept along with it. Like dust in the wind. That's all we are, like the man says."

"You're so full of crap," said Steve Two.

"I'm not the one they call Number Two, dude," said Steve One.

Then later that day, Steve and Steve happened to tie me to the tetherball pole with skipping ropes, then went away again. They only meant this as a joke, and it was kind of funny, it just happened to be me they played it on that day. It could have been anyone, even one of the boys. Once I'd seen Steve Two pick up Luigi and turn him upside-down, and dangle him head first over a big trash can. It was only a joke. Everybody laughed except Luigi. But there's always somebody who doesn't get the joke, that's the person the joke is *getting*. Now it was me, and I didn't get it either.

The Steves used one skipping rope to tie my hands behind my back, another one to tie my ankles to the tetherball pole, then one more across my shoulders to hold me upright. That's three skipping ropes. I just let my body go limp like those people who chain themselves to trees on the news. Other kids were laughing, which had the same effect as eating three whole packages of cherry-grape Lik-a-Stix. A giddy rush of happiness followed by a sick and empty feeling. Their purple faces laughed like a bunch of grapes, and for a moment I felt deliriously happy that everyone was laughing at me, which proved I was there.

Then Steve Two called, "Well, everybody who wants to go down to the soccer field for a game of Red Rover, raise your hands!" Everybody screamed *Me-ee-ee-ee!* and everybody's hands shot up in the air like pirate's swords. *Me-ee too,* I said, breathing through my mouth and twisting my shoulders to free my arm. But that was supposed to be the joke.

"Aw shoot, I guess Agnes doesn't want to play," said Steve Two, then he mussed up my awful haircut with his hand which was humiliating. Like being bathed. *Don't talk, you'll get soap in your mouth. Don't open your eyes, you'll get soap in them. Let me just finish your ears. Don't squirm so much.*

So I'd let my body go limp like those tree people on the news, and soon I'd be floating over the tub like a soap bubble, with none of my parts touching the ground, watching myself being cleaned. I became very proud of this ability, to float away like a bubble, and kept it a secret. I believed that one day I'd meet other creatures who could do it, too.

I had recently learned something about boundaries. That they are very narrow. Also something about the difference between inside and outside, between me and not-me. It seemed a very fuzzy border, very simple to cross it, very simple for somebody to erase it like a chalk circle. That's when I would float. Feet in blue sneakers sinking very far away, as the head floats up like a plum, and the green trees blur into one fluffy leaf. A nervous grey squirrel would watch me, I could see her finger-bones moving as she wrung her hands. Then at the end of it, I'd hear the footsteps of the Walking man shuffling in my ears, walking in time with my heartbeat as it moved up into my ears. He'd appear just as I looked up to see somebody coming looking for me, feet walking with no sound.

I could see them all, down there on the soccer field, from where I stood casually tied to the tetherball pole. The kids were divided into two teams wearing green and orange pinnies, the Peas and the Carrots. They looked like two armies of ants, who build complicated houses to live in and have complicated systems for food storage and waste disposal. Army ants who wear helmets like soldiers or children with skull injuries.

My wrists were weakening in their circular work, I twisted and turned them, gaining only rope burns. I think it must happen to everybody, that *blip* in time when you suddenly see yourself as two people at once. The one who's participating in the game, and the one who watches quite separate from it. Even though my wrists worked automatic circles against the rope, I could not feel wholly miserable. My face caught sparkles of mist in the air, my body was still and steady as a wooden lady on the nose of a ship. I could remember few examples of feeling so bound in *space*, so rooted to a particular *place*. Tied to a pole I couldn't get lost, I knew exactly where I stood.

There may also be something about having your hands tied behind your back which emblazons an emblem of defiance on your chest. Perhaps it's simply that the posture requires some jutting forward of the chest, as those who are brave or proud are said to do. My memory flipped through movies and World Book encyclopedias, segments of the news and historical documentaries, finding dozens of these people tied to poles, among the din of those who either loved or hated them, or both. Then the countless other faceless tied-up people to whom nobody paid much attention at all, not even long enough to learn their names.

Finally I chose *Joan of Arc*. I knew almost nothing about her, except a black and white poster of a beautiful movie star gazing skyward and wearing armour. I knew she could hear angels' voices, as my father was able to do, and that no one believed her either. And that she wound up getting burned for it all, just like I was getting rope burns on my wrists.

I listened very carefully. I heard the shrieking of ants in the field, the gulping mouth of the wind swallowing their shrieks like a sea monster. I heard three croaks from a crow, then my own runny-nosed sniffling, which I hadn't noticed up to that point. I listened harder until big purple veins stood out at my temples. I heard the footsteps of the Walking man pumping in my chest, the creaking of the rope against the pole. But no angel voices came sailing in on the wind, as far as I could tell, none at all.

So either the angels were frauds or I was one, but more probably it was me. Just like vampires couldn't be seen in mirrors, and werewolves could not be shot dead with ordinary bullets. There no longer seemed much point, then, in trying to be polite about things.

Enough to wake the dead, as my mother would've said, I hollered and thrashed about like a doomed escape artist. The black crows flew away with swooping wings, and all the ants looked up from the field. One of the Steves came running, but it was too late. I'd already shaken loose the skipping rope holding my shoulders to the pole, which was also the rope keeping me vertically inclined. But my ankles were still tied to the pole, and my hands were still tied behind my back, so there was no way to stop myself from falling smack on my face on the concrete playground. It leaped up at me like a barnacled whale, then salty shards of splintered calcium were rattling around in my mouth, then my useless lips inflating.

Suddenly I *could* hear voices on the wind, drifting in and out and upward as my body was unbound and lifted up, carried to a better place where everything would be all right, the voices said, everything will be all right. A thick thumb lifted up my swollen lip and whistled *Holy mackerel*, then fished around in my mouth for the barnacles I was hiding under my tongue. The voices carried me to the stack of blue gymnasium mats in the equipment closet, which smelled of musty sneaker rubber. They set me down and told me to stay put until my mother arrived.

I waited for about three days. On the first day, other kids came and looked at me until they were shooed away again. *Blackout*. On the second day, Steve One came in and handed me a Tupperware container with my two front teeth inside it. *Blackout*. On the third day, Steve Two started peeking in at me every five seconds, saying *Ohfuckwhaddarwegonnado?* I wished he would stop saying that *word* before my mother got there. She would've taken me out of after-school care for sure, then I'd have to start going *home* after school again, where I wasn't supposed to bring my head or my ears or my eyes or anything else inside the house, and now not even my two front teeth. I kept losing bits of myself all over the place, and wondered when this would stop.

"Well, I'll be double-damned," Dr. Spektor would say, whenever something happened which he'd never have believed unless he saw it with his own eyes. Like the baby goat born with a double-branching backbone and seven legs, or those photographs which proved the existence of Sasquatch. Or when my mother showed him my mouth and told him how much she was suing the school to pay for my dental surgery. My busted teeth got a *double-damn*, which helped me understand why the Steves had tied me to a pole in the first place. It was what they did with the damned just before they got set on fire.

I jutht fell, I told my mother again. I held the Tupperware container very still on my lap so its contents wouldn't jangle.

"Don't give me that story again, pet, you just *fell*," my mother said, her face very close to my face. "Fell *where?* Fell from *what?* Wasn't anyone there? Did somebody *push* you?"

"*Eb'ry* bothy wath there," I said. "Wha cud they *do*? I jutht *fell*."

Dr. Spektor pressed an unseen pedal, and I descended back. "Just lean your head back and close your eyes. There you go. And you might as well leave on those big sunglasses, Agnes, we'd've had to put some goggles on you anyhow. You can pretend you're sunbathing in the Bahamas," he said, smiling briskly and showing his teeth, before disappearing behind a partition. Dr. Spektor's smiles were meted out sparingly like electricity, switched off abruptly whenever they seemed unnecessary in order to save energy. Maybe he so seldom showed his teeth when he smiled because any normal person would be half-blinded by them. This was why I was wearing the sunglasses in the first place, so I wouldn't pee my bed from nightmares about Dr. Spektor's radioactive teeth. From behind the sunglasses, they looked mauve.

Shortly after Dr. Spektor disappeared, my mother came in and placed some metal instruments on the dental tray.

"Here you go. I'm just going to stick some sticks in your mouth. Open up. Let's just pull the curtain round so we have a bit of privacy." My mother stuck three or four wooden swabs in my mouth, under my top lip. The swabs had been dabbed with sweet and sour pinkish paste, supposed to be cotton-candy flavour but just not. My gums began to go numb. Then my mother left and Dr. Spektor came back with a steel syringe.

"This'll pinch a bit," he said automatically as he lifted my lip with his index finger. I closed my eyes tightly and held fast to the vinyl armrests with sweaty sweaty sweaty hands. *Lips inflating like a balloon.* My whole mouth was spreading across my face as though I were an oyster, with a siphon-suction tube stuck in at the corner, and the sound of rushing water. There were mincing picks and prods, the tapping of tiny hammers, the fastening of shackles. I opened my eyes and caught sight of a green grinning crocodile on one of the posters from the Canadian Dental Association, which was my usual cue to go somewhere *else*.

Now I was sunbathing far far away in the land of Lilliput, where I'd never been before. The trip required transport of body and mind, the sinking into some other element, a sleep and a forgetting. If I opened my eyes now, I would find that tiny creatures had tethered me to the ground with miniature tent pegs and cables. They would be scurrying over my body like ants, examining, fastening, tapping. They would flee and shriek and scramble when I blinked my monstrous eyes, ant mothers scooping up aphid-sized babies, hurrying off to their walnut-shell homes. I will awake and crush them under my feet as they try to get away....

"The swelling *will* go down, you know," Dr. Spektor said as I grimaced at the mirror, catching my first glimpse of the phony new teeth. My gums were bloody and puffy and beginning to thaw. The new teeth looked a bit long and pointy, and they were not quite the same colour as the other teeth in my mouth. They seemed to glow a bit, I felt, like Dr. Spektor's teeth.

Vere my other voneth ath long ath theeth? I asked.

"You'll grow into them," smiled Dr. Spektor.

12

SIMIAN CREASE

When Buffalo man opens the passenger door of the red Gremlin, two long sinewy arms reach out to embrace him. The hands at the ends of the arms are black with pinkish palms, the knuckles gnarled, the skin covered with coarse hair. They sling themselves like jute rope about Buffalo man's neck, drawing the body toward him, a puffy flash of pink rump. The creature shrieks like an excited girl.

"Okay, Mae, it's all right," the man whispers in her ear, bouncing her up and down in his arms. She's still wearing the teal satin gown I'd seen her in earlier, when she'd begged my lynx-quarter from me in the park, but the lace bloomers have been removed and are now hanging torn from the rearview mirror. Styrofoam coffee cups lie bitten and strewn about like puzzle pieces throughout the interior, lip prints thick as Boston Creams on all the windows. She's apparently been eating a box of Shreddies; she has demolished the cereal and shredded the box.

"You haven't been a patient girl, Mae West," says the man. The chimpanzee makes a series of soft *boo* sounds as the human attempts to relocate her to the back seat.

"Go ahead," he says, watching me wanting to touch Mae. "She won't bite, just try not to startle her." Then, crossing round to the driver's side, "She's never bitten me."

My persisting inability to drive convulses my hands in tense little fits on my lap as if swatting wasps. Again I find myself in the passenger seat of a vehicle driven by somebody else. A car remains a country whose language my hands do not speak. To my left, my weak side, Buffalo man sits colossally hunched with the steering wheel like a pretzel in his hands. Further left is the familiar passing of cedars and totems, and Canadian geese with black chin straps. Further still is the inlet, the glittering sash of a mysterious countess, who disappears as soon as the car turns toward the purple tunnel of skyscrapers downtown. The mountains have disappeared also, into that misty amnesia within which only very large things are able to conceal themselves.

Concepts of *left* and *right* are typically beguiling as well, unless I remember that I *write* with my *right*, while the thumb and index finger of my illiterate hand form a capital *L*, as in *left*. But this was hopelessly relative, when the twin behind the mirror could just as easily make an *L* with her right hand, relative to her own universe. And probably most people's universes were pretty relative, our relatives being pretty universal in the end. There is something in notions of perspective, logic, and proportion, which don't come naturally to me. I occasionally wonder if this condition is a sort of idiocy. I am likewise unskilled at giving directions to anywhere from anywhere, even to the house on Dormier Street. So when Buffalo man asks me, *Where to?* I only shrug and say, *It's up to you,* as though I am not idiotic but merely free-spirited.

Aside from right and left, the other choice of scenery is the road straight ahead, with Mae's face hovering above in the kidney-shaped mirror. She is waggling her head to and fro, projecting her lower lip out as far as she can, studying its length like humans study the length of their tongues. When she looks directly into the mirror, the glint of her copper-brown eye settles not on Buffalo man but on me. When I turn away again toward the window, she makes sucking sounds through her teeth.

"Can Mae sign?" I ask Buffalo man. I'd read about apes who were able to do it, some of the mothers were even beginning to teach it to their offspring.

Buffalo man casts snake eyes at me from the driver's seat.

"No," he says flatly. "No, Mae can't sign. That's not the sort of education she was fortunate enough to receive. Hope you're not disappointed." He turns abruptly onto another street which I don't recognize.

"She can play peek-a-boo," he continues, "she may sneak up from behind and cover your eyes, it's a favourite trick of hers with new passengers. Humour her, you know, try guessing a coupla other names before you guess hers, *Betsie* or *Bozo* or *Rasputin* or whatever. She'd love you to mistake her for a martyred Russian holy man."

Mae West seems a bit neurotic. Buffalo man had cautioned me

about her several times during the walk to the car, each time to remind me not to do something-or-other which would upset her. *"Don't* mimic her sounds if she doesn't know you yet. *Don't* swing your arms too quickly around her head," as if I was going to do that anyway. "I'd ask you not to smoke cigarettes, if you don't mind, I'm trying to get Mae to forget they exist." He tells me that Mae West used to smoke, and I want to ask him when and why, and how she feels about his pipe.

"I'm not trying to stress you out, she just doesn't know you yet," the man says.

"Neither do you," I say, still a bit stuck on the phrase *new passengers*, and wondering who they were. Probably there are lots of other girls with poor senses of direction, poor judgment, and no driving skills. Maybe I am a member of a group he calls *new passengers*, consisting of young women who appear not too difficult to pick up, appear to be lonely, appear to be gullible. Appear to be *sending out signals*, those grazing suggestions that one is a specimen of a *type*. It isn't that I'm always making *bad* choices, it's that I'm scarcely aware of making choices at *all*. It seems more like a body just gets pushed along.

"You a student or an artist?" asks Buffalo man. "I saw you sketching earlier."

"Really? No, I'm no artist. I'm a student. Biology."

"Biology, eh? That's sort of my field as well, or used to be. I was into wildlife photography for a number of years. Still got a lot of the gear at my place, specimens and photos and tons of other stuff I've collected over the years. Not too clear on what you're thinking, to be honest. I mean we could go there if you wanted to, or we could go to The Railway Club or someplace, or I could just take you home."

Some interesting biological specimens at his place. Okay, so he's got a freezer full of heads, or, no, maybe it's an eight-foot creature laid out on a slab, made of stitched together parts collected from graveyards and charnel houses, which he reassembles at home then waits for an electrical storm. Or maybe it's just an ant farm or something, some guinea pigs in a hutch in the backyard, unless he's making a lewd insinuation, I didn't even think of that. Some fine biological specimens to show me.

But why should I be surprised?

"I live over there," I say, pointing vaguely out the window of the Gremlin toward Chinatown. I can't take my eyes from Mae West as she watches from the mirror above, but neither can I bear to look at her for very long. She's still wearing that tawdry satin dress and now I have a mental picture of her smoking cigarettes. Do chimps have a sense of irony, or is Mae West just as earnest in her whore costume as I'd been dressed up as a bumblebee on my first Hallowe'en?

"Does she ever put her hands over your eyes while you're *driving*?" I ask, just as Buffalo man makes a sharp turn. "So where are we heading, in the end?"

"Back to your neck of the woods," he says. "Might as well just give you a lift home, is my impression."

"Yeah, umm… maybe that would be best. Sorry, it's nothing personal, you seem really interesting. I just don't want to give you the wrong idea… I still live with my mum and have a bunch of homework to do."

So he drops me off downtown because I lied about where I lived. I walk home across the Cambie Street viaduct in the dark for ten thousand years, the slope of my forehead changing as I walk, my lower jaw jutting forward, a lumbering fixity in the pelvis, a looseness and a lengthening of the arms. By the time I get back to the house on Dormier Street I am a primate incapable of speech and intricate manual dexterity, but sign to my mother that I am going straight to bed now, grabbing yellow plums from a bowl on the way to my room.

Pull, release. In the middle of the night I wake up to the remembered sound of my father in the basement on his rowing machine. I can hear it, the sound still echoing in the walls, though my father hasn't lived here since I was eleven. I creep from bed, down the hall to the living room, where the ghastly hand of the spider plant sprawls across the walls, shadows of the mesh drapes casting webs over the floor. I've been semi-dreaming about minotaurs and longing and following string to a very dark place where I can't see anything. Without thinking I grab my parents' wedding photo from where it was stuffed under a bookcase and take it back to bed with me.

In the photo, my mother's white shoes peak out from beneath her long straight dress, so small, her sleeves hanging down like freshly-laundered linen dish towels. Her folded arms meet at her navel like a geisha, with a froth of white carnations and baby's breath where her hands should be. She is smiling without showing her teeth, her closed lips smirking crooked like a girl holding her breath. And there is my father, uncomfortable in a suit with his hands behind his back, his body craned slightly forward like the politely curious. But gallant, in some old-fashioned sense, if a bit out of place. His teeth are a hem of white grazing his lower lip.

When the photo was taken, he was still intending to become a minister of the church, and my mother would become a dental hygienist. Things should have gone well for them, they could've afforded two kids with clean teeth and clean minds, annual polishings and the occasional root canal. I was never too clear on whether my father actually completed theological college or not, he'd lived mostly in the basement for as long as I could remember. I was only two or three when my brother arrived, a time period my mother refers to as "when I started feeling a bit fed up." Sometimes she used metaphors concerning equestrian equipment: she'd had "to take the reins in her hands," and "wear the pants," though most people seldom saw her wearing pants. She wore a blue nurse-like uniform at work, and at home she'd taken to wearing those floor-length polyester house gowns which zip up the front and are usually purple. It seemed that wearing the pants often involved not wearing them, for the sake of something like appearances.

13

THE BACK OF MACKENZIE KING'S HEAD

The day before my eleventh birthday, just before leaving the house to have my teeth cleaned and scraped by my mother, I went into my room to put on a short tartan skirt which hadn't been worn since I was nine, a pair of bright pink knee-socks, and sneakers made of clear blue plastic with sparkles. Then I sat on the floor with a set of poster paints, and painted bees on both my knees, one bee on each kneecap. Then I glued more glitter to their wings. This was part of an experiment into the relationship between insides and outsides. The difference between how a girl sees herself, and how she is seen. I wanted to know if a girl who has bees on her knees would get any special attention which other girls didn't get. And if so, whether the special attention would have any effect on who she thought she *was*.

After painting the bees on my knees, I crept into my parents' room, while my father was still downstairs banging at a lawn mower. I quickly found a bright red fifty dollar bill in an envelope taped beneath my father's underwear drawer. On the back of the bill were fifty men in crayon-red coats, and fifty glossy horses, black as wet slate, standing in a ring on some very green grass. I folded the bill up accordion-style and stuffed it in my sock.

Stealing the fifty was part of the experiment as well. I wanted to know whether hidden thefts were borne on the skin, like a peculiar smell. Or whether they were virtually undetectable from the outside, like hairline fractures. Whether my mother would sniff out my theft as soon as I sat down in the chair and opened my mouth, the fifty red coats like cinnamon-heart stains on my tongue, the smell of uniforms and horses on my fingers. Or whether she wouldn't even notice. Some things only get noticed when they go missing, while other things don't even get noticed when they are right there in the room.

I ran out of the house and let the screen door slam behind me, listening for a voice to tell me not to slam the bloody screen, but didn't hear one. I kept running all the way to the intersection at Kingsway and Victoria where I hailed a cab. I had never done this before, but I'd seen ladies do it in movies, holding up their pretty hands so their skirts inch up their thighs a little. Hailing a cab seemed to be one of the things you could learn from watching movies, like kissing or firing a gun. A black and yellow cab stopped almost right away. It was *that* easy. I hopped into the front seat right beside the driver, in a style my mother called *flouncing*. I was out of breath from running and my mouth tasted of old pennies. But I figured out which of the levers on the door was for the window, and rolled it down six inches, where it stopped and would roll down no further.

"You okay, girlie?" said the man. I nodded my head that of *course* I was, then looked for a clue of what to do next. I looked at the man's face. It was several shades of pink and rough like a peach stone. His hair reminded me of fried eggs, mostly white with yellowish tinges and slicked back behind his ears, which were large like curls of bacon. He was wearing a blue short-sleeved shirt with an Esso patch on the pocket. I thought he had a very interesting face, in profile it looked like a fist.

The cab smelled of something like brewer's yeast, greasy celery sticks, Styrofoam, smoke, and coffee. There was a greasy paper bag on the seat between us, and a packet of cigarettes with a camel on it. Stuck above the dashboard was a small plastic bust of Smokey the Bear, about the size of a charcoal briquette, with a hole in the top of his hat to stick a pen in. A ribboned plastic scroll formed the pedestal of the bust, inscribed with the words *Only you can prevent forest fires*. It reminded me of the firemen's calendar in the kitchen at home, with the words *Always know where the nearest exits are*. This was good advice if a fire was already burning, but preventing one was a new concept, sending a quick hot chill up my spine. How was a person supposed to know what was going to happen before it even happened?

The driver was looking at me. His eye-beams made a bee-line straight to my almost-eleven-year-old knees, the bees on my knees, the bright pink knee-socks which were slipping until I reached down and pulled them up a bit. Still looking at me. I was beginning to understand something about being looked at, why people went out of their way to be looked at, or not to be looked at. I began to see more clearly what it was I was trying to do, with the socks and the bees on my knees. It came in sudden colour like the door opening into Oz, way more garish than you ever expect. There was a shift in perspective, having to do with the difference between being a pair of eyes looking at things, and being the thing which a pair of eyes is looking at. Being *watched* seemed to have the power of transporting a person's awareness someplace else, *outside* of the body.

Perhaps it was possible to split off entirely, to relocate your own point of view in somebody else's head. It might feel consoling to do this, at times. It might even feel like a type of desire, to be secured in space that way by somebody's eyes, like the belt which holds you safely in your seat. Or a stickpin securing a shiny green beetle, it might feel rare and ecstatic to be pinned by someone's eye-beams that way. Surely this could feel like a type of love sometimes, when you aren't sure how else to recognize it. At least the green beetle could be labelled, then. It could be given a name, like the red flag on a map reading, *You are here.*

"You sure you're okay, kid?" the driver said again.

I sunk my head into the upholstered headrest and said, "Take me to St. Paul's Hospital, please."

Dr. Spektor's dental clinic was located just inside the lobby of St. Paul's, but the potential drama of the destination didn't strike me until the driver said, "All right, missy, you don't have to talk about it if you don't want to. I was just checking in because you seem a little nervous, is all."

So I thought to myself, now here's a person who doesn't know me from a hole in the wall, as my father would say, and probably I'll never see him again after today. I could tell him any story I wanted, really, it wouldn't do any harm. I could chalk it up to experimental research.

So I lied.

"No I'm not very okay, actually," I said, looking down at my feet as though they were dead sparrows. "I'm going to visit my mother in the hospital." Technically this was true, and it didn't seem to require too big a leap to say, "She's very sick, actually. It's kind of an emergency."

"You got it," the man said, his hand flicking the switch on the meter.

I liked that. *You got it*. I settled myself in for the ride like it was a role in a movie I just got. Outside the universe of the cab, nothing either of us said or did would have any relevance to the other one. A taxicab was like a changing-room cubicle where a girl could try on different personalities, before actually committing to one. And the driver was the mirror.

"So what seems to be the problem with your momma?" the driver asked.

"Uhm.... Cancer." I was thinking of the constellation. Whoever first saw a big crab in the sky must have been a fisherman who caught them every day, because I'd never seen a crab up there, without it scuttling away as soon as I looked at it directly.

"Is that right?" he said. "What kind of cancer's she got?"

This was a more challenging question. I didn't know much about cancer. I didn't know which kinds were the worst ones, the ones you'd hear about in movies where the person dies.

"All kinds," I said. "She has all kinds of cancer." It would suit my mother to have a variety on hand, I thought, recalling the cupboard in her kitchen where she stored all kinds of cans, tomato soup and creamed corn and whole baby beets.

"That's a terrible story, kid," said the driver.

"I know it is," I said.

The car turned onto a gravelly street lined with rainy-looking houses. I saw an old woman struggling with an umbrella as though it were a fishing rod with a large-mouth bass at the other end, then I saw a frog-boy in green boots hopping from puddle to puddle. I could see them but they couldn't see me. I could look into people's living rooms, and even watch them watching Phil Donahue on TV.

"Do you like being a cab driver?"

"Sometimes, I guess. I just got out of the hospital myself, though. You're only my first fare since quite a bit of time ago."

"Oh. What was wrong with you?"

"Nothing life-threatening. Nothing like cancer. Let's just say I was over-tired."

The man told me he was originally from Florida and had a family there, a wife and a daughter about my age. He didn't want to break my heart with sad stories since I seemed to have plenty of my own, and he was very sorry to hear about my mother. I was starting to feel an unpleasant green twinge in my stomach. I told him I was sorry, too.

"It's a shame," he said, "how people could get shut up in hospitals and forgotten about." He told me that my mother was lucky to have a little girl like me, who'd come and visit her at least. I let my eyes wander from his face up along the frame of the window on the driver's side, stopping at that plastic hook to hang dry cleaning on. A driver's identification card was hanging nearby, with a picture of a taxicab driver. The man in the picture had long hair tied back in a ponytail and brown skin. He was not the same man as the man who was driving the car. They didn't even look alike, they didn't even look alike at all.

When a person is pretending to be somebody else, it doesn't necessarily occur to her that somebody else might be doing the same thing. Was it the man in the picture who had a wife and daughter in Florida, or was it the man who was driving the car? Did he really have a little girl my age, or was she as make-believe as I was?

I looked out the window again in search of familiar objects. There was a big red dog who looked familiar, but none of the stationary things did, none of the houses or trees. This may have been only because trips to the dentist were usually erased from my memory, like confessions under hypnosis. Trips back home again were usually blurry as well, my tongue all frozen and monstrous, slurring my words all over the bus.

The cab driver hadn't done anything wrong that I could see, except pretending, which was what I was doing myself. I remembered hearing my mother say, *Never trust a man who keeps his hands in his pockets*, but the driver had one hand on the steering wheel and the other one hooked through it hanging limp. I looked at his pockets. They were pouchy and walrus-looking but they weren't doing anything strange as far as I could tell. The only problem was a wordless sense that we were driving in the wrong direction.

"Are we lost?" I finally said.

The man looked over and puffed out his cheeks in a way which seemed to mean that he thought I was joking, or that we were lost, or that he was taking me someplace else.

"I remember being taken to the Kingsgate Mall once, to get a decent pair of sneakers, even though I didn't need them," I said. "My mother got me into the car by saying we were going for cherry-lime slushes at the DQ, then suddenly we were at Zellers in the shoe department. *You're not going to tramp around in the slush with those old things on your feet,* she kept telling me. She was talking about my favourite shoes from Chinatown, black canvas ones with..."

"What is this, story time?" said the driver. "You gonna tell me about your socks and underpants next, or what?"

"They were my favourite shoes, black canvas ones with aluminum buckles. My Great Aunt Hilda bought them for me in Chinatown when she came here once. My mother didn't like them. 'You'll catch your death, you'll catch your death, you know,' she kept telling me, like death was an old boot..."

"D'you wanna relax a bit?" said the driver.

"Well, that was the end of the story, anyway," I said. The shoes on my feet seemed like moot points anyway, seeing as they were no longer carrying me. In my mother's car, I was carried by her feet, her size five blue pumps like the feet of a church organist on the pedals. We had left Zellers with squeaky white tight sneakers on my feet, having left my Chinese slippers in the store. Now it was the driver's shoes, dog-brown and battered, doing the footwork for the both of us, while my blue plastic shoes didn't even touch the floor. I sat forward in my seat.

"Okay, how come that picture of you isn't even *you*?" I blurted. It was the only ace I had but he couldn't argue with it. Later I learned that this trick was called *calling someone's bluff*, it was a trick I'd have to remember. It might be necessary to use it again, someday, and when that day came I'd be prepared. But I'd also have to be prepared for it to backfire.

"You just came from a little birthday party, is that right?" said the driver.

"No. No birthday party. I'm going to visit my mother, I told you, in the hospital. She's very sick."

"I do remember you saying that," he said, slow-smiling. "I just wondered why a little girl would worry about painting glow-bugs on her legs when her mother's dying in the hospital. You gotta admit, it's a strange little dee-tail."

"To cheer her up?"

"Nup, don't think so."

I tried pulling the tartan hem over the bees on my knees but it wouldn't stay put. The skirt kept inching up all on its own, like the skirts of ladies hailing cabs, as though being looked at were less of a matter of deliberate make-believe than I had thought. First the antennae peeked out from beneath the hem, then both bees would creep into view, their sparkly wings nipping at the light. I covered them with my hands.

"I asked you *first*," I said. "How come the man in the picture isn't you?"

"Your mother isn't sick in the hospital, is she?" The fist of his face seemed to be tightening, his lower lip getting fatter and trembly.

"How do you know she's not? Can you prove she isn't?"

"Nope. But she isn't, is she?"

I turned away from him and looked out the front window. I could see the street, the rainy, red tail lamps of the car in front of us, the streetlights suspended like cheap costume jewelry from criss-crossing wires over everybody's head. Slowly space was shortened to a very small area, extending no further than two feet in front of my face. All I could see were smudges on the windscreen, the two ghostly arcs where the wipers travelled like moons. My eyeballs were turning to tongues, thick and monstrous, slurring my vision until it staggered like a drunkard into the traffic. My eyes drooled and blubbered all over my face, knowing I'd been caught.

"Where are you taking me now?" I asked quietly.

For a long time he said nothing. He reached his big hand over and shut off the meter, freezing time at eight dollars and eighty-eight cents, and we glided quietly through unmeasured space. My face was hot and wet as though I'd been holding it over a steaming bowl with a towel covering my head, like my mother sometimes did *for the skin*, she said, though her skin would emerge ruddy and rubbery-looking. I was sitting on my hands, tapping my knees lightly together and apart, together and apart like a butterfly.

"I'm not sure what to do with you," the driver finally said. The cab rolled along for about three hundred years with both of us inside it, the face of the driver brooding moonish cycles. Then suddenly he dragged the steering wheel in a wide arc like reeling in a net, swooping the car in a horseshoe back the way we came.

"Where are you taking me *now*?" I asked again, my feet like dangling limp rabbits, not touching the floor.

"I'm taking you to the damn hospital," he said. "That's what you said you wanted, isn't it? St. Paul's Hospital?"

We drove back down the rainy-looking street where I'd seen the old woman and the frog-boy, but they were gone now. I saw the same red dog again, barking its lungs out from one end of a chain attached to a tree in the yard. I hadn't noticed the chain the first time round, seemed I hadn't noticed a lot of things.

I couldn't be sure anymore that the driver was taking me to the hospital just because he said he was, but felt somehow relieved for the change of direction. We seemed to be going back the way we came, as though it were possible to wind time back to where we'd begun. I looked at the meter to see if it was moving backward as well, erasing numbers all the way back to whatever number it started with, but it was still frozen at eight dollars and eighty-eight cents. I thought of the red fifty-dollar bill folded up accordion-style in my sock. In a certain way it was comforting to have it there, it was something Driver man hadn't figured out about me yet.

Initially my plan had been to give the fifty to him and tell him, *Keep the change,* because I'd always wanted to do that. Just because I liked the phrase *keep the change,* the way it contradicted itself. There were things you could *keep* and other things which would *change,* but altogether it seemed that *change* was the only thing you could *keep.*

My mother had special creams and lotions to make her skin last as long as possible, like the grease she put on our boots in winter. Almost everything she did had to do with making things last longer. Winter boots, people's teeth, rhubarb and string beans put up in the deep freeze. It had been ridiculous to tell the driver my mother was dying of cancer, it was like telling him I had a new dime in my pocket which *didn't* have the Queen's face on it. The Queen's face appeared in every pocket of change I'd ever had, her face will probably still be there when I'm old. Something about my mother was like this as well, she seemed as immortal as a penny. The cab pulled up to the curb and stopped beside a tall building with rows and rows of narrow windows, like the holes along the edge of a roll of film.

"St. Paul's Hospital," said the driver. *"Get out."* He flicked a switch on the dashboard and the lock-peg beside my right shoulder popped up, like one of those plastic darts in turkeys which pop up when the bird is done. I got out of the cab, walked round to the driver's side, then crouched down and reached into my sock for the fifty-dollar bill. When the driver rolled down the window I held out the money. I didn't want it anymore, but I wasn't going to tell him to *keep the change,* either. After everything else it seemed obvious.

"Don't give me that, kid," the driver said. "I don't even want to know where you *got* it. Go give it to your *mother."* He quickly glanced down at my knees then squinted ahead through the windscreen. "I think you should wash that glitter off your legs, too. You're too young to walk around with glitter bugs on your legs. It doesn't *look* good, do you *understand?* Now get out of here." He rolled up the window, then reached back and yanked the phony driver's permit from where it was hanging.

But I didn't get out of there right away, I stood and watched him while he searched his cab for somewhere to hide the permit. Soon he was rolling down the window again.

"In case you don't *real*ize it, kid, I just let you off the *hook*," the man said. "Doesn't your mother ever tell you anything? And listen, one more thing. If you're going to be a liar, you have to learn to tell better lies. Don't give yourself away unless you mean to. Because they'll always be some part of you that wants to get you caught. I just figured that out today, d'you get me? You don't seem too clear on why you're telling stories in the first place, so better try to figure out what part of you is trying to give you away, before you even start out. Then steel that part, or get rid of that part. And be ready for it to call your bluff. Do you get me?"

The man rolled up the window again, then bent down and pulled up one of his trouser legs to shove the phony ID card down his sock. He sat up and shot me a glance, then took his foot off the brake and pulled away from the curb. I could see the back of his head and shoulders framed in the left corner of the rear windshield as he drove away like a picture of Mackenzie King's head, as if fifty-dollar bills were reversible, showing both the front and the back of the man.

14

Hide and seek

During the winter I go to slaughterhouses, and look for thick-coated, large, Black Angus cattle. The winter hair of the Black Angus is almost identical to that of the black bear. I purchase these hides and have them tanned. Most of the time I sell the hide as is, once it is tanned. I tell my customers what the hide is, and also what it looks like.

Then when they take the black hide home and put it on the floor, most of the time we two are the only ones who know that they don't have a real bear hide lying in front of the fireplace. Now if they want us to, we'll even cut the hide in the shape of a bear skin, so they really have a trophy to show off.

— from *How to Make Extra Profits in Taxidermy*

The day after meeting Buffalo man in the Stanley Park Zoo, I spend all day wandering around campus when I should be attaching electrical devices to the skulls of white rats. I eventually wander into the Science building, and inside the service elevator with me is a technician carrying a bucket of rats. Each rat is capped with a shiny metal device, like a beetle with a lot of metal legs fingering into its closely shaved scalp. I don't even know exactly what the devices are *for* because I haven't done the reading, but I thrust my hand between the metal jaws of the elevator door to make it open, and leap out. *Always know where the nearest exits are.*

There are laminated maps on every floor of the Science building, indicating washrooms, exits, and public telephones, with corridors branching off like those rat mazes in the lab. No self-respecting rat would bother tackling these corridors at all, without the provocative introduction of controlled stimuli, whether positive or negative. These could be crunchy food-pellet dispensers installed in every hallway, or mild electrical shocks to our feet when we're late for class. Lab rats can't really go where they want, but they can learn where they're expected to go. After a while they just go where they're supposed to, even if it doesn't get them any crunchy food pellets anymore, or save them from a thousand unnatural shocks to the feet. They learn something so they keep doing it, even if the way they learned it is totally unnatural.

I go through two more double doors into a smoky vestibule, duck past the furtively puffing neurology professor whose class I'm just about to skip, then out into the faculty parking lot. Once outside the doors I run rather than walk through the parking lot, and stroll too-quickly over a too-green lawn, statued with studious forms hunched over books and sandwiches like figures in a famous pointillist painting. In the foreground a woman's lunar face is turned over her shoulder, looking directly at the viewer, indifferent. The clock tower in the courtyard is just a toothpick through an olive, and Time an electrical device attached to the head. Is this device responsible for sudden mental floods, collapses of perspective? Was it because of this device that Time sometimes moved very very quickly and other times as slowly as the heart of a hibernating lungfish?

Maybe I'd lived too long in an attic room at the back of my mind, and now felt distracted from that place by something from *outside* the cranial frame. There was a distinct electrical charge between what-had-come-before and what-would-happen-next, it prickled on my neck like a moth. I remembered the calluses Buffalo man had on his hands, as though he'd been digging a hole, or as though beams of light had singed his skin on their way out.

At the bus stop I tear several phone numbers from posters. All of a sudden fringed posters with phone numbers were leaping out at me, fluttering all their little legs at their own possibility. *Sublet loft to share, female preferred. Futon for Sale, nearly new. Desk and Chair, best offer.* Then more of them, *Massotherapy, Adventures in Indian Cuisine, Ski-Weekend on Whistler, All-Included. Golden-Ages Bible Study, Same-Sex Ballroom Dancing.* I grab up all of these indiscriminately because you never know, choice based on ignorance of options is no choice at all. Then suddenly another poster leaps out, more fatalistically than the others, and again I tear away the number, already knowing I will call it. *Your subjects stuffed & mounted on site. Most species welcome. Call Noah's A-1 Taxidermy.* There's an address near

Gastown and a photocopied image of a raccoon standing on a chunk of bark, holding a piece of fruit, which somehow or other I recognize.

❦

Buffalo man is half-buried in a crawl-space when I first arrive, our arrangements over the phone having been as ambiguous as a door left open, when you can't tell whether someone has just come in or just left. Fried eggs, formaldehyde, sandalwood, sweater wool, vanilla pipe tobacco, dust. These are the first smells I am able to identify, though there are many more smells in Buffalo man's studio apartment, overlapping like fish scales. Then there are the auxiliary smells, the temporary smells, those smells which come and go like visiting relatives. It's a smell I dimly recognize but don't care to name. Like a litterbox but not one. Like a peat bog but not one. Like old false teeth, but not those either. At first I wonder if the smell is chimpanzee-related but it isn't. It's more like the smell which makes an antelope stare suddenly into the trees for an instant then spring away. The smell which makes animals nervous, human beings included.

Mae West is sitting on the top rung of a wooden ladder propped against a red brick wall, cleaning her nails with her teeth. That used to get me a slap on the hand. *Don't bite your nails, Agnes, it's filthy.* Mae West seems indifferent and immune to whatever germs are living under her nails, but she looks pretty much as nervous as I am. She shuffles on her perch a bit, and makes a few soft *boo* sounds.

There's an old wooden apothecary's cabinet standing near the door, with dozens of drawers like the storeys of an old building, a few of them standing open like tiny balconies. Tip toeing over to the drawers, I find that the open ones are mostly full of artificial tongues and teeth, unconnected to any animal, disconnected from consequence, speaking, swallowing, spitting forth nothing. I poke at the mouth objects in the drawer with my finger, studying them. The rubber tongues are the exact colour of raspberry bubble gum, but smell like condoms. I do not have any condoms. The artificial gums are a paler pink, like that fondant at the bottom of a cherry cordial, while the false teeth are like pine nuts, or slivers of untinted butter. Altogether a delicious mouth.

Now Buffalo man backs out of the crawl space like a bear, on his hands and knees, sitting back on his haunches when he sees me. Until now I'd completely forgotten what his face looked like. In minotaur-dreams of the previous night, his face blurred and bled into other faces, bearded faces, brushes of coarse hair on the muzzles of buffalo, the chin straps of helmets, the bearded faces of men who were thought to be wise.

"Wow, great, glad you decided to come. Good to see you again," says Buffalo man with his whole face lighting up. "C'mon in, grab a seat. You're already in… been here long? I'm just looking for some crap in the crawl space, there, no clue where stuff gets to." He wipes off his grubby hands on an even grubbier cloth and extends a paw. I reach out mine to shake.

"What were you looking for?" I ask.

"Um… it's sort of a leather cap," he says, "like the ones worn by WWI flying aces, with a chinstrap and flaps over the ears, 'cept this one's got a pair of goat horns attached to it, fairly large, curly and ribbed. Made it myself, that hat. First thing I made."

"Too bad," I say, impressed. "I'd have liked to see that hat." I cross the cluttered room and sit down on a trunk. "What made you think of it? I mean, I'm always looking for stuff I can't find, but there's usually some *reason* why the particular stuff is suddenly meaningful. What made you think of your goat hat?"

"I don't know, a prop," he says.

"Prop for what?" I ask.

"For your *head*! Use your head, I'm sure you can come up with something." He's not being mean but he's smirking a bit. He reaches back into the crawl space and drags out a smallish wooden crutch with yellow foam duct-taped to the armpit.

"There's no end to the useless *junk* I've collected over the years," he says, balancing the crutch upright on his palm until it topples then catching it in his other hand. "I was actually just trying to find something fun to do today in case you didn't come over, if you want to know the truth. That's why I was looking for my goat hat."

"That's admirable," I say sincerely, "I mean your collection of useless things. The best things are things which are useless. I've never had much use for useful things."

"Would you have much use for something to drink?" he asks, quasi-hobbling past me on his short crutch to the kitchen area, then hanging his useless crutch on a nail. He's doing a kind of show for me, which makes me wonder what I should be doing. I look around and notice now that there's a black bear hide on the wall behind me, mounted on a red felt mat. It draws me over to it magnetically.

"Is that a bear you actually *shot*?" There isn't any particular judgment in the question at all, more of a perverse fascination. But no, the bear isn't one of his, he tells me, though the guy who'd done the work told a fantastic story about the hunt, second-hand again from the guy who actually shot the bear.

"This fella was quite a fighter," says Buffalo man, saluting the skin with his scotch and ice. "Cost me a bit to acquire him," he admits, "but my buddy did the work, and anyway I owed him a favour and a bit of money on top of that. Still got a pretty good price for one-hundred-percent kick-ass black bear hide." He tells me he bought the skin before he'd ever dreamed of doing taxidermy himself, even before his first marriage, at a time when his buddy needed the money. Then later when he needed some himself, the same buddy informed him of just how much cash certain rich bozos from the States were willing to pay for a chance to shoot a polar bear, and that he knew one of these guys who'd shot *two* of 'em and wanted them mounted. The buddy wasn't set up to handle such a big job but he didn't want to lose the contract, so Buffalo man had apprenticed in taxidermy with two polar bears as guinea pigs. He tells me one polar bear paw was about the size of my whole torso.

"But back to the black bear," he says, "turns out I always end up telling people it's a Black Angus cow just cut to look like a black bear. Because times change, and people aren't too impressed anymore, to hear how this incredible beast continued to barrel through the forest for a good twenty minutes after he'd been shot, finally collapsing from exhaustion and sliding down a ravine. They had to bring in a helicopter to air-lift the bear out of there, the poor bastard didn't make it easy for them. But my ex-wife thought the story was *awful*, hated me more every time I told it, so I was forced to start telling people it was just some old cow up there on the wall."

Privately I was noticing that buddy-the-other-taxidermist had removed both the head and feet of the animal, which made me curious because you'd think he'd want to leave the head and feet on if it were really a genuine bear. The most impressive features of an authentic bear hide would have to be the head and the claws, certainly those were the most impressive features of a living bear. Claws and teeth like those could shred a man to ribbons if he didn't have a gun, possibly even if he did have one. Because what would be the fun of killing something which wasn't able to kill you first, unless you were terribly terribly clever?

Regardless, one of the first things I do, while Buffalo man is busy fixing drinks in the kitchen area, is move even closer to the skin on the wall and run my fingers through the thick black hair. I peek at the pale floor of skin beneath the hair, scanning for a tattoo or a brand, like my mother searching for lice eggs on mine and Gavin's heads. If I find the branded initials of a cattle ranch, then buddy-the-other-taxidermist and I will be the only ones who know that it really is a Black Angus cow disguised as a black bear, disguised as a Black Angus cow. Something always gives you away. You can snake an empty inner tube through fingers and thumbs all day and never find the hole, but sink it underwater and it breathes bubbles from the place.

All I really want to know is how ridiculous I should feel about wanting to be seduced by this man I don't even know, and at a deeper level what I am doing here. It was a fantasy which wasn't happening *willingly* but it wasn't *unwilling* either, more like *will-less*. The will was not engaged, somehow not aware that it even should have been engaged, like an idiot receptionist who puts you on hold for a million years and then goes on a coffee break. The situation didn't feel completely *good* but it didn't feel *bad*, it was the interim state between. Who's to say there hadn't been dozens of cows like me, dark-eyed Agnes-cattle like me whom he could easily corral into his red Gremlin and steer home to graze? Or did he view me as a solitary creature like himself, somehow cut off from other humans, hunting alone with tooth and nail, staking out her own territory? Who could say whether he viewed me as a brave and sacred skin or just another silly cow posing as a predator?

Buffalo man never actually kills anything himself, according to him. His subjects have mostly been found in ditches by the side of the road, begged from cosmetic laboratories, stolen from among the euthanized at dodgy animal shelters. A few had been entrusted to him by bereft eccentric pet owners, some had been rescued from pre-incineration bins at universities.

"I think it's a bit weird that you broke into a university laboratory to rescue *dead* animals instead of *living* ones," I say.

"Yeah, well, you might think so, but there are no consequences for stealing a *dead* rhesus monkey because I never get caught. If I stole *live* monkeys someone would likely notice, they aren't as quiet as dead ones. Anyway it's not my job to free all the animals, Agnes, in case you haven't noticed I don't work for Greenpeace. I enjoy taxidermy because it's fascinating and it doesn't hurt anyone, the animal is already dead when I meet it, get it? I learn tons about anatomy and a fair amount about human psychology to boot. And it's a personal challenge to make the specimen look like it did when it was alive. I used to name my subjects after dead famous people because they're basically the same thing, taxidermy subjects and famous dead people, they're frozen in time and they can't change, and usually we try to preserve them as we'd most *like* to see them, regardless of whatever unpleasantness might've been associated with their passing."

Above the door, therefore, is a great horned owl called Catherine the Great, and on a lower shelf is the raccoon, whose name is Voltaire, standing up on his hind legs and polishing the same wax plum in fruitless perpetuity. Voltaire was one of Buffalo man's very first subjects. I take a yellow plum from the bag of fruit I've brought and try to wrench the wax plum from the raccoon's hands, to replace it with a fresh one.

"You won't get anywhere with that," says Buffalo man, watching me from the kitchen area. "The plum's strung through with steel wire looped round his hand bones, there. You'd have to break at least his thumb for him to let go of that plum."

There is also a marmalade Persian, stiffly languid on an adjoining shelf, her mouth half-open on one side like she died of a stroke, dreaming the after-life in static and colourless cat dreams. The stuffed cat purrs audibly through the hum of unseen wiring beyond the walls and the more distant murmur of traffic, she absorbs your expectations of a purring cat and mirrors them back. Watching her, you could believe her ribs rose and fell with every breath, though she's breathless. She can't disappoint as long as you don't try to touch her.

"What's your cat's name?" I call to Buffalo man in the bathroom.

"Marilyn," he calls back, mouth full of toothpaste, then the sound of expectoration. A twinge of domestic feeling, so soon. At the old house on Dormier Street, there'd been no such expectorations. Whatever was clogging the family throat was meant to bloody well stay put like the running gag it was. So I welcome the sound of Buffalo man's spit, it isn't excessive. I balance on a chair and reach up to stroke Marilyn's head. There is no give. Flesh is meant to have a certain amount of give, it's meant to be responsive. Even very firm flesh draws itself around a touch and touches back. There's supposed to be a sort of *charge* between flesh and flesh, but stuffed Marilyn lying there sprawled on her shelf has not a spark of it.

"In life she'd belonged to an elderly lady, who opted not to keep her after she saw the results," calls Buffalo man from the bathroom.

"I was pretty pissed, you know," he continues, "because it hadn't been too pleasant to stuff an old lady's kitty cat, if you see what I mean. But the lady didn't want it, after she saw it, said it didn't look natural. Said Muffo or Puffo didn't *look like herself*, like no kidding. Still didn't have the heart to toss the thing out so I adopted her. Least ol' Marilyn doesn't need to be fed, just vacuumed now and then, and I brush her just like a regular cat, still check her for bugs. Bugs do all right for themselves, torment you when you're living and eat you when you're dead, it's all the same to them. I'd like to come back as a *bug*," hollers

Buffalo man from the bathroom, then the upward scritch of a zipper.

He washes his hands at the kitchen sink then hands me the virgin *mojito* I asked for, then he goes to unlock the door at the far end of the room and the metal grate behind it. He motions me to follow him through the door into the garage, where his taxidermy studio is. The first thing I see when I step through the door is the enormous head of a twelve-point buck hanging above the deep freezer.

"That one there's a white-tailed deer," he says.

"How can it be a white-tailed anything," I say, "if it doesn't even have a butt?"

The deep freezer is also locked, its key hangs from a sink-chain around Buffalo man's neck. Currently stored in his freezer, he tells me, are three yellow-bellied marmots, two rabbits, some red squirrels and a beautiful silver fox, a pheasant and a pair of raccoons and a pot roast. I tell him there used to be a deer head in the shed at my Great Aunt Hilda's house, when I was little. The first time I saw it I must've been three or four years old. My Great Aunt Hilda says I ran outside the house like a shot, behind the shed all excited, expecting to see the back half of the deer out there.

"And it wasn't," says Buffalo man.

"Course it wasn't," I say, "heard me coming and ran away."

On Buffalo man's worktable is the skin of another deer head, a young buck, turned inside-out like a sock. Skin-sockets round the eyes and nostrils are turned up in small hollow cylinders, like empty barnacles. The interior surface of the scalp, extending all the way down the animal's neck to its shoulders, has been rubbed with salt and borax, then set to dry.

"This one here's a mule deer," says Buffalo man. "Properly looked after it could last for decades, could still be around when you and I are gone. I'll leave him to you in my will, just remember to rub him down with cornmeal now and then."

"Guess the mule deer didn't have a will," I say.

"I see," says Buffalo man, "well, as long as we're on the topic of *abrasion* you should know right now that I'm not one of those guys who thinks humans are better than everybody else just because we write wills and have free wills which we then impose on everybody else. I look at Mae and it's plain she's looking right back at me, making decisions and feeling things, telling me things. I live with a chimp, for crying out loud, so don't get all animal activist on me like I don't know shit. Humans are often *less* tuned in to what's really going on than less evolved species are. *Instinct* is how other animals operate all the time. Only humans would decide that maybe we should repress or redirect things like instinct or intuition, because we're not entirely convinced by them. We usually like to head-muscle through everything. I mean, look at a dog. Anyone who has a dog, if he loves his dog, will tell you that a dog takes it on as his full-time job to absorb your whole emotional state and chew it up for you. When you're happy, your dog is happy. When you're miserable, so is your dog. Your dog has devoted his whole domesticated life to reflecting back to his human all this stuff about himself, really for nothing but some pats and a few bags of kibble, but does the human necessarily bother to return the favour? Some of the reflections we offer back to our dogs aren't very nice, it's incredible if they don't think we're just a bunch of hypocrites. I think every dog should get to feel like the best dog in the world. It's only fair, since we're the ones who brought them into our charming society in the first place."

"I read that Cro-Magnons and dogs met around the same time, and found hanging out together to be mutually beneficial," I say.

Buffalo man comes over to where I am standing by the deep freezer and crouches down on his haunches in front of me. He lowers his voice like a campfire story.

"You're looking like you want to know how I can say all this, when I stuff dead animals for a living," he says, "like I should talk about offering up a bad reflection. In fact, it's the work's made me think about it more. There are spooks around us all the time, is what I've sussed out. I'm pretty sure that goes for animals too, or it doesn't go for either of us. It has to be both or neither, I figure. If only *humans* have souls, and we invented the concept ourselves, then it's like we have no *faith* in souls at all, we only believe in them for the sake of security. It's like humans can keep rewriting the rules however we want, without any significant consequences, because we're the only ones that matter. I have dreams about Voltaire, that damn raccoon waxing his plum for the rest of eternity, he shows up in tons of my dreams, and can he *talk*. If there *are* ghosts hanging around here, they're probably trying to tell me something useful, or else they want my help. More likely they have something to teach *me*, since it's kinda too late to help *them*, don't you think? Might as well invite them for tea, I reckon, might as well listen."

15

CEPHALOPOD

"Just scoot your bum forward a bit and lie back... there you go." My mother bent over me to fasten a pale blue bib around my neck, a flash of fuchsia lace between her tan freckled breasts. The bib was a paper towel laminated on one side, fastened with alligator clips on either end of a sink-plug chain. She ran the cool chain round the back of my neck and under my hair, clamping the little jaws on the other side. *There you go.*

She then pressed an unseen lever with her foot, and my head sank back below the horizon while my feet rose up like a see-saw. My pelvis was a fulcrum, a fixed point on a lateral plane. It was as though my head, my neck and shoulders, were submerging underwater, bibbed in blue and staring through jellied yellow light. The light in Dr. Spektor's clinic was never breathable. It had no air in it but seemed to be a gelatinous mass, through which things swam unnaturally. Pale things of artificial yellow, blue, and pink, Styrofoam-white and chrome. My head was a pale stone, underwater, looking up.

I saw another set of jaws. That sea-monster lamp on its long mechanical neck, the gummy yellow light inside its mouth like melted glass. My mother placed her hand on the back of its silver head and drew it closer to my face, squinting down at me as though I were difficult to see way down here. There was another set of jaws clamped to her breast pocket, a serrated clip holding her photo ID in place, like a postcard with her picture on the stamp. *Berenice Underhill.* Like the taxi driver, the photo looked nothing like her.

When she turned her face away, I saw another set of jaws at the back of her head. There were jaws everywhere. These ones were the pale blue jaws which gathered my mother's frothy hair between long curving teeth, like a sea monster will a mouthful of foam.

"Hang tight a minute, pet," my mother said. "Don't go anywhere." Then she went away. I didn't know where she thought I was going to go. The only other place in the hospital I knew how to get to was the bathroom down the hall, where I'd just been, to scrub the painted bees off my knees. The glitter-glue wings had peeled off whole, like fake fingernails, but the paint didn't come off as easily. When I'd left the bathroom my kneecaps were rosy red from scrubbing, as though I'd spent the morning kneeling in a chapel, or scrubbing floors like Cinderella. I had hidden the stolen fifty-dollar bill in the sole of my shoe, which now felt uncomfortably conspicuous, sticking way up in the air like that. *There'll always be some part of you that wants to give you away.*

She wouldn't read my theft in my *face*, then, she'd read it in my *feet*. I was inverted, had supplanted two eyes with two sets of eyelets, lashes for laces, a pink fleshy tongue for two nylon tongues rudely protruding from shoe-mouths in which I had stuck both my feet. I was a two-faced cephalopod, with two foot-heads and one head like a foot. Those soles were exposed which should have been hidden, which should have been connected to the ground. *Astronauts in space must feel like this*, I thought, *also deep-sea divers. They must feel monstrous and displaced, like plaster narwhals suspended in glass tanks at an aquarium.*

There were numerous sets of jaws on the walls as well, on molar-charts. And posters of green cartoon crocodiles with gleaming white smiles, and tiny pink trochilus birds whose job was to hop about the crocodiles' mouths and pick out the plaque. In a lower corner of the poster was a small insignia, a circle and a triangle entangled with each other, and the words *Recognized by the Canadian Dental Association.*

I recognized the insignia from toothpaste tubes. It also appeared on the green crocodile bookmarks my mother brought home from Dr. Spektor's clinic for my brother Gavin and me. Anything bearing the crocodile and the crest was *Recognized by the Canadian Dental Association*, of which we assumed my mother to be an essential part. *This product contains sodium monofluoro-phosphate which is, in our opinion, an effective decay prevention agent, and is of significant value when used in a conscientiously applied program of oral hygiene and regular professional care.*

My mother might have written the official toothpaste message herself, most of the words were the sort she might say, or sounded that way. *Effective. Decay prevention. Significant value. Conscientiously applied, professional care. In our opinion.* As though my mother were a queen, referring to herself in the plural, to account for her several faces on coins and stamps. Any product bearing that official CDA stamp was recommended and approved, which was no small accomplishment with my mother. *Recognized & Approved by the Canadian Dental Association* and my mother.

I wasn't sure what to make of the twisted snake, maybe a relative of the crocodile on the posters and bookmarks. That smiling reptile who reminded me, *Brush your teeth twice a day, Put the bite on tooth decay,* every time I looked at the wall or opened my book to the place I'd left off. There was a crocodile bookmark hidden in the *Secret Garden,* and another one waiting at the centre of *Charlotte's Web.* The crocodiles had no meaning to any of the characters in the book, in fact they were rather intrusive. *Imagine.* Mary Lennox turning the key in the rusty lock to open up the Secret Garden for the first time in ten years, finding the gnarled tree with the broken bough, the dormant roses, and a crocodile. Or astonished farmers staring up at Charlotte's web to find embroidered there the spindly words *Some Pig,* and a crocodile.

Sometimes the Dormier Street story seemed no more believable than those other ones, often it seemed less. Like the other stories, the real one also required that I wrestle disbelief and break its jaw, force it to swallow its own tail until it disappeared like the final pixel before the screen goes dark.

Crocodile Dislocates Agnes. Every time I saw the initials of the CDA I had to wonder whether the scenery I was walking around in was real, or whether I'd painted it myself. There was the voice of my mother at dusk, when I was out playing with my brother in the empty lot across from the house, skinning my knees on blackberry bramble and tasting the cool copper taste of my own blood in the air itself; finding emeralds in the green glass of broken bottles and Roman coins in bottle caps; seeing crouching lions in every matted clump of yellow grass. Suddenly out of nowhere the voice of my mother would snap the air like a crocodile, calling, *Come to dinner, Agnes. Can't you see it's getting dark, Agnes.*

Call it a day, Agnes.

"Catch you daydreaming, Agnes?" My mother's blue-uniform breasts were sloping over me now like low storm clouds, to which were pinned a shiny brass emblem of the CDA. Her bare arm reached across and picked up a metal instrument from the small sidetable, attached by a mechanical arm to the chair. In her other hand she held a plastic cup, the size of a shot glass, half-filled with tiny cotton balls soaked in bright pink fluid like spider eggs pickled in grenadine. My mother set the cup on the table and began to unscrew the jaws of the metal apparatus, which was a sort of clamp or vice, to hold my mouth open. *Okay, I know how much you love this part, but try to co-operate, all right?*

My mother fastened the clamp onto my lower jaw so that my mouth was held open, my tongue propped up from its natural bed. She then picked up the cup of eggs and a set of tweezers.

"I know it's not as bad as you pretend," she said. She picked out a pink egg with the tweezers and placed it in the bed beneath my tongue, then swabbed it back and forth along the inside ridge of my lower teeth. A sour shockwave attacked the glands at the back of my throat and my tongue started flailing about like a naked mole rat.

My mother swabbed another pink egg along my upper teeth, then another, until I could feel their sharp little dendrites creeping in between all my teeth and sliding down my throat. I could not tell whether she was leaving the eggs in my mouth or taking them out, but envisioned them clustered in there, nestled soft and leathery, and wondered what sort of creatures would hatch from them. I let my head sink to the bottom of the ocean, and dreamt of a thousand baby sea turtles flapping down the beach. At least one of them was bound to make it to the water.

16

INN OF THE THREE MONKEYS

> Each year thousands of deer feet are thrown away by sportsmen who fail to see the value in the cloven hooves of the white-tailed deer, mule deer, and elk. These feet can be washed, preserved, and made into many useful items such as hat racks, letter openers, knife handles, thermometers, and gun racks.
>
> — from *How to Make Extra Profits in Taxidermy*

Parting the red hair, I see stitches. Amazing that a man whose hands are so large, fingers thick as thumbs, could sew such tiny stitches up the belly of a squirrel, concealing them in the tufted scruff of its throat. His fingers look too rough and blind to find those anatomical places which make the toes curl. Yet pulling at a certain tendon, the toes of the squirrel open and close like the claws of a cat before it sleeps. His hands see clearly how to tuck in the eyelids so the eyes are alive and not dead-looking. Glass squirrel eyes glint in lamp light side to side, not up at him as I do. Squirrels need a wider periphery to know when something with a net is creeping up from behind.

But parting the red hair I can see them, sutures like scriptures on the scalp. Buffalo man sits in an amber cone of light, the shade of a calf-skin lamp, stitching up the belly of a red squirrel. It lies in his lap flipped on its back, forepaws extended like a pose in martial arts. Buffalo man bends the wire-bone legs of the squirrel into a comfortable sitting position and sets it on the table. We look at it, its beady eyes, its motionlessness. The expression on the man's face makes me think of a clown who's just made a balloon animal, and now can't tell whether those bumps he's constructed are meant to be a pair of legs, a pair of heads, or something rude. He rubs his eyes and asks me if we should just leave the squirrel until tomorrow.

There's a turquoise fluorescent tube installed along the headboard of Buffalo man's king-sized waterbed. The bed swooshes and laps in a black-vinyl frame like a puffy cartouche, the frame making hissing-sounds when I sit down on it as though deflating a snake. When I shift my weight from the frame to escape the sound of hissing snakes I sink into a turquoise-lit aquarium, surfing back and forth on its surface by clenching and releasing gluteal muscles. I've never been on a waterbed before, nor any bed at all aside from my cramped little twin at home which still has a scratched decal of lambs on the headboard.

"Aren't you afraid Mae West will bite a hole in the mattress?" I call to Buffalo man, who is back in the kitchen area slamming an ice tray. Until now, she'd been dozing all evening, sprawled out on an armchair and looking quite peaceful, unless she's just avoiding me. I noticed when I first came in that there were numerous locks on things, the old apothecary cabinet had a padlocked bar across it and there was also a lock on the fridge.

"Nahh," he calls back, "Mae wouldn't do that. She'll often just crash there in the same bed with me. She's more in tune than many humans are, as to what's in her own best interest."

Hsss. Buffalo man takes an X-acto knife from a pencil holder and sits down on the hissing bed frame while I surf the wavy mattress looking very very calm. He pulls a navel orange from a deep front pocket then scores two meridians of longitude along its skin, at right angles to each other. He peels away the first quarter and hands it to Mae, who's now sitting, rocking back and forth on the floor. She snatches the peel from him and sticks it in her mouth, under her lips but over her teeth. She grins an orange slice, shiny and dimpled like an advertisement for Florida juice.

"If you were going to stay awhile, I could find something else for her to do," says Buffalo man. "She likes to look at National Geographics, pictures of apes and pictures of humans she likes, pictures of elephants and trees..."

"Really?" I say. This surprises me, that she's able to identify elephants in photos.

"Um-hm, really," he says. Mae West makes a soft *boo* sound through extended *O* lips. I stand up from my wavy seat not easily.

"I wasn't necessarily thinking of staying," I say. "I just felt like I had to meet you again, I needed to talk to you more than we did at the zoo." Buffalo man hasn't asked my age. I wonder how old he is and how old he thinks I am. There are no clocks anywhere, except for an hour-glass which sits on a tree stump by his bed. Is it supposed to be decorative, or does he actually use it to time something? It is constructed of two stout green bottles fused together lip-to-lip, on a stand made from four deer hooves lashed together with twine. Four additional hooves point up from the top of the hourglass like the turrets of a medieval castle, to become the feet of the thing if it were flipped over. That made a total of eight deer feet for one hourglass. It looks as though it hasn't been flipped over for a very long time.

It is hard to estimate how much time is represented in a cup and a half of sand, how much a body can actually get *done* before the sand runs out. By tomorrow morning I am supposed to have completed a diagram of a fetal pig, with its skin peeled back and pinned according to specified incision lines. I am supposed to identify its internal parts with neatly-drawn boxes and arrows, and to write up a report of what I learned from the experience in terms of the pig's similarities to human anatomy. I'd decided to copy all this information from a book, after a violent turn of nausea prevented me from performing the actual dissection. Things had been fine until the moment the aluminum baking pan was set down before me, thickly lined with yellow wax resembling congealed bacon grease, scored and sliced every-which-way like a hockey rink from previous dissections.

Lying in the middle of the pan had been a fetal pig, of course, but I hadn't expected it to look like the most depressing thing I'd ever seen in my life. The exact colour of Silly Putty if you leave it in bath water overnight, with creases where the eyes were pinched shut. Other creases where the tiny hind legs met the folds of skin beneath its body. The half-grimace of disturbed sleep and dark internal regions visible right through the skin, like the closed blue eyeballs of newborn mute swans.

What on earth was I thinking majoring in biology? I couldn't even bait a hook. Obsessed with what went on beneath surfaces, I still couldn't be the one to make the cut, I couldn't risk finding out more than I wanted to know.

"I can't stay, I gotta to go home and draw a dead pig," I mutter into my hands as Buffalo man comes back with jingling tumblers.

☙

The first step of a laboratory experiment is to write down a few predictions under the heading *Objectives*. This is done so that you can later compare what you predicted you'd learn to what you actually observe. With the dissection of fetal pigs, *Objectives* and *Conclusions* were roughly the same, usually, because they basically tell you what to expect anyway, the experiment having been performed a thousand times before.

Performed a thousand times before, but not by me. This would be my first time. The first time I would not come back to the housing unit at Salmon Court, would not let a soul, not even my mother's, know where I was. The first time I would look at desire retrospectively, my head on a pillow turned away, comparing expectations with conclusions, wondering where choice occurs or whether it does not at all. *Because they basically tell you what to expect anyway, don't they?* You basically know what you're going to learn from the experiment, don't you? *Everybody* does, but *no*.

But *yes*, when Buffalo man's hand slips behind my neck and lifts my whole head toward him like a living goblet, surfaces do fall away, giving rise to waves and the zip of linen against the grainy scritch of the vinyl mattress. If I wanted to, I could sink into the crevasse between the bed frame and its quivering viscera, I could disappear like a penny in its folds. But I don't want this, to disappear, for the first time I don't.

☙

Amazing. Like watching a sea turtle laying eggs is amazing, or like a man escaping from an underwater box where he is chained and handcuffed in a straight jacket is amazing. I thought that something would burst, something would puncture, thought the water we were made of would rush and merge with the water we were tossed upon like stripped barks, thrown one against the other in surges and ebbs.

Or really what I thought was that the water mattress would burst and we'd be soaked, and I'd arrive home at my mother's door like a drowned thing returning from the deep with strands of kelp in my hair. I didn't realize how unlikely this was, any more than I could admit the secret plan of never returning home at all.

He seemed to be wholly large, the whole ceiling descending, at least in the sense of things seeming very large when seen very close up. Like those visual games where they take a close-up photograph of some object or surface and you're supposed to guess what it is, assuming you're not accustomed to seeing it from such intimate perspective, which I wasn't. The body of Buffalo man was a whole series of these photographs. *Can you guess? Hirsute surface, smooth dome, puckered crease, bony projection, mobile elastic fold.* And my responses, reciprocal, *mobile elastic fold, bony projection, puckered crease, smooth dome, hirsute surface.*

But separately and above all this, I sensed another part, suspended above us among the wooden rafters. From this remote perspective we were creature-small, pale and strange, jerking like puppets. From there I had to wonder who he was, what manner of beast he was, and how I came to be there in the room with him. This suspended part, this imp-in-the-rafters was not hungry for the longing to be touched like the parts below. This impish part watched and laughed and thought, *What fools, these mortals, why would they? Why do they? Tomorrow, conclusions will be drawn up. Objectives will be proven true or false, just as they have a thousand times before. And then what is to be done with the specimens, once they're splayed open and named, once it is done, what do we do with the bodies?*

I don't try to fake any conclusions. I couldn't have done this anyway, didn't really know what it was supposed to feel like on the inside only what it was supposed to look like from the outside. Women in movies always said *Yes yes* while at times I found my voice straining toward *No no*, though I knew these things were supposed to mean the opposite. Then comes a moment like a stroke when the body is caught, delirium tremors in suspension then does she *fall* or does she *not?* Either one as easy, as impossible as the other. *Don't push me,* no, yes, *push me down* down and up *up out of myself* into myself *into you* and you and I disappear entirely. To become another sort of beast entirely, with two of almost everything. Two backs, two mouths, four legs. Narcissistic parasitic epileptic hermaphrodite. Two hearts and two livers and two of those oyster-like spaces beneath our two tongues, where pellets of poison may be hidden, or pearls.

Amazing, too, that masks of tragedy and comedy fit together so well on a bed, framed as on a stage, *beatific and low, febrific and slow, pelagic libido, catastrophic placebo, conspecific peepshow, geomorphic yo-yo, anthropophagic tic-tac-toe, magic deathblow, protomorphic echo, tragic curio, sudorific tremolo, soporific airflow, heteromorphic counterglow...*

Then all at once a sharp intake of breath, a seizure in the throat, and something has been split. Recoiling like a violin string, a torn tendon, retractable tape measure spinning back into itself. Looking up into his eyes in turquoise aquarium light, I do not see my trunk and lower limbs, do not see the upper and lower incisors of a primate creeping to the primal scene, joining like the third wheel of a triangle, now nipping my extremities, a bite to the Achilles, then the primal scream...

Whaddafuck... whatizzit!? comes the voice of Buffalo man like a man thrown from a horse, a man in a phone booth which suddenly blows up. "Agnes? What the hell's wrong?" His face over mine is a mask of concern, lunar and turquoise, and I am grateful for it.

"It's my *foot,*" I say, "I think my foot's snapped off."

Buffalo man is up on his knees now, surfing the bed with his hands spread, looking me up and down as though trying to locate my foot.

"*This* one," I say, gesturing with my head, unsure as ever about what was right and what got left. *His right? I'm left?*

Holy crap, he says once he's located the problem, then whistles through his teeth as though my ankle's a falling bomb. He tries to move me but my foot blows up like a big red dirigible, a million smithereens in my head, my breath coming ragged as birth. "She's done quite a job on your ankle, Agnes, you shouldn't try to move it just yet," he says, as though I even could. "I'm so sorry, it never occurred to me she'd ever do something that."

"Why not?" I ask.

"Stay right there, I'll go get something," he says, then he disappears.

From where I am lying I can hear Buffalo man in the bathroom, where the toilet seat is made of transparent resin poured into a mold with two garter snakes, some shiny beetles, and a scorpion suspended inside like the swirls in a Bundt cake. He is rummaging through his medicine cabinet, scolding Mae West simultaneously. "What's your *problem* you crappy monkey? Agnes is a perfectly *nice girl*, she's my friend and she's done nothing to you. YOU MUST NOT BITE PEOPLE, DO YOU UNDERSTAND ME? NO. LISTEN TO ME. NO BITEY. DO YOU GET IT? LOOK AT ME, COME ON, SAY IT WITH ME, NO BITEY...." Mae was simultaneously hoot-panting *Ooh-ooh-Ah-ah-ah* and I could hear the soft muffled thump of her body over and over as though she were turning somersaults on the floor, which it turned out she was. It was one of the things she did when she was extremely distressed.

Soon Buffalo man comes back to the bed with a bottle of hydrogen peroxide and a roll of gauze, enough to do me up head to toe. *Hiss*. He sits down naked on the vinyl frame and unscrews the cap of the bottle. His body is shrunk back in contemplation of itself, hooded and sulky, his face gone quite red.

"Where's Mae?" I ask.

"Locked in the bathroom," says Buffalo man. "If she's going to *act* like an animal I'm going to have to *treat* her like one." I consider this statement while Buffalo man dabs peroxide on the fresh arc of tooth marks half-encircling my ankle, the fluid fizzles and spits like seltzer tablets. "Nasty bit of luck, Agnes, I'm really sorry," he says.

"Has she ever done that before?" I ask him. I am sitting up now and studying the imprint of her teeth, wondering if they will leave a scar and what an unusual scar it would be, a bite from a jealous chimpanzee.

"No, I've never seen her bite anybody that hard the whole time I've known her. She's taken little nips at people, gets a little possessive when

I have anyone over, any guests at all I mean, not that I have that many...."

"It's okay," I say, "I know I'm not the only girl you've ever taken to bed, but I'd like to know whether I'm the first one she's ever attacked like that. Just for personal reasons I'd like to know." Buffalo man scowls at my heel and appears not to hear me, swaddling my ankle round and round with gauze. I start to laugh and can't seem to stop.

"Oh look," I say, "I'm going to be a *mummy*."

"That's not funny," says Buffalo man. "Quite a wicked bite you got there, it seems it's gone to your head, laughing like that. Suggest you don't move yourself until morning at least. Hate to say it, but you might want to look into a tetanus shot, just to be on the safe side. Mae's pretty clean, but...."

Lockjaw? Well wouldn't it be hilarious to catch a disease with a name like that. Locking the jaw like a diary and concealing confessions, sealing memory inside. Wouldn't it be funny to flee that sort of creepy secrecy only to find it repeated again. I keep thinking how funny this is until two red birds cover my eyes with their wings, and I fall asleep.

❧

Well, of *course*. Of course there'd be a third party hiding in the rafters, waiting, watching, bearing witness, baring teeth. Of *course* that imp in the rafters was bound to be dragged into the mix *just* at the point of crisis, *just* in the nick of time by a jealous set of simian incisors. Even here in this room God-knows-where. *See-no, hear-no, speak-no.* Mae's stealth had been remarkable, I'd neither seen nor heard her approach, as though she just dropped in from the ceiling like a giant hairy arachnid all flailing limbs and gnashing mandibles. For how long had she been watching us, that imp in the rafters, looking down and snickering, *What fools, what fools?*

In the dream there are three of us up there, who share a single set of grinning teeth, a single pair of eyes and ears, passed from one to the other among us. We three monkeys are Mae West and my mother and myself, or some remote-control version of myself, perched up in the rafters, watching the coupling below. The twisting and writhing of limbs, the grunting and smacking of lips, the hairy thrust of muscles and the glistening of fluids, the engorging of flesh, such a curious spectacle.

"But she is one of us," says Mae West in slow motion to my mother and me, pointing a curving index at the humans below. I am able to hear her say it, because presently Mae has the mouth and I have the ears, while my mother has only the eyes and hears nothing. She watches furiously but cannot turn away, because there are also eyes at the back of her head. The female body below is hidden from view, beneath the hunching haunches of the male, while we three monkeys take turns trying to guess her identity. "But she is one of us, can't you guess?"

Then all at once the sharp intake of breath, a howl heard above and below as the man throws back his head and looks up, the bed sheets incarnadine as the wounded scrambles out from beneath on all fours, her gleaming teeth concealing something in her mouth.

My tongue, is the first thing I say when I finally wake up. *It's as dry as a stick.* On the tree stump by the bed stands the hourglass and a terry face cloth full of melting ice chips, and a gruesome stack of bandages more red than they are white. "You've been sweating out a fever all night," says Buffalo man, lying beside me propped up on one elbow, mouth set in unworded thought. He reaches across me for the blue glass pitcher and pours a glass of water as I squirm semi-upright to drink it. "I've been quite worried about you," he says. "Has anyone every told you, by the way, that you grind your teeth like crazy in your sleep?"

"No, I wouldn't say anyone's ever been in a position to tell me so."

"Really? Are you serious? Huh. D'you mean...?"

I nod my head without opening my eyes. From the bathroom, I can hear the soft thump of Mae West's body turning endless somersaults over the black and white tiles. Thump, whump, until I fall into sleep again.

"I can't believe how hard you grind. I've never seen anything like it." Buffalo man smiles mildly down on my waking face, blurry-edged in the morning light as though he were haloed with peach fuzz. I am sure I can smell peaches though there aren't any. I read that the brain can be manipulated into sensing smells which don't exist at source, that certain areas of the brain may be stroked or poked to produce the olfactory experience of peaches or burnt toast. In a disappearing dream, I see Buffalo man tickling my brain with a feather from one of his stuffed mallards.

"You've been listening to me grind my teeth all night?" I ask.

"I've been watching you for the last half-hour or so," he says, "You really go at it. I'm no expert, but it sounds like you're lugging around some stress you don't need."

My head still heavy on the pillow, I place a closed fist on my forehead like an apple and make a mental note never to let my mother watch me sleep. She'd have me fitted with one of those latex bridles for sure, like a gag in the mouth of a person with seizures. The theory was that the teeth would eventually exhaust themselves, grinding against nothing but the smooth surface of the mouth guard. Eventually they would stop doing it, allowing the muscles to release all their tensions. The mouth guard would teach the taut jaws that resistance was futile, the only freedom from stress was relinquishing control. This general concept is terrifying to everybody, no less because it is true.

I struggle upright in bed, hop on one foot to the reptilian toilet seat, and am sick. Buffalo man and the bite from Mae have combined to nudge something awake, either that or I really am becoming ill. There was a churning as of dreams or nausea, or simply the continued contractions of sex-muscles which hadn't released themselves completely.

"That's not unusual, for a first-time experience," shrugs Buffalo man. "With many women it doesn't happen at all," he says, "for emotional reasons." When I ask him what sort of emotional reasons those are, he says he wouldn't presume. He just wants to make sure I'm taking care of myself if there's anything wrong. He looks a bit freaked out when he brings me the phone so I can call my mother's house at Salmon Court. I don't expect there to be an answer and there isn't one, she'd already be at work at the clinic.

"I fell asleep in the lab," I tell my mother's new answering machine, "even the janitor didn't bother waking me up. I must have been pretty exhausted." Then for some reason I say, "Things are going great at school, Mum, don't worry about me." I should have called her last night, before there was anything to hide. Before there was any unspoken thing to creep through the phone line. Something always gives you away.

"You could crash here until your ankle heals, if you need to," says Buffalo man. "I noticed that you didn't leave the phone number. Thanks for that, must admit I was greatly relieved."

So I stay with him in his taxidermy studio all weekend and learn that there *is* more than one way to skin a cat. In fact, there are three. He shows me hand-drawn diagrams of three unique cutting strategies for stuffing and mounting a bobcat, with dotted lines on splayed cat-shapes, named after the taxidermists who invented them. The cats look as though they are reaching up their arms and praying.

17

To a Field Mouse

> As in water face answereth to face,
> So the heart of man to man.
> Hell and destruction are never full;
> So the eyes of man are never
> satisfied.
>
> — Proverbs 27: 19-20

It was on my eleventh birthday that he left, and in leaving, left the green chain-link gate open behind him. I came home from school to find the gate flagging open as though the invisible albumen sheathing the house had finally ruptured once and for all. As soon as I saw the open gate I knew that my father was not there anymore, but a stray malamute had wandered into the yard and was digging a hole beneath my mother's wisteria.

Inside the house, in the kitchen, a chair had been pushed away from the round melamine table. Not quite directly, at an oblique. A knobbly mug of cold tea was sitting there as well, like a gnomish monk in meditation over half-full and half-emptiness. Near the mug, a paper napkin lay crumpled like a tiny temple, where the card or the note should have been. Really should have been. But I knew even without a note, that my father had left for good. The mug and the chair and the napkin and the tea had a strange familiar presence which had never been there before.

It had not been unusual to perceive my father as a present absence meant to signify something. But here, now, was a new presence which seemed to signify absence, nothingness embodied, disembodied. It did not seem asymmetrical. My father seemed suddenly more comprehensible as a mug of cold tea, than he tended to be as the unseen resident of a basement room. I could move up quite close to the objects on the table, look at them closely and pick them up in my hands. Still I thought there should have been a note. It was my birthday. I was eleven.

I sat down in the vacated chair. There seemed some wrongness in this, as though sitting in the last place he sat were some affront to the respectful observation of time. The empty chair, the paper temple, the monkish mug were familiars of my father. I fancied they were what he'd left behind, for me to find. I might have approached them more respectfully, instead of sitting right down in the chair as though the absence of my father weren't already sitting there. I might have offered pennies and fruit, let this new presence of his absence sink into my bones for a while, my bones which felt familiar and strange.

But somehow my first incentive was the physical imperative to sit down. Like when a policeman phones somebody's house asking to speak to the nearest relative of such-and-such a person. The heart stops for a moment and burrows way down low. I kept thinking how I wished he'd at least left a note. I would have accepted any words at all to be his final ones, any at all. I'd crouched on chicken wire outside the card-boarded window of the basement room, listening to his mumbled words I couldn't even understand. Obviously I would have accepted anything. I unfolded the napkin to see if there was even one word written there. There was a greasy stain, some crusty sugar from a doughnut, but not a single word.

I looked away at the kitchen wall, the blurry kitchen window, the undulating curtain patterns of fish and chopping boards. My vision swam outward in breast strokes and finally clung to something on the wall, some folded pages. From the pages, seven words dropped into my eyes like plums into a silver colander. *Always know where the nearest exits are.* My father had not written the words himself, they were not hand written, but printed in a tiny font on glossy paper, in the bottom corner of the page hanging open on the wall.

The pages were a calendar. It was splayed open to the month of September, with a picture of a Dalmatian dog wearing a fireman's helmet beside a red hydrant. Someone had drawn a blue X on the 17th, which was today, which was my birthday. The calendar had been purchased from a fireman who came to our door, selling them to raise money for burn victims, who might have been people who hadn't known where the nearest exits were.

But as final words they would have to do, and I did keep them, concealing them within myself like a hearing aid. I would become quite adept at listening for the possibility of exits. In later years, it would become more a problem of where the exits would lead to, ultimately. When one's only thought is to flee a burning building, just about any exit will suffice. But for how long can one go about solving one's problems by leaping from third-storey windows? After a while a body has to start thinking about where it is going to land, or if anybody else will be there to catch it.

Anyway, this was not at all the manner of my father's departure. Nothing so gaudy as a leap from a window, nothing so abandoned as that. Only a mug of cold tea, a sugary napkin, a gate left wide open. I arranged these details in various ways, as though they were wooden blocks with pictures on them, until I could make them represent an embarkation on a quest. In any case, I preferred to think of him as a man who had someplace more important to go, than one who had been forced to leap from a burning building.

The difference was a matter of perspective. My mother had no time for embarkations upon spiritual quests, literally no time. She was busy scraping plaque from people's lower incisors to support the three of us, my brother, my father, and I. Our family had been more supported by the decay of people's teeth than by spiritual questing, that was the truth of it. Perhaps my mother had little choice but to think of spiritual longing the way she thought of dental nerves. It was best to keep them as unexposed as possible because poking at them was extremely painful unless the subject were heavily sedated. Nerves needed to be frozen, in order to be examined comfortably. More deeply rooted questions of freeing one's soul might have seemed counter to the stronger imperative of keeping surfaces clean and white and free of cavities. You only started poking at nerves if there was a visible problem, and you didn't liberate a tooth from it roots unless the tooth was clearly dying or already dead.

My father's departure was like the roots of his teeth, many of which had to be extracted after a rugby accident when he was twenty-one. He didn't have many roots left, being the only one is his family to make the trip across the water, more or less on a dare because none of them believed he could make anything of himself. No one, especially his own father, expected my father to growl or to hunt, to bite down with bared fangs. For this reason, he might have thought it best that he simply disappear. *Mysteriously* would be best, like the crew of the *S.S. Marie Celeste*, leaving their cups and cutlery on the table, salt herring still on their plates. As though the possibility of abandoning ship had never occurred to them until the very moment it became mandatory, when they simply extracted themselves or were extracted like teeth.

Yet for several weeks after my father's departure he continued to make his presence felt, like sensation in a limb which has been amputated. He'd kept his set of keys, and now and then I'd notice small signs of his having passed by. Personal possessions he'd left behind would go missing from the house, or there would be three fewer doughnuts on the Styrofoam tray in the fridge. There'd be another light fixture newly and badly repaired, so that it vacillated between light and darkness, or I'd notice yellow bald patches on a newly-mown lawn. A pen or two would disappear from the jar beside the phone. I'd find doodles of spoons and spirals along the margins of the message paper, or a few cases of empty bottles would be gone from beneath the basement stairs. At last, the three-wheeled shopping cart disappeared from the pile of junk behind the house. I imagined my father dragging it along the beach like the shell of a giant tortoise, and wondered where he slept.

No comments about my father's visits ever arose from my mother, except for one time when a crystal mouse went missing from on top of the fireplace mantle. The mouse had been part of a collection of lead crystal animals given to my mother by Dr. Spektor. She received a new animal every year on her birthday. Their bodies were geodesic domes of many facets, glinting blue like the low flame of a gas stove. She'd collected an owl, a baby seal, a baby chicken, a turtle, a rabbit, a mouse, and a duck.

My mother would never have addressed the matter of the missing mouse to my father, because doing so would make implicit reference to Dr. Spektor, of whom my mother preferred not to speak. The absent mouse aroused comment only because my mother thought I'd taken it myself, as I'd been known to take things occasionally. Small ornamental things which could be stashed away in my school bag, and given as anonymous gifts to teachers I had crushes on. But I swore to my mother I had nothing to do with the disappearance of the mouse. Which was true, or half-true, if knowing its whereabouts made me accomplice to my father.

I knew where the mouse had gone. I had found it in the basement, on my father's workbench. It was wedged between the steel jaws of the vice, with its beady black eyes starting from their sockets. One of its crystal ears had been broken off and repaired with Super Glue, then left to set in the vice. And this is what I mean about the way that memory works. Sometimes I remember it as my mother's vice and my father's mouse, when really it was the other way round.

I had turned the lever to release the grip of the vice, letting the weight of the crystal mouse fall into my hand. The repair was not very successful. The wad of dried glue was yellow and mucusy-looking, there was enough of it to repair a dozen mouse ears. It was not even in the right place. The ear was stuck fast to the mouse's neck like a gill. I could have done a better job myself, I thought, and it bothered me very much to think that I could have done a better job myself. I would rather have had a father who was good at fixing things, especially since he persisted in fixing things. His workbench was piled with rusting tools he'd collected at yard sales here and there over the years. I'd rather he had learned to use them properly, or had found something else to do. I frequently told kids at school that my father could bend spoons with his mind, and half-believed it. But I replaced the mouse to the grip of the vice, and turned the handle back the other way until the jaws slowly reclosed around the tiny crystal head.

18

How to stuff a squirrel

Be sure to follow these five basic rules:
Observe the position of the animal before shooting it;
this will be useful when you stuff it.
Never aim at the head. You could shatter the skull,
and you would then have to reconstruct it later.
As soon as the animal is killed note the colour of the eyes. Always
have a notebook with you when you go to the woods or to a zoo.
As soon as possible, pack with wadding the openings through which
blood or excrement could escape.
Wipe the fur or plumage carefully with wadding, so that the blood
will not coagulate on it. It is very difficult to remove it later.

— Jean Labrie, author of *The Amateur Taxidermist*

Buffalo man's toolbox contains tools from several other trades thrown together in one. From the carpenter's toolbox, one cross-cut saw, a tack hammer, and a vice. From the artist's toolbox, tubes of oil paint of the best quality, modeling clay, Plaster of Paris. From the tailor's toolbox, cotton padding for stuffing, an assortment of sewing needles and non-putrefying thread, a pair of scissors. From the surgeon's, one bottle of hydrochloric acid, a No. 3 scalpel with a No. 10 blade. From the cosmetician's, some tweezers, a soft-haired brush, an aluminum comb. From other, miscellaneous toolboxes, some paste, some table salt, some galvanized wires, a pen knife.

Only one item on his list of equipment didn't need to be borrowed from anybody's toolbox. Artificial eyes. Buffalo man kept them in one of the wooden drawers of his apothecary's cabinet, bundled together on their thin stalks like a colony of mushrooms, or a bouquet of Martian camomile blossoms. There were a few larger orbs resembling horse-chestnuts in the drawer as well. These were fake deer eyes.

Borax was mixed with alum and salt and rubbed into the skins of the animals to dry them. The solution could be used several times, each time picking up a little bit of the animal whose skin it scoured, until it was too saturated to absorb any more and had to be discarded in sealed containers. In the garage, Buffalo man had a large cardboard canister labeled *Borax*, and a smaller canister hand-lettered *Arsenic*, more traditionally used for the same purpose. Buffalo man now only used it to kill the beady-eyed rats who sometimes found their way into the garage at night, before they could gnaw the ears off drying deer pelts. The rats would die anyway from gnawing arsenic-encrusted ears, but the damage to the deer pelt would already be done. In the morning, there would often be the bodies of rats flipped belly-up on the concrete floor, frozen with their paws suspended in the air like commas. Unnatural pauses, in comparison to the posture of the deer who'd been stuffed according to *Basic Rule #1*, which recommends that the animal be arranged to resemble how it had appeared when it was alive, just before a bullet tore through someplace other than its head.

Yet if I twisted the key in the padlock and tiptoed barefoot into the garage, early in the morning before Buffalo man was awake, it would be the rat and not the deer I would be more drawn to. To check whether or not it might still be living. It would be the rat, with its pained grimace like an open wound, its paws held stiff in final gesture, which more closely resembled the expression of creaturely life. The deer, though it had been molded to look like a living deer, looked like a picture of a deer, or like a deer who'd been hypnotized, its final expression not even its own.

PG Warning. This next section features some images of skinning a squirrel, which images I would have avoided myself, if it could've been helped. But as it could not, and as these images of squirrels are tangled up in the immediate environment, I've included the squirrels here, as much to exorcise as to present them. You may not wish to see them. Like the image of my father on the aeroplane to Winnipeg, the skinning of squirrels is an image I sometimes wish I had not seen. But having seen it, there is nothing else to do but find the words to name it. The most frightening image of all is the one which has no name. I had watched Buffalo man move through the various procedures enough times to have stuffed squirrels in my sleep. I had also begun to refer to the specimens as *it* instead of *he* or *she*, because otherwise the whole process seemed unbearable.

A staple gun. A spool of shoemaker's thread. An instrument called a skin holder, and one called a skin adjuster. A tool called a bone snip and another called a bone saw. Surgeon's needles. Flat-nosed forceps. Straight forceps. Needle-pointed forceps.

First, Buffalo man lays the squirrel on its back with its forepaws in the air, and measures its length from head to tail. He takes cotton wadding to plug up every opening through which blood or excrement might escape. Mouth, nostrils, anus, open wounds, holes from bullets or shot. Its mouth stuffed with wadding, the squirrel makes me think of a roasting pig, and then of an ECT patient.

The specimen is now ready to be skinned. This involves making a vertical scalpel incision along the abdomen to the anus, then carefully turning the animal inside-out like a pair of socks. Special care is required in removing the tail nerve, which is elastic and pale as a willow switch when the bark is peeled away. Finally, the skin is gently pulled forward from the head, as though removing a balaclava, taking care that the eyelid holes are not damaged by delicately cutting round the orbit of the eye.

At this point, the specimen is released from the small triple-fishhook from which it has been hanging on a chain. Now there are two squirrel shapes lying on the newspaper, connected nose-to-nose like a pair of circus seals kissing. One of the squirrel shapes is a body without any skin covering it, while the other is a red inside-out squirrel costume with no body inside. It's a wide-eyed squirrel connected nose-to-nose to its empty-eyed reflection, as though staring into an enchanted pool which turns everything inside-out.

Buffalo man now severs the head at the neck, freeing its muscles and bones once and for all from the squirrel suit which had contained them. The head itself is left connected nose-to-nose with its skin hood, then carefully cleaned of tongue, eyes, and brain, which are all replaced by artificial replicas of themselves or modeling clay before the head is tucked back into its hood. The skin is now rubbed with borax and salt, and left overnight. In the morning I will wash the squirrel skins in a basin of cold water and laundry detergent. They cannot be wrung out, but must be carefully pressed like angora sweaters. Then I will hang up the squirrels on the laundry umbrella which Buffalo man has set up in the garage for this purpose.

Looking over the leftover squirrels, I remember the bucket of rats I saw in the service elevator at the university, the last day I was there. There'd been two experiments planned for those rats, both hinging on faculties of memory. In the first, rats were introduced to a maze of blind alleys with only one exit, where a reward of food awaited. It had taken even the smartest rats several false starts and retracings of steps to figure out the maze, while other rats were never able to figure it out at all. The *maze-bright* rats were subsequently able to remember the correct way through the labyrinth with few errors, and were soon interbred to produce rats who were even quicker at learning the maze than their parents had been. The offspring of the *maze-dull* rats, conversely, were even stupider than their parents.

The other experiment had involved removing half the brains of *maze-bright* rats in order to see whether any specific area of the brain could be localized in which memory of the maze was contained. Those beetle electrodes were to measure their tiny diminishing brainwaves. What they'd found was that almost any rat with half a brain could still figure out where the exit was, eventually, so they removed half of the half that was left. They found that some rats could still remember how to do the maze, though more slowly. Their hypothesis was that memory is not localized in any one area of the brain, but rather seems to involve an unpredictable activity of communications, a network of neural ivy branching madly off in all directions. So, what if Agnes Underhill turned out to be one of those *maze-dull* rats who could never remember where she'd come from and therefore where she was going? What if she were never able to find the exit at all? Would she pass this loser gene on to future generations?

In dreams, I am taught tongue-twisters by a highly intelligent rat, who laughs at my failure to repeat them successfully. *Round and round the rugged agate Agnes ran a ragged rut.* Repeat. Round and round her ragged brain, Agnes ran a tad insane. Round and round the memory maze, Agnes wound her dance hall days. Round and round a state forgotten, Agnes sensing something rotten. Those who did not know history were doomed to repeat it. Repeat. Those who could not remember history would run round and round and never find the only exit, never find it at all. Were there even any exits, or would she need to invent one?

19

MASTODONS

> Little Luther Underhill
> Is a loathsome poet
> His unrequited loved ones
> All seem to know it
> But oh, the bounty they would reap,
> If only he could sow it.
>
> — Agnes' father, on a matchbook cover

"I've left a note for your father to move the rest of his stuff out," my mother said, as she left for Dr. Spektor's clinic that morning, a few weeks after my eleventh birthday. *Please see that he does so.* And so my father had been coming to the house almost every day lately, from God-knows-where, to creep about, and snoop into things. The same way I did, when no one was around.

I could hear my father banging his tools at his workbench in the basement, or else locked in his locked room muttering God-words to himself, just like he had when he still officially lived here. At five-fifteen he would leave again, then soon afterward the green Torino would pull into the driveway with my mother inside. It made me nervous to never see both my parents in the same place at the same time. Maybe they'd become the same person, the one having been absorbed into the other. Now even my father's *things* were vanishing from the house on Dormier Street, piece by piece, like a staircase in a dream.

Whenever I could, I went to Effie's house after school, which was pretty seldom because of her ballet classes, and because she didn't really like me anymore. I still went to see her every couple of weeks, when she was sick at home with the flu or something. She seemed to get sick a lot. Those sick days she didn't do much except throw her dolls around the room and cry. So mostly I went home after school, and stayed in my bedroom drawing zoo animals.

The day of the mastodons, I was lying on my bed in my room, caging an elephant in a box with red crayon, when I saw the shadow of feet through the crack beneath my door. My father knocked once before opening it, then stood there in the doorway waving the note from my mother like a baggage claim in his hand.

"Did your mum say which stuff she means me to move out of here, please, or am I supposed to guess what's mine?" he asked. I closed the book on my red elephant and sat up on my bed.

"Uhhm. Well, she said whatever was no use to her was probably yours. All the stuff in the basement, I guess, and your dresser-things."

"I don't know how your mother expects me to remove the things from the dresser," said my father, "since the bedroom door is bloody locked. With a brand new lock. Who installed *that*, by the way, and with whose *tools*?"

"I know it's locked," I said. I also knew it was possible to break into my parents' bedroom through the window outside, by bracing your palms against the window then pushing up and over. I considered telling my father this. But it would have been asking him to acknowledge a sensibility I often suspected him of having, the desire to pry into things, to break open seals and examine contents. I would have been asking him to confess that he thought that way, like I did, with an insatiable curiosity of mysterious sources. So I didn't tell him what I knew about breaking in through windows, when all the doors are locked.

"I guess you'll have to wait until I can convince her to leave her bedroom unlocked," I said, "which she probably won't do." I reopened my book and picked up a new pencil crayon, to fill in the red elephant's body cavity with pale mint green. "Or else you'll have to come by when she's actually here, Dad."

My father made a sound like a dog when it sneezes.

"Well, I'm not bound to *do* that," he said.

"*Fine* then," I said, because it was what my mother would've said.

Scr-rr-ews, like the ones my father said I had loose in my noggin. Like the ones I'd have on either side of my neck just below the jaw line, if I were a creature stitched together of parts. Now I was sitting up on my father's workbench, picking screws from a shoe box, dropping them in a Mason jar. *Clink, clank.* Separating them from the nails, which I am picking out and dropping in another Mason jar. *Clank, clink.*

My fingers could tell the difference between nails and screws, more quickly than my eyes could, the metal shafts either smooth or grooved. Nails went in straight, screws twist in spirals. This was why I had *screws* loose in my noggin and not *nails,* because nothing in my head ever followed a straight line. Nothing ever went *straight to the point* as my mother put it, but wound itself dizzy around some central axis I was never quite able to drive home, and wasn't sure I should. There was always a fear of what the point might hit, behind the walls.

"Well then, Agnes, d'you know how this broken mirror came to be under the carpet?" The voice of my father came from the adjoining spare room. This might be the last time he came back to the house on Dormier Street, to pick up the last of his things, and mess about as though the house were a holey sock which needed mending.

It came from that old medicine cabinet, idiot, I said in my head, *which was busted like seven hundred years ago.* Why did parents ask questions they already knew the answers to, or thought they did, or acted like they thought they did? From where I sat cross-legged on my father's workbench, I could not see my father but I could hear him. *Rrr-rrip-rip,* like the amplified sound of someone removing bandages. I could hear but could not see my father tearing up the rug in the spare room, where all the family skeletons were buried. The monster-doubles who haunted the ground the house was built on. It was just as well, I wouldn't have wanted to watch. Only bad things came from tearing up burial grounds, surely my father of all people must have known that. I wished that he would tear more quickly and have done with it already, instead of jerkily yanking. It might have been less painful that way.

"Agnes? Do you know anything about this broken glass, here?"

Curse my bad luck. I jumped down from the workbench and went over to the wooden vestibule dividing my father's half of the basement, where the locked room and the workbench were, from the spare room where my brother Gavin and I daily tortured each other. It was this room, the spare room, that my father decided should be stripped of its carpet, in a final gesture of his departure. My mother probably didn't know he was going to do this, but neither would she care very much. She thought the basement was a pit of despair and she hardly ever set foot down there.

Mustardy scabs of foam floor padding were flying about the room. Some were clinging to the underside of the carpet, some still stuck to the floor in curious shapes resembling continents, with the cool concrete ocean beneath. My father's eyes were bleary-looking from the dust of the orange shag, as he rolled it up tamale-style, then stepped over to tear up the other side. He found it had already been torn up, and that *someone* had hidden a broken mirror under there.

I had hidden the remains under the orange shag in the spare room, instead of throwing them away in the trash. They hadn't been forgotten about, exactly, except in the way that hidden things are conventionally forgotten about. Pickled in a Mason jar labelled *F* for *Forget about it*. You still know the preserved memories are there, but manage to un-know it most of the time. My father had likewise seemed to un-notice that there were only *two* mirrors left from the original *three*, though they were right there over his head, when he puttered around at his workbench every single day. Now he stood over the bones of the missing one, reflecting back parts of his face, which looked reddish. It was what happened to my father's face whenever he bent down over something, such as a dysfunctional lawn mower or some onions he was peeling.

I brushed nail rust from my fingers onto my jean pockets and went over to my father. Then I was there, too, in sharp pieces on the floor. Only bits of me, and bits of him too, tapered long and sharply curved like elephant tusks. Or what were those hairy prehistoric elephants? *Mastodons*. There they were, *mastodon tusks*, buried here under the orange shag carpet, since, like, seven million years ago.

"Were there mastodons on the Ark?" I asked the top of my father's head, as he stooped to gather up the pieces of the mirror. "D'you know anything about mastodons, Dad?"

My father didn't look up, he was thinking with his tongue, I could see that. He was one of those people who move their tongues around when they think. When he finally spoke, his voice was like a minister's, turning every sentence into a tune and pronouncing everything very precisely.

"I think what happened was this," he began, then recited one of his famous poems, one of his un-famous poems, one of the dozens of poems he wrote which nobody ever saw.

> The mastodons were almost gone
> When Noah built the Ark.
> Indeed, the only one remaining
> Was out stampeding in the park.
>
> "This flood theory," quoth the beast,
> "Is both unpleasant and unproved."
> No matter how much Noah badgered,
> The brute would not be moved.
>
> So Noah watched him from his deck chair
> And as the water level rose,
> He saw the last mastodon was swallowed up
> Feet-first, then ears, then nose.
>
> And so it vanished in the deluge,
> And never more was seen.
> Which is why elephants are wise
> And can't forget the mammoth fools they've been.

My father finished his poem but still didn't look up, just kept on piling the shards of glass in a staggered stack like a natural mica formation. "That's not bad," I said, not sure how good it was, but it wasn't bad if it was right off the top of his head. Still, I couldn't help remembering having heard the same story before, in a song about a unicorn.

Every time my father left the house, I didn't know if it would be the last time I ever saw him. And there didn't seem to be any script I could recite, to prevent a peculiar father from leaving forever. The only ones which came to mind involved soap opera lovers, and taxicabs madly pursuing departing aircrafts down runways. But weeping just then seemed as out of the question as calling him *Daddy* right to his face. I felt my jaw muscles tighten like a spring, and stay that way for a million years.

The specifics of pain do not accommodate themselves well to language. Perhaps this is why many people don't remember the most painful things, but remember all the little things surrounding them. Memory is similar to language, in its selection of certain details, its arrangement of details into patterns, which are supposed to mean something. But pain is mute, and lives in the muscles of an animal. Often not one photograph exists, in the mind, of the most painful thing. There are dozens of peripheral photos, domestic scenes where pain is not manifest, but still it's somehow visible anyway.

I could see it plainly in the eyes of my mother and father and brother, when I stared into their eyes in photographs, as I would never dare to do right to their faces. In photographs, I could see the way pain is stored in a body, in the chronic tension of a jaw muscle, the stoop of shoulders, the cloudy screens over eyes. The more I tried to explain the strange shadows cast on the walls of my dreams, the more I could see how everything is connected to everything else, like a magician pulling endless scarves from a hat. Dig forensic holes all over the lawn of history, if you must, but know that the skeleton you reconstruct, even if you are able to find one, and identify all its parts, might not be able to speak to you. And in the end you might not want it to.

20

A BIG FAT HEN

After my Achilles heals, Buffalo man and I take morning walks along Commercial Drive. He wears those molded sandals with the rubber-tire soles and fitted straps, like he could unravel his shoes and repel down a cliff with the parts. I wear canvas shoes from Chinatown. The Buffalo man and I do not notice the same things when we walk, this is something I notice. I also tend to notice things like cappuccino cups with foam scum still on the rim, and dogs who've run round the pole they're tethered to a few too many times. Red leashes getting wound round like a barber shop pole, with the dog clinging close and whining whiskered like a drunk.

Buffalo man notices a sticker for a local hardcore band on a crosswalk breaker, with a picture of a red Dr. Seuss fox carrying an axe. Then he notices a woman who looks exactly like Tippi Hedren, she just got on that bus, he swears to God. He can't understand how I could've missed her. Then in the window of a junk shop we both notice an old tin sign, bent and rusty with the words *Tattooed Poultry* in black block letters.

For several blocks we talk about what *Tattooed Poultry* might mean. Buffalo man thinks it's an advertisement, that you could once have gone to this place and got your hens tattooed, so no other guy could claim they were *his* hens. Or maybe these people sold exotic hens, and had the whole coop of 'em tattooed as proof of pedigree.

So then I start talking about what-all *misery* the hens of the world were subjected to, foot diseases from standing in overcrowded dirty coops, and being made to lay eggs constantly. Poultry fowl being executed with electric probes inserted under their beaks. I must have mentioned the electric probes at least a half-dozen times, even a full dozen, I couldn't make the image go away no matter how quickly we walked.

"You could *slow down* a bit, you know," says Buffalo man.

"There's something so personal about beaks," I continue, "so intrinsic to the identity of hens. So much depends on beaks. It's because of beaks that we got to pick out the yellow and orange crayons to colour in pictures of chickens, instead of just red for the wattle and comb. Because most chickens in pictures are left white, for some reason. You felt like you were supposed to leave the body white, like the White Spot hen. And the colouring books never said *boo* about electric probes."

Buffalo man cuts in and says he wants me to stop dwelling on electrocuted hens, but I *cannot* stop dwelling on them until I understand why the image persists. So much depends on understanding why an image does not flow away into grey matter, like so many of them *do*, but gets caught in some mental appendix and inflames the place. Demanding to be extracted, expressed, or at least identified. Relative heavens and hells seem to seed in the naming of pictures.

"I remember this bird Miss Gristle drew on the board in grade three," says Buffalo man. "Gristle probably wasn't her name, just how I remember her. She drew this bird on the board then took a ruler and caged it in a grid, six squares across and six down. This was to help us understand how to draw a bird. If we studied each of her squares individually, then faithfully reproduced no more no less than the contents of each square, into the corresponding square on our own little grids, we would each end up with a perfectly perching bird just like Miss Gristle's but smaller. Then after class I took scissors from her desk and cut up my bird into thirty six squares, like one of those puzzles, you know? Where the squares are all mixed up and you have to slide them around 'til you find the scrambled picture? I cut up the bird because it was the exact opposite of what Miss Gristle wanted me to do.

"So anyway, I discovered that Miss Gristle's bird could be reassembled with its feet on top of its head like antlers and its beak sticking out of its ass. At the end of the year, she wrote on my report card that I showed an aggressive personality and probably always would, and that I'd have to learn to follow instructions, because she herself was not about to back down. *Not about to back down!* Imagine, being caught in such a battle of egos with a nine-year-old. Poor woman, probably never got laid in her life."

"I'd like to get one of those beaded curtains, one of the bamboo ones," I say, when a golden haired woman walks past, fragrant of amber, with sand-soft bead sounds rustling in her hair, and silver toe-rings. Probably she had beaded curtains as well, and could read a person's palms, with all of her exits entrancing through shimmering sheaves like a goddess of wheat. And I was a goddess of beaks. A goddess of ungainly mouths, which squeak and squawk and are frequently heard to say nothing. A goddess of shock-mouth hens who don't peck back, electrically pecked in the pecker.

The mouth of a cup, with dried cappuccino scum. Round. Open. Receptive. Silent. I didn't want to emulate these qualities, wholly, but when I saw their expression in objects, even the foam on the mouth of a cup, I did feel a tug in my chest like I'd open a robe to receive them.

Later, lying back in the tub, I wash my hair with egg shampoo and dunk my whole head to rinse it. I am tempted to taste it, and do so, but it does not taste like eggs at all. While my eyes are still closed and my ears underwater, I imagine the sound of a drill, and for a moment I am drowning in a dentist chair at Dr. Spektor's clinic. My mother is rinsing cherry fluoride from my teeth, with a shiny metal water-pistol, another trigger shooting off only cold air. Cold air and water hitting my two front teeth, the fake ones, and splashing up into my nose. If the teeth are fake why can I still feel them? If something is not real, why can you still feel its breath on the back of your neck when you walk home late at night?

I sit up suddenly in the tub, streaming egg shampoo from hair tendrils, the water tepid and soupy. *Egg drop soup.* By accident of nerves, I drop the cool egg of soap into the tub and feel around in the suds until I find it. Like an eel it eludes, drawing eddies in my brain, again to the place where I am always reaching beneath the surface toward something unseen and unremembered, into the warmish dampish depth it dwells within. When I bathe, or wash dishes, or pry open the drain with a dinner fork to dig out the carrot coin which is clogging it, I expect to find lost memory in such places.

The sound of the drill starts up again, and the bathroom door shimmies on its hinges. The room is tilting sideways perhaps. I hold onto the water fixtures, hot and cold in my hands, as onto a world which is fixed when the mind shimmies. But no, not much of the world is *fixed*. The world is a stray cat who prowls the alleys and sires many, bears many, buries many. Nothing is fixed but all is in need of fixing. Fixing is the state of desire, moving toward completeness. A fine fix is what we all are in, we are.

I watch the door, fix eyes. It tips toward me ajar, a crooked jar, then the barbarous face of Buffalo man, grinning with a ball cap on backwards. There's a strap across his forehead where I might expect to see a spot light, like he's one of those guys in mines who blow holes in walls, breaking through to hidden caverns.

"Why'd you take the whole bathroom door off?" I say. Aside from the taxidermy studio, the bathroom is the only closed space in Buffalo man's place. But now, in the empty doorway, he stands on a barstool and hammers two nails above the frame with the Hammer of Thor, a small steel hammer which came attached to the hand of an eighteen-inch action figure. Buffalo man uses Thor's hammer to free Thor from his usual hanging place above the door, before driving home the two new nails. From my seat in the cold bath, all I can see of Buffalo man are his hands, and his slouchy trousers, his American bison belt buckle, and the unbuttoned belly of his green work shirt. Now that the bathroom door has been removed I am prickly with a cold draft.

"What are you *doing*, anyway?" I ask.

"Shhhh," says Buffalo man, "it's supposed to be a birthday present. I bought it for you today, when you were conversing with stray dogs on the Drive, Miss Doolittle."

Then, from the two nails, Buffalo man hangs a shimmering sheaf of bamboo beads. There is the sound of a rain stick as they settle plumb. Once the beads have stilled, I can make out the picture painted on them. There are two elephants, with green foliage all around. They are either walking side by side or they're mounted on each other, it is difficult to tell. But from certain angles, or when there is too much back-light, the elephants seem to disappear entirely like the purple Two Lions across Burrard Inlet.

Before leaving the bathroom, I catch sight of my face in the steamy mirror. If time continues to co-operate with gravity, I will look exactly like my father in twenty years. If vision fixed *upward* continues to be made impractical by perpetual clouds, or I fail to learn to laugh at things, my brows will continue to knit a low-creased awning over my eyes and I will look exactly like my father, in twenty years or maybe *ten*. I know this, not from a very clear memory of my father's face, but something more akin to a haunting in mine. Yet finally, when the mirror speaks, it is with *his* voice and not mine.

"Don't go *back*, Agnes. You're obsessed with going *backwards*. *So you think you're changed, do you?* Whose face do you seek when you look into his eyes? The past is a garage sale, Agnes, you pick the things which *seem* to be valuable. You take them home. And in time comes *meaning*, like a holy garage sale grail. But remember, you could have picked other things instead."

Walking through the beads makes a sound like hidden rattlesnakes when I leave the bathroom to join Buffalo man in the lighted loft. The painted elephants disperse, they shimmy between sheaves and disappear, reassembling themselves only after the sway and hiss have passed. But looking back a bit later, I see them there again, the pair of mountainous elephants, still shaking slightly.

21

THE HEADLESS BRIDE

When would I start to see the connections? Only once I start making them. But a jar of beads could be strung together in any order, and still reach round the circumference of a neck.

— Agnes Underhill, on a napkin

My first real object of desire was a severed head. I was seven or eight, if memory serves, which it generally doesn't, things tend to work the other way round. More often I find myself playing chambermaid to my own recollection, rearranging objects on its vanity table to look as functionally generic as possible, moving mental furniture according to its changing fancy.

But I do remember desiring the head, after my father's perennial, *I'd like to see you get ahead, you need one.* Which limping pun was not even original, I found out, when I saw it printed on a dozen T-shirts in the window of a Water Street souvenir shop. The T-shirts make a fitting souvenir of my father, who figures in memory as a sort of spatial concept, or emblem. Bearing little physical resemblance to the man himself, but easily transferable onto other things, and other people, like an iron-on decal, or a phony tattoo.

And I did get a head, the Christmas when I was seven or eight. It sparkled from beneath the low-hanging boughs of the tree, a food-processor-sized box, wrapped in zig-zag pink and silver paper, tied with a frothy lepidopterous bow. The bow had made similar appearances in previous years, like a lacy fading ghost of Christmas past, moldering to naphthalene. But under the warm burlesque of the tree it remained lovely, its whispered proposition ever the same, *open me first.*

Strictly speaking, the bow was not tied to the box at all, but stapled to itself in multiple loops and stuck with a daub of rubber adhesive. It was slightly disillusioning to learn this, when I'd thought my mother was able to tie such elaborate bows herself. She was resourceful, and believed strongly in the importance of presenting agreeable packages, regardless of means. She also believed in occasionally reminding us that her resources were pinched, like the nerve in her back was pinched, and that it pained her.

So I unwrapped the box carefully, knowing the bow would be preserved to reappear on some other object of desire, in some other time. I slipped my father's penknife beneath the bands of tape and sliced through until the paper fell away, then clamped my hands like forceps over the temples of the lovely head to lift her carefully out of the box. A small plastic bag of pink hair ornaments and play cosmetics fell out as well, like those bags of internal organs found in turkeys. For a few moments I could only sit staring at the head, until my mother said, "Well, if you don't like it, kitten, we could always exchange it for something else. Such as a decent pair of slippers, as per my original suggestion."

"What do you say, Agnes?" said my father. Then I was all praise and thank yous. The head was more perfect than I'd ever imagined, the most lovely head I had ever seen, the most perfect of presents. And it wasn't really severed at all, severance being predicated on some original attachment to a body, which this head had never known. It was blond, female, single. Its only attachment was a starchy, phony ponytail, which could be fastened in place with a pink plastic barrette, and as easily removed. Unlike my own head, this one was pliable and weighed almost nothing. A thumb pressed into its forehead left a dent, which gradually re-inflated when the thumb pressure was removed. It smiled with sealed lips, as I was encouraged to do, so as not to expose my crooked teeth.

The head stood about a foot tall. She had long shiny locks of celestial platinum, while my hair was as dark as peat. The eyes of the head were the flat blue of postcard skies, while mine sank back to oily brown, then black, then deeper to infinity, or less profound than that. The colour of drugstore sunglasses, beguiling the pupil into wide dilation as though it were protected, the retinas only getting more burned for their openness.

At seven or eight, my eyes sucked in radiance like a vacuum. The world burned its blueprint silhouettes onto my retinas, corresponding in negative to the shapes of objects on the landscape. By the time I was nine or ten, I had collected an entire shadow-pantheon of objects, and constructed frames around them in my mind. I saw their forms represented everywhere, as though every woman's face were trimmed to fit a silhouette-portrait in the back room of my brain, or every man were Alfred Hitchcock, lumbering into an ink-sketch caricature of himself and sublimating there. These shapes projected themselves from my eye-beams, like a magic lantern, and I saw their ghostly forms reflected in everything.

The head exactly filled a silhouette in my mind of a certain aspiration, or a risky possibility. I loved her detachment, her severance from butterflies in the stomach, from clumsy feet and other appendages which couldn't be relied upon to function with any grace. If desire to flirt with this sort of possibility were a glass slipper, then the head was that dainty foot which slid in smoothly and fit perfectly.

The head was supported by a pink plastic pedestal, embossed with curly designs. In place of shoulders, the pedestal looped out into epaulette-compartments, to hold hair ornaments and play cosmetics. The face of the head floated luminous, like a spider egg case, pale and gossamer, self-contained. I thought of spiders because of her hair, which was practically white and slightly sticky, like webs. When I flipped the head upside-down, to peer through her hollow neck and into her cranium, I could see rows of egg-like baubles, where the sticky strands of hair were pushed through perforations in the scalp, and heat-sealed in place. There was nothing else inside the head at all, except two blue concave bruises, which corresponded to her eyes, and a tiny dimple where her nose was. The face of my head, in negative relief.

I envied her freedom from attachments, and that she never had to shut her eyes to sleep. She was always wide-eyed and eager, yet registered no change of expression whatever. She did not have to drag around a body, like certain other species who spend their lives tethered to their own larval cases, or to communal shell structures, or to arms and legs.

Her empty-headedness appeared to mean that she had achieved something, in thinking nothing, in conceiving nothing, in seeing-hearing-speaking *nothing*.

I could stick my fingers up the slender tunnel of her neck, and hold her aloft in one hand; like a ballerina, she was easily borne. Were she ever to bear progeny, I imagined these as baby spiders, which would float away immediately after birth, to make their own way in the world, independently and elsewhere. Perhaps I loved this head for having, no for *being*, no body. Her birthright or copyright was to remain attached to nothing, and nothing, for its part, could remain attached to her.

After dinner, I carried my head into my room and closed the door. I draped a pale blue chiffon nightie from my mother's dresser over the pink plastic pedestal which stood in place of the head's shoulders. Then I cupped the back of her graceful nylon scalp in my squarish hand, and lead waltzes about the room. I admired how gracefully her blue chiffon no-body flowed in time to music it could not hear at all, and how she never trod on my toes.

I was always treading on my mother's toes, though I scarcely ever saw them. They were hidden in fluffy blue rabbit-fur slippers, or raised out of harm's way on the footrest of her big mustard armchair. This didn't seem to stop me from *always treading on her toes*, but at the same time I was *always getting underfoot*. I didn't dare point out the apparent contradiction in this, my dual identity as both treader and trodden upon. I simply understood that as a subject I was an imposition, and as an object, an encumbrance. All in all I was too much of a *body*, and this I had to bear in *mind*. "Mind your tongue, mind your manners, mind your feet you great horsey girl, mind you stay out of harm's way." Enough to make a girl wish for a body which occupied no space at all, so that it could be kept out of harm's way. Enough to make a girl long for a body which occupied negative *space*.

How delicious then, to be a severed head, transcending all of that. Immortal women were often bodiless. Preserved behind glass inside tiny gold lockets, or framed on gallery walls. Embossed on boxes of chocolate and cake mixes, bottles of pancake syrup, backs of coins, packets of cigarettes. Preserved on postage stamps, or suspended above the gateways of stone castles. More memorable as heads than they ever were as bodies, and not in anyone's way.

❦

Boxing Day, my little brother Gavin and I were packed in the dusty back seat of the green Torino and driven a million miles north to spend New Year's at my Great Aunt Hilda's house in Soapspit Bluff. My father stayed home, to care for the house, or to repair something at his workbench.

I had brought my head to Great Aunt Hilda's, draping my best red corduroy jumper over its pedestal-shoulders and fastening the six pearly buttons up to its throat. My mother had laid out the jumper on the motel bed for me, with a new pair of white tights, and shiny black shoes with gold buckles. I was supposed to wear them for New Year's. I did wear the tights and the shoes, but my head wore the jumper. I wore a brown cable knit sweater of my father's instead, and was swimming in it. But I pinned my hair back from my eyes with two of the head's pink barrettes, and hoped my mother would not be too cross about the jumper.

"I don't know why you persist in doing these things, Agnes," my mother said as she drove, "I don't know why you *persist*. Your Great Aunt Hilda hasn't seen you the whole blessed *year*. It would have been nice if you'd made an effort to look more presentable. You're not a bad looking little girl, in that jumper." She frowned at me in the rearview. Those eyes at the back of her head.

"I hope we won't live to regret giving you that ruddy doll head," she muttered, swerving into the passing lane.

My brother sat crumpled in his best navy blue polyester suit, beside me in the back seat. He was bent over a game which fired marbles at pictures of jungle animals, when he released a spring-lever. *Antelope, fifty points. Hyena, one hundred points. Tiger, five hundred points.* He had killed the same antelope at least a dozen times, and was still trying for the tiger. The game rattled endlessly.

"Gavin, let's leave off with that for now. I mean it, pet. You can pass that up to me, if you like." My mother's green-gloved hand appeared at her shoulder, reaching into the back seat like an eyeless puppet, opening and closing its mouth. "Gavin, let's have the game, please."

Gavin handed her the game and asked again why our father hadn't come with us. I watched the back of my mother's hatted head, and half of my own face in the rearview. The head lay smiling on the seat between me and my brother, its pale hair coarsely spiralled for the occasion, the red jumper lying limp across my lap like a grounded parachute.

At New Year's dinner my brother made the announcement that both of us had got pin worms. My mother caught him quickly by the elbow and escorted him from the table. The grown-ups had been talking about absent persons and suspicions of illness, and other suspicions which couldn't be verified as the persons were absent. Great Aunt Hilda was listening with what appeared to be distaste. I couldn't tell whether she disapproved of the people who were being spoken about, or of the fact they were being spoken about behind their backs. She hadn't seemed to mind about the pin worm report, she'd even smiled a bit. Enough that I was encouraged to pursue the subject, as soon as my mother returned to her seat, leaving my brother to do his five-minute time-out in the kitchen.

"But it's *true*, we *do* have, I *saw* them," I said, convinced it was some exotic ailment we had, maybe evidence of genetic dysfunction. At the very *least* it was a sign something was wrong. There were worms in rotten apples, and crawling inside dead groundhogs at the side of the road. I knew of such things. Great Aunt Hilda would know something of them too, I guessed, she was very old and had seen the death of many things. She would certainly know how to tell if a body were dying. She'd have known it better than I did, that dead bodies can't speak, nor do much of anything else. And that they were generally disposed of by someone, being unable to dispose of themselves.

But my mother reached for my arm under the table, and pressed a discrete trail of slender half-moons in it with her small, pointed nails. Above the table, her mouth was smilingly explaining that at times I tended to forget myself. This was why she was digging her nails into my arm, I thought, to remind me of myself. That I was there, and that I had arms, which were under the table where no one could see them, so no one would comment.

I was keenly interested in things upon which no one would comment. Despite the turkey and stuffing, the sparkling cranberry-orange relish in its clear crystal bowl, despite the candied yams, the green beans in butter and cream, the turnip mashed with carrots, the polished silverware, the best bone-china, despite the festive paper tablecloth embossed with bells and red bows, all I could think of was that there was a mangled dead bird on the table.

That night I slept on a cot in my Great Aunt Hilda's kitchen, beside the old washing machine which featured a device called a *mangle*. The mangle resembled two rolling pins, pressed together like tight white lips. Wet laundry was fed between them to wring it out and press it flat. The clothes would emerge pristine and two-dimensional on the other side, as though the machine ate dirty laundry and shat sheets and shirts. I had heard stories of women getting their arms caught in mangles, and tried to imagine what got spat out the other side. Long thin arms, pressed flat, like the long red satin gloves my mother complained of never having occasion to wear.

Great Aunt Hilda's kitchen smelled of dusty steam and turkey fat and laundered flannelette. The folding cot made me think of an ironing board, it creaked when I shifted my weight to avoid the metal beam at my tailbone. My mother had pulled it down from a tall cupboard by the cellar door, unfolding its jointed legs to stand it up on all fours. Great Aunt Hilda had contributed a pale green night light, shaped like a cat face, winking. She had plugged it into the wall beside the old washing machine, making the barrel glow mint green like an enormous jellied salad.

The night voices of Great Aunt Hilda's house had not changed in nearly two hundred years. Night time spoke in crickets and creaks, like the slow turning of a wheel. The groaning of the rafter beams like slumbering oxen, the ticking of the wall clock, and my own pulse pacing back and forth in attic rooms. Green light washed the contours of the walls, sliding over the oval frame of a portrait hanging above the cellar door. Surprising. I was sure that portrait had once hung upstairs.

In the sparse green light, I could see the head and shoulders of a sallow young girl in a lacy-necked pinafore, her high lunar forehead and low-sloping brow, shading the bright little eyes which peered from beneath. Her short curly hair clung close, like a plaster cast of itself, while her tiny tapioca teeth glowed green in the half-light. Her face was green-tinted as well, like the face of a girl who is sick. I knew the portrait had once hung upstairs, because I had slept in the same room with it before, or had not slept. There'd been a staring contest I couldn't win. *Just close your eyes, there you go.* Eventually I would begin to nod off. Then my eyes would open with a start, and there she'd be again, her oddly veiled smile, her eager little eyes still staring at me. I had run downstairs to wake my Great Aunt Hilda, who kindly climbed back up the stairs with me to save me from *the girl with the tapioca teeth*. I had hoped Great Aunt Hilda would stay, at least until I fell asleep again, but my heart sank as I watched her simply reach up and turn the portrait to the wall.

"I don't think that will help me much," I'd said quietly. In truth I thought it was much worse, the girl's sallow little face pressed to the wall like that. She'd be furious. She'd try to flip herself back over again with her tongue and I'd have to lie there in the dark listening to the thumping.

"Well now Agnes don't be silly," my Great Aunt Hilda had said. "*Imagine* making such a fuss over a *portrait*. Your grandmother, poor soul, had that portrait done when your mother was just a little girl, you know. It's your own mother, after all, when she was just little like you."

But this night, it was my mother who had that upstairs room, with my brother on a cot at the foot of her bed. The portrait had mysteriously moved downstairs where I was, apparently to watch over me in my sleep. I shivered, and pulled the grey woolen blanket up to my neck, then turned away from the portrait toward the beautiful blond head in bed beside me, her pale green nylon profile. Over her shoulders was draped my pink flannel nightie, which quite became her. Being only a head, she quite became whatever she was dressed in. The pink flannel no-body lay limp and flat against the cot like a paper doll, or like a fairy tale princess pressed flat between the pages of a book.

I was the opposite of this. I could not see my own head, but the rest of me was a grey mass of woolen blankets. Peeking beneath them, I appeared to be a naked cluster of pale and rounded shapes, like cheeses. The milky smell of my living human body, warm and slightly damp, was in contrast to the cool artificial scent of the head. Like those products advertised as *unscented* which are not. Each of us, the head and I, seemed to have what the other one lacked.

I sat up creaking in the cot and set my bare feet down on the chilly linoleum, its twisting pattern of cabbages-roses strangling themselves in lovely ways for nearly two hundred years. I nestled my blond head in the crook of my arm, letting her pink gown flow to the floor like a veil. She smiled sweetly with sealed lips. I placed her up high on my head like a basket, steadying her with one hand. I draped the grey woolen blanket over both of us in such a way that my body was hidden except for my feet, with the plastic head sticking out the top. I was still able to peek through a crevice in the folds of the blanket, to avoid bumping into things, as I shuffled our feet over toward the cellar door. Then I made the head look up.

The portrait of my mother would serve as the Justice. The cellar door above which she was framed reminded me of those lofty wooden podiums where judges sit. I fed the portrait her lines one by one like tea cakes, while her tapioca teeth grinned green over the proceedings. It was the first time in memory I'd ever put words in my mother's mouth.

We are gathered here in the green sight of the winking cat face to witness the joining of this head to this body, holy macaroni. If anyone present knows a reason why these two should not be united, let them speak now or forever rest in pieces.

There was adequate pause. The house creaked, the clock ticked and my pulse paced, but no one spoke. I fed the portrait her next lines.

Do you, head, take this body to be awfully yours, to have and to hold things for you, for better or for worse. For richer or for poorer, in sickness and in health, 'til death does its part, or however the words went; they seemed to anticipate the worst. And I was conscious now that the worst parts of the vows referred more to *me*, the body, than they did to the head, who would never be sick, would never be dead. But I tipped the head back and forth, like one of those glass-ampule birds filled with red fluid which dips its beak into a wine glass. In this way, the head slowly nodded, *I do*.

Beneath the blanket it was dark, and becoming very warm. My arm was beginning to tire from holding up my head like that. But cool against the floor were the soles of my feet, pale and green as phosphorescent fish, among the tangled vines of cabbage-roses. This was all I was able to see clearly, a pale green island with my two feet planted on it, while everything else was cloaked in thick woolen darkness. *Our two feet.*

I was beginning to get cold feet. The head had nothing to lose if this union failed, never having been attached to any body in the first place. Or the head might begin to miss having no body, having done very well for herself with no body to weigh her down.

Blonde, female, single. Bodiless, bloodless, non-biodegradable. Though immortal women were often figured as bodiless heads, I'd never seen a picture of a headless body on a postage stamp, nor a coin, nor a box of chocolates, nor suspended in an oval frame above a cellar door. There were a few old statues, but they'd been headless for such a long time, who could really tell if they were gods or goatherds? It seemed that a body separate from its head became basically anonymous.

Do you, body of Agnes, take this head to be yours, for better or for worse, for richer or for poorer, in sickness and in health, for as long as you both shall live?

The lines came unbidden to my mind, as though automatically, like the workings of an infernal machine, having only one switch to set it into motion and none to shut it down. It became difficult to tell where the words had come from, in the beginning, just who was feeding the words, and who had to eat them. The tapioca-girl could speak words simultaneously with their appearance in my mind, as was usually the case with putting words in someone's mouth, or taking them from someone's mouth. *Do you take this body? Do you take this head?*

Then I lowered my head and let her rest in the crook of my arm, like a helmet, then gathered the blanket around the two of us as though we were standing on a bridge watching the last of the fireworks. The tapioca-girl on the wall was a chattering ventriloquist, not moving her mouth. Like trying not to think of a purple cow, I couldn't make her stop.

Is there any body present who objects to this onion? Who will give away the bride-head? Are you with the parts of the bride or the parts of the groom? It seemed the only way to stop the talking head was to accept her terms, or at least say that I did.

I do, I said, then looked up into her soft eager eyes which did not blink, did not weep as the eyes of mothers are said to do at weddings. I spoke the words again.

I do, I said, *I do take this head.*

I now pronounce you head and body, said the tapioca-girl on the wall. *Let no one tear asunder what herein has been conjoined.* Then I was permitted to kiss my new head on her small pink lips, which were cool and hard like buttons.

22

THE CAMEL'S BACK

Mae West continues to interrupt us, pulling my hair or grabbing my ankles right in the middle of things. Buffalo man's explanation that she's just a little jealous and needs some time to adjust to my presence does not console me much anymore, she seems quite certain my rivalry can be overcome. Then one night she absolutely pushes things to a crisis. She's crept up to the rafters again as she often does, to spy on us from above. Lying on my back in bed I can see her. Mae's eyes are the only living eyes in the room other than mine and Buffalo man's, but even artificial eyes can hold light and propel it through space. Marilyn the stuffed Persian, Catherine the Great horned owl, and Voltaire the raccoon, all have eyes which still catch sparks and fire them back at us.

This night I am rocking myself to strange oblivion, looking down into the face of Buffalo man like a face underwater in the blue-green tube-light along the headboard. He talks as we move, holding onto my wrists so I don't fall forward. Then he closes his eyes. Just as I am about to tell him to open them and look at me, just as I was *about* to, *Mae peed*, her aim rushed and unfailing. In the next frame, I'm standing naked and shaking on the bedroom floor, wringing chimp piss from my hair, wiping droplets from my brows, pinching my eyelids against the sting. I can hear Buffalo man slooshing back and forth on the waterbed, stifling laughter.

"It's so not *funny*," I spit, while he gasps, "I'm sorry, I'm so sorry," over and over again.

"That's it," I sputter, "I've *had* it. That's *it*."

He sits up in bed and hunches his shoulders in a type of shrug, palms open, facing me. "She's a *chimp*, Agnes," he says. "You should try having a little more patience with her, plus a little compassion. Try thinking of her as your little sister, just to see how it feels."

"You're arguing *compassion*, here? I wouldn't let any little sister of *mine* climb around in the rafters and piss on people. Besides, she's what, almost *nine* years old? That makes her a mature young adult. In ape years, she's about the same age as I am."

Buffalo man is still squelching a smirk as he gets out of bed and walks right past me to the fridge. It's the walking right past me which makes something sort of *snap*. Standing there drenched in chimp urine, my eyes send poison darts flying right at his naked butt as he opens the fridge and bends into it, rummaging around like a bear in trash cans. A sort of howl arises from my throat as I run at him, start pummeling his back with my fists.

"*Listen*, you. *You* brought her here, and taught her to wear dresses and kiss you and do funny things to *amuse* you. She's *not* just a chimp anymore, so you *can't* have it both ways, you jerk, you *asshole*...." I am blathering freely now in a voice I don't recognize, or my own voice from some other time. "She can't be your *precious little Mae* and still be just a chimp running free in the freakin' *jungle*, don't you see? She can't be owned by *your* ass and also own her *own*. You might just as well've stuffed and mounted her like the rest, so she could stay your own little Mae forever, Noah, you big jerk."

Another first. I never call Buffalo man by his real name, I could hardly believe it was his real name, Noah, who saved all the animals.

"As to whether Mae gets to behave like a little girl or a chimpanzee," I say, wiping mingled tears and urine from cheeks, "I think you made the decision yourself, the first time you put a bonnet on her."

Seven storm clouds hang over Noah's eyes as he turns from the lighted fridge to face me. "That's *totally* not fair, Agnes. Mae had already been subjected to much worse treatments than bonnets when I got her, I promise you. I'm not the bad guy, Agnes. Mae was taken from her mother when she was just barely born, she grew up in a laboratory. She had a brief career as an entertainer but wound up back in the lab because she got too depressed to perform. Depressed chimpanzees aren't entertaining. Even the lab was just going to get rid of her, she was so maladjusted by that point she was useless to them as well. I met her when she was on death row and brought her home. I'm not the guy who hurt her, I'm the dude who rescued her from an appalling situation and put her in a more comfortable one. Given that her chances for survival in the wild or even in a zoo were pretty much ruined...."

Ruined? I am struck by the word. Reputations are said to be ruined, as well as careers. Characters are said to be ruined by the mere telling of tales.

"Anyhow maybe it's not really me you're pissy at, pussycat," says Buffalo man, standing behind me and placing his heavy hands on my shoulders. The dome of my head fits easily in the curve of his neck, my cheek against his chest. "But if you've ever worried about losing your wildness, you don't need to," he gravels, "I've got tooth marks to prove it." He takes me by the hand to the bathroom, where he draws a frothy sink-full of Dr. Bronner's Peppermint Castille Soap and warm water.

"You're quite a lunatic, you know," he says.

"Why do people always say that to me?" I ask.

"Oh really?" he says. "Do they?"

Over the next few days we reach a compromise and make a plan. We will erect some sort of metal grid dividing Mae's section of the loft from other areas where we spend our private time.

"In some sense I can understand why Mae's been so pissed," says Buffalo man. "Before you moved in, she used to sleep in the same bed with me. You've pushed her out, Agnes." I ask him to please stop saying things which make it sound as though I am losing in an amorous contest with a chimpanzee.

The next afternoon Buffalo man goes out alone to buy the materials to build the partition, while I stay home with Mae West. I try to explain to her about the unanimous separation referendum in which she's ineligible to vote on account of her species. Today Mae stays as far away from me as she can, lying under the vent with her blue ducky spoon and a torn book. Hours pass this way, Mae West ignoring me while I sit and fret about it.

Buffalo man looks a bit sheepish when he gets home.

"Well, it'd be far too expensive to put up the grate exactly according to our original plan," he says, "but I figured out a compromise we can afford. I'll draw you a diagram."

His diagram indicates that the most convenient and least expensive way to solve our problem would be to build a sort of cage around the bed, with a door, which could be padlocked from inside. Buffalo man already has plenty of padlocks. We could install a curved roof of corrugated tin like a bus shelter, with a gully so that if Mae ever peed again it would simply run off the roof into a bucket on the floor. Buffalo man has already brought home the three walls of extended steel from the hardware store, grey sheet metal scored then stretched to open a million little eye-shaped apertures all over it. The three sheets are strapped to the roof of the Gremlin outside.

"I say we set up the walls tonight," he says, "then go back to the hardware store tomorrow together to pick up the roof. It's actually going to look kind of cool, Agnes, I got it all sussed out. With the blue light from the headboard coming through those fish-scale cracks in the steel? It'll be like we're sleeping in a giant fish."

◦৵

"But wouldn't you say there was part of you which *always* wanted to be a taxidermist?" I ask Buffalo man in the hardware store next day.

"No," he says, "of course not, I told you this already. I used to take *pictures* professionally, in my heyday, but that heyday was short, then I got divorced."

We unchain a giant orange shopping cart and skateboard down an aisle of aluminum siding, braking at a variety called *Silver Lining*.

"We should get some of this stuff," I say. "Never know when you're gonna need some."

"I think it's just some kind of insulation," he says, "which is not really what we're here for."

So we buy our sheet of corrugated tin and drive it home like a deer strapped to the roof of the Gremlin.

"So what kind of pictures did you *take*? You've never told me specifically, just that they were wildlife and that it didn't work out. What was the real deal with that?" These questions about Buffalo man's past are becoming a running gag of sorts. I've asked him a dozen times about his photography and what his ex-wife's name was and what she was like, but just like with the question of God he always leaves those spaces blank.

"It's like pulling *teeth* getting answers out of you," I say. "I can never tell when you're being straight with me."

"I'm pretty straight, if you haven't noticed," he says, "I just do things differently than you do. But all right, since you won't leave it alone, you gotta promise not to make me sorry I told you. Here's the story. I thought I was going to spend my life travelling the world taking pictures of wildlife, become a famous photo journalist and eventually start a whole institute in support of wildlife preservation. So now I stuff and mount them and they last forever. Irony's pretty blunt, like that horrible story of the monkey's paw. You have to be careful *how you wish* or you end up with some perversion of what you wished for."

Back at Noah's A-1 Taxidermy we carry the tin cylinder inside and unroll it. We then prop it up against the pre-assembled bed cage like that scalloped drive-in movie attachment on the Flintstones' car. The plan is for me to climb up to the rafters where Mae usually sits, then help guide the bumpy roof into position while Buffalo man feeds it up from below.

"After a few years of setting everything up, though, with the wildlife photography thing," he continues, "I started thinking it was pretty hopeless. I couldn't stop the clock, the whole world was going to crap with or without me, it really looked that way.... Could you slide your right-hand-side over the corner joint, just one or two bumps, baby?... I was past thirty and still hadn't really, you know, *nailed* it. And I wasn't going to be stuck saving puffins on some craggy island by myself at the end of the world.... Wait, don't move, I want to see if it will balance by itself yet. Perfect.... And I wasn't going to end up like my father."

"What about your father?" I say, then, "It's balancing, I'm not touching it. I can get back down this way." Buffalo man steadies the tree stump by the side of the bed as I step down on it, he takes my hand as I jump to the floor. He lifts my hand like a glass of wine and brings it to his lips, and lets it fall to my side again.

"You know what my dad did, Agnes. I told you the first day we met what my dad did for a living. He was a puppeteer, a ventriloquist."

"Oh, right. The girl-puppet who was a ghost. Ruthie."

"Dad's character was supposed to be a ghost, too," says Buffalo man. "That was the act, a dead girl and her dead uncle. Toothpaste in his hair, Ihle's Paste on his face, smelling like the school nurse. And now he really *is* one, a ghost I mean not the school nurse."

"I'm sorry," I say. "I didn't know that."

"Not your fault. I know you don't see much of your father anymore either," he says. "Anyway I told you I've been recently reconciled to ghosts," he says. "Losing my dad had a lot to do with that. I'd lose my mind if I didn't talk to ghosts, living in this place."

Buffalo man rolls the tree stump around the bed to each of the corners by turn, standing up on it to drive holes through the tin, bolting the roof to the frame of the cage. When it is finished, we stand back and look at it. The waterbed is now contained in a long rectangular box, with a curving roof and a door in the front. Now that the roof is installed, it looks less like a cage and more like a type of house.

"Covered bridge?" the Buffalo man suggests, "kinda reminds me of a railway bridge."

"Sort of," I say, "but bridges are open at both ends whereas ours has, like, a wall at one end and a metal grate at the other, with forty gallons of water inside it instead of under it.

"Oh yes," says Buffalo man, grinning and nodding, "I can see it now. Think floods, Agnes, think cubits."

"Oh *no-oo*," I say. "You're right, you know."

֍

Noah finally shuts the door of the Ark and locks it with a padlock. He'll pull it open again in the morning when light will hit us like unsolicited advice. But now it is night. Mae West is turning slow somersaults over the floor as she does when she is very upset, which she increasingly seems to be. *Thump, whump.* She is upset because us humans have built a cage around ourselves and now we are arguing. *Whump, thump.* We've been arguing about Mae West herself. *Thump, whump.*

"She's totally miserable," I say. "It's obvious she's smart, she's probably smarter than me but she seems deeply screwed up in some way. Don't look at me like that, please. How much do you think she likes parading around in a dress, if the first thing she wants to do when she gets home is tear the thing off?"

"So do most healthy people," Buffalo man says. "We only put up with clothing because of genitals and weather. I'd happily get arrested for walking around naked, if I had a bannered cause to do it. *Listen,* I know the situation isn't ideal, for Mae. You seem to think you're the only one who's ever come along to tell me that. But you didn't see her when I first got her, okay? She shrank whimpering from every damn thing, skinny as a chicken wing. So I took her around with me everywhere I went. And for weeks I phoned zoos all over the country trying to find one that would take her, but when they heard about her history they basically said that it'd be impossible to place her with other chimps. Too risky, she'd probably freak totally out. Look at her, Agnes, she wouldn't have a clue what to do in a zoo with other chimps. They probably wouldn't like *her* any more than she'd like *them.*

"You say she doesn't look happy," he continues, "well no duh, she isn't very happy. But I took her on, and I intend to see it through. How do you think the guy feels who ends up with a dog who pisses everywhere? Doesn't mean he gets rid of his dog, unless he's an asshole. And contrary to some people's opinion, I'm not one. The guy tries to teach the dog not to piss everywhere, and he learns to love the dog. Now imagine if we're talking about *kids.* Would *you* know what to do if your kid drooled all the time or got beat up by other kids, or was never able to go to the bathroom by himself? It's scary how patient some people are supposed to learn how to be."

Mae climbs up to the high shelf where Marilyn the stiff Persian lies permanently sleeping. She begins to groom the stuffed cat, parting the fur and scanning the skin for removable motes. These would mostly be dust mites. Finding little, she grunts softly to herself.

"Why do you insist I don't like her? Seems to me right from the start, it was the other way round," I say. "Oh God, could you please stop her from stroking that dead cat while we're talking about this? She almost has me in tears."

"Wouldn't hurt you none," Buffalo man says, standing up now and pacing before me with his arms open wide as salvation. "You never pick her up in your arms. You see me do it a dozen times a day, I pick her up and talk to her, but you never do it yourself. You turn into a cactus as soon she comes near you."

"She *bit* me then *peed* on me," I say, "I'm allowed to be a little reticent of her."

"Yeah, but still," he says, "she's a chimp and not a human being, like I say. She's still an animal who, under certain circumstances, *may* bite. That would seem obvious, Agnes. She's still a wild animal. Or maybe a perfectly civilized one who's suffering from cultural dislocation. But it's still our responsibility not to forget that the animal has both emotions *and* teeth."

"How can you say that and still have her out curtsying in the park?" I ask. "If she's a wild animal, then she has no business wearing dresses and learning how to beg money from human strangers."

Buffalo man crosses over to the shelf where Marilyn and Mae West are perched and scoops up Mae in his arms. She embraces him and kisses his head making soft hooting sounds.

"She doesn't hate to do it, Agnes. She certainly likes it better than where she was. Those first weeks, when I carried her around everywhere in one of those Guatemalan baby slings," he says, drawing the shape of one over Mae's body with his hands, "she got so much attention. People stopped everywhere to meet her. At first she was terrified, like no kidding. But after a while she genuinely seemed to enjoy the attention, or some of it. There were people she liked and people she didn't, but very few she trusted."

Buffalo man lets Mae's body fall while still holding onto her hand, so she swings deftly to the ground and knuckle-scurries off to her corner.

"Then after a while she became almost as curious about the human-monkeys as they were about her. I never coerced her, Agnes, you know."

"Of course you coerced her," I say. "She didn't have any other options, or none that she was aware of, so isn't that coercion? She had to learn how to put coins into slots, and curtsy."

"Well actually, we had a pretty good time learning to curtsy, Mae and I," Buffalo man grins. "And there was nowhere else that would take her, Agnes, that's the bottom line. Her only other option at the time was a lethal injection at the lab, if she didn't find some way to hang herself first. That'd make a really happy ending, wouldn't it? Just like Flipper the dolphin."

"Flipper hanged himself?" I ask.

"No, she drowned herself," he says, sitting down in the chair near the amber calf-skin lamp, his beard turning bronze like a mask. "You may laugh but it's true." He stuffs fraying wads of Black Bart tobacco into the bowl of his pipe and lights it. The lighter has a frieze of Greek warriors along the side, and finally sparks after about seventeen tries. Then the smell of vanilla pipe tobacco. "Some official record claimed that Flipper's cause of death was swallowing too many nickels the tourists had chucked in the pool or some such crap. But that wasn't it, according to this documentary I saw. After Flipper retired from the TV show, she was relocated to a cruddy little tank in New Mexico or somewhere. So then one day, her old trainer from the show goes to visit her. She recognizes him, of course, knows *exactly* who he is. He's that prince of a man who made her work for a whole decade, then totally abandoned her. Then, and this is the thing, the dolphin swims out to the centre of the pool, holds her breath, and sinks. Apparently they even try to hoist her back up again, but she just does the same thing. She just sinks, on purpose."

Buffalo man then attempts three smoke rings which resemble amoeba, clicking his jaw like a dolphin.

"I can see why people get all choked up over stories like that," I say. "They kind of say something."

"Oh yeah? What do you s'pose they say?"

"I'm not sure. Maybe just that you're better off making more than *only one* decision in your whole life, such as lifelong loyalty for instance. Unless you're a dog or a captive dolphin who doesn't have much say in the matter. Or you'll end up waiting, like, forever, until you die."

Buffalo man relights his pipe and exhausts the ceiling with a blue cloud. "You know," he says, "there's some people believe UFOs are actually mental projections from sea mammals, whales and dolphins, in a last-ditch attempt to get us humans to sort things out. Humble ourselves a little before the force of evolution." He makes an ambiguous dismissive shrug, from which it's impossible to tell if he's one of those people who believes this.

"Still," he says, "you're right there's no cause worth wasting your whole life over, I know it from my own experience. It would've been stupid of me to isolate myself on some craggy Arctic island in the middle of nowhere, with nothing but a tent and a tripod and a dwindling species of puffins. Would've been a stupid thing to do. At that point in my life, I guess I thought it was pretty important." He knocks the ash out of his pipe with a certain violence. "But I'd've never met you, or Mae West either, if I'd spent my whole life saving puffins."

Mae has again climbed up to Marilyn's shelf. I watch her groom the stiff cat, while Buffalo man talks and attempts more smoke rings under the amber cone of lamplight. Suddenly, Mae pushes Marilyn from the shelf. The stuffed cat falls to the floor. *Thump, whump.* I go over and pick up the cat and replace her on the shelf. Mae follows me to the kitchen where I take a green plastic basket of strawberries out of the fridge and hand it to her. She places her hand briefly on my foot before settling into her chair with her strawberries and a fluffy pillow.

"You should never keep clinging to an idea you once had, in the hope that it'll some day work out," he says. "If it's never been shown to work, then the idea's clearly dead, right? It should be allowed to rest in peace, right? You don't try to resurrect plans once they've become obsolete. That's the real reason I'm not out saving puffins, and it's why I got divorced, too. Bottom line."

"You can't make time stand still," he says, "You just can't *do* it, so you shouldn't try. You can spend your whole life inventing crutches to support what might come down to a single bad decision. Being married, or buying some crappy real estate. Isn't it better to keep as many options open as possible, I mean with your life in general? You don't want to go through endless grief and anxiety over some decision you made when you were too young and stupid to understand the implications of it. Do we have any more cranberry juice? Am I making any sense?"

"No," I say, "grapefruit. I get what you mean about not being too wedded to ideas, but it's just as impossible to keep all your opportunities open like spinning pie plates. Eventually you have to set down a few of the pies, or you end up dropping *all* of them. Say you end up dropping all of your pies except one, and *bingo* there's your decision made for you. You get to choose the only thing you didn't screw up. What kind of a decision is that? Wouldn't it be better to plan ahead a bit? Take *one* pie at a time? How many pies could one person need at one time?

"For me, right now, it's finishing school," I continue, "and getting away from my mother for a while. That's two big-ass pies. I just need to catch up on my *work* and get *away*. Because up to this point I feel more like my life has gradually shoved me into this exact position, not like I've had much to do with the process. You wouldn't believe how clumsy I am, for instance. I don't know how I turned out that way. If anyone's going to bang her head on a cupboard door or fall down the stairs or get bitten by a chimp, it's me. I just have bad luck."

"Do you need help with those glasses, then?" grins Buffalo man.

"Not from a dude who can't tell he's been drinking pink grapefruit juice and not cranberry."

"They taste exactly the same to me," he says. "They both have the flavour of doing something healthy for my urinary tract."

"But listen," I say, "it's incredible to me that a man who stuffs things for a living could say something like *you can't make time stand still*; isn't that *exactly* what you're trying to do? You make dead things look like they're alive, what else is that? And you might think you're protecting Mae from something, but in some respects she's only slightly luckier than the other animals here, she's still supposed to be this little girl or something who doesn't change."

"I'll pretend I didn't hear that, Agnes," says Buffalo man slowly, "because you don't have a fucking clue what you are talking about."

"You told me you rescued her from maternal deprivation experiments at a lab," I say, pushing back stray hair with my wrists and sighing like my mother does. "That's why she's so pissy, according to you. It has nothing to do with the satin dresses and the parading around, according to you."

"Shut up, Agnes," he says. "You have no idea what you're talking about."

"Fine," I say, "so enlighten me."

"Mae was tortured. There's no other word for it. She was taken from her mother when she was just born, then introduced to a series of mechanical monster-mothers to cling to. That's what they *called* them. Monster-mothers. The first robot-surrogate shook violently, while the baby chimp just kept trying to hold on, barely a newborn, mind you. Then the second one dropped to sub-zero temperatures. The third charming lady had a nice soft terry-cloth body, which could eject metal spikes at the push of a button. This was all to see whether the babies would continue to cling to the robot-surrogates regardless how negative the reinforcement. Which they did, as predicted. The subjects were chosen precisely because of their similarity to human children. Makes you wonder why they had to do the damn experiment. Anyway that's the story."

"That happened to Mae?" I say, watching her pick up my salmon-coloured toque and pull it over her head, walking about on her hind legs with her arms in the air.

"That definitely happened to a bunch of rhesus monkeys around the same time I picked up Mae West," he says. "A janitor at a lab gave me a tip so I went to pick up this dead monkey they had. I'd never stuffed a primate before, didn't really know what to say to the chap. Usually it was white rabbits he had, a few dogs and raccoons. There weren't even any diagrams of primate anatomy in my taxidermy books, only in the books which point out the similarity between monkey skeletons and human ones. Wasn't sure I wanted to see that thing skinned in my sink, you know?

"Anyhow, I go there, and there's this chimp in a cage by herself, cringing and screaming, while this technician-woman in a lab coat is trying to fasten her drinking bottle to the metal holster inside the cage. The woman is obviously upset about it, she keeps saying, "I know I'm not your mother, I know I'm not your mother." So I go up to her and she says, "There's nothing much can be done about this little one." After that it wasn't difficult. I just said I'd take her, promised to take care of her as best I could. That's it, that's all.

"So, no, I can't prove to you that Mae West was subjected to the same treatment I described," he says, "but what does it look like to you? I mean, you've seen her. Aren't you allowed to just go on what it looks like in some cases, when proof is something which just isn't going to happen?"

"I'm not sure," I say, "I don't know the answer to that question."

23

Metaphormosis I: Ammonite

> It is for good reason that snails have attracted as many collectors as have postage stamps, coins, or beetles. Their whorls may be coiled in various ways; they may be flat like a disc, slightly raised in the shape of a flat cone, or piled high like a steeple; their interior space may increase gradually or rapidly; they may sport ornamentations, such as scallops or spikes.... [Their] colors may delight collectors, but because of their poor vision the snails themselves are hardly in a position to appreciate their own beauty.
>
> — from *Animal Architecture* by Karl Von Frisch, zoologist and Nobel Prize winner

Under my pillow at night in the Ark I've lately been keeping a fossil, a flattened spiral cephalopod resembling a reddish-brown ear. Specifically it's an *ammonite*, extinct relative of octopus, cuttlefish, nautilus, and squid. These animals are classified as chordates just as humans are, because their bodies contain spine structures. Many of them also carry around their personal brand of ink, with which they conjure cloudy apparitions to conceal themselves within, like writers do. Meanwhile, they can dart away in a pulse of chrysanthemum-legs in the opposite direction. This appears to be a marvelous ability.

Unlike the writer the squid has both a spine and a beak, both of which are removed if the squid is to be eaten. The spine of a squid resembles the rib of a salmon, translucent, the texture of fingernails or quills. The beak is also translucent except for the very tip, which is dark-tinted. If these two thorny parts are removed from the squid and reassembled next to each other, with the beak forming a nib at the thicker end of the spine, they very much resemble an ink-stained quill.

The ammonite under my pillow was stolen from a dusty wooden box of them at the university, where it'd been buried for mere decades. How quickly these ammonites were able to move around now that humans were here. Whereas for millions of years, they'd remained heavy and manifest proof that stillness existed. That foundations existed, as unconscious spirals in the bones of stones.

When I first got home to Buffalo man's place with the stolen ammonite, I took off my clothes and dove into the slooshing waterbed of the Ark while he and Mae West rolled about like leather medicine balls on the floor. They rolled and wrestled, the curve of their spines, the somersault whump of bottoms. I am glad to be naked in bed with the stolen fossil, and glad that Mae and Buffalo man seem in a good mood today. Since the introduction of the Ark, he's built Mae her very own bed out of a wooden sled with a decal of red rosebuds on it.

"What do you know about ammonites?" I call to him. I want to know if he has any interest in spiral stones as a possible God-image, or maybe a trans-dimensional hearing-aid, or whether he'd think a person were out of her mind to be considering these possibilities.

"*Children of Lot,*" he calls back. "And a bad lot the lot of them, or at least so I remember I was supposed to think. Huh. Why d'you want to know *that,* Agnes?" He's now wiping his hands with what looks like my Spiderman T-shirt and walking toward me. People always look menacing walking toward you while wiping their hands.

"Because I'm interested in patterns," I say, "basic *patterns*. And where they might come from and what they might possibly mean. And I'm worried about my intelligence. I think intelligence has something to do with the ability to *notice* patterns. These days I feel like one of the stupider people, who doesn't notice the patterns because she doesn't even seem to realize that she's part of them." I flop flat on my back on the waterbed and cover my eyes with my arms. This gesture has something to do with consciousness of vagary.

"So you're interested in basic patterns," repeats Buffalo man. "Well, I'd say that sounds like a little less concrete an interest than a few weeks back, when you were still sacrificing pigs to the gods of Science and actually showing up to your classes once in a while."

"I never dissected a single pig," I say, "who were already dead by the way, at least by the time they got to the lab. But if you must know, I've been very busy lately wondering about the source of the universe and whether ammonites have any functional metaphors to lend. Do you like that any better?"

"Oh," he says, "well...." Then he sits down beside me like I'm eleven and just about to get the sex talk. About the basic patterns of hormonal development, and how I should welcome the strange natural changes I'll soon be going through. But just like those adolescent sex talks, what he tells me has nothing to do with what I thought I was asking.

"So, from what I remember," he begins, "Lot lived in a cave with his two daughters and they both got pregnant by him. And one of the baby sons was called Moab and the other was called Ammon, or something close. Benammi. So the descendants of Moab were the Moabites and the descendants of Benammi were the Ammonites and they all were cursed idol worshippers and enemies of the tribes of Israel. That's about all I can remember."

"What are you *talking* about? I was asking you about *fossils*, man." I was quite a bit creeped out to be offered *this* kind of story out of nowhere and out of context, it fairly spun my brain.

"Oh," he says, "*those* ammonites. I know even less about those than the first ones."

"Never mind," I say. "What's all this about a cave?"

So we blow the dust off King James and bring him into the Ark with us. Buffalo man is surprised at how quickly we're able to locate the passage about Lot's daughters, the book practically falls open to the place, but this doesn't surprise me a bit. Lately things like that seem to be happening all the time, as though someone were leaving me breadcrumbs to follow.

Buffalo man has padlocked the door of the Ark from the inside so that Mae is unable to come in, but we can hear her shuttling back and forth outside, sometimes lurching at the metal grids and rattling them a bit, trying to get our attention. We're finding that it's nearly impossible to behave like creatures living in their natural habitat when we're being watched by a curious fellow primate on the other side of the bars.

"So here goes," says Buffalo man, bent over the book and reading ahead, paraphrasing like mad. "Looks like Lot was warned by angels to get out of Dodge, because God was going to destroy everything again. Not everything in the world, just everything in the general vicinity. The angels tell Lot to take his wife and his two daughters, and leave. But wait here, it looks like there were two other daughters as well, married daughters, who had to stay in town, I guess so much for *them*. Don't get married, is all I have to say."

"Get on with it," I say.

"So God says, *Go to the mountains, Lot,* and Lot says, *Can't I just go to Zoar?* and God says, *Okay, Lot.* Then Lot's family gets escorted to the city gate by angels, who send them on their way. But Lot's wife looks back, probably because she's freaking out about her two married daughters who got left in the ruins. Maybe she's also a bit worried about her husband, who, only a few paragraphs earlier, was offering the two remaining daughters as a sexual bribe to some thugs. So anyway, Lot's wife looks back and you know the rest. That's all she wrote."

"Bloody hell," I say, "that used to be one of my biggest nightmares, except it was my mother instead of me, and she turns into a pillar of dental ceramic material."

"I don't know what to say to that," says Buffalo man. "So then okay, after that, Lot is too scared to even live in Zoar, so he goes and lives in a cave instead, with his two unmarried daughters. In a cave. Then his daughters get him drunk and *LIE* with him, it says, this is freakin' twisted, they *deliberately* get their father intoxicated in order to conceive by him. They do this on two consecutive nights while the father is passed out drunk. He isn't even aware he's committing incest."

"Oh, no? How the hell does he think his daughters got pregnant, then, if they all believed they were the only three people left? God was going to *destroy* everything else, isn't that what it says? I'm sure Lot's daughters would never have done such a thing if they thought they had any choice in the world. It must've felt like the absolute end of the world, and it sounds like the end of the world, to have a mother who's turned into a salt lick and a father who has to hide in a cave for the rest of his life. The girls must've felt like it was their responsibility to prevent their own *extinction*. The whole story might've been a pack of lies to smear these peoples' reputations, which is quite possible, if they were sworn enemies. I'm not defending the daughters' behaviour, mind you. Okay, but really I *am* defending the daughters. Maybe it was Lot all along....

"Anyway," I continue, "all I wanted to know in the first place was whether you knew anything about this *rock* I found," I say, opening my hand to show Buffalo man the fossil ammonite. It lies quietly in the bowl of my palm, like an artist's ear.

"Where'd you find *that*?" he says.

"In a cave," I lie.

"C'mon," he says.

"I'm not going to tell you then," I say.

I've started keeping the fossil ammonite under my pillow at night in the peculiar belief that it will help me hear my dreams, so I can write them down in the morning. I really don't care whether or not I can prove this theory to anyone, just believing it helps to make it work. I divide a page in my biology notebook into three columns: *Hypothesis, Observations,* and *Conclusions.* In the *Hypothesis* column, I write, *To explore the theory that keeping an ammonite under one's pillow at night will assist the sleeper to hear her dreams.* The first night of the experiment, I dream a matronly fishmonger in swaggering burlesque selling six spiral-shaped bagels from a glass wheelbarrow, *singing* all the while, and I can hear her very clearly.

So instead of digging out my textbooks and catching up on how well lobotomized rats are still able to run a maze, I spend days in the library reading about spirals and fossils. I look up *Ammonites* in the card catalogue and find references leading to two different floors, and decide to wind downstairs to *Prehistory* in the basement. The other reference would have taken me up three flights to *Religion.* There'd still be time to go there, some other time. Did the Bible ever make reference to fossils?

There must've been fossils, back then. Fossils of subaquatic creatures, fish and sharks and trilobites, the ones who didn't get into the Ark because they already knew how to swim, or how to breathe underwater. They'd been just *fine* where they were, through forty million floods, and where were they now? The ones who'd already *seen* the end of the world once, and kept right on evolving?

Downstairs in the basement, I find an article by a Japanese paleontologist who'd discovered the beaks of ammonites inside the bellies of Plesiosaurs, the latter of whom appear to have resembled underwater reptilian geese. Up to that point, I hadn't known for sure that ammonites even *had* beaks, never mind that these were indigestible to Plesiosaurs. According to the illustrations, the creature under my pillow had once been a sort of spiralling squid. Some scientists believed a meteor hit this planet, covering everything with a dark cloud of iridium dust, blocking out the sun for several months. Creatures who relied on light to photosynthesize suffocated in darkness. Downstairs in the dark basement of the library, I wonder whether my father is sleeping in a doorway these days or what, because I haven't heard from him in years, and now it appears that not everything which disappears for years does so without a trace.

24

Aeroplane Bones

Like the small bones of chickens, aeroplane parts lay grey and bleached on the concrete floor, in the basement beside my father's workbench. My brother had been too young to construct the model plane by himself, but he was not too young to have destroyed it already on its maiden flight. Gavin at four stood by like an intern at my father's side, while the man requested tools and glue, paper towels and tiny screws, or another peek at the instruction sheet translated into seven languages with equal lack of clarity. My father cursed tamely, blamed the work of careless or malicious translators, blamed illustrators who must've never laid eyes on a christly aeroplane their entire lives. He blamed my Great Aunt Hilda for deliberately presenting Gavin with a gift whose assembly she *must* have known would fall to him.

"*Fancy* giving a model aeroplane to a *four*-year-old," he muttered. "Who'd she think was going to inherit the task of putting the blamed thing *togither*?"

It was true, there was no way my brother would have been able to decipher the instructions and all the myriad parts. My father was scarcely able to do it himself. The finished plane was peculiar looking, bearing horns and appendages which surely were meant to have been internal mechanisms, and the tips of its wings sagged a bit. My brother was not too young to sense this discrepancy between the flashy picture on the box and the thing it yielded up. He must have known it was some flightless satire of aeroplanes which my father finally delivered into his hands with some disgust, before going to wash his own in a pink oily preparation which smelled of sheep.

Perhaps the tragedy of the craft's maiden flight had been a type of mercy killing after all. Gavin lifted the thing into the air and ran swooping circles through the basement, up the stairs and back down again, turbulent engine sounds sputtering from his lips. He guided the nose of the craft in the direction of the workbench as though to a safe landing, then suddenly drew a magnificent figure eight in the sky before plunging it into the concrete like an egg.

The model of providence might have been my mother's. It was best to do away with failures, best to consign them to dust and sweep them under the carpet; best that they should descend in silence and be spoken of never more. Especially concerning my father, who could little afford to collect such trophies on a shelf, nor recount their stories again and again to curious relatives at dinner. It was best that the plane sign off with a final figure eight, a reclining infinity symbol in the basement-sky, before resolving itself to pieces.

৫৯

"Why doesn't your daddy just take it back to the store?" whispered Effie. We were crouched beneath a card table in the basement, listening to my father as he shook his fist at the small aeroplane in the next room.

"He can't do that," I whispered back. "He'd have to tell the saleslady that the instructions don't make sense, but he doesn't have any *proof* that they don't make sense. Anyway that aeroplane was a present from my Great Aunt Hilda. She'd have to send it back to the Sears-Roebuck warehouse *herself*, and she'd hate that."

"Why can't your daddy just *tell* them the instructions don't make sense?"

"But what if they do make sense?"

"That's not possible," Effie said, "he's your daddy. He'd be able to tell if the instructions don't make sense."

Effie's father earned a living building motorcycles, it was *he* who'd have been able to tell if the instructions made no sense. He'd have been able to take the merchandise back to the store, slam it down at the check-out counter, and convince the saleslady that it was a piece of *crap*. She'd find herself apologizing to him, offering him a new model aeroplane or his money back or anything else he wanted. So then maybe he would ask for her phone number. This was my impression because it was Effie's complete conviction.

I could almost believe it too, having seen the man, his big leather hat with the Mexican turquoise set in silver on the band. He wore a sky-denim shirt and pulled his chunky-heeled black boots off his feet like he was skinning a seal, when he came in the front door smelling of bike parts. He called Effie *princess* and me *her little friend*. He unbuttoned his shirt and sat down on the couch with his big denim legs spread wide open, drinking a stubby brown bottle of Extra Old Stock, or cleaning his fingernails with a penknife. One of his fingernails was very long and curved like the tooth of a dog. Effie and I danced to *Rumours* in the living room a hundred dozen times until her daddy tore it from the turntable and flung it off the porch like a frisbee, singing, "*Now there you go again, you say you want your free-e-dom...*"

But today we were at my house, and it was *my* father we were studying. We crouched beneath a card table draped with mosquito netting in the basement, listening to the muttering of my father and the clatter of plastic aeroplane bones from the next room. "How the *dickens* d'they get from figure eight to figure nine here? There's a whole extra *part* seems to've slipped their kind at*ten*tion..."

"You can do it, Dad," I heard Gavin say only once, hoping Effie hadn't heard him or maybe hadn't understood what he meant. Effie believed that anything in pieces could be put together again, and that fathers were the people who knew how to do it. They had tricks up their sleeves and presents in their pockets, they were that imperative quantity greater than the sum of parts.

The mosquito netting was verdant by tint of our imaginations. We were deep in forest green with sable trim, the skirted velvet robe of a Christmas ghost with the two of us crouching like urchins beneath it.

"*I* thought you said Christmas *presents*," Effie grumbled, disappointed that our invisible banquet, with its candles and cooked geese-with-the-beaks-still-on and pyramids of coconut snowballs and crackers with prizes inside and shiny apples and steaming plates of figgy pudding, whatever *that* was, was not even intended for us.

"This doesn't sound like a very fun game, Agnes. Why'd we bother imagining all this stuff if we're not allowed to imagine eating it? And why are we hiding under an old man's bathrobe?"

I didn't know how to answer Effie's questions unless we played the game. Playing the game was the only way of finding out what the point of it was, if there was any point at all. Sometimes the only present you get is an idea in your head, then you have to build the rest yourself, with no instructions. All I kept thinking about were the two children under the ghost's robe in that movie Great Aunt Hilda made us watch every single year. I wanted to know who they were, and why they were there, and just who the man was whose robe they were hiding under.

I had one theory that the *ghost of Christmas Present* was the same person as the *absent guest,* that invisible man who came every year to Christmas dinner, for whom Great Aunt Hilda always set an extra place. When my mother rubbed that magic spot on her throat to strike the company mute, it was he who was able to laugh it off to the tune of tinkling cutlery, it must have been he who was speaking when the rest of the table fell silent. I was disappointed that she did not love him more than she seemed to, the absent man who licked his platter so clean it need never be washed, and always left his Bloody Mary standing in the glass, until the end of the meal when my mother would pick it up and drink it herself.

The ghost of Christmas Present. The ghost of Christmas presents. In the tumbler of dreams, what midnight penance would come to haunt my childish eagerness to tear the pretty paper and ribbons from mysterious boxes bearing my name? Were they really presents, if they came with strings attached? If they arrived in the company of a ghost whose job was to remind the little girl what she might someday owe for them? If a little girl were given a plastic model of a little girl, for example, did this mean that someday she'd owe somebody a little girl? Was there a debt to be borne in the giving of gifts and, if so, then to whom?

Effie was still cross that the feast we'd dreamt up was not even for us, and also she hated the names of our characters. *"Ignorance?* and *Want?* What kind of names are *those?* This is so *whatever,* Agnes, but at least let me be *Want.* Then maybe we can do what *I* want. And I *don't* want to play this game. I don't want to be stuck here with you under some old man's bathrobe and I don't want to be horrid and miserable-looking either. And I think your daddy is weird."

Miserable-looking was about the last earthly thing Effie was. She didn't even look like an earthling girl. She looked like a cartoon of a girl, one of those girl-creatures who really look more like praying mantises or baby deer, with huge eyes like half-avocados and thin elegant limbs blurring to a silk fringe when they run. Effie's eyes were the colour of green tea flecked with gold, and her eyebrows were scarcely there at all.

Her face was cordiform, not the shape of an actual heart muscle but the shape of the hearts on playing cards, with a wide forehead tapering to a pointy little chin. Her mouth was a baby's mouth, two perfect peaks above a pink lozenge, drawn close as though by a drawstring. Her long yellow hair had a life of its own, slinking about her shoulders like a sable, or like kestrel wings it swooped when Effie stooped to tie her shoes. There was way too much hair for such a little head, and it just kept growing.

In school photos, she was always the girl who got seated in the very centre of the front row, with her knees facing forward, while all the other front-row girls had to turn their knees slightly inward toward her, like neon chevrons directing motorists to the entrance of a fancy motel. It was because of this that Effie consciously sat with her knees pressed more tightly together than many of us did, because otherwise the camera would be aimed right up her skirt. And Effie always wore skirts, *every single day.* Skirts with multiple flounces and tiers like wedding cakes; skirts made by her mother out of cranberry calico and purple velveteen, with satin ribbons and Scandinavian braid around the hem. Effie wore a hair-comb with a large and poisonous green bow on it, peeking above the crown of her head like an Egyptian cobra. I thought she was beautiful and strange, just as everybody else seemed to, only more so I think.

Sometimes I wished that I didn't find Effie so beautiful. I might have been happier to be ignorant of the fact, and less troubled by the desire to be that way as well. I had no *proof* that I was not, but neither proof that I was, which tended to be stronger evidence in these cases. It seemed true that a little girl was not beautiful until somebody told her she was, and everybody told Effie. She herself seemed completely ignorant of how people watched her wherever she went, unless she had simply learned to take it for granted. But taking something for granted was the opposite of desiring it. It seemed that being watched left little to be desired, in Effie's case. It seemed more to leave her listless.

"That girl should be a model when she grows up," my mother said. I told her I knew that because everybody said that. Effie's own mother said the same thing all the time, and her father called her *princess*. They'd put her in beauty pageants and twice she had won, and twice she got sick from how much hair spray she'd swallowed.

But years later, in grade seven, when we had to write compositions on what we wanted to be when we grew up and why, Effie wrote that she wanted to be a model but that she didn't know why. Miss Shoemaker wrote in red that Effie's composition was too far below the standard length, and was therefore unacceptable. According to the school's own model of compositions, hers was too short.

Models have little to say about the way things really are. Take model aeroplanes, for example. A model aeroplane has almost nothing to say of actual aeroplanes, being of different substance and function and size. Many model aeroplanes are not even able to fly, though flying is the first function of aeroplanes. In effect, a model aeroplane only says something of the person who *builds* it, how well she can follow instructions, how well she can assemble a predetermined quantity of parts into a cohesive whole, or a cohesive model of a whole.

My Composition by Agnes Underhill

When I grow up, I would like to work in a factory which manufactures model aeroplane kits. I would like to include with each kit an anomalous part, secretly and without corresponding instruction, as a sort of spanner in the works. The usefulness of a spanner depends on what you understand to be its purpose. If I hadn't learned from my father that a spanner is a wrench, which can be useful if you know how to use it, I might have thought a spanner is a sort of virus, which, when introduced to the works, causes them to cease working. The purpose of my experiment would be to observe how the person who eventually builds my model aeroplane would incorporate the anomalous spanner into her construction. I'd have to figure out some way of getting in touch with these people, perhaps I'd include a sort of homing device in the engine of the plane. I would like to observe whether the people would be able to find a way of including the new part, or whether they'd be at a loss. Whether they'd dream of the spare part for many consecutive nights amid floating question marks....

At the heart of it, all I wanted to know was whether the spanner would then become an object of obsession, simply because there seemed to be no place for it where there ought to have been, because of simple faith that there had to be a place for it, somewhere, but no one had invented the proper model yet.

It was hard to say which was worse, in the long run, *not knowing* something or *not having* it. Or *having* something, but *not knowing* it, or *not having* something and *knowing* it. Perhaps the most balanced person in the world was the one who didn't have anything and also didn't know it, maybe like my brother Gavin. He seemed as content to play with sticks and stones as model aeroplanes. My brother could have his picture taken hanging by his knees from the monkey bars if he wanted to, without having to worry about, *I see London, I see France, I see someone's underpants.*

But later in the afternoon that day-after-day-after-Boxing Day, my mother swept the parts of Gavin's plane crash into a dustpan and disposed of them in the kitchen garbage bin, whose lid opened like a rude mouth when she pressed the pedal with her foot. Gavin returned to building cities with mashed potatoes and peas on his plate, making functional vehicles of his knife and fork. We would all say he forgot the plane almost immediately; it seemed that he had. But when my mother wrote a thank you note for the model aeroplane to my Great Aunt Hilda on his behalf, my brother Gavin signed it, in shaky awkward letters large as dimes.

25

Covenant

Sometimes I wanted to unplug the water mattress inside the Ark and drain it, flood the place. I'd finally located the plug, the umbilicus of the quivering thing, and was often tempted to just unscrew it and pull it out, jump up and down on the mattress with forty gallons of water spurting out in geysers, send it cascading over the floorboards and engorging them.

The Ark at its gloomiest is also comfortable. When Buffalo man is asleep, I can amuse myself by clenching and unclenching alternating buttocks to make my body sway slightly to and fro on the water mattress. The sway begins very subtly, scarcely more than the *thought* of swaying, but soon my legs align themselves as two sides of a vacillating balance, my shoulders beginning to sway as well. Then my head and even my ears become conscious of a central meridian. I've never felt this before. If I sway long enough, the whole mattress will slowly sloosh into motion, with a wave and a current running through the water beneath and the water we're made of. I send subaquatic sonar messages to Buffalo man through these channels, when he is not awake to hear.

Just now he's lying face down on the bed with me sitting straddling his butt, facing backwards studying his calves, which resemble those clubs carried by cartoon cavemen. If I do not move, do not tilt to either side, the waves will still and he won't wake up. But if I shift my weight even slightly to the right, I'll lose my balance and he'll wake up. Like a shipwrecked prince, awakening to the face of the lady who rescued him. The tongueless fish-tail woman from the sea, or the earthbound impostor who suffers him to *think* it was she.

Buffalo man's left calf is branded. He has a scar the size and shape of an iron on his left calf because he'd once tried to remove a tattoo with one. When I'd asked him who in his right mind would do something like that, he'd said he wasn't in his right mind at the time. The original tattoo could only be seen as a greenish wrinkled shape at the centre of the scar like the pit in a peach. Somewhere embedded in the scar tissue was a picture or the possibility of a picture, maybe even a word. But it was impossible to tell what it had once been.

When we are in bed Mae West still comes to watch us through the slats of extended steel. I am very aware when she watches us. Certain sounds I make, certain facial expressions, I have to admit are partly addressed to Mae. She is included in them in some way, just because she's the third person in the room, and female like me. Sometimes she rolls off to the kitchen on her knuckles, and returns with snacks to eat during the naked human show. One time it was a whole watermelon whose remains were later found gutted and pitted on the floor outside the Ark, the cool juice of it seeping between my toes when I got up in the middle of the night to pee. I saw Mae West sitting there in the dark as soon as I stepped out of the Ark, sucking on a melon rind, her golden glinting eyes. And if I ever forgot to shut the door of the Ark behind me, she'd shamble past and replace me in bed. She'd sling her arm over Buffalo man's back and he'd make a sound but wouldn't usually wake up. Then I'd think to myself, she loves him more than I do.

Although our tin roof was quite effective in preventing Mae West from peeing on my head or dropping things on us, it failed to prevent her from trying. There were hailstorms of myriad objects, at first only sock-rolls and the odd fruit, then keychains and coffee mugs, then came the thud of Marilyn the stuffed Persian. Then came Mae's *grande finale*, a jar of pennies which had been collecting on top of Buffalo man's fridge since biblical times. The coins hailed down gradually at first, in single ear-ringing pellets, then all at once the full metallic artillery of them came showering down on the Ark.

"Cut it out," bellowed Buffalo man. "This *sucks* Mae, you're totally not playing fair." He was banging the walls of the Ark not looking at me, not even opening his eyes, sunk inside himself and clearly tormented there, leaving me wondering what really needed to be cut *out*. I'd asked him about forty times, over just as many days, whether Mae had been like this before I came along or only after. He'd pretty well avoided answering the question, so I pretty well knew. He was at the end of his rope with her. It had got to the point where it was either the chimpanzee or me, the Ark wasn't big enough for three. One of us girls had to think about finding somewhere else to live.

❦

During the day Mae becomes evasively resigned to me. She brings me an empty tea cup then goes away again, which moves me practically to tears. She never comes to me with open arms, wanting to be picked up and embraced like she does with Buffalo man. There are always three characters in my dramas, never only two. I've been feeling a bit like a home-wrecker and am not too clear on what I'm even doing here. I've left messages for Berenice every few days so she knows I'm not dead, but haven't spoken to her since I left. I tell her answering machine that school's fine and that I'm staying with a friend and that maybe we both just needed some space.

At last I pull a box of National Geo's from behind the water heater, where they've been moldering ever since Buffalo man changed his whole approach toward wildlife preservation. I find pictures of gila monsters and giant pandas, marine iguanas and blue-footed boobies, a North American woodpecker and some African termites, and tape them all up inside the Ark. I plan to cover the entire interior, once I gather together enough species. Then Mae West the chimpanzee will no longer be able to see in.

By about mid-afternoon it occurs to me that neither will we be able to see *out* anymore but at this point the walls of the Ark are thickly papered with panthers and puffins and tapirs and vampire bats, sandy bowls of moon-eggs left by sea turtles, young gorillas orphaned by poachers, and a giant aardvark standing up on its back legs like a clawed alien.

That night, Buffalo man admires my handiwork until we actually try lying down in it for a while.

"It's really hot in here," he says.

We can hear Mae West pacing about outside, trying to find a way to see us. Finally she punches her index finger through one of the eye-shaped slits in the steel grate. I watch Mae West's finger tearing through the belly of the giant aardvark, then again come projecting out the open mouth of a marine iguana. From inside the Ark I watch her finger probing the reptile's mouth, tearing the paper and widening the hole, reaching inside-from-outside and outside-from-inside both at once. I lie there worrying she'll cut her finger on the sharp edges of the grate.

A few minutes later the turquoise fluorescent tube along the headboard goes out with a spark and a fizzle.

"And dark, too," says Buffalo man.

We can't even see the perforated animals anymore except as a glossy sheen on the paper, when spindly light comes nosing in through Mae's finger-holes. We lie side by side, sweating and assessing the darkness in silence for several minutes. If either of us says anything we'll end up fighting, so we don't.

Three rainy days later we find a soggy old globe of the world, in the back alley behind Noah's A-1 Taxidermy. The globe is only slightly damaged. There's a hole punctured in the middle of the Pacific Ocean, a few hundred miles southwest of the Hawaiian Islands, and also an electrical cord dangling from the South Pole. After we dry out the globe, we unscrew the metal plate covering most of Antarctica and screw in a sixty-watt light bulb. Then we set up our globe on the tree stump beside the bed and plug it in. The globe glows. We discover that the hole in the Pacific beams a tiny spotlight onto a picture of a weaver bird's nest, so intricate and perfect you'd swear it was made by human hands. Buffalo man shuts the door of the Ark again, sealing us in with the old globe, three bags of animal biscuits, and the deer-hoof hourglass. Mae West is left outside, rattling the walls and making a sound I've never heard her make before, like a person screaming the word *Raw* over and over again.

"She sounds furious," I whisper.

"She doesn't often make that sound at all," he says. "Sounds like the chimp version of a war cry. Sure she's furious, Agnes, what'd you expect? I'm her sole support and she didn't really plan on sharing me."

Nevertheless I've taken time to stock the Ark with provisions, like a bower-bird designing the best nest to attract a mate. I light the scented candle I've set up on the tree stump, and we're suddenly enveloped in the smell of pumpkin pie. I don't bother repairing the holes in the Ark since they seem to help with ventilation, but have packed a picnic basket with two navel oranges and two clingstone peaches, two elephant-ear pastries and a couple four-packs of Giraf beer, two marzipan mice, two boxes of Goldfish, and a bottle-opener shaped like a bottle-nosed dolphin.

"You know," I say, cracking open a Giraf with the dolphin, I was thinking how there wouldn't have been any dolphins on the original Ark, because they just stayed in the ocean."

"We've already talked about this, Agnes, it was me who came up with that idea. Anyway I think dolphins used to have feet. What happened to those Goldfish, by the way?"

All our favourite things to do involve our mouths. With lips of books and orange peels spread open wide we lie about like gods, reading aloud the entry for *mnemonic device* in a dictionary of mythology. Daring to eat a peach without use of opposable thumbs. Making games of passing it mouth to mouth, until only the pit is left to suck. *Resuscitation.*

Resurrection. He slips his thumb in the shallow enclave just below my sternum and holds it there, pulse feeling for pulse. We bring things to the surface, the nerves of the skin which jump up at each other, magnetizing one another like iron rubbed together. We are shipwrecked then crawl back to land, then crawl back again to the ocean. We lie at the bottom of the deep deep blue, mouthing goldfish-words. *Open, close. Open, close.* There are only two channels and these are they. I always find myself confessing the underbelly of my thoughts to him, my fried-side of sunny-side-up. So he sees me as a pessimist while he is the optimist, even though his profession involves stuffing dead things. At least he tries to create something lasting.

"Why won't you ever tell me what the hourglass is for?" I ask Buffalo man for the umpteenth time. It stands on its four deer hooves on the tree stump by the bed. I'd been asked not to flip it over because it is fragile, so I never have. The upper cone of the hourglass has been empty since I met him, except for the dozen-or-fewer grains which still cling to the mouth of the hole, like the dozen-or-fewer things I could say with any certainty I know anymore. Meanwhile, in the lower cone, pyramid sands slope in a gentle dune around a central point. One of those top grains had been the very last one to fall, but having fallen, it was indistinguishable from all the rest.

"If you could fire a lightning bolt at anyone in the world right now, and know it would never be traced to you," I ask Buffalo man, "where would you have it strike?"

We'd recently taken to playing games of Truth or Dare to kill time in the Ark. *Killing time* was an expression Buffalo man used frequently because he thought it was hilarious. Our games of Truth or Dare are pretty loose, since we're allowed to make up the answers if we need to but only once per game, although we don't have to say which bits are made up.

"What's the most disgusting thing you ever put in your mouth?"

This question flips the scan of my recollection over myriad dental procedures, stops briefly at an obscure file which appears to be a childhood trauma concerning eggs and earthworms, slips by those and lands on *a tongue.*

"A tongue," I say. "A cow's tongue. There's this old memory of being served one on a white plate smothered in raisin-mustard sauce, and not being told what it was until after I'd eaten it. It haunted me for years afterward, the thought of tasting something which could've been tasting me back. What about you? Same question."

"A person can choke from swallowing his own tongue," says Buffalo man, rolling over like a seal face down in the pillow, the smell of human oils there. "I know it for fact," he continues, sitting up suddenly, swaying and swallowing back the rest of his Giraf. "But don't ask the question unless you want to hear the story, and it's a real pretty one, all about your man lying in a gutter puking on himself."

"Okay then I won't ask. How about this one? What would you call the worst nine-month period of your whole life since conception?"

"Well since you're *asking*," says Buffalo man, "I'll tell you." So he tells me about a bartending job he'd had for nine months at the Casino, when he was twenty-eight years old, right after his divorce. How his slurred hands couldn't work fast enough, and about the hovering man who always wore the same banana-yellow tie every night. Then one night the banana-tie man dangled capsules which looked like bumble bees, and they did make him work faster for a while, as fast as a swarm of spinning roulette spokes. When people *spoke* his mind would *spin*, and *stop* at the perfect witty reply every time.

"But as times go," he says, "it went wretchedly." His clothes, his sheets, his sweat, and sex, he says, all reeked of gin. Then one night he poured a whole half-bottle of Gordon's London Dry into his fish tank because he felt like *What's the difference?* When Ted and Texas died he left them in there, stinking of dead fish and pickled juniper for days and days, until finally checking himself into a clinic. Actually, his ex-wife found him unconscious in her garage and told him if he didn't check himself in she'd have him arrested for stalking.

"From the day I started working at the Casino to the day I crawled into the clinic was hands-down the worst nine months I ever spent," he says, "not spent, more like *killed*. So there you have it. That's what can happen, if the kid you *were* marries the kid you *married*. Then ten years down the road, you both want to take back all your toys and go home. Only there's no toys and there's no home, which had been the whole root of the problem in the first place. This is a stupid game, Agnes, can we play something else for a while?"

"What was her name?"

"I just finished saying I don't want to *talk* about it, Agatha. *Agnes*. Jesus. Sorry."

26

A HOLLOW LEG

The morning after my marriage to the severed head, my mother stood at Great Aunt Hilda's cast-iron stove frying eggs, potatoes, onions, bacon, bloody-pudding, and candied yams left over from the night before. The stove also stood, on four stout legs like a black bull in the corner by the kitchen window. I could see the bony fingers of the crabapple tree outside, frosted white like piped moldings on a ginger-bread house. My mother's hair was pulled back from her steamy face by a set of blue plastic jaws, gathered in frothy champagne curls at the back of her head. This was also how she wore her hair to work. The short blue housecoat she was wearing reminded me of her dental uniform. She worked quickly over the frying food with metal instruments, slotted spoons and spatulas, occasionally pressing back tendrils of hair with her wrist. My mother informed each of us by turn that her head was *killing her* this morning. But when Great Aunt Hilda shuffled in and asked how everyone had slept, my mother said *like the dead*.

"Well, so which is it?" said Uncle Vernie slowly, coming in from the shed with an armful of logs the size of pigs' legs. "You're either being killed or you're already dead. Got to be one or the other, Berenice, can't be both."

Uncle Vernie was Great Aunt Hilda's son. He was around the same age as my mother but acted younger, and always spoke very slowly as though his tongue were too big. He had a permanent slightly crooked smile on his face, even though he hardly ever said anything funny.

"You're right, there, it's always one or the other, Vernie," my mother said. She scraped some dark round slices from a frying pan and piled them on a platter. "Who's interested in bloody-pudding, anyway? I've cooked up this mess but must admit I've never seen the attraction."

Great Aunt Hilda was sitting in the rocking chair by the window, looking critically at the backs of her hands. "It used to be a favourite of

Arthur's, dear," she said softly, then flipped her hands over like pancakes to examine the palms. Then she rubbed them together and set them down on her lap. Upstairs, I could hear the endless rattling of that mini pinball game shooting marbles at jungle animals. My brother was still trying for the tiger. *Five hundred points.*

I was foggy and ravenous this morning. My dreams had been about honeymooning with the head. She and I planted a secret garden in the cellar of Great Aunt Hilda's house, then watched it grow up before our very eyes. Enormous purple and green cabbages, blooming from hanging vines, with looping trefoil footpaths all around, and a deep well, yellow-green like a cat's eye at the very centre. I set up lawn chairs, then the Head and I sip elegant green drinks from stemmed glasses with sugar-crusted rims, through candy-stripe straws with goosebendy necks. In the dream, I am watching all this from outside the frame. I can see my headless body, sipping serenely through a tidy hole, like a teardrop pendant at the throat.

Meanwhile, my lovely Head sits like an Easter basket on her own lawn chair. She looks at me and smiles. She has no trouble at all accepting the mouth of the straw between her lips, and I watch the fluid level in her glass go down as she sips. I have to wonder where all the liquid is going. But when I look down, the cellar is filling with green liquid, already up to my ankles and rising. The Head's fancy drink flows straight through her neck, swooshes out the bottom of the pedestal in a minty-green cascade like mouthwash. It looks marvelous.

"You see," says the Head precisely, "having no *body* means never having to take responsibility for anything!"

My mother piled the browned steaming food onto platters and set them down heavily on the table, then unreeled herself in a straight-backed chair. Hers was slightly removed from the other chairs around the table, and she hadn't set a place for herself.

"Well, that should keep you going for a while," she said tiredly, pouring pink grapefruit juice into a small fluted glass. She sat sipping it with her knees crossed, her one extended foot switching back and forth like a cat's tail. A blue, rabbit-fur slipper dangled from her toes. *Well.*

The leg-switching was particular to my mother. It was a gesture which made her seem perpetually impatient or slightly cross, the way cats and birds and certain fish can puff themselves up to intimidate predators. The word *Well* was common to all grown-ups, and could preface almost any statement. It appeared to mean that listeners had the option of not paying attention to what was about to be said. *Well, I guess I'll drive into town today and find out about that steer manure. Well, I don't suppose anyone's interested but I'm going to say something now.* When grown-ups spoke only the barest bones for what was on their minds, it was necessary to invent elaborate systems of signs, to fill in the spaces between what they did and did not say.

My mother's foot switched more furiously as she watched me stack my plate with potatoes and refried yams. Then she lit a long skinny cigarette, and blew out a thin gust of smoke aimed sharply at the ceiling. Uncle Vernie passed the platter of steamy bloody-pudding to a visiting girl from a neighbouring farm, who had wispy blond hair, and a name I could never remember if I ever knew it. Uncle Vernie called her *Missy*, a name I could only associate with a cat Great Aunt Hilda once had, who had died of feline leukemia. "Oh I couldn't, I really couldn't," said Missy, gently declining the bloody-pudding. She was smiling shyly at my mother, and drawing a tiny infinity symbol on the sunny vinyl tablecloth with her finger.

"Well, you could take a tip from our Agnes there, Missy," said Uncle Vernie, with his famous humourless laugh, half-whinny half-wheeze, his upper lip curled back. "She's got a hollow leg or two to fill."

My mother raised her chin slightly and touched the tiny enclave between her collarbones with her fingertips. This was the most subtle and magical of my mother's sign-language. Touching her throat that way seemed to sever the possibility of speech, her own speech as well as anybody else's. As though the gesture were a stylized *Cut*, a silent slicing of the throat with the fingers, the director's directive to stop the scene. My mother was a great director of silent films. When she touched her throat that way, a grainy silence would descend like scrolling acetate, and everyone's motions would turn jerky and artificial and mute.

This technique worked very well with my father, because often the speech which my mother withheld touched him in some way, unless it touched me. Perhaps it would be his locked room in the basement which she was not commenting upon, or the trousers which didn't fit him properly, or his inability to fix things so that they functioned better than before the repair, or his persisting unemployment. We were creatures of a common species, my father and I, like those dogs who don't seem to fit their skins very well. I would watch him dance round my mother's glass bell of silence, condemning himself as cautiously and doggedly as possible.

"Well, pet, they did ask me if I might pop by the manse again next week, which I will do. I think even Reverend Forster will eventually take a shine to me, once he's had a chance to see me with the little folks. I think prospects are good, all things considered...."

Prospective congregations were apparently moved by my father's earnestness but unable to summon much faith. It would come out later that he hadn't got the position as Sunday School teacher, that perhaps there wasn't any budget to create such a position in the church at the present time. My brother and I would come home from school to a silent house, with my mother standing by herself at the living room window, one hand pressed gently to her throat like a Queen Midas of quietness. The silence would hang in the house like lingering paint fumes, making the furniture uncomfortable to sit on. My father would remain in the basement until another position came up, or else he'd go for long walks through alleys and empty lots, searching for junk to drag home and toss on the big heap in the back yard.

"A fellow does what he can, *doesn't* he?" my father would say, while my mother silently built a language of crossing her knees and switching her foot.

"Now Vernie, don't tease," said Great Aunt Hilda to Uncle Vernie's remark about my hollow leg. "Agnes is a growing girl," she said, intending kindness, while the arch of my mother's right eyebrow said, *She certainly is.* Looking down at the mess of leftover potatoes and yams on my plate, the segmented coils of fried onions like translucent earthworms, I wish I could say I lost my appetite. Appetites of all sorts were distasteful to the arch of my mother's eyebrow. My brother, unmoved, was scarfing down his third helping of bloody-pudding. Uncle Vernie was sucking his teeth, while Missy, whom no one ever saw again after this date, was carefully smoothing out her region of the tablecloth, sweeping her toast crumbs into a discrete little continent.

I'd like to say that I was not an overly large child. I'd like to say that, but in truth I can't be sure. Anyway *size* wasn't even the issue, *capacity* was. Up until you were born, Rose, nobody in the family took many pictures, and the ones in my head were quite faded and unreliable. When I remember scenes like the fried yam scene I'm not really in the picture, the same way the person holding the camera is not in the picture, except as an occasional blurry thumb in the corner of the frame. I relied on my mother to supply me with some clue as to how I appeared, though her reflections tended to be ambiguous, variable, contradictory. So I learned to see myself this way, as a sort of blurry mist, whose shape was defined by whatever it happened to condense upon. Or like water, conforming to the shape of whatever receptacle it is poured into.

Rose. I could tell you a funny story which happened not too long ago, while you were sleeping here in your gauzy yellow crib. I had my head buried in the hall closet, and was going through boxes trying to find something or other. I didn't find whatever it was, but I did find a monstrous wooden shoe. It was a Dutch clog, stashed at the very back of the closet, behind other boxes of boots and shoes. The clog was the size of a cinder block if it was an inch. Later, when your Mum-Mum, as she calls herself, came home, she found me weeping so hard I could scarcely catch a breath to tell her why. It was that I'd been convinced the shoe must've been mine. Why else would it be hidden away like that? I started blithering on about Clementine, blowing bubbles soft and fine beneath the surface of the foaming brine into which she had fallen. She wore *herring-boxes without tops-es* on her feet, because there were no proper shoes to fit her. I had no idea how big herring boxes were, but I couldn't reconcile *light she was and like a fairy* with *her shoes were number nine*, which seemed very large to me considering that my mother's feet are size five. I wasn't even sure what size my own feet were since I tended to pick up my shoes second-hand, after the sizes have already been scuffed from the soles.

Anyway, it turned out that I hadn't had giant feet as a child. The wooden clog was a window box in which my mother had once intended to plant geraniums. Of course it was, how silly of me. But I've been thinking lately, that I must have a somewhat skewed vision of scale, maybe always have. I look at T-shirts intended for terriers and wonder if they will fit me, or again at table skirts and wonder the same thing. Something is missing from my ability to understand *scale* very clearly. But what I want to say about this, Rose, is that maybe things like clothing and identity are better described in terms of relative function than absolute size. There is no such thing as an absolute identity or an absolute size five anywhere in the world, except in outer space, where these might exist as floating conceptual balloons. Somewhere in outer space, there is a size five dressmaker's dummy which resembles my mother, as I had come to see her, but the woman herself is not this article.

If a person were to tell a story about somebody called *she*, then that *she* could be described as fat or thin, by the storyteller's estimation. She would be the object of that person's vision. But in a story about a person called *I* there is no one to watch the watcher, and no one to take her picture as she sits at a kitchen table eating fried yams. What's in an I? A blind spot, the centre of a lie. A relative truth. Watching frenzied drops of condensation fret their way down a bus window, I am monstrously huge. Looking up at similar configurations in a clear night sky, manic points of light a million miles away, I am tiny, or nothing.

My mother was switching her foot to the tick of the wall clock, while the rusty skins of yams curled round my teeth like peanut hulls. Uncle Vernie was out in the yard now, loudly telling weepy Missy that she should think about becoming a nun *right away, today*. Great Aunt Hilda was still napping like a cat, in her chair, maybe dreaming of Arthur shaking apples from the uppermost boughs of the crabapple tree, the fruit falling into her lap.

From my chair at the kitchen table I could see into the living room, as I scooped forkfuls of fried yams into my mouth. There was a farmer's calendar by the phone, with a picture of a prize Charlais bull, the colour of butterscotch-ripple ice cream, and beside it was the window onto the porch. Propped against a window ledge out on the porch sat an old wooden boomerang, decorated with aboriginal designs in black and maroon. Beyond it, the snow-covered hayfields expanded like a pale and monstrous underbelly.

Objects which Great Aunt Hilda found too backward or too exotic to be fathomed were generally exiled to the porch. There was a little rubber Chief, with feathers and face paint, out there as well, who beat a drum when you wound him up. Also a set of camel teeth on a leather thong, which somebody somewhere once had worn, after the camel had given them up. The porch was a capsular limbo between inside and outside the house, containing articles which Great Aunt Hilda could neither reconcile keeping nor throwing away. She was interested in things from faraway places, but only insofar as they retained that dear strangeness which made them interesting yet undemanding.

Inside the living room, things were lacier, more delicate and more demanding. Things which needed to be dusted frequently but seldom were. Lots of teacups and doilies, and ceramic figurines of lovely ladies, storybook animals from Red Rose tea packages. There was an avocado-green chesterfield, with curly wooden legs and little *bouclé* pommels all over it. But the thing I was fixing upon, rather than looking back at my mother as she watched me chew my yams, was the framed print hanging over the chesterfield. It was red and garish and completely flat, like a window into a world of two dimensions.

The print was an enlargement of a 1916 Vogue cover, showing a mother and daughter in a glamourous red salon. Every time Great Aunt Hilda looked at it she muttered about having always wanted one, either a daughter or a glamourous red salon. The daughter in the print was about four or six or maybe eight. The girl looked tiny from here, seated behind a round table in the foreground with only her head and shoulders showing above the red table top, her two little hands placed on the vivid surface as at a séance. Her hair was the colour of pennies, cut short in a Prince Valiant skullcap. Her purple smock had criss-crossed stitches at the throat, her milky-blue eyes were without pupils.

The mother in the picture was pressed flat against an encroaching backdrop of swirling peacock feathers, with her long hands wrapped round an elegant bowl of fruit. She was tall and pale and bone thin, her body bent over the bowl like an ivory shepherd's crook, the embodiment of a question mark. Dressed in billowing white sleeves with a tangerine bodice, a black velvet bow drooping from her bony cleavage. The bow resembled melting tar. The mother was pushing the bowl of fruit coolly across the table toward her daughter, with the black bow looking as though it would drop like a massive arachnid to nest among the fruit.

Whoever painted the picture hadn't thought to include any viable way for the girl to exit, unless she were to scoot beneath the table and stay there until the mother took the questionable fruit bowl away. I might have taken a bite of the apple myself, if there hadn't been that nasty bow drooping over it, all spidery and poisonous looking. But surely normal little girls would never suspect their mothers of feeding them poisonous fruit.

27

Lunar Unicycle

"It'll be no use their putting their heads down and saying, 'Come up again, dear!' I shall only look up and say, 'Who am I then? Tell me that first,' and then, if I like being that person, I'll come up; if not, I'll stay down here 'till I'm somebody else."

— Alice

The next night there's a violent storm, it flashes and sobs like I've never seen. The power goes out and everybody in the neighbourhood is powerless. Still the lightning flashes, an electric reaper's hand slapping the sky then erasing itself. Finally the thunder becomes a mumbled afterthought, as the storm rolls noisily over and goes to sleep, leaving slick the black back of the asphalt. The plumbing at Buffalo man's place runs all night like a babbling brook, the fridge is the buzz of cicadas. The sound of a leaking faucet becomes goldfish kissing the meridian between two dimensions, hauling in clear beads of oxygen underwater where they live. *Pearldivers*.

When the storm has passed, the sirens begin wailing, not luring but lured to the peril of others. Some body in the city is like any other body. A person's life is an intersection, where dimensional planes and trains converge, a station erected there. You can get to any body from any body, but some routes are more direct. You can take this whole metaphor to the very end of the line, if you like, I'm sure it goes there by now.

After the rains have stopped I leave him sleeping alone in the Ark, and step out onto the wet fire escape with my notebook. Bliss beneath my feet, the cool sleek iron. I sit moony and half-naked on the top step, moonlight filtering silver on my limbs. Passing headlamps fall across my kneeling knees and thighs, as I slip behind the lush green tongues of a potted heptapleurum. My ears prick up at passersby, as though to induce some gallant in helmet and plume to pause beneath the balcony and look up, whence I'd let down my hair, else drop the potted hepta-pleurum upon him.

Outside in the alley beneath the fire escape a black umbrella goes for a circular walk, blown point-over-point by the wind. Like those spiders I used to draw when I was a child, with too many legs pointing every which way. My spiders were identical to my suns. Both were rendered as circles with multitudinous rays, fringing the entire circumference of the body. The only difference between suns and spiders was the colour of the crayon, black for spiders, orange for suns. The sun is an orange spider with eyes and legs all around, casting a web all around to catch us in its light. The spider is a black sun, spinning stories in the dark and casting them into the fire.

"Spiders have only *eight* legs, Agnes," my grade two teacher Miss Shoemaker said. "Yours has twenty-seven."

"My spider is running very fast," I said.

My Father is of the Sun, my Mother is of the Moon. This is supposed to make sense on some mythical level, yet I can only get the gist of it by selecting certain details and ignoring other ones. *Moon Mother.* Her coolness, polishing teeth like a moon woman polishing luminous stones. *Sun Father.* The infernal pressure inside his head, how even the walls of the locked room couldn't prevent it from radiating throughout the house. The shaft of light slipping from beneath the door, the sound of the rowing machine like a great bellows.

But I could just as easily look at it the other way round, with my father as the lonely satellite, whereas my mother tried to keep on the sunny side of things. She bustled constantly, smiling brightly, preserving the impression that she ran her daily course above the world of men, when in fact *she* was the solar centre around whom everything else revolved.

Now look again. At the end of the storm there are gifts, reminders from another realm of sense. The moon is so beautiful and close I could hold it on my tongue like a pearl. The moon is full, and like she is, always changing, always constant. Some nights she is an engagement ring while other nights she's a hole punched in the night sky. You can see only a spot of that lighted page beyond where nothing has been written yet.

The morning after the big storm I wake to another cataract East Van sky, milky blue like the eyes of a blind dog. I stretch on the water mattress every direction my limbs will reach, touching my toes to the cold vinyl at the foot, the vinyl at the head, and those new fixtures on the walls to which my wrists could be affixed with silk scarves. It amazes me, that this day could begin like any other, when it is fundamentally different from any other day.

It's first conceived as brooding indigestion, which becomes worse as soon as I creep out of the Ark. From the kitchen comes the smell of frying bacon, the sound of Buffalo man whistling tunelessly, the sizzling of fat like falling rain. Then comes the thought of that fetal pig I'd been dreaming about, bedraggled in formaldehyde, lying on its side in an aluminum tray amid all the glittering instruments. I climb out of bed, skirt the floor trailing bed sheets, slip between the beads of the bathroom door and am sick.

Buffalo man's knuckles set down two egg holders like bishops across from each other on the table. He then sets down two soft-boiled eggs inside the egg holders, so their tops can be split diagonally with a spoon and their contents dabbed at with toast fingers. I sit wrapped in my sheets like Lazarus, staring down at the bald pate of my egg. I tap at it a few times but can't bring myself to break the shell.

"Not hungry this morning?" he says, dipping a toast finger in the runny egg yolk and flipping it into his mouth. Mae West sits quietly rocking back and forth on the floor. There's a jar of strawberry jam and her baby spoon with that blue ducky on the handle.

"Are you sure that's good for her?" I ask, wringing a chafe mark on my wrist. Sometimes one thing and its own opposite feel exactly the same.

Over breakfast Buffalo man reads a newsletter from the Jane

Goodall Institute, citing the genetic difference between humans beings and chimpanzees being not much more than one percent. That humans are more closely related to chimps than chimps are to gorillas, and that blood transfusions between humans and chimpanzees are perfectly possible. He feeds yolk-soaked toast fingers to Mae West, smiling at the egg spit running down her chin.

"It's so obvious we share almost everything," he says, leaning back in his chair. "I often regret that extra one-and-a-bit percent of whatever-it-is that makes up the difference between us. I'm pretty sure I'd be much happier as a chimpanzee."

"I don't know," I answer, "pretty sure I wouldn't want Mae's life as it is now, to tell you the truth." It strikes me right between the eyes as the worst possible thing I could have said. I go back to bed without breaking my egg, and sleep through half the day again with my fossil ammonite and my biology textbook under my pillow. I dream of scalping soft-boiled eggs and finding fetal pigs inside.

༄

There are places on the hands which correspond to internal body cavities, and which, when pressed, can inflict sharp pain in those regions, or even cause an opponent to pass out. Yet we shake hands with people, we allow ourselves to be touched by strangers and we touch them.

I stare at the chest of a young man on the bus as I come home from a blood test at the Pine Free Clinic. He is closer to my own age than mine is to Buffalo man's. I can see the young man's heart thump under his Chilliwack T-shirt like a sub-woofer, while Buffalo man's heart is a slow buried clock which can't be seen from the outside. But at night when we're still, and the floods have stilled, he and I are an island. Then with my ear on his chest I can hear it. A low rumbling, not mercurial and clean, but stomping the clods like hooves.

Sometimes I think about the bodies of other women Buffalo man has known. Their pirate mechanisms, secret levees, how these had to be learned anew every time. I had none of this knowledge myself, only knew *his* body intimately other than my own. Now the bodies of all other men walked into his shape and were somehow measured there. As though Buffalo man were the original King, against whose foot all other feet became commensurable.

When I get home from the Clinic, and when the words finally come, they come like every bottle of beer I've ever tried to open, messily, surging up in quickly bursting bubbles slipping over the lip, then flowing down like grains of sand moving quickly. A person running fast in the sand, looking down at her feet. When the words come, they *do*. They spend themselves, spill themselves, and the throat is left dry. It seems to me that he and I are forever telling each other slightly *more* or slightly *less* than we really intend, too much or not enough, or not at the right time, or not in the right way.

"You are *not*," he says.

"Yeah," I say, "I'm afraid I *am*."

"No, Agnes, please, are you *serious*?"

"Yes, Noah, I am."

He lights his vanilla pipe again, and for some minutes puffs away without speaking. At last he unfolds his arms, takes the pipe out of his mouth, and says, *So you think you're changed, do you?* He grins grimly, knows I know it's what the smoking Caterpillar says when he first meets Alice.

"It's not unusual to be *wrong* about these things, Agnes," he continues, knocking ashes from the bowl of his pipe into an ashtray shaped like an open hand.

"What'd you do, buy one of those piss-kits at Shoppers Drug Mart? Yeah, I bet *those* are reliable," he says. "I mean, I don't want to call myself an *expert* here," he says, but on the other hand he loves to call himself an expert. He can sew the tiniest stitches up the belly of a yellow-bellied marmot, sealing in the sawdust with no seams showing. He could split a tree in two with one sweep of his axe, probably, though I'd never actually seen him do this to any tree. I'd seen him do it to a park-bench once, said he was going to splinter wood to make bean poles but then he never ended up planting any beans.

The avocado pit I try to sprout in a jar on top of the water heater bursts its leather case and sprouts mold. The single green shoot looks strong enough, but has black spots all over it like pictures of lungs in films from the Cancer Society. I take the pit and bury it in some soil packed in a cinderblock in the back alley, and plant a pair of tethered sticks in memorial. It seems terrible to bury a seed not to grow it but because it's dead. I worry myself sick every morning, that there's no way my present environment could possibly germinate life of any sort which is not grotesque.

If something does not have a name there is less ceremony attached to its death. There is this bundle of cells, more than a bundle, I am worrying myself sick about it. It is not getting smaller with the passing days. Now it is practically weeks, maybe a few of them. Not just a bundle of cells anymore, probably. There were pictures of embryonic chickens in my biology books, their large heads, and the chart which showed what they looked like, after how many weeks. I couldn't bring myself to look very closely at the chicken chart, the nursery of tiny beings, and pick out my own little tadpole in there.

But there, I have named it anyway. As a period of time, as a tadpole, as matter, as internal to myself, and as growing. When Buffalo man is inside I try not to think about it at all, I pretend not to think of it. Until afterward, when he draws lazy helixes on my belly with his fingers, and I watch as though it is a glass unicorn he holds in his hands. Be careful, you might break it. If anyone is going to break it, let it be me.

28

Isis Millipede

My friend Effie's house was bordered by a tall hedge. Among its lower limbs were numerous irregular chambers, leafy cupolas with branching buttresses, fluttering windows filtering green shafts of light in harlequino patches on the moss. In winter, Effie's hedge was a cage of frozen spines and barren ribs, the picked carcass of seasons past. But now, finally, it was spring. Throughout the winter we played mostly inside, in the basement at my house, or nestled in the downy comforters of the upper bunk of Effie's bed. Effie's sister, Robin-Mae, was a quiet elf dwelling on the lower bunk, with her crayons and her smooth pretty stones, while Effie's bunk rose transcendent like the long thin legs of a stork. Or like the long thin legs of her seven Barbie dolls, who all had jointed knees and could sit discreetly.

Effie's mother made us doll-sized sandwiches, with mini melba rounds and raspberry jam, then sliced apples into slender crescents. She filled the doll's teapot with apple juice, to serve in the tiny china cups. We perched up in the top bunk and dressed Effie's dolls for tea, then sat them around a table made from a hat box, with yellow place mats cut from J-cloth.

Effie had the most extravagant harem of Barbies I'd ever seen. There were seven of them in all, like seven sisters who looked exactly the same, except for differences in hair colour. They all had sky blue eyes, insectival waists, hands resembling lobster claws, and hard exoskeletal breasts which had no nipples, and didn't spring back when Robin-Mae bit them. The more advanced dolls had stigmata through their hands and ears, which could be plugged up with rhinestones on pegs, to represent diamond engagement rings with earrings to match. Effie's Barbies were named Pinkie and Silky, Petals and Creamy, Tulips and Rosehips and Cherries. Silky, Tulips, and Creamy were blonde, Rosehips was a redhead, and Cherries' hair was black. Pinkie was bald.

She had once been blonde like three of her sisters, but Robin-Mae cut her hair off with pinking shears, to make a nest for her family of feather-wing beetles. Whenever Effie needed a doll to be male, for a wedding or a lion hunt, the role would fall to bald Pinkie, then later to my doll Isis Millipede.

Isis Millipede was three times the size of a Barbie doll but looked a third Barbie's age. Her body was a knotty trunk, not an hourglass, and her hair was mutantly white. Like that fibreglass cotton candy called *angel hair* wound round the trunk of the Christmas tree. Her eyes were yellowish-brown glass, and they opened and closed slightly unevenly, making her look potty and slur-eyed like grown-ups on New Year's day. Unlike the lips of the blond head I had married, this doll's lips were parted, revealing small painted teeth. I called her *Isis Millipede*, after the goddess who has a thousand faces and the bug who has a thousand legs.

Isis Millipede wore a spangled pink and yellow mini-dress which was too short for her, her pink underpants with lacy ruffles on the bum plainly visible underneath. Her legs were not jointed at the knees but set stiffly into her hip sockets, so she had to spread her legs open in a wide V just to sit down, as most little girls were taught not to do. Girls who sat that way were teased by boys and scolded by their mothers.

After the shearing of Pinkie, Effie kept her dolls safely locked in a carrying case resembling a great thick book, with the seven sisters packed away like entries in a dictionary of synonyms. There was a separate index for dresses, and a smaller appendix for the plastic shoes, paper umbrellas, purses, stethoscopes, cameras, dumbbells, ski poles, snorkels, and suitcases which came with the various outfits. The cover bore the title *My Secret Fantasies* embossed in gold on pale blue vinyl, and it locked with a tiny heart-shaped lock, with a key Effie wore on a string around her neck.

"You are never *ever* to look in that book, do you understand?" Effie warned her little sister Robin-Mae. "That's my *one* rule. I shouldn't even tell you what will happen to you if you do, because it wouldn't be nice. But probably a man will come and cut off all your hair and glue it to your chin. Then you'll have a beard and be bald like Pinkie."

On non-rainy days, we left the nest of Effie's upper bunk, and went outside to play in the hedge. I learned that it was possible to suck up apple juice through a cocktail straw, then inject it back out the straw and through the tiny hole in Isis Millipede's mouth. The straw was one of those jointed types, with a flexible ringed segment like the clitellum of an earthworm. I dangled the tip of the straw over Isis Millipede's mouth and let the juice fall in small gulps, gradually seeping down through the hole between her teeth. I managed to feed her eight tiny tea cups of apple juice this way. Then I peeked under her skirt to see if she'd pee.

"Do you think I should make a hole down there for her to pee through?" I asked Effie.

Effie's green eyes grew as wide as saucers, she looked like she was getting ready to cry. "You shouldn't *say* things like that," she said, "it's not *nice*." If Effie said something was not nice, she meant it wasn't to be spoken about.

"But wouldn't it be much less nice to have only one hole which everything went into, and no holes for anything to get out?" I asked. "It would be like keeping a secret for way too long, until it started to turn poison on the person." Once I'd seen an old movie where some Roman soldiers killed a guy by force-feeding him a whole cask of red wine through a funnel in his mouth, until he swelled up like a leech. Then he exploded like a waterfall when they poked him with a spear. The only way of avoiding such a catastrophe is being very very careful what you put into yourself in the first place, and how much of it.

This wasn't only true for apple juice, but for other things as well. Effie always closed her eyes when she undressed her dolls, for instance, so she wouldn't have so many pictures of naked ladies filling up her head. She shut her eyes as soon as the tiny snaps were undone, then I would talk her through the change until the doll's body was covered again. Then she'd open her eyes. I'd have to talk her through all the sleeve-holes and neck-holes with *you're getting warm, warmer,* or *you're getting cold, colder* when she was missing the holes. A lobster-claw thumb would often get caught in the lace of a sleeve, or hair would get tangled round the metal snaps, pulling the pliable face askew when Effie tried to force the head through.

I would watch all of this, the horrible contortions, the smooth shiny plastic, poreless and pinkish like skin that's been steam-burned. I'd seen all Effie's dolls naked though she never had, as far as I knew.

Beneath the leafy flying buttress of the hedge, I helped Effie undress her dolls for their naps, changing seven evening dresses into night gowns. We laid out the seven of them in a row inside a pillow case for a bed, with Isis Millipede on the end. When Effie opened her eyes again, she laughed at the sleeping arrangement.

"Well, no one's ever gonna mistake *your* baby for one of *mine*," she said. "I hope Isis Millipede doesn't roll over in her sleep, or she'll crush everyone."

In contrast to the other dolls, Isis Millipede was a cuckoo bird, the one who pushes the others out of the nest one by one until only she is left. Baby cuckoos grow to be three times the size of their surrogate parents, wearing resources thin with their insatiable appetites.

"No wonder you always eat all the sandwiches," said Effie, "your baby is a *monster*."

Effie was right, my baby was monstrous. The apple juice I'd fed her was now fermenting inside her body cavity, giving her breath a peculiar, alcohol smell. Furthermore, the metal axis holding her eyes in place was rusting slightly, tinting her tear ducts like those religious statues who weep blood. Her rusty eyes could no longer open and close without some assistance, I had to either pick Isis up and shake her or physically pry her eyelids open with my fingers.

The seven sisters didn't have this problem because their eyes were painted permanently open. They had a different change of clothes for almost every hour of the day, while Isis had only one dress which she had to wear all the time, because it was very difficult to find dresses for dolls of her size. At nap time, she wore just the ruffled pink underpants she came with, instead of nothing at all, which Effie said wouldn't be very *nice*.

"It would be okay if she were only sleeping by *herself*," she said, "but it's just that she's in bed with all of *mine* and she's not even covering herself."

I was beginning to dislike Isis Millipede. Though she towered above the others, she had the body of a child. Sitting down, she came eye level with Pinkie, Silky, Petals, Creamy, Tulips, Rosehips, and Cherries, but still there was the problem of her legs, which spread open almost at right angles, like a nutcracker.

"Does she have to sit like that?" Effie would say. "It doesn't look very nice." But things didn't look much nicer if I stood her up again, when she became a slur-eyed monster Snow White among seven gorgeous dwarves.

Suddenly Robin-Mae hopped down the front steps in a pale green gingham pinafore with *appliqué* apples for pockets, carrying an empty mayonnaise jar and a nail. She sat down under the question mark tree and began digging an embedded stone out of the earth, which she used as a hammer to pound holes into the lid of the jar. She pulled up a fistful of grass and stuffed it in the jar as well, then disappeared behind the hedge. Effie was singing to her seven dolls who lay passive and smiling on their backs, staring up at the ceiling of leaves through eyes of blue paint. Isis Millipede had one eye open and one eye closed, because one of the eyes would no longer open at all, no matter how much I shook her or picked at her lids.

"Isis Millipede is in a coma," I announced, propping her up in the corner with her arms stretched out like a sleep walker or mummy in a horror movie. I watched Effie's thumbs and fingers climb up an invisible waterspout as she sang:

> Itsy-bitsy spider climbed up the waterspout
> Down came the rain and washed the spider out
> Out came the sun and dried up all the rain
> And the itsy-bitsy spider climbed up the spout again.

The tiny voice of Robin-Mae echoed *itsy-bitsy, itsy-bitsy* from some corridor inside the hedge, then her two little hands suddenly burst through the leaves, hanging there for a moment like the antlers of a moose head. Robin-Mae clapped her hands for the spider song and got a little slap from her older sister.

"*Don't* stick your hands through the walls," scolded Effie. "Hasn't anyone ever *told* you? You can't stick your hands through the walls."

Robin-Mae pressed the fingertips of both hands lightly together, so they made a little cage with an empty space between the palms, then she pumped her hands so her fingers moved together and apart like the spokes of an umbrella.

"Guess what *this* is," whispered Robin-Mae. "Can you *guess*?"

"You're so *retarded*," Effie said to her sister's hands. "Anyway I was the one who taught you that in the first place. It's a spider doing push-ups on a *mirror*."

"No, it's not," chirped the voice behind the hedge.

"Is too," said Effie.

"Is not," chirped the voice, the hands disappearing into the leaves again.

"Is too," muttered Effie finally.

What the pumping hands had looked like to me was a rack of moose antlers fighting with itself. But I was now trying it myself, the hand-spider joined by five fingery legs to its own reflection. The motion felt curious. There is no way of telling which hand is supposed to be the spider and which the reflection. The imaginary plane between them remains flexibly solid as long as the fingertips are connected, they continue to mirror each other. I was learning that if something or someone you are touching follows your motions exactly, even a single point of contact can feel like a solid plane.

Under the hedge, I wondered whether this phenomenon was only true with one's own hands, or if two pairs of hands, or even two whole bodies connected in this way, could experience the same thing. If touching somebody could feel like a continuing surface of support, which extended beyond the particular points of contact, then this was a marvelous thing.

"You should try this, Effie," I said. "It really feels like there's a solid surface there, between your fingertips. It's like a wavy mirror."

Effie clucked her tongue and pulled Tulips out of bed to have her hair brushed.

"Robin-Mae just wants you to pay attention to her," Effie said, which was the first reason not to pay attention to someone.

Mirror mirror on the wall, who's the real spider after all? said my right hand to my left, or my left to my right. It didn't matter, was the whole point. I looked over at Effie, who'd moved on to Silky now, stroking the nylon hair, electrically clinging to the comb. They weren't interested in my hands. So I looked to Isis Millipede, standing in the shade propped against the undergrowth, arms outstretched and eyes rusted shut. *Monstrous.* She was my only doll and she was monstrous. I began to see how Isis Millipede would become a poor reflection upon me, as my mother said I could sometimes be, when I was acting in a way unlike the way she liked to see things.

Isis Millipede was not a nice little girl. It was in her sluttish way of sitting, her unco-operative eyes and her sleepwalking, and the hole between her lips and the bad luck teeth she was born with. The flirty ruffles on the bum of her underpants, and the peculiar smell of her internal humours, and the fact that she held everything inside. The fact that she wept rusty blood. The fact that having no genitals, nor any other orifices besides her eyes and her mouth, did not make her more pure after all, but in fact had caused her body cavity to ferment. And the fact that her name was Isis Millipede, after the goddess who had a thousand faces and the bug who had a thousand feet.

She was not the model daughter any mother would set loose in the world without some modification. Her multiplicity of character would only confuse people, many would dislike her for it, few would care to marry her. There she'd be, poor little thing, living out in the wild with God knows how many maniacs and dwarves and women with shaved heads. *Imagine!* She'd end up not finding many who'd take her, once the dwarves tired of her, she'd make a square peg of herself. Any mother who *cared* would do her damnedest to correct this, nip the problem in the bud before the day the daughter sees herself and is properly horrified at what she's become.

I decided that the best strategy would be to carefully amputate Isis Millipede's legs. This would be helpful in two ways. It would create two large lower orifices, through which the fermented apple juice in her body cavity could be bled, and it would also assist in normalizing her height. She'd be able to look other dolls straight in the eyes, without having to splay her legs to do it. The operation would not be as grisly as it might at first sound. Isis Millipede's legs were only shallowly set into her hip sockets, and could be popped out as easily as undoing a button.

I picked up Isis Millipede and held her close for a moment. Her outstretched fingers lightly chafed my skin as they brushed my neck, her plastic torso beneath my chin was like the cool smooth body of a violin. Then I sat her down on the ground in her usual way, with her legs spread open wide, the earth and the grass like a private baseball diamond between them. I sat her down with her back turned away from me. Then, all I had to do was push her head forward to the ground, and probably the legs would pop right out. With a bit of help, they did. Effie made a sound like she was choking on a cherry pit, then she started to cry.

"I can't believe you just *did* that, I can't believe you just *did* that, why would you *do* that?" she said about seven times, twisting Creamy's hair into tight little knots, until the whole body did a full flip like those jointed wooden acrobats.

Robin-Mae suddenly popped her head through the doorway of the hedge.

"What did you see, Effie? Can I see too? Do you and Agnes want to see what *I* just found?" Then Robin-Mae held up the mysterious mayonnaise jar, which now had a huge hairy spider inside it. Effie screamed and scrambled past her sister, then ran up the front steps in tears. I picked up Isis No-Legs and stuck her in bed with her seven stepsisters. She now fit *perfectly* and seemed to be resting comfortably. I gathered up her legs and tried to bury them behind the hedge, with Robin-Mae and the spider watching.

"Is that lid screwed on tight enough?" I asked Robin-Mae. She nodded her head.

"Then let me have a look, but not too *close*." The spider was standing up on her back legs, tentatively tapping at the glass with her front legs.

"Are you going to let her go, eventually?" I asked.

"Of *course* I am," said Robin-Mae, as though it were obvious.

29

Metaphormosis II: Sea peach

> The process of paedomorphosis is one by which immature larvae suddenly become sexually mature and reproduce. However, the development of the organism then ceases at that stage.... The mature adults of these free-swimming organisms may resemble the immature larvae of other species within the same group.
>
> — from *Biology*, Raven & Johnson editors

Buffalo man's fingers draw double helixes on my hipbone like silvery stretch marks, while I hold my biology book up in front of my face tanning-reflector style. I can't see him, but now and then can see myself from his perspective, a headless body invisibly growing. There's this *thing* come between us which wasn't there before, a cluster of cells so very near the end of the alphabet with only the *Z* left to come. But just now I'm arrested by the slip of his fingertips below, and above by a picture in my biological textbook. I dwell on the latter. *Halocynthia auranthium.* I long to say the beautiful name out loud but this would involve speaking, and just now Buffalo man and I are not speaking.

Halocynthia auranthium. The sea peach. The sea peach is a creature who resembles a human heart almost exactly, and appears to live a brainless but balanced existence rooted to the ocean floor by way of a sucker on its underside. Its evolution has chosen this sort of lifestyle. Its flesh is luminous peach colour, with a pair of truncated branches at the top, resembling the aorta and the pulmonary artery. These two branches function as *incurrent-siphon* and *excurrent-siphon* respectively, there being no other entrances nor exits to its body. Through its two siphons, the sea peach feeds, breeds, and breathes, taking in food and oxygen and reproductive products, expelling breathless water and waste and tadpoles.

I dwell on the image of this heart-shaped creature for quite some time, until I begin to dwell *in* the image, for all intents and purposes *as* the image. There seems little risk that I'll actually turn into a sea peach by dwelling upon its qualities, but I may learn something from the experiment. There's no vivisection involved unless it is to myself, examining my parts as they're mirrored in the parts of a sea peach. *A heart, rooted to the ocean floor.* I would like to be one of these creatures, would like to have a sense of this, at least. The sea peach appears very peaceful.

I study a cross-section diagram of its interior. The body cavity of the sea peach is horizontally divided into two separate chambers, a small basement and a considerably larger attic. The attic is spacious and airy, open to watery elements through two semi-lunar windows on the ceiling, these being the valves of the branching siphons. The attic chamber is mostly taken up with a delicate breathing apparatus, the gill structure and pharynx of the sea peach. This breathing apparatus consists of a graceful slotted cylinder, like the inner bowl of a salad spinner, or an upside-down chandelier.

The basement is a small room where the sea peach keeps its heart. The creature itself resembles a heart living in the very basement of the planet, and it keeps its own heart in the basement of itself. The heart of the sea peach is a small red turnip, its root gently curled around its sex gland and stomach. The heart and sex and appetite, these are organs which our own species also keeps in the basement.

Phylum Chordata. The sea peach is a chordate, whose body is headless. Its body resembles the hearts of larger chordates, such as a caribou or human beings, who both have heads. All members of *Phylum Chordata*, which would include guinea hens, marine iguanas, great horned toads, wide-mouthed bass, chimpanzees, all other primates, elephants, giant squid, gerbils, and the sea peach, to name but a few, look very, very similar in our prenatal form. Each of us in this group begins life as something resembling a tadpole, with something resembling a *head*, and something resembling a *tail*. This is because we share the common feature of a spinal structure, at least in our immature form.

As humans beings, we appreciate and retain our spinal structures throughout our lives, though often they pain us. The sea peach, however, loses its spine when it reaches adulthood. In infancy it resembles other members of the chordate group, darting about in a similar fashion, headstrong and wriggling just like the rest of us. Chickens, gila monsters, arctic perch, and a hippopotamus. But when the sea peach reaches maturity, it gives up its spine and sinks to the bottom of the ocean, where it stays put. When a sea peach grows up, what might've been its spine turns into a suction cup to hold it in place for the rest of its life.

Subphylum Urochordata, the Tunicates. The sea peach is a tunicate. In addition to a sucker, the adult also grows a rough tunic to protect itself, in lieu of an exoskeleton or bones. This tunic is comprised partly of animal matter and partly of cellulose, which is a substance very common in plants but quite uncommon in animals. As a grown-up, therefore, the sea peach becomes a spineless creature who is half-animal and half-vegetable. It successfully evolves into something headless, brainless, footless, and faceless. It's got a sucker to root it in place, like a spouse or a mortgage, and two siphons to wave about like those wind-tunnel puppets at rock concerts, or the truncated arms of a goddess. Through those two open vessels, the sea peach feeds by caprice of the tides, scatters tadpoles like seeds to re-root themselves in some other place — where the brood soon loses mobility, loses spine and loses face. Human beings on the other hand, begin life with tiny gill structures like the sea peach has, but we forget how to breathe underwater quite early. We do retain our faces and spines, however, then spend a lot of time complaining about, destroying, and reconstructing them.

Gradually I become a cordiformarian. I develop the habit of eating only heart-shaped food. Red Delicious apples, roasted red peppers, cinnamon hearts and a million little strawberries, clingstone peaches and persimmons and plums and small green squash. I cut the peaches in half and marvel at their flaming veined interiors. I eat hearts made of maple sugar, and hearts with tiny amorous sayings printed on them. *Kiss me. Wild thing. Lover boy. Beat it.* I eat so many strawberries Buffalo man starts using those green baskets to store his false eyes, tongues, and teeth. The little green leaf-caps litter the floor like sea stars, squelching red trails when we step on them.

I eat those elephant-ear pastries, which really look more like hearts than ears. Stratified hearts, allowing you to trace their progression of growth, like the heart of the Grinch which grew three sizes that day and burst the whole frame. *Sproing.* I try to imagine my heart feeling bigger but all I keep seeing is this hard little plum, still green at both ends. More of a gallstone than a heart. I try imagining my heart as a luscious peaceful sea peach. Buffalo man tries to poach an egg in a heart-shaped cookie cutter so at least I'll get some protein, but the egg balloons up like a tumor and I start crying for no reason at all.

"*Why* do we have to eat so many *eggs*?" I keep saying over and over again as though it represented some global crisis.

Since our conception Buffalo man has withdrawn. He had done this before the conception as well, which somehow satisfied us that there'd be no such conception. I marvel now that he'd never asked, but marvel more that I never took care of the issue myself. *It's too late now,* I kept telling myself, after the first time, though this makes no logical sense. I don't completely understand this detail but will have the rest of my life to ponder it. One tenacious cell had decided for itself then, since higher decision had been relinquished.

He could've predicted it himself, he says, this desert of desire, this flatland-of-the-heart where nothing arises on the horizon. No blue oasis, no lookout point. Whoever got away with a lousy forty days, he says, couldn't have been dealing with the brink of yet another break-up, in addition to what the Clinic had tentatively described as *unwanted*. This was the ultimate destination of reckless pairings like ours, he says, meaning not the pregnancy but the desert, and addressed more to his bourbon than to me. I should probably just go back to my mother, he says, she probably wonders where I am.

Unlike other men who became absent from my life, Buffalo man is one whose picture will remain clear and solid in my mind. I'll always see him standing naked in fridge light, the blue glow spreading over his belly like a cool breeze. Earlier on there'd been ice cubes to suck, thrillingly chilling our tongues. Then later fewer cubes, unless they jingled in bourbon. When he opened the door to the freezer his head would disappear, and leaning from the bed I could see the rest of him, headless and naked and blue. He'd raise a paw and scratch himself with it, tug at the soft folds as though they were a map which kept curling up before he could read it. Then he'd sleep very deeply, exhaling a faint pine smell like pillows in cabins.

More recently he's been doing everything he can to persuade me he's diabolical, and I'm near the brink of persuasion. Then suddenly he hits me below the belt, going on about how he used to have this whole strategy with younger women, which strategy I really wasn't so much of a departure from, in many ways. It wasn't something he was proud of, he tells me, or even something he felt he'd chosen. As though the scripts were already written ahead of time, and not even by him. The strategy went like this, to convince a girl that she's somehow not well or not safe or not in touch with herself on some level, then to offer himself as a sort of saviour. It usually paid off both ways, basically, he tells me, but only for a certain amount of time.

In the biscuit section of the supermarket I find animal crackers, and purchase three bags of them to stash in the Ark. By the time Buffalo man and I have eaten halfway through the second bag, he has devised a whole new astrology based on them. Critter Cracker Zodiac. We make another game of it, which is about all we do in bed these days. The rules state that you can draw no more than three animals at a time. Then the other person has to make up some sort of horoscope or fortune based on those animals. On my very first try, I draw a rabbit, a tortoise, and an owl.

"That one's obvious," Buffalo man says. "You've practically got the Serenity Prayer right there. Got the tortoise and the hare, those're the two ways you can go, fast or slow, and the owl's the wisdom to know the difference. Nice one. Something to think about, eh?"

So I do think about it, standing naked and pregnant in the phonebooth-sized kitchen, boiling three brown eggs in an aluminum pot. Or not boiling them but watching them boil, bumping softly against the bottom and floating up again like uneasy porpoises. I rescue one with a soup spoon and set it in the dish rack to dry because I still can't make myself eat an egg. The other two I put in egg cups and walk them to the table. There you go, dears.

Buffalo man is combing his beard with one hand and picking his teeth with the other, which combines to make him look like a walrus. He sets down the party-pick he's been picking his teeth with and scratches his belly. He laces his fingers behind his head and stretches his shoulders. He sets one hand on the table and scratches his nose with the other. He drums his fingers. He coughs, loudly, twice. Finally he asks me, "So what are you planning to *do* about this situation?"

Love could be a little death or a very large one. Totalizing, like a wrecking ball you're holding onto, he tells me, and I can see it quite clearly when he puts it like that. I can feel it happen, the change, a chillier strain in the veins. I can hear it creeping, the toothy clawsome scurry-worm of love.

30

THE TOWER

Dream. Mae West and I climb stone steps, eroded spoon-shaped, like the steps of the tower at Pisa. Mae is carrying a pale blue book, with a heart-shaped lock and key. The key is to open a diary which is actually a box of secret treasures. But when we reach the top of the steps, Mae grins and uses the key to open a tiny door, instead. I try to wrench the key from her hands, because I know we're not supposed to look in there, but the door recedes like a lateral elevator shaft and disappears. In grainy bluish light I can see seven or eight dolls, the size of human mortals, hanging in cocoons.

Buffalo man has been mounting a lot of heads lately as they're in season. Half-finished head mounts are generally not hung up on the walls of the shop, but sit around on horizontal surfaces, staring up at the ceiling with glass eyes or empty sockets. This gives the shop a peculiar sense of dimension. The current white-tailed deer head has been sitting there all afternoon, on the counter by the sink, with its sockets fixed upward as though the room were tilted on its side. Just now, from where I sit watching Buffalo man fill a glass of water, it looks as though the running faucet pours directly into the deer's mouth.

Add to this the fact that I'm sweating like a horse, and have not been feeling at all well lately, I'm about ready to climb the walls, as Mae West would've been able to do. As doubtless she would do, if she ever saw for herself what really goes on in here. This is why there's a grate across the door soldered with globules of lead and a big padlock. Buffalo man is quite scrupulous about preventing Mae from ever seeing his handiwork, but surely she can smell it on him anyway, the borax and the dead things. It's the smell of the biggest fear, perhaps the only fear there is. Unless Mae has become desensitized to it, just like I have, if I actually have. I'm starting to think it's stupid to protect her from things she may have seen more of than he has.

Funny though, that first night when he drove me home from the

Stanley Park Zoo, and asked if I wanted to come over and see what he had in his freezer, for petesakes, body parts were the first thing I thought of. Which perhaps is my own problem, no less so when it turned out to be true. It's something Buffalo man has in common with Dr. Spektor, the desire to preserve things by probing at them with instruments, a proclivity toward peeking at the stuff inside. Buffalo man's job is to take dead things, and make them appear to be living in suspended animation, which requires that the degradable contents of the body cavity be removed and replaced with a synthetic substance. Which is exactly like filling a tooth.

Just now I am sitting on a steamer trunk full of pelts in the taxidermy shop, watching Buffalo man pull a hood of skin over the mounted skull of a white-tailed deer. There's something in the way his veins pop out on his arms and forehead as he works, so heated and dog-earnest that I somehow lose and gain respect for him both at once. It can happen that way in a moment, you suddenly see a person differently. Maybe it's not nice but it's true. The veins at the inner vale of his elbow stand out like the sheathed penises of dogs, just before they protrude like lipstick plants.

Now I'm recalling those embarrassing situations when you're looking at the dog and wondering what exactly is arousing this expression in him. Whether it's the smell of you or what, or something humans can't identify at all. Whether dogs think erotic thoughts about humans, and whether the dog is conscious you are looking at his penis. Whether you have any reason for feeling ashamed.

Buffalo man stands holding the deer pelt like a man holding his derby hat in church, turning it over and over in his hands, feeling the brim with his thumbs. He's been struggling all morning with stretching that skin over the frame, but the button-hole eye sockets keep sliding cock-eyed over the skull, the mouth hanging open drunk. The skin is not fitting the skull at all well, and he has no idea why.

"Maybe they aren't from the same deer," I suggest. "Or maybe the hide, y'know *shrank*, probably it would, you'd think."

"That's not possible, it has to *fit*," he says through his teeth, "or I'll bloody *make* it fit." Then he punches the deer in the side of head. His bare fist hits the deer skull square in the brow bone and it appears to hurt only one of them. He hops about sucking the third phalange of his right index, the same place he sometimes chews while he reads the news. There seem to be as many reasons to love him as to run from him. The losing and gaining of respect can happen in the same instant, like two racing blood vessels which overlap each other, one carrying red blood, one carrying blue. One moving away from the heart, satiated, the other racing toward it, needy.

I often wonder what Mae West would think, what she'd feel, if she ever saw what her best buddy does in here. What she'd do, if she knew the man who saved her life earned his living by pulling skins over artificial skeletons and stitching them shut. I read that chimps are capable not only of rational thought, but also the ability to attach symbolic significance to things. They have the capacity for mental pain and despair as well. I'd seen Mae West studying the belly-seams of Voltaire the raccoon, I'd even seen her try to pull out his tongue. But Voltaire would just keep on grinning, rubber-gummed and bone-still, waxing his plum. One time I'd seen Mae stroking Marilyn the stuffed Persian and looking equally mournful, but perhaps she's only imitating us. Humans beings often behave as though we understand the significance of things, even when we don't.

Mae West is just as haunted as Buffalo man is. It's clear enough she's seeing ghosts. She watches things which don't appear to be there, except as bodiless eddies in the air. At first I'd taken these to be tricks of the light, shadows of a ceiling fan circling the floor. Now I'm certain they're spooks.

Although Buffalo man keeps unfinished mounts well hidden from Mae, I'm still certain that some day she'll find a way to break in and see them. That she'll just barge past him, one day, knocking him right over. Mae West is very strong, probably stronger than Buffalo Man, and soon she'll be of the age when she might just stop obeying him.

So *imagine*, if she breaks in here one day, what with all the hanging skins and skeletons in the sink, and him standing there with a blue beard and bloody hands. Wouldn't it be one of those external pressures which the primate skull cannot withstand? To finally penetrate the master's secret cell and see what you most feared to see but knew all along was true, other hanging specimens similar to yourself? And might not a cry come then? The screaming figure on a bridge, the scream of monkeys sprouting electrodes? The buried screech which people seek therapy to release, like a howling moth from a jar? The scream of a baby hauling in oxygen for the very first time? *Imagine.*

That afternoon, we take Mae West to the vet, under the pretext of inquiring if there's any point to having her spayed. The free pamphlets in the waiting room list *Prevention of Mood Swings* as one of the advantages to having your females fixed. So she wouldn't prowl and yowl any longer, pining at the moon in moony cycles, chewing on things which shouldn't be chewed, her butt up in the air like a tent pole. Much like humans do when their hormones send them on a bender.

Mood swings. Reminding me of swooping vines, great green veins in the heart of the jungle. With primates brachiating from tree to tree, hollering and howling just as much as they please, as long as they live, as long as there are trees. Now, if we just clip back a few of those swinging hormonal vines, perhaps the female primate in question will learn to simmer down a wee bit.

"Does she have contact with any fertile males?" Dr. Fowler asks, and I don't know whether to laugh or cry.

"Not so many," says Buffalo man. "It's not that, we just read that sometimes emotional volatility can be curbed by, you know, adjusting her hormones a bit. I mean, is this a good idea, or what? Probably wouldn't be such a good plan for Mae to have kids anyway, even suppose there was a suitor, she's had a rough enough time as it is."

"We just want to do what's best for Mae," I add, as though I have any say in the matter. "She really goes crazy sometimes, and then gets really depressed. Surgery would be our last resort, but...."

We wait in the waiting room, while the vet examines Mae West. Buffalo man picks up a full colour pamphlet entitled *Canine Heartworm.*

There is a photograph of a heart, from a dog who died of the disease, looking just as bad as the name sounds. Run through with evil thin things like mung bean sprouts, translucent and tubular. It strikes me as a picture of the biggest fear, perhaps the only fear there is.

And probably the only reason we've come to see the vet in the first place is some dumb-animal sense that things are going wrong, but probably those things have nothing to do with the fertility of Mae West. So when Mae returns from the examining room with a clean bill of health, we decide to bring her home intact of all her parts and hormones, successfully postponing for another day the more pressing question of our own.

31

ZOOSE

Buffalo man and I are canned in rush hour traffic, because neither of us has the foresight to leave the house in reasonable time to get anywhere. We can never find the keys, or we take too long dressing ourselves, all in shapeless black these days as though we were already mourning each other. I don't have much time left until I have to decide. We seem to heighten drama whenever we can, now with only seventeen minutes before the store in Chinatown closes and we won't be able to buy a lucky cat for Duncan Folger, a renowned artistic director I've never even heard of, who has invited us to a dance recital in Shaughnessy at seven o'clock. I had suggested getting him a lucky cat, one of those white ceramic cats with red ears and a raised forepaw and gold calligraphy on its belly prescribing long life and good fortune.

"As though the dude needs a lucky cat," grumbles Buffalo man. "He doesn't carry himself like a guy who's lacking much, in any department. Maybe we should get him an *un*lucky cat, for the sake of karmic balance," he says.

"Whose karma are we trying to balance?" I ask.

Mae West sits in the back seat, tearing the spine from a Golden Book about a woolly lamb who wanders away from the farm and meets forest creatures who talk about their respective lives as frogs and squirrels. Mae West chews at the spine and studies her free hand as though making plans for herself.

"Is the clock on the dash working properly?" I ask. "It hasn't moved in ages."

"Prob'ly because we haven't moved in ages," says Buffalo man.

The red Gremlin sits for chilly minutes like hours on the Cambie Street bridge, a cork of cars wedged motionless in a chilled bottle. Buffalo man starts cursing like he'll pop a vessel, while Mae West pant-hoots until the cars begin to flow again toward Main. I look out the side window at the pelagic parking lot below, at a black dog running tiny as an ant between the painted yellow stalls. I'm convinced that I cannot hear anything as I watch a cloudy flurry of pigeons in the sky like fresh ground pepper in chowder.

Finally clearing the bridge, we see a scrap of tire rubber at the side of the road. Or no, it's an errant garbage bag. No again, now we're only hoping it's a garbage bag. We've both seen the thing. Buffalo man slows down the car and no, it's not a garbage bag, but a black cat, stalk still. We stop amid applause of angry horns and pull to the shoulder. I leap out, go over to where the cat is lying, and crouch down.

There is a mask of death you can tell on sight, a snarl frozen permanent. No skin is broken, but black-red droplets fall from the cat's mouth when I move it, its final utterance. The body is still warm and malleable like a living cat, a particularly floppy and trusting one. It flops in my arms when I lift it up and carry it over to the grass. There's a pigeon skeleton scattered in the gutter nearby, the skull resembling an extracted tooth, the open beak like tapered roots, eye sockets empty as eggshells, nestled in a matted aura of dryer-lint feathers.

"Don't put the cat beside a *dead pigeon*," calls Buffalo man from the car window, as though it might be somehow inauspicious to do so. Meanwhile, I was just about to lie the cat down beside the pigeon, because it seemed somehow auspicious to do so. But I relocate the cat to a grassy vestibule in front of an approachable-looking house, then notice a phone number in faded blue ballpoint, scrawled on the cat's flea collar.

I go back to the Gremlin to find my centennial quarter with a bobcat on it, and a black Sharpie marker in the glove compartment. I write the seven digits like a tattoo on my hand, along with the address of the house where I laid down the cat. Then I take the bobcat quarter and run to a phone booth. The kind which is not a booth at all but a sort of Plexiglas wind visor, which is great unless the wind is coming from the other direction. Now I am pinned to the visor by wind, amid the rattle-dirge of rush hour traffic. I insert the coin in the slot and dial the number on my hand.

"*Hello?*" a child's voice answers. And I find myself saying it, the thing I vowed never to say to another child, when I was about the same age as the voice sounds. "Is your mother or father there? Could I please speak with your mum or dad?"

When I was ten or eleven, I hated it when people asked to speak to my mum or my dad, as though parents were the ultimate authorities on everything. I'd often respond with something cheeky like, "Well, I'd like to help you today but my mother and father are both quite deaf, and mostly people just tell me what they'd like to say to them. Is that okay?"

The girl on the other end of the line says her mother is downstairs, but she can give me the downstairs phone number if I want. The concept of a downstairs phone has a futuristic ring to my ears, I am sure there was no such thing when I was ten or eleven.

Meanwhile, Buffalo man is circling the block for the umpteenth time. The din of rain and traffic is atomic impatience, while I try to decide whether or not to tell the little girl about her dead cat. It has to be a snap decision, quick as impact. I realize how seldom I'm aware of any such authority, the decision to tell or not tell. Or decisions in general, especially lately, despite how many crises I've tried to bring myself to. Running away from home, dropping out of school for no apparent reason, moving in with a man old enough to be my father, and getting pregnant. I am one of those girls I used to think was a total ditz.

So much fuel can be used up trying to manoeuvre the landscape so that it forces the hand of crisis. So that choice appears relinquished and orgasmic. You can choose to set things up so that there appears to be no choice involved. It seems to be a peculiarly human talent, to approach certain things in this way. The afterglow of such experience is humble and grateful, and utterly baffled. Or tragic and utterly baffled. And if you're lucky, you can find a way to assign some meaning to it all.

Probably the black cat was the little girl's cat, since this was the number on the collar. If I were ten or eleven again, and it was my black cat who'd been hit, would I want to know about it, or not? From the vantage point of several years later, I would want to know about it, definitely. But that's not the same thing.

"I might have some bad news for you," I finally say to the voice. "Can you hear some bad news right now?"

"Yeah," says the girl, "I guess so."

"My friend and I found a cat on the road, a black cat, all black. He'd been hit by a car and I'm sorry to tell you he didn't make it. This was the phone number on his flea collar."

I am practically shouting above the traffic, while the girl's voice is very quiet, becoming quieter. Mostly she just says, "okay, okay, okay," as the bits of information reanimate in her ear. Sometimes you can feel this process happening right through phone cables, the electrical connections happening in the mind of the person on the other end of the line. It is not possible, however, to tell exactly what information is being received. The other person has their own associations with *black cat*, or *mother* or *father*, or *bad news*, but you still can hear the crackle of neural connections like distant geese.

"We moved the cat to a yard," I yell. "The cat is not alive anymore, do you understand that? I have the address here, where we moved the cat to. I have it written on my hand. Do you want me to tell you the address?"

"Yes," says the voice. "Yes, please. Tell me where he is."

"Do you have a pen?"

"No, I have a pencil. Please tell me where Zoose is."

"Zeus?"

"Yes. Z-o-o-s-e. My cat's name."

I tell her the address of the yard where Zoose is lying and she says, "Okay, wait, okay." Then she repeats the address to me about six times in a voice which sounds like hiccups. Each time I listen carefully to make sure we both have it right, checking the digits on my hand. The ink from the Sharpie bleeds between the creases of my skin, the number becoming less clear the larger it swells. But no sooner have I told her about the cat than I start fantasizing other possibilities. I start worrying that the girl's parents will soon be hating me, the silly anonymous woman who phoned to tell a *child* that her cat had been killed by a motorist who didn't even stop. They'll probably think *I* did it. Or who knows, maybe Zoose had already been missing for a month, and the little girl had finally been persuaded by her loving parents that he'd gone to live with some other little girl for a while, and was still a happy living cat.

If it'd been me, I'd have wanted to know the truth, I think, but truth can only be divined through what's known. So the question of whether to know or not to know spins in circles like a tail-chasing dog, god-chasing tale. Whatever you know becomes the truth, because you can't factor in what you aren't aware of.

After I hang up the phone, I go back to the Gremlin to find Buffalo man's scalp being groomed by Mae West, in the front seat. She is also wearing my scarf so I get in the back instead.

"Store's gonna close in seven minutes, Agnes," he says. "We'll have to go to Duncan's place pretty direct, whether we get the lucky cat or not."

"Poor little cat," I say. "Poor little girl. I didn't even ask her *name*."

"Sure, poor cat, poor girl," he repeats, "but we're still late." He keeps talking as he drives, loud and grandiose, the way some people smoke or chew pen lids when they drive.

"Everything has its own secret lifespan, Agnes, you can't *do* anything about that," he says. "Even a *Bic pen* is an entity of certain features and behaviours, and it has a lifespan.

"The death of a pen might mean nothing more than mundane action," he continues, "but that's reason enough to pay attention to it. The pen begins and it ends. It has what might be called a lifespan, which is no more and no less than any *living* creature has. Is this the shop you were thinking of?"

We do make it to the shop in time, just before it closes. A woman is taking down the paper lanterns which hang outside like giant tomatoes from the eaves, and taking down the bamboo curtains, the rushy swoop of entrances and exits. Inside the shop, on a high shelf, we do find two white ceramic cats. One with the left forepaw raised, and one with the right.

"Do you think it makes any difference which one?" I ask.

"If there's any significance to a lucky cat at all," says Buffalo man, "then of *course* it makes a difference. But I have no idea what it is."

32

DAS BLAUE LICHT

The backs of people's heads, row on row, like coffee beans. I read the stencilled numbers on the backs of wooden seats, which resemble the stencils used for serial numbers on army paraphernalia. The suggestion of artillery in trenches, the orchestra pit, jagged bayonets of the violin section. The kettle drum is a shining bomb, its low rumbling forward march. Instruments are drawn up under the chin and secured like helmets. Noah and I are positioned side by side in the dark, facing straight ahead, this position familiar by now. Without exchange of words we choose respective sides, I always to the left of him, whether walking down Commercial Drive or lying in bed or sitting in this draughty old theatre. In bed it would be the tin roof of the Ark I'd be staring at, instead of the orchestra pit.

But here we both are, launched on this mission to spend more quality time together, yet at every turn projectiles rise from the darkness and hurl themselves at our faces. People keep thinking Buffalo man is my father, for instance. This makes me pointlessly annoyed but there is nothing to fuel the feeling but its own containment. So I've been sitting here feeding it the kindling of petty complaints, gathered from every sour corner of my mind.

We wait. People cough now because they can, in order to be heard, to have the final word in the shuffling calm before the storm.

Once the house lights fall much of the scenery disappears, a sketch torn from an easel. A circle of blue light begins to grow on the stage. Now it's ovular, a blue lozenge growing wider, diffusing like a tablet of Easter-egg dye in water and vinegar. Easter-egg blue. Voices trail off and we wait some more. For a moment I'm distracted by the red *Exit* signs on either side of the stage. This distraction is compulsive, like checking pockets for keys or holding your hand to your chest to make sure you're still breathing. *Always know where the nearest exits are. Be aware they may be behind you.*

The theatre seats are wooden and uncomfortable. The tongues of them snap the back of the knees when you stand up. *Sit down, Agnes.* I've already tried to leave once, but there's no sense making a scene in the middle of a theatre unless you want everyone to watch you.

I look around at couples who appear to be on actual normal dates, and wonder why I never had any dates until suddenly I had the whole tree. I'd tended to avoid dates because I couldn't understand why people always went to see movies or plays, where you're not even looking at the person, unless this were basically the point. The couple-on-a-date could pretend to meet in the empty space between their opposing ears, imagine a floating mind of common experience they're shouldering together.

As it turns out, there might not be much common experience after all, even to the same person seeing the same movie twice. But the couple can *imagine* a common experience binding them ear to ear, shoulder to shoulder as the music swells, and this might be comforting. To people other than me and Buffalo man, it looks like. We've become *remote* and *controlled* like astronauts with glass domes over our heads. His white sleeve lies on the armrest like a radioactive pod to be jettisoned into space. *Remote. Controlled.*

Then out into the blue oval of light steps a black leotard, lithe as a leopard. Her toes pluck at the blue like the legs of a spider, or again, a leopard. She leaps with one long leg lashing up and back, a sinewy tail, her body jointed where surely mine is solid bone, surely she's almost boneless. I hear the hair at the back of Buffalo man's neck prickle, feel his spine leaning forward in his chair. In front of me, another man raises his eyeglasses to scan the programme for her name. In these ways, I imagine that each man is trying to invent some personal connection, because each in his mind fancies himself alone with her in the large room.

The leotard covers the dancer's head, like a black olive with a hole for her face to peek through. I think of those hand holes in magic boxes, where a lovely lady gets sawed in half, waving a hankie to prove she's still alive. It's incredible that any living woman could twist herself in such ways, and so gracefully, as though half-serpent half-bird. Anybody seeing such a creature between the trees would follow her deep into the woods and become fatally lost. Through the hood of her leotard I can see the tight little bustle of hair at the back of her head, knotted like thoughts preying on the mind. She stands like a diver, gathering height. She lifts her arms above her head like an exaggerated shrug in slow motion, the elongation of uncertainty into grace.

Seal. The blue-lit lady drops to her knees, then slowly rolls forward along the tops of her thighs, bracing herself in a C-shape as though by cables. Her head lolls back, neck arches shiny to the light. Her mouth opens at a slant to the downward swoop of cellos, an audible yawn. She presses her palms flat to the stage, lowering down on her elbows, holding herself over the floor with forearms at flipper-angles to her body. Long moans and short grunts from the horns and strings. *Now a seal, a spider, a serpent, a bird, a lioness. The blue dancer shifts her shape.* When the music stops and the house lights come up, the blue light contracts around her feet like an iris, and she is the pupil shrinking in the light.

"My very best pupil," I hear a Shakespearean-looking man say in the crowded lobby during intermission, "though she must *never* hear me say so. They seem quite to fall from grace if their egos are overfed." His coven of congratulators chortle and sip wine while he toasts them as the Life-Blood of the Arts and Dear Dear Friends.

Everything about him reminds me of coffee. Robust, full-bodied. Aromatic roast. Carefully selected from only the finest quality beans. Vaguely colonial as well, as though he were presenting as his own special blend an exotic merchandise harvested elsewhere, at the many hands of insignificant others, whose names are not listed on the programme, and are poorly recompensed. I can picture him in the borrowed robe and turban of the Nabob man, a striped sash around his full-bodied middle. His picture appears in the programme with a snowy van Dyke beard and a black turtleneck, leathery laugh lines stray from his eyes:

> Duncan Folger, Artistic Director. The dance recital *Shape-Shifter* written and arranged by Duncan Folger. Choreography by Duncan Folger. Special thanks on behalf of the performer and technical staff goes to Duncan

Folger for his tireless dedication. All donations to the Theatre may be made out to the Head Office, care of Duncan Folger. *Shape-Shifter* performed by Fancy Garland. Music adapted from Mueller.

Also on the programme is a storyline of the choreography, written by Duncan Folger:

> Our interpretation of Chinese Taoist mythology depicts a young female shape-shifter, who both celebrates the power she has gathered from her numerous lovers, as well as lamenting her inability to ever give herself completely to any of them. As she recounts each of the men she has seduced, she transforms into the animal-familiar of each by turn, beginning with the Leopard, shifting then to the Seal, then the Fox, moving on to Owl, Snake, etc.
>
> Ultimately, she realizes that she has lost herself among them, ensnared by them just as she ensnares. She sees that she is doomed, never to find ecstatic release in love. At last, stricken, she surrenders herself to the god of Thunder as his mistress. As he ravishes her, she is drained of her own vital essence as well as the essences of all her previous lovers, until, a frail and empty husk, she crumples and dies in his arms.

During intermission Noah feeds me drinks, and I drink them. Cranberry and tequila, with ice cubes like wind chimes in a rut. *Drink me,* he writes in the frosty condensation, scarlet letters on tall pink glass. I wish for a paper parasol to spin and shrink behind, until I am tiny and can bat my lashes like a doe. I sip red drinks and become increasingly preoccupied with inconsequential things. I rearrange items in my handbag, believing this will illuminate all things. I drink three double red drinks in fifteen minutes and he orders me a fourth.

Passing people are tourist postcards spinning on a display tree. Noah introduces his "young ladyfriend Agnes" to a large purple woman with a harlequin-face brooch made of painted plaster, pinned to her cowl neck sweater. Her name is Aretha or Althea. I am far too flattering over the brooch, have scarcely looked at her face for staring at her sweater.

"It's so *lovely,*" I slur, "I've always *wanted* a brooch like that, you know, *two beds are better than one,* you're wise to carry a spare. You're a *wise owl,* Urethra. *Athena?*"

The woman moves away without shaking my hand. Noah catches me by the arm as the lights flicker off and on, off and on again. *That's two minutes,* someone says. Until the air raid. Or until I will be asked to step up onstage and spell a difficult word. *Crepuscular.* C-r-a-p-u-s-c-u-l-e-r. *Crappo-skewler.*

I think of the woman with the harlequin brooch constantly, in agony throughout the second act, during which I mostly watch colourful coffee beans on my inner eyelids after staring too long at the floodlights.

What had I said? Was I ridiculous? Could she *see* the beginnings of you through my dress, Rose, as a tiny shrimp with stumpy fingers and bulbous eyes and a pulse? Did she see me *pickling* you in cranberry brine, you brine shrimp, you sea monkey? This is the bottom of the ocean. This is the lowest point. I don't want you.

I follow crepuscular rays from the stage to their colourful source, the bucket lights tilting like the spilling paint on the Colour Your World sign. Then I see the after-image of an embryonic creature, dancing before my eyeballs like a taunt. A luminous curl, floating in space. No matter where I look I see you floating, even if I close my eyes you float before me. Yellow, magenta, turquoise. You unimaginable thing. You nightmare. I feel sick, I am sure I will be sick....

Once, long ago, I was one of those kids who fell for the ads in the back pages of comic books. I believed in them, the X-ray specs I could send away for, which would enable me to see curves through women's dresses. I was delighted by bars of soap which promised to lather black like foaming coal on the faces of unsuspecting house guests, and the candies which would taste like rotten fish. For this reason, I never sent away for any of them. I wouldn't have borne disillusionment well if they failed to deliver.

But who could resist sea monkeys? The illustration rendered them as mermaids in tiny pointed tiaras, whole families of them, happy and slender and fish-tailed. They would build small castles out of coral, on the sandy beaches of their tank. They would raise happy families there.

They would gyre and gambol in their waves. There'd be so much I could learn from them, those happy sea monkey offspring who inherit the perfect toothy grins of their parents. *Who could resist?*

So I'd stolen a stamp from the desk drawer and folded a dollar, cut out the coupon and sent it away. Then I waited.

I waited for weeks, developed an agonizing superstition that the day I forgot the sea monkeys would be the day they arrived, which was like trying not to think of a purple cow. Whenever I checked to see whether I'd forgotten about them yet, there they all were, grinning at me in tiaras.

When they finally arrived, in a packet like pansy seeds, they resembled tiny dessicated spiders. And I followed the instructions exactly, it couldn't have been my fault, what happened. They never really hatched exactly, or rehydrated, or whatever-it-was they were supposed to do. Rather, they arose from the bottom of the bowl to become an unpleasant-smelling pinkish substance floating on the surface of the water, like the pulp from pink lemonade, when it floats like skin round the rim of the glass, then sticks to your lips like a blister. Or like spitting up cranberry drinks. None of these were what I ordered, but they're what I ended up with.

Buffalo man and I leave the theatre before the end of the second act, shortly after he'd come out to the lobby to see what the hell was taking me so long in the ladies' room. I was fine, wasn't drunk anymore. But when I ask him, "Why did you keep feeding me all those drinks?" he responds quite reasonably, "Why did you keep drinking them?"

So the conversation stops there, and we walk across the blue parking lot just as applause explodes from inside the theatre like water from a broken pipe. We walk side by side and listen in silence. Then, just before he ducks into the driver's seat of the red Gremlin, he says, "You *did* say you weren't necessarily thinking of keeping it, Agnes. Don't do this, please, make me out to be some ogre, I'm not that guy. D'you have any idea what you're *insinuating?* Why are you even *with* me, if you think I'm a guy like that? It's your decision, Agnes, nobody's twisting your arm either way."

33

Red Delicious

Northern Spy. Red Delicious. Braeburn.
Spartan. An apple a day keeps the doctor away.
Pippin. Royal Gala. Granny Smith.
Red Rome. How do you like them apples?
Strudel. Pie. Cider. Crumble. Brown Betty.
Dumpling. Juice. Sauce. Pine. Road.

With the exception of the bathroom, Great Aunt Hilda's house was two hundred years old. Someone long dead had picked out the pattern of twisting cabbage-roses on the kitchen floor.

The bathroom floor, by contrast, was covered with knubbly orange-brown tiles, in a dizzying pattern of concentric circles. The bathroom had been built in the early seventies, tacked onto the side of the house and stuck out like a dewclaw. Somewhere in my head were memories of being taken outdoors to the outhouse, before the plumbing was installed, and looking up at the limbs of cedars reaching through the outhouse ceiling, waving shadowy hands in the lantern-dark.

Physical surfaces are what memory condenses upon, like drops of mist on a window, taking shape there. Because of Great Aunt Hilda's bathroom, I am able to remember being less-than-three, standing in the kitchen, beneath the upper incisors of a gaping mouth where one of the kitchen walls had just been. Creeping as close as I dared to the ragged jaw where the floor abruptly ended, I peered down into a pit being dug by two men. Probably Ed Sullivan, not the famous one, and Uncle Vernie. Perhaps I remember this only because the bathroom was tangible proof that something like this must have happened, whereas other memories seem to vaporize for lack of physical *proof*.

It must have some effect on a person's neurological development, when early childhood is associated with the introduction of plumbing.

Had I not seen the men in the pit, swinging shovels and pick-axes, connecting bony pipes together, it might have taken me a lot longer to figure out how it was possible that I could turn a faucet and water would rush in. Flush, and water would rush out. Where did it come from and where did it go? Witness to plumbing, I'd learned early on that buried things could have mobility underground, and could be brought back into presence simply by opening the proper valve.

But this did imply that there really was no difference between inside and outside any more, these boundaries as permeable as skin. I'd seen with my own three-year-old eyes, that a gaping hole could be knocked right through the wall of a house where people lived, a pit gouged into the earth, and subtle passageways constructed between inside above-ground and outside below-ground.

After the bathroom was built, I did notice that strange things began to come into the house through the pipes. Microscopic things which turned the water red and rusty smelling like dried blood. I believed that the microscopic things were parts of my Great Uncle Arthur, who was supposedly buried beneath the crabapple tree out back, quite nearby the scars on the lawn where the men had dug the pit. Sometimes I'd even find thin red veins inside the crabapples themselves, close to the core, like the tiny blood vessels at the corner of an eye. I was convinced that Great Aunt Hilda was slowly siphoning bits of Great Uncle Arthur back into the house, which was why I could still see him, why his presence here was so strongly sensed.

Great Aunt Hilda used to refer to those tough, translucent casements covering the seeds in apples as *apple teeth*. I called them *apple fingernails*, which they more resembled. But whether tooth or nail, they'd apparently evolved to protect the seeds.

My mother's fingernails, though not long, were strong and beautifully shaped. They tapered to crescent moons, like those knives used to scrape residual flesh from deer pelts. During the work week they remained unpainted, to avoid nail polish chipping off into the mouths of her patients. But on weekends and New Year's she polished them red or mauve or fuchsia or frosted mahogany. She took gelatin supplements to keep them strong and hard, gelatin being made of a similar substance to fingernails, the boiled-down resin of hooves and hides. When my mother drummed her nails impatient on the table, I saw the painted hooves of carousel horses, flashing round and round, not going anywhere, running out of fuel then coming to a stop.

In the fall the crabapple tree out back was heavily boughed with small hard fruit which Great Aunt Hilda would boil down to make crabapple jelly, transparent and salmon-coloured like sunsets. My brother and I would be sent out with ice cream pails to gather crabapples from the ground. Sometimes the apples would look perfectly discrete from a distance, red and picturesque in the dappled green grass, until we picked them up and found a wasp or a horsefly or a large black beetle gnawing caverns inside.

Often the crabapples would be rotten underneath, the colour of caramel, and our grabbing thumbs would thrust right through the skin into the softened flesh. *Gross me out*, my brother would shriek, chucking the bad apple as far as he could in the direction of the wooden fence post dividing Great Aunt Hilda's land from the encroaching woods. His exiled apples never gained the outskirts of the yard, though, the yard being large and my brother's throwing arm being short, they never landed that far from the tree.

"God's truth, Agnes," my Uncle Vernie once said to me, "you know my papa, your Great Uncle Arthur, is buried out under that crabapple tree. God's truth he is, I can remember when they buried him." I never dared to ask Great Aunt Hilda whether or not this was true. Great Uncle Arthur was a topic you were not supposed to mention, like that cousin who was found hanging by the neck in the garage with his pants down around his ankles. In photographs Great Uncle Arthur looked a bit like the man on the five-dollar bill, but less sour and less blue. I didn't dare to think what he looked like now, waiting and waiting for decades beneath the old crabapple tree.

Yet it seemed to be exactly this image Uncle Vernie was meaning to conjure up, since he mentioned his buried papa so persistently. I wondered whether it was possible to conjure an image in someone else's head without having to look at a similar version in your own head. And if not, as I suspected, why Uncle Vernie would want to dredge up pictures of his father turning to dust underground. But mostly I wondered why he wanted to pass those pictures along to me.

"Where else d'you think they'd bury him, Agnes, down cellar?" Uncle Vernie said, biting into a crabapple, then another. Great, so now I had a picture of Great Uncle Arthur buried down in the cellar *inside* the house, but still Uncle Vernie wouldn't stop.

"It was just lucky for Ma and me that he went in the spring instead of earlier, or he would've been laid up in the *shed* all winter 'til the thaw."

So now there was another picture of Great Uncle Arthur frozen solid in the shed. I learned when I was eight or nine that things don't need to be *true* to produce ghosts, nor need they necessarily be false. But from that point onward, whenever I was in the shed, I would see him, suspended in a block of ice like the abominable snowman, waiting for the thaw.

"How old were you?" I asked my Uncle Vernie. "When they buried your dad under the tree, how old were you?" But my Uncle Vernie patiently ate the rest of the crabapple, laughing the whole time. I thought he would choke. Then he stopped and told me very seriously he didn't know how old he was, he didn't have a clue how old he was, and that I knew very well he couldn't remember shit about anything.

Sometimes I thought Uncle Vernie was only pulling my leg, the hollow one where I supposedly stored all the fried yams I ate. Part of me thought Great Uncle Arthur was probably buried in the Soapspit Bluff Cemetery just like anybody else. But then I'd find those thin red vein-like things inside the crabapples, and I wouldn't be sure anymore he wasn't telling the truth. It seemed quite likely that buried things didn't lose their ability to affect the world, only their ability to speak in the usual way.

On top of the toilet tank in Great Aunt Hilda's bathroom sat an old woman whose purpose was to conceal a spare roll of toilet paper beneath her navy gingham skirt. Her head was a dried apple, brown and wizened. Two push-pins with pale blue heads had been inserted into her eye sockets, and a blue gingham bonnet sewn to her head. Her hair was made of frayed grey yarn or lint, and her face had been coated with spray starch to keep it from rotting. Like that plastic doll's head I was married to, the old woman had no *body* beneath her dress. Only a spare roll of toilet paper which was never used. People seemed to forget it was there, as in that rhyme my father used to sing:

> Oh dear, what can the matter be?
> Two old ladies locked in the lavatory
> They've been there from Sunday to Saturday
> Nobody knew they were there.

I imagined that the two old ladies would have been dead by then. Deaths to which the song did not refer, unsung deaths. Yet people have been dying ever since there have been *people,* they've wizened and dried and reverted to objects like the toilet paper apple woman. There was ultimately no point to saving a roll of toilet paper forever. Yet Great Aunt Hilda would put up dozens of jars of crabapple jelly every year, as though there would always be another year, if not for her then for somebody else. She'd store the Mason jars of jelly on shelves down cellar to last through the winter, which came after the fall. Also after the fall came a sink of sin and iniquity, according to the church guy on TV. Looking at the rusty water gathering in the new bathroom sink, I wondered if there was the proof.

Adam's apple. At eight or nine I wondered why, if it was Eve who ate the apple, it was men and not women who possessed that bulbous protuberance in their throats. My mother's throat hollowed to an enclave, while my father's throat bore an apple which bobbed up and down when he spoke and stuck out as large as his nose. This was the type of theological question I might've once asked him about in a note tucked under the door of his basement room. Eventually I would find his reply, folded up neatly in my retainer container or inside the box of Shreddies:

> Adam took the bite to please his wife
> instead of his own guts to follow
> But doing so was the curse of his life
> 'twas more than he could swallow.
> The fruit sits to this day like a frog in his throat,
> or chewing gum gathered in a wad
> It could've been him whom God would
> protect, but now he must take care of God.
>
> The moral of story, Agnes, is this: Don't swallow your chewing gum, for the sake of all that's Holy, unless you favour a ruptured appendix in the coming years, and that's the truth of it.
>
> Love, Dad.

Well, what an idiot Adam was, I thought. Now, if my mother had been God, she would never have accepted the excuse that his wife made him do it. "Well, if Eve told you to jump off a bridge, would you have done that as well?" my mother would have said, if she'd been God. Then she would pour herself a glass of sacred wine, and pronounce the languid decree that it be Adam who should painfully bear children for the rest of eternity, in appropriate consequence of being so gullible. She'd toast to that.

34

HOLE IN THE MIDDLE

Elephant, Cat, Chicken. Buffalo man's *I-Ching* of animal biscuits offers these three in the final draw, which he interprets to mean that I should finally go see my mother. And finally tell her about it, and that I am planning on keeping it, if I'm really *really* sure that's what I'm planning on doing. But really, if it were anything close to *planning* we were doing, we wouldn't be drawing animal biscuits from a bag as a method of arriving at decisions. Or then again, maybe we would. Buffalo man thinks the animal biscuits can't lie because it's still our job to *interpret* them, but doesn't that mean we're just rehashing stuff we already know?

Chicken, Cat, Elephant. He picks up each of the animals by turn and hands them to me, then talks about them as I chew them up. He thinks eating the animal biscuits as they're being read will help internalize the issue.

"*Cat.* This one's your mother, Agnes," he says, "trust me. She's the cat who doesn't come when you call, who sits around all day like an ornamental vase polishing herself. Hope you're not too horrified if I picture her that way, I've never met the woman except through stories from you." And he's right, I *am* a bit horrified if I described her that way.

"Not all cats are like that," I say, biting off the head of the cat biscuit. "Many of them are friendly. Anyway, it's *teeth* my mother polishes, not *vases*, so she doesn't exactly sit around all day. Did you know that the highest suicide rate is among dentists? Well, my mother's been working for that Dr. Spektor guy for, like, twenty years now, and he still hasn't hanged himself. If he were really such a model citizen he'd take some initiative."

"Let's just pretend for the time being that the cat is your mother," says Buffalo man patiently, "so you're the chicken, Agnes."

"Thanks," I say, "I always wanted to be a chicken."

"Hear me out," he says. "This is serious business. So, you're the chick who's running around headless, sorry, *feels* like she's running around headless. You follow, when prob'ly all you started out wanting to do was *cross* the freakin' *road*. And you're a bit of a nervous bird, you know, you're flightless and you're edible."

"And you're creepy," I say, biting the chicken biscuit butt-first so I won't be left holding a headless chicken.

"Then there's the elephant," says Buffalo man. "We already know what *that* one means, you told me yourself. Whatever that *thing* is you never talk about, the big invisible elephant in the room. Your personal avatar of pseudo-amnesia, there, who takes up more space in your head than it sustainably can. Your mother probably has her own angle on it, *whatever* it is, maybe you should ask her about it some time."

"I think you're assuming a bit too much," I say. "What makes you think my mother knows anything about it? You're making it pretty obvious you think it's some deep dark creepy secret and what if it isn't? If I can't remember whatever-it-is-I-never-talk-about, well maybe there's nothing to remember. I'd rather die than name it and be wrong, but I'm not the ticking time bomb you seem to think I am."

"Right," says Buffalo man. "So there you go, Agnes, those are your biscuits. If I were you, I might interpret them to mean you should go talk to your mother, since apparently she's not gonna come looking for you. Doesn't mean she isn't sick to the heart wondering where you are."

"I've left her quite a few phone messages," I say, sucking the whole elephant until it dissolves to a semolina paste on my tongue. "She knows I'm not dead, already."

"Well, that's a start," he says. "You might almost have something in common, after all."

⌘

The air smells like autumn just after nightfall, when I climb up the grassy hill out back of Salmon Court to the student housing unit where my mother lives, its rows of sliding patio doors lit up like boxcars in the lumbering night. Most of the drapes are drawn, in the manner that drapes are drawn after nightfall, not so much to escape the dark as to avoid being exposed by the light. After night falls, uncurtained windows become television screens into the strange interiors of people's lives.

I can't *guess* which of the curtains has my mother behind it. It's quite dark and I haven't been back to Salmon Court since my previous incarnation as a virgin biology student who attended classes regularly and was not pregnant. But instinctive navigational devices in my feet are able to narrow the choice down to three possible curtains from which I, like a game show contestant, could choose. If I knock on the wrong patio door, I may be greeted by a goat or a donkey instead of my mother, and will then have to choose between keeping the prize and gambling it for possible improvement.

As fond as I am of goats I'd still have made the gamble, which illustrates something about parents. It's difficult to imagine having different ones than the ones you've got, however often you might wish they'd turn into farm animals. This may be because the possibility for certain types of light and energy is particularly strong between members of a family, even when the spark is dull. Some flint might remain or fossil fuel, though often not both of these at once. Each person is supposed to bring something different.

So I am surprised and unsurprised and grateful, when the curtains of door number three are suddenly drawn open like a bathrobe just before it slips to the floor, and that right between those sloping folds stands my mother. Buffalo man was right, her arms *are* open wide, if only in an act of drawing the curtains aside and sliding open the patio door. She hasn't seen me yet. I stand still as a shrub on the dark of the lawn, while she's lit up in a frame like an ambered damsel fly.

My mother steps out onto the patio in bare feet, then takes cigarettes and matches from opposing pockets in her frilly blue dressing gown. It always surprises me to see my mother spark a cigarette, though the brand she smokes looks as delicate and thin as rabbit ribs, with floral patterns like ankle tattoos around the filter. Despite how elegant they look, I've never been able to reconcile them with my mother's contempt for tarnished surfaces, the stained enamel of teeth and of the kitchen appliances to which she applies such vigourous abrasion. It is strange to see her light a match when she looks to be made out of wax.

My mother turns over a yellow milk crate and sits down on it. I can see the mauve silk scarf she wears tied around her head, the pupal tubes of hair curlers cocooned beneath it. She leans forward on her elbows and exhales a narrow angle.

Mother? comes my voice in darkness, barely. The scarf might be covering her ears after all. Or she might not recognize my voice, scarcely recognizing it myself. But why would she happen to open the curtains at exactly the moment I happen to be standing here? Couldn't this be taken as some kind of synchronous connection? I'd take any sign at all, really any.

Her glowing tip swells red then thins to grey at intervals.

Mother, I say again.

Then in one animal motion of limbs she stands up, pushes the milk crate out of the way behind her with her foot, gathers her robe about her throat, and peers like a deer at the scope of my voice. Had I been a person come to harm her, somebody only pretending to be her child for instance, wouldn't she be able to tell instinctively? Wouldn't she bolt back through the door and shut it fast? Definitely this was a good sign, she hadn't run away at least.

"Oh my God, *Gavin?* Is that *you?*" my mother whispers. As far as I know, Gavin is still in Turkey or somewhere, learning how to shoot a gun if not actually shooting one, or else getting shot by one. My brother Gavin might be a ghost, for all I know. My mother may think she is seeing a ghost.

"No, Mum, it's me," I say, "your wretched daughter."

"Oh my God, *Agnes*? Is that *you?*" she whispers again, accents thickly like the first.

But time and space do collapse, between us. We do move toward each other to close it, each to each enfolding arms around the other. Then immediately, the touching truth in human limbs, the pointedness of shoulders and of elbows, the gracelessness of our inability to bear the weight of one another for very long. I catch the red-tannin scent of her tongue warm on the side of my face as she slides away from me again. Then I catch the familiar smell of her hair-setting lotion, made from the placentae of Danish sheep. We allow each other to take a few steps back again, recompose ourselves before the imperative of speech.

"You look well," my mother says, though by her usual standards I'm certain I do not. My eyes must be heavily circled from weeks of nauseous insomnia, my skin a display case of things my mother bought lotions to prevent. Ruddy, spotty, tired, puffy, and suddenly I feel that way. I missed out on the famous radiant skin some pregnant women get, plus I'm wearing Buffalo man's big fishing jacket which smells like his car. I am attempting to camouflage myself but her eyes are always quick, and always I feel an instinct to shrink from them. There's an urge to blurt out the news of my condition immediately, if only to account for any changes in my body she might have felt when we touched. Some hormonal scent I bear which she detected, whose origin she recognized, having been there before.

"I'd intended to drop in for an afternoon visit," I say, "and here it is the middle of the night already. I was wandering around in the woods for a while, saw a couple of raccoons though."

"Really?"

"Yeah," I say, "an older one and a younger one. So, you're just hanging out on the patio in the middle of the night, Mum?"

"I've been doing this for days, coming out here in the middle of night," my mother says, sweeping away the lost days with her hand. "Well, d'you want to come in, Agnes? We have to be quiet, though...."

"Why do we have to be quiet? Isn't this your own place? Who's here?"

My mother silently draws the curtain and holds it aside. I can see several familiar objects in the room, the wood-panel credenza with her Johnny Cash records, the brown macramé wall hanging of an owl, her mustard-coloured armchair. Excess clutter is arranged in tidy piles or else still taped up in boxes since Dormier Street.

There are unfamiliar objects as well, such as the hanging basket-chair which dangles from the ceiling like a wasp's nest, cut at cross-angles so you can creep inside. My mother's famous spider plant is hovering above it, now grown monstrously huge, with some of its slender green legs feeling their way through the lattice rattan and into the hull of the chair. Other unfamiliar things include a stack of golf magazines, and a pair of reading glasses, shiny green and mantis-like with bifocal lenses. These would be Dr. Spektor's, who is apparently upstairs in the bathroom. I can hear the endless gush of rushing water.

"Why don't we just stay out here on the patio for a while?" I say. "Unless it's too chilly. You're barely dressed."

"Just two secs," my mother says quickly, disappearing behind the curtain with me unsure what she just said. But a few seconds later, she reappears with her slippers and a brown knitted Afghan, a pair of cranberry-coloured goblets, and a capless green bottle half-empty, half-full. When I shake my head at the glass, she digs into her pocket for a roll of Lifesavers, and hands me that instead. It seems necessary that I have something in my mouth, every meeting with my mother involves putting something in my mouth. Dental instruments or various kinds of baked buckles and crumbles and crisps, fried yams, Nanaimo bars, and wintergreen Lifesavers. If I were drowning, would you throw me a mint? I hold the roll like a hilt in my hand, while my mother swallows a discrete glass, then pours herself a more sloshy one.

"Funny," I say, "feels like we haven't seen each other in months, and now here we are...." I can't bring myself to say *just as though I never left* or *just like normal*, these make no sense, but *here we are* seemed safe to say.

"Here we are," she repeats, though it seems she's gone quite elsewhere. Above her head and behind her on the stucco wall, a patio lamp attracts a confusion of flying insects. There are multitudinous flying ants in their winged sexual phase, that phase which seems to compel them to fly stupidly into candle flames, or drown themselves in pooling wax. My mother shoos a few away.

"Don't suppose it occurred to you, the whole time you just took off without telling anybody where you were, that I might be out of my mind with worry," says my mother slowly, lighting another skinnyankled cigarette.

"I'm sorry Mum," I say lamely, "I really, really *am* sorry, I never should've gone."

My mother's hand waves away my apology like a small quick windshield wiper, which also means she has something more to say once she's finished exhaling.

"I just want you to understand that I'm no fool, Agnes," she says. "I know all about girls wanting their freedom and all of that, Heaven *knows* I know. I've been there, don't forget, dashing off like a silly little colt in all directions. You can't hold it against me for not reeling you in, pet, when I'd bet dollars to doughnuts you'd've only taken off again." She holds up her two hands as though to show me she's just washed them. "I wasn't going to be the one to stop you, kitten, you're a big girl now. But I'll be waiting for some explanation, just so you know." I nod my agreement then we're silent for a moment, long enough to make it clear that I can't answer her question just yet.

"These kind make sparks when you bite them," I say, handing her back her Lifesavers. I'd heard that they *did*, that some ingredient peculiar to wintergreen mints would produce sparks when you bit down on it, but I'd never tried it out for the same reason I'd never again send away for sea monkeys. Certain types of disappointment just seem to hit you harder.

But then we *do* try it. My mother disappears again to turn off the light inside the house, so the patio becomes very dark.

"Okay, watch," I whisper, turning my head to the side and pulling my cheek out of the way so she can see my teeth in the moonlight when I bite down.

"When was the last time you had those scraped?" she asks.

"Just *watch*," I say, and she watches.

Well, sometimes they do spark, I promise you, or maybe they don't bloody spark at all. I'd put so much energy into this picture of my mother and I sitting on the patio with our teeth making little sparks, I couldn't shake the image and I still can't. That's how I'll remember the night on the patio almost a year later, even though my mother told me several times, *Sorry, I can't see them. Sorry, I still can't see them.* So I must be *disassociating* again, remembering sparks where there were none. Perhaps it was only that the sky was particularly speckled that night, or perhaps I really am a crazy fool, expecting to see pretty sparks which are not there, reading constellations in biscuits and paint splatters.

But mother, didn't you weep like a baby when I finally told you? And didn't you know as well as I did that I'd never seen you do that before, not *ever*, not even when Dad left and not even that Christmas when Great Aunt Hilda said you were just like your mother. You wouldn't let me see your face, but I could see your shoulders shaking, your cheek turned and pressed against your wine glass like it was the window of an aeroplane three miles in the air.

At some point I'd sat down on the woven rug by your chair. I'd rested my head on your lap like a golden retriever, hadn't I? You'd reached over to shake a paw, we must've at least done that. Hadn't we finally fallen asleep on this very couch and chair? Hadn't it been illuminating not to be strangers?

Look, Mum, they *do* spark when you bite them, they do, they do, they do, they do.

Book III

35

GLOBAL WARMING

After the first few weeks of sleep and forgetting, Buffalo man and I take to phoning each other at frequent sporadic intervals. Sometimes several times a day, as though reporting mutual contractions to one another. *Contraction, release.* In turn, we are seized by sudden swimmings of the eyes, constrictions of the throat, spinnings in the head, convictions we should curl up and play dead, there seems nowhere else to go from here. In turn we are overcome by waves, set loose by something as small as the scalding of a pot of milk or the loss down the drain of a silver chain. These overcomings seldom happen simultaneously, one of us is always prepared to be present and heavy as an anchor. *Contraction, release.* Most often we're both dragged down, regardless who triggered the deluge. Regardless who'd *again* been unable to resist the compulsion to *pick up the phone, push the buttons, hear the voice....*

"I'm just calling to say *hello*," the more imperiled one would say, and the other one would say, "*Hello*, how *are* you?" Then the first voice, the trembling one, would scarcely make it through the first note of *I'm fine* when something would burst behind the eyes, in the throat, the pit of the stomach, and the beloved would drown right there on the other end of the phone line, while the other could do nothing to save them anymore. "Rather throw myself at the wreck of this," he says, "than watch it sink from the shore."

Buffalo man's cries sometimes come as a frightening chord, low and sustained, like the creaky opening of an old wooden door. A castle door, a barn door, or the door his namesake lowered onto dry earth to let out all the animals. I was privately frightened by this, the initial part of his cry, the force of the hinge which held it back. Soon they would all come forth, the wounded birds and limping oxen, the elephants with patches over their eyes, all the sad inhabitants of our sad Ark. I want to collect them to me in my arms, crossed over my own chest rocking back and forth so slowly and dumbly, so tightly that the last drops of water are wrung from them.

Human Error. As though there were any other kind. As a species, we are quite proud of our memory and foresight, but it is only in relation to these that the concept of *error* can be said to exist at all. Mistakes appear to be a human invention. Technical errors, or mechanical errors, or even acts of God which are thought to be unfortunate, are only erroneous according to *human* faculties of memory and foresight. It's only relative to some sense of where you've *been* and where you want to *go*, that you can possibly go in the wrong direction. Otherwise, you're just *there*, like a protozoa, always in the right place at the right time because there is no other possibility. If you are to be preyed upon, so be it, you can't foresee it, so amen then. If the will of God is unerring, perhaps it is also unconscious, like a protozoa.

Coral is unerring in its industry, building cities upon its own bones. Over time the bone pile takes on independent force, a reef, a barrier to those who so name it, those whose easy transit is endangered by its very presence there. Neither is there error in the trajectory of a meteor hitting this planet, nor any other planet, nor in shifting angles and proximities of tectonic plates, nor any other meteorological variations making it too hot or too cold or too wet or too airless for us to live here. These are no body's error but all bodies participate.

Someone said that if humans were to assess our own species in terms of the criteria by which we tend to assess other species, that is, in terms of observable behaviour, we'd find that the animals we have most in common with are germs. Germs continually build up resistance by destroying the function of the body which sustains them, and for them it seems to work quite well. There's always another body to move to, like a brand new planet, once the original host is eaten. This is why human beings are so keenly interested in space travel.

Metaphormosis III: Radiolaria

Rose. Today here at Salmon Court I study drawings of protozoa skeletons in a smuggled biology textbook. They strike me as the most beautiful creatures I have ever seen. Some protozoa are able to pick up traces of silica from the sea water in which they live, through any of their impermanent mouths, like anonymous beachcombers collecting bottles and cans. They process the silica inside their bodies and re-secrete it as an exoskeleton, that is a shell or house to contain themselves within.

Radiolaria. The exoskeleton of the single-celled *radiolaria* is one such fabulous architecture, forming an intricate construction of three concentric spheres. Imagine three concentric horse chestnuts, their green spiny hulls, but tinier. Very, very tiny, as tiny as a star. A sphere within a sphere within a sphere, each thinly hollow, and delicately dotted with holes like a wiffle ball. The outer surface of each wiffle ball is prickled with spikes, like the spines on urchins or the spyres of churches, the spikes on the surface of one sphere poking up through the holes of the next outer sphere.

The outermost sphere is an explosion of spikes, some upon the outer surface, some jutting out from inside. All this has been built by an animal who does not think, only absorbs what it finds in its environment and recycles it as a house. And the shape it comes up with is something resembling an apocalyptic premonition.

God, I write in the *Observations* column of my biology book, *If God is anything, then may be something resembling a diagram in a biology textbook of a microscopic creature. Or something resembling a galaxy, something which you would not normally be able to see with the naked eye, even though it's everywhere.*

How to become a protozoa:

The method of the experiment will involve some splicing of the real and the imaginary, hopefully yielding some hybrid form of truth. The osmotic process by which this truth evolves will henceforth be referred to as Metaphoric metamorphosis, or Metaphormosis, in that the change which occurs in the human being will not be literal, or structural, initially, but something akin to lighting one lamp in a darkened basement.

Some of the hypotheses under investigation are these:

That it is possible to learn to move in the world with simplicity and grace, like a protozoa. It is possible that there are natural windows between the single cell and the ocean of its environment, and that these windows do not threaten the integrity or discretion of the organism, but in fact are necessary to the creation of its house. It is possible to unburden oneself of the impression that the world can be held at bay, once one has deeply absorbed the truth that the world is the bay.

Buffalo man and I had that old globe of the world which lit up when you plugged it in. It sat on a tree stump by the Ark. I'd once watched an illuminated insect jump suddenly northwest, from Poatowchen to Biisk, then down southwest to Khandahar.

A few hundred miles southwest of the Hawaiian Islands was a hole in the middle of the ocean. It was roughly the size and shape of Spain. I could stick my whole thumb through it, and feel the heat of the light bulb at the Earth's core. *Sixty watts.* Buffalo man'd kept telling me to remind him to change the bulb. He'd intended to take out the sixty watt bulb, and replace it with a forty watt. Because as it was, the centre was too hot and was causing surface melt in certain locations. The names of the countries were turning brown and incinerating themselves, and the borders too. Buffalo man had asked me to remind him to fix this.

Every night I'd watched the meridians of longitude rust and widen, like iron weldings on the side of an old ship. Would it fall apart in sections, then, like an overripe orange? Or would it melt on top, and cave in, like a jack-o-lantern?

When I look at tombstones, I think of rotten teeth. Death is that point where we cease to ruminate upon the world, and gnash our teeth. Finally through consuming it, it consumes us. Not as a human consumes, in gobbles and slurps, and not like gnashing mechanical jaws. The Earth eats like a bird. Constantly, and in small units, grinding us between the tiny and cumulate grains in its gizzard. The Earth is a hen, it has no teeth, but finely it grinds us. It grounds us.

All pushing is pushing toward an end. All pulling is pulling toward an end. Like my father on his rickety rowing machine in the basement, *Pull, release. Pull, release.* He was stasis in motion in my mind. So I had *not* reminded Noah to change the bulb at the centre of the Earth, I had not. How many would it take to change it? I had not reminded him, but had *pulled* him down to the flood of the bed, and pushed the switch of the globe to *off* with my thumb. *Pulling to a crisis. Pushing to a crisis. Release.*

Now that old globe grows more and more implausible with the passing weeks. It becomes inconceivable that so much space exists, countries inhabited by so many others, while here beneath the sheets in my room at Salmon Court, my own body sprawls like continents. I could map out my body as a small planet unto itself, my belly a continent, swelling large and uncharted, foreign to me.

The growing creature is beginning to hum tunes. I can hear its meandering melodies when I go for walks around the sea wall, past that corner where the sea leaps up and speckles your face. A sign there reads, *Caution: Beware of Falling Rocks.* For the first time in my life I have the sense of being self-contained, not dispersing outward onto everything like a tide, but folded within myself. I could not imagine leaving this creature behind at this point, like an egg does not imagine leaving. Like a rock does not think about falling, until it falls, and then it is only falling.

Inside and outside. They slide together in a Möbius loop, you can't always tell whether a person is more the insides or more the shell. These are obviously connected but don't necessarily match up. Still, almost everything is divided this way, according to insides and outsides, so the least a body can do is learn to label itself legibly, because there seems to be no predictable relationship at all, between the way a body *sees* and the way it is *seen*. The heart leaps forth, the feet step back. The mind grasps outward while the guts shrug themselves into a burrow. Maybe the tougher the shell, the softer the nut.

I think of the empty husks of flies which peppered Great Aunt Hilda's window sill, and how she used to blow eggs every Easter. Shells and hulls and the stuff that fills them. Eggs are fragile and need to be carried very carefully, like those races on Sport's Day where you balance an egg on a teaspoon all the way across the soccer field. The ribbon goes to the kid who doesn't drop her egg, while all the loser eggs are left running all over the field, until the janitor comes and hoses them away.

The shell of an organism, or at least the necessity for one, must arise from *within* the organism, in relation to its environment. But I am beginning to wonder if it is possible to open up tiny apertures of sense between the two realms, inside and outside, without them collapsing into each other and making a great bloody mess of the whole situation. Whether it is humanly possible to live in the world this way, porous and receptive, and what this might feel like. There are single-celled animals who can do it, I'd read about them. My books describe protozoa as having *no permanent mouths*, which means they can open up mouths on their bodies any place they need one. Wherever opportunity met necessity along the jellied contour of its tiny body, a mouth would open there, to absorb some tasty plankton or a fragment of silica with which to build a shell. Conversely to dispose of things.

This is the only way I can possibly begin to understand the effects of loving someone. Surely love is among those simple life forms which can never become extinct, in an age no matter how cynical, when it operates according to such elementary principles as opening and closing, inside and outside. Love appears to possess the magnetic quality of water, rushing to join larger springs of itself, then moving on more powerfully.

36

SHADES OF YELLOW

Azure. Cobalt. Navy. Robin's egg. Powder. Sky. Baby. These were the shades of those days, that pregnant pause before your birth, Rose.

"Why don't we get you a new pair of sunglasses?" my mother suggests, because it would be one of the things guaranteed to cheer *her* up. "At the very least it'll stop you squinting like that, save you a few wrinkles." So we walk up the flashing flank of a shopping mall and down the other side, stared at by sunglasses on spinning display trees. I pick out a yellow-tinted pair of lenses and put them on.

"For one thing," I say, looking up through the glass ceiling, "everything that used to be blue now looks sort of yellow-green, even the sky. So how do they look?"

My mother squints at me and says *hmm* so I pick up a hand mirror to see for myself. The hand mirror looks exactly like the one our guidance teacher brought to class in grade eight, encouraging us girls to employ such mirrors, sitting splay-legged to examine our parts, not right there in class but when we got home, in our own rooms, with our own hand mirrors. And despite the contracted groan which came from the class at the time, I always wondered how many of us went home and did it anyway, suddenly given permission to look.

"I can't tell whether they look good or not," I say of the yellow sunglasses.

"Uhm... well, pet, I have to say they look a bit like you should have a Band-Aid wound round the bridge of the nose," my mother says. "A bit geeky and pigeony-looking."

"I don't have a problem with pigeons," I say. "These shades are fine." I'd got to see how they saw before I saw how they looked, and I liked what I saw.

"The world looks *gorgeous* through these," I say, "like it's *magic* light all the time. That twenty-five minutes of light just before sunset on summer nights when everyone looks gorgeous and people just want to take pictures of each other? Like that, but all the time."

"Suit yourself," my mother shrugs. "I still don't think they really suit you, so you might just as well suit yourself." She takes back the hand mirror and snaps her spearmint gum at a pair of tortoise frames with rhinestones in the corners.

"Honestly, Agnes, you're in your own little world," she says, "like a person living underwater, aren't you, dear?" She frowns at the tortoise-glasses and takes them off her face. "Which reminds me to look into that water-birthing thing, Agnes. I promise you I'm not wrong about this, you're the perfect candidate. I know you've been a little nervous this baby will tear your life apart, so, well, it seems to me a gentler, more natural approach might be a great help."

"Natural if you're a dolphin," I say, but actually it really does sound like a good idea, and I'm grateful to her for offering. I just assumed I'd be in a hospital and I hate hospitals. "Seriously, Mum, thanks. Let me know what you find out."

She seemed completely right. In our opposition we're very similar people. Despite running away from her, my mother was still someone who could step right through the mirror with news from the other side. But I wasn't so sure my fear was of tearing apart, more like I was afraid of solidifying.

"Maybe you mean *confiding*, because you're afraid of even *trying*," comes the voice of my father from a pair of Clark Kent frames on the display tree. The frames would've suited him well, until the moment he whipped them off his face and tried to leap a tall building. It'd been unreasonable to expect this of him. But I have no trouble believing the Clark Kent frames are able to speak in my father's voice. I'd begun to accept all objects as potential mnemonic devices. When I stand alone at a bus stop or sink my head in the bathtub, I remember him, the ubiquitous wash of his absence, but just who he is, is never distinct. It's beginning to seem that, even when something is absent, there are still ways of communicating with it.

A pregnant body, or even an unpregnant one, can become a region of the paranormal, and annoying paranoia. *A noise annoys an oyster,* as my father used to say, and in that cloister of my pregnant state I wondered what noisy sediment might be filtering in from outside, tainting the shape of things. And whether the sediment would form smooth ocean pearls or misshapen freshwater ones. Fingers and toes become wrinkled in bath water, bath water can seep into the ears and obscure how things get heard. Changes and choices can enter the body from outside, as particles or voices or sense, to be recycled and expelled as something quite different.

The fear was this. That what my father was calling *confiding,* and what my mother promised would be *gentle,* might really be something more akin to Great Aunt Hilda's egg blowing. She would puncture the egg shell at both ends, then blow the contents into a glass in a slimy scrambled mess. Somehow I feared that transformative processes such as pregnancy might do this to a person. I was afraid that this alien creature conceived from *outside* would scramble the contents of some other entity *inside,* who hadn't even been hatched yet. How could something like that offer any backbone to anyone else? Especially a baby. A *baby,* for heaven's sake.

The psyche is a house of rooms. Creatures of memory creep and turn somersaults over one another, howling in the corridors. Memory may be this, a sort of zoo, a semi-natural habitat meant to house imaginary creatures who had once been living experience. They later become the *shades* of this. Ghosts who represent the original animals, but substantially changed in form and habit. So the question is, should I just ignore them or climb down there and offer them something to eat? Will they be happy to see me or try to strangle me?

Basically I lack faith there *is* any soul-satisfying way of reconstructing the past. There seems to be no way of reassembling lost time as though it were actually standing there in the room. You have to piece the thing together according to conjecture and laws of probability. You can't go attaching a set of horns to somebody's head if you have no proof they had horns. Even if memory leaves you with a spare pair of horns which don't seem to fit anywhere, you can't just attach them to some poor unsuspecting skull and make a demon of it. Blame is the tail of the donkey, right after you've been spun in circles with a blindfold on. It's not so easy to find the right place to pin it.

A story about memory might aim itself toward some singular revelation meant to explain everything which has come before, some rolling away of the stone, some throwing aside of the curtain. Revealing *there*, once and for all, the single missing piece upon which everything else hinges. *There*, the prehistoric elephant in the room. *There, look quick*, the culprit who hoped to slink away before the lights came up, shedding culpability like bloodstains on his hands. *There*, beneath the romantic dinner table, the pair of cloven hooves which everyone half-expected to see anyway. *There*, the shadowy figure on the shore holding a fishing rod in his hands, the one who's to blame for the irrational thrashing of the fish. It's all so seductive.

But maybe memory doesn't work this way at all. Maybe there's no single place in memory where a rupturing experience can really be contained. By the time a person is ready to undertake the reconstruction, the missing piece may have already dissolved and been reabsorbed by fertile ground. Perhaps there's no single malignant part which can be extracted and held to the light like a gallstone, only a network of how pain has rerooted itself within the person.

I can't remember any of my pregnant dreams. Only that they've been large and sad, like a sad slow elephant, moving singly as a thousand truncated parts. I can trust that some process is underway, present in how I seem to have sobbing fits every morning, the nausea of things unremembered. Waking up is like being washed up on a beach, choking on salt water, water in the eyes, water in the throat, water flowing warm through those internal channels behind the face, back to the body of water it came from. But there's only so long a body can tread water. Everything returns to it eventually, and there's only so long before the levee breaks between private tears and public smiles. Suddenly it bursts wide open and the body is swept along by the force of the currents, the teeming accumulation of decades. Somewhere in every body is an entire ocean of sense and sensibility, and it remembers *everything* in its own watery wordless way. Then there are always some cerebral despots who keep trying to build a parking lot over the whole thing. *Imagine* trying to build a *parking lot* over the whole ocean. A person's brain would have to be an *idiot* to even think it was possible.

From what I can tell, a person's memory can be changed as easily as turning on a light switch or turning one off, or putting on a different shade of sunglasses. *Look,* the story looks different again. There seems to be an oceanic region where faith and belief are not quite the same after all; where faith is the older genus of belief's evolving species. *Faith* is your grandfather who saw the end of the war and came home from it alive with a metal plate in his head. Faith is your grandmother with Alzheimer's who still knows that in February there will be crocuses and in November falling leaves.

Belief has to do with resolve and it is a sand castle, it routinely dissolves. *Resolve* is that long ashen casting, hanging like a dirty snowdrift from my mother's cigarette as she sleeps with her eyes half-open, half-listening to the late night TV psychic who tells her, *There will be love in your life if only you will reach out for it.* She reaches somnambulant for the ashtray but the ash falls, breaking in two on the taupe carpet, where it resolves itself to dust beneath her polished big toe.

There is something humourous about whatever evolution or process is. One seems to call *process* those aspects of fate over which one has no control whatsoever, which, from a certain distance, is almost everything. The web of what a body feels bound to is called *process*, its plot widening and thickening daily, as the body becomes more of a character and less its author. Less able to make rational decisions, perhaps, but more able to respond to what's there, and to somehow come into alignment with it. It may be this process called *process* which buoys us all along, or else it may be God.

Pathos is that clown who comes in at half-time, to offset and poke fun at human tragedy. Pathos is that character who scans the floor beneath bar stools at the end of the night, picking up pens and lighters, finding that none of them work. It's weird that pens and lighters are often disposable and commonly lost, when they correspond to two of the most valuable evolutions in the human species. Perhaps we've been making fires and scribbling ciphers for so long we kind of take it for granted.

I made an accidental fire before I ever wrote a word. I was three or four, and a housefly was floating on its back in candle wax. Its struggling legs were a confused thought bubble, a cartoon scribble reading *confusion*. The fly's wings were a gluey boat as I tried to rescue it with my thumb, watching it cling with all its legs to the giant peach of my thumb. *Clingstone peach*. But the fly couldn't get a grip, and I couldn't keep holding my thumb so close to the flame.

See how pain makes a body determined. I sought about my mother's vanity table for any object which could assist the fly. *The use of tools.* I found a fine-toothed comb, which my mother had bought when Gavin and I had head lice. She called it a rat-tail comb and it was made of stainless steel. But the comb got too hot when I tried to rescue the fly, so I dropped it and accidentally knocked over the candle, setting fire to the flounce on my mother's vanity. The flounce was made of thick knubbled fabric like a polyester pant suit. It didn't burn so much as melt, yawning holes like it was being eaten alive by invisible moths.

The smell of smoke and melting fabric woke up my mother. She'd fallen asleep just before the part where the third Billy Goat Gruff goes trip-trapping over the bridge, just before the Troll bellows, *Who's that trip-trapping over my bridge?* I'd been lying beside my mother waiting for the Troll, until eventually all I heard was my mother grinding her teeth in her sleep. So I started imagining different voices for the long awaited troll, high squeaky ones and low rumbling ones. It was then that I heard the screaming fly, first in a high squeaky voice then a low rumbling one.

Help me, I'm melting, I'm melting.

37

BRUXISM

Dr. Spektor has a voice like a prolonged yawn, as though he is half-Australian and half-Texan trying to do a posh British accent. Whenever my mother troubles me about eating too much cheese, how it produces excess mucus in the throat, Dr. Spektor in his chair comes yawningly to my defense from behind a monthly journal about dentistry or golf. "Perhaps *dah*iry is neces*sah*ry for culi*nah*rily *hah*ried vege*tah*rians," he says, chortling to himself. Like most of Dr. Spektor's verbal intercourse, these comments seem put forward mostly as tongue exercises.

"Culinarily *harried*?" my mother says. "Well, if you're pointing out that our Agnes is no magnificent chef I can't argue, but what's she got to be harried about? She scarcely lifts a finger around here." Which is hilarious, because lifting a finger was just what I wanted to do as soon as she looked the other way, but never would on account of those eyes at the back of her head.

I'm ticked off this morning because I'm being sent to the clinic to have my molars filed down again by Dr. Spektor. They both believe that this treatment will help me stop grinding my teeth in my sleep, apparently because there'll be less enamel to grind against. But after several treatments I'm still not convinced, unless the rationale is that bruxism becomes exceedingly painful when the enamel is no longer there. I've been given a special toothpaste which will gradually numb my dental nerves, because according to my mother even my teeth are over-sensitive. I imagine my back molars as shoes with the soles worn right through, letting in all the elements.

While Dr. Spektor waits humming in his Volvo, I go to the kitchen to look for my cardigan. The dusty-rose one, with the shredded and mended and reshredded elbow. I find it lying like a strip of raw salmon belly on the white kitchen table. Wouldn't it be better to simply see a sweater? When I look for a sweater, instead I see a strip of flesh from the belly of a tenacious fish who never forgets where she came from and will kill herself trying to get back there. I see a sweater and I think a fish.

From my mother's brightly lit kitchen I can hear her voice on the patio, calling cheery hellos to neighbours, drinking excesses of moderate scotch in the still forenoon, curiously mixed with pink grapefruit juice for the sake of appearances. But when I reach for my cardigan I notice a black speck on the sleeve, a patch, morphing into a moth when I peer down to look at it more closely. It rises in flutters like campfire ash, settling on the shade of the overhanging lamp. There are six white spots across the span of its wings, the central ones like oval eyes, the needle-thin abdomen pointing downward like a nose. The moth is a Mardi Gras mask of black feathers with rhinestones, white ovals for eyes. I wonder if seeing a carnival mask when I should see a moth is symptomatic of a larger problem.

But now and then just lately, I've been remembering your birth Rose. As though particles of memory could be held in a translucent casement which suddenly bursts open to express itself like a gelatinous bath bead. I'd been unable to remember anything very specific about your birth at all, but still had never spoken with my mother about it, even though she was there. Now I am wheeled horizontally down a corridor in the obstetrics ward of memory with my mother trotting along beside, holding my hand until her purse strap falls from her shoulder and severs our connection. "I'm not much good with extractions," I murmur, which makes me suspect this memory is fraudulent after all.

"I'm really afraid," I say truthfully.

"Extractions?" she repeats. "She's long past being an impacted wisdom, Agnes. Your job from now on is only to help her." Mantra. My *only* job is to help her, my job is to *only help* her, my job is to help only *her.*

The truth of the matter is, my mother's furious at me for being so clueless about my date of conception. As though I haven't been clueless about dates my whole life. So you are born over *two weeks late* because *someone* wasn't paying proper attention. Now things are a big emergency, and my mother's plans for a beautiful water-birth are ruined. I can tell how upset she is, even as they wheel me down the corridor, although she's trying so hard to keep it hidden. She's brought me ice chips made from diluted cranberry juice, lugging them to the hospital in a small beer cooler. It was a sweet thing to do and so like her, but those ice chips are driving into my dental nerves like pins on top of everything else.

In the delivery room every face but mine has a white mask on, covering the lower part. The doctors and nurses look like the opposite of Mardi Gras, where nothing is colourful and the eyes are all you can see. With their noses and mouths covered, the doctors and nurses look quite frightening but beneath all of these masks all I can focus on is your unseeable face. What you could possibly look like, whom you will most resemble. Meanwhile my knees are a fleshy divining-rod pointing straight up, and the air appears to be liquid. It wouldn't surprise me a bit, if the space ship lamps hanging over my pelvis suddenly burst open and poured out a flood. Framed in the circular mirror above and framed in sheets below, the widening opening sectioned off as a *sterile space*. Because who knew what-all germs could be transferred down there, if I were to reach down to touch her crowning head, the place where it would come from. My only fear is this. That whatever divinity had us balanced on her tongue will suddenly close her mouth.

So you spend your first earthly hours in a sectioned-off room where they keep babies who, unlike you, have arrived too soon. Baby books had warned not to be startled by the first sight of a premie as it could be unsettling, best to be prepared. There were babies who weighed only two pounds, less than what a modest-sized chicken in a supermarket would weigh, as one book pointed out. Babies with tubes stuck in their mouths and noses, tiny intravenous needles in their scalps. Little birds with worried parents whose arms seem to ache to fly to them.

But you are not one of these early birds, and the book was less precise about babies born too *late*. If a baby remains unborn for longer than the usual two hundred and eighty days, she doesn't necessarily continue to gain weight after that point. In fact, she often starts losing it, like a person who is very anxious. Her hair grows and her nails grow, and still she does not move from where she is. Still she is not born.

Finally when you come you are thin and scrawny, your skin loose and wrinkled. You have a full head of hair and your fingernails are quite long. Your eyes carry what the book calls *a very alert look*. I worry that you have been born with a look of innate cynicism, like a cat who's been locked out on a rainy night, or a dog who's been locked in. One of the most important days of your life was postponed for *two whole weeks*, because *one* of us wasn't ready. We could spend the rest of our lives bickering over which one had been so reluctant at the threshold of life-long commitment. Maybe you had read it in my blood, that the compulsion to vault into experience has its treacherous points. Life-long commitments may be lying in wait at every corner. Things can happen which weren't anticipated, weren't prepared for, unprotected against. I could hardly blame you for wanting to take your time, as your mother had not.

"You had to want it more," my own mother says, in tears, trying to explain to herself how badly I'd botched up her plans. According to what I'd told her, you would've appeared to be right on time, but it didn't take long for the water birthing clinic to figure out that things weren't quite normal and rushed us to St. Paul's in an ambulance.

"You *said* you wanted it, but then some other part of you completely ignored your own decision," my mother says. "Why did I *bother* with all that *planning*, if you weren't even going to do it right, Agnes, you stupid, selfish girl? You had to *want* it more. You have to *want* her more." She is hugging me as she says this, whacking my back as we hold each other. The doctors and nurses have just taken you away to siphon the meconium out of your lung-cavity, and I have a panic attack in the Recovery Room because I haven't even held my daughter yet.

But later, even through the pane of a window and through the skin of your plastic bubble, I recognize you right away. Your hair is dark and curled like your fathers, and your bumpish nose suggests his, while your eyes are opaque and perplexed like mine. Probably most mothers can easily recognize their own in there, as though by simple binary instinct of who is and who is not the same blood. My mother often tells people that I was born face-first with my head tilted back instead of curled in, over-curious and gullible right from the get-go. That's why my first baby pictures show me with a very bruised face, puffy eyes like a prize-fighter and clenched little fists. You, on the other hand, were forced to wait, and your eyes make you look almost older than me.

❦

When I get back to Salmon Court after my tooth-grinding appointment with Dr. Spektor, I find you asleep in your crib and my mother nestled among purchases of pale green yarn with silvery filaments. She is studying patterns for twin cardigans, one baby-sized and one her own size.

"Okay," I say, "I have to ask... why don't I get a new cardigan?"

"Well, kitten," she says, "when was the last time you wore *pale green*, now really? I'm not trying to be unsympathetic but ever since you started your Italian widow phase you won't even *look* at pastels, if you recall. And I sure wasn't about to see Rosie done up in black for her first birthday, pet. Black is for cocktail parties and funerals."

It seems that a woman secretly gives birth to several people when she gives birth. One daughter becomes a grandmother, another daughter becomes a mother, and yet another comes into being as both a daughter and a granddaughter and herself. It's quite possible to trace the lines between these figures, like a chain of paper dolls patterned by what's come before and what comes after.

But Rose, it must still be possible to rewrite your own story, or at least change the ending if you're able to catch yourself at a crossroads in time. This is why I don't like fast moving cars. People in movies are able to leap out of moving cars if they need to, but most days this type of escape would appear a bit extreme. Especially when no immediate danger is present. Maybe you're just being taken to Zellers to get a new pair of sneakers, but you wind up being kidnapped by an insane cab driver. Maybe you find yourself in a car with someone who's going to change your life in big big ways forever, ways you didn't even consider and hadn't taken precautions against.

Always know where the nearest exits are. If this remains sound advice, Rose, I'm proud to teach you just this one thing. But I should stop here, drawing too near something I don't mean to say. I can't forget how ambiguous it sounds when my own mother says to me, "You know you'll always be my little girl." In some ways it tells me exactly nothing and leaves me with a lot of guesswork. I could say I love you, Rose, and also say I didn't mean to, and these statements could fall like weights into each hand, leaving you to measure one against the other, searching for any difference between them.

But it's not really like this. Most times when I'm holding you there's no question of what I meant to do, or did not mean to do. Only the wonderful truth of your arms and legs, the grateful reality of your ten fingers, ten toes all intact and accounted for. Your smooth round face in sleep, your wakeful eyes. When I watch you seeing things I know you're both a part of me and quite apart. *What colour is the sky in your world, Rose?* Through the yellow gauze of your crib cover, the sky's divided into tiny little squares like a grid. Will you learn to measure space this way?

But clear nights on the patio, I sway you to and fro and we witness an eclipse of what was *meant* to be and what *is* in fact. On the clearest nights, these two align themselves perfectly and suddenly the way seems brightly lit on either side, as though by rows of torches, the city lights gaining speed and running up the distant purple mountains before leaping like an Olympian at the sky.

38

Happy the Ghost Boy

> Could we with ink the ocean fill
> And were the sky of parchment made,
> Were ev'ry stalk on earth a quill
> And ev'ry man a scribe by trade,
> To write the love of God above
> Would drain the ocean dry,
> Nor could the scroll contain the whole
> Tho stretched from sky to sky.
>
> — Rabbi Mayer of Germany, written on the wall of the institution cell where he died

This is how the second birth happens. The squiggly lines in my mind, the ones my mother claimed were hysteria or something more sinister, gradually migrate like faraway geese heading south, down into my hands, where they perch and become restless. They slap their leather feet into the meat of my palms, and peck along the small bones of my fingers. I feel them ruffle and settle themselves. I see their footprints, and know them like the back of my hand, their webbed toes figured in bones on the back of my hand.

I become extraordinarily conscious of my hands. I wring them, wring out diapers with them, rub ointment into their knuckles, which are red and cracked like udders. I hold you and your stuffed giraffe in them, pace the floor, stop suddenly and weep for all and no reasons. I am seduced by a goose-down comforter, but seek out a mummified storage closet instead, and start hauling out boxes. The back of the closet is full of giant insects, spindly broom-bugs and bucket-beetles, and a machine which cleans carpets with its million legs, and a plastic cocoon to wrap up my mother's head until it is dried and set.

Finally I find it, the thing I didn't know I was looking for. That large black beetle of a typewriter my father used to tap out his God-words on, all his weird little parables. I pull the typewriter out of the closet, then have to reach back into the mustiness to feel around for one of its feet, which has broken off. It is very surprising to find my father's old typewriter here at my mother's new place. I don't understand why it's here, moldering in storage, instead of with my father. There comes a mute anger, that he'd be so pathetic as to leave his favourite thing behind. Similar to my mother's annoyance at him for adopting so many three-legged hamsters. We never heard the end of that.

"Your father is one of those men who believes it's morally *superior* to have only three legs, even if you're supposed to have four," my mother would say. "He seems to think *handicaps* indicate depth of *character*."

"Tha' hamster is nae *handicapped*," my father would defend, "it is merely *challenged*."

If a thing which is missing is exchanged for a thing which resembles it minutely, it is unlikely that most people will notice the switch. This was why my little brother Gavin believed our parents were actually aliens, and why every hamster who ever lived at the house on Dormier Street had only three legs. Because the first one had only three legs. But I always wondered how my father managed to get in touch with so many three-legged hamsters.

Discovering that he had left his typewriter behind, though, I did feel a bit of my mother's exasperation. Her fury that he seemed to find so much beauty in challenging situations, or especially hopeless ones. Not taking his typewriter with him, as parting gestures go, was a pretty hopeless one. It was even more hopeless than not leaving any good-bye note. As though there were something very noble about leaving behind the one thing which embodies your whole dream plan, my father's highest aspiration, his typewriter.

Still, I wouldn't have gone through the whole storage closet looking for that spidery old machine if I didn't half-expect to find it there. I wasn't sure whether this half-expectation was a form of disrespect or a form of understanding. People's expectations can cause dizziness if they are too high, but they are crushing when they are too low. People's expectations can be like second-hand snow suits, which don't fit you particularly well and are ugly, but sometimes you're forced to wear them anyhow.

On the other hand, my father's typewriter could only be here at Salmon Court if my mother had taken the trouble to bring it with her during the move. Instead of liquidating it, with the rest of my father's leftover personal effects, when she sold the house on Dormier Street. I am a bit surprised that she kept it. She never mentioned there being any typewriter at her place at all, obviously, since I was not to over stimulate my brain with things like words until I was quite quite well again.

But back to the original hand, I wouldn't have found the typewriter at all, if my mother hadn't for *some* reason decided to keep it. My father had abandoned it, deliberately or not, then my mother had preserved it, deliberately or not.

So I am learning to type, Rose. Hands have their own memory, and are hopeful. They reach, they hover over keys trying to remember, they find their pace and scuttle along with purpose until they hit another glitch. But I notice there are certain words which my hands insist on misspelling. *Mother,* whenever my hands try to type it, always comes out *mouther.* And *father,* when I have cause to write it, comes out *faither.* The typewriter ribbon is bi-chromatic, bisected bilaterally in two colours of ink. I turn the spindles upside-down and type in red, to see if this changes anything. Whether typing in red opens more direct channels to the heart of the matter.

Matter, fodder. I set up the typewriter on a yellow milk crate, on the kitchen floor, in the faith that planting myself on the ground will help me connect with what everything is built upon, where everything finds its roots. I have to keep my mouth shut about reasonings like these, having learned that people don't so much care what private eccentricities you cultivate, but they *do* care if your reasons for cultivating them are too unironic.

My mother assumed, for instance, that the row of drying apple cores on my bedroom window sill was simple depressive messiness, until I told her that I planned to collect three hundred of them and plant an orchard some day. Now the row of apple cores is like a pentagram on my door, and my mother suddenly develops superstitions about every living thing in the house.

Mouther. Faither. I move the milk crate outside, behind the trees a bit, so my mother can't see me as I watch her sitting and coddling Rose and breathing in my daughter's breath. The milk crate makes harlequino patterns on the grass. The froth of spit bugs, and the furred helmets of tall grasses brush my bare legs. My little brother Gavin and I used to fight wars with those grasses, the ones whose heads could be struck off when you whipped them with another piece of the same type of grass. It had been a bit of a shock to be holding forth your bobbing head, then suddenly be struck and left holding only the stem. The heads had snapped off so cleanly, like asparagus.

Mouther, mother. Faither, father. U and *I.* Those are the extra letters, the ones my typing hands fill in as a joke on my two half-brains. *Faith*, the awareness that one's thoughts and activities participate in a pattern, perhaps even that *meaning* can be discovered, or invented, by paying attention to the pattern. *Faith*, like the rhythm of pulse, or the sound of my father rowing back and forth on his rickety rowing machine in the basement. *Pull, release.*

Mouth, an aperture, a simian crease. A dragon's cave where stalactites and stalagmites grind themselves in sleep. The dragon tongue lies coiled, licks fire, spits sparks. It plays with the place where a tooth is loose, the chink in her armour. *Mouth*, the eventual gateway of utterance. *Faith*, the rhythm of pulse sustained.

⁕

Happy leaps back and forth over the yard, swooping past my yellow milk crate. He's wearing a thick woolen balaclava despite the midday heat. A hood of winter white, with windows for his eyes and mouth. His father has gone away to Los Angeles and left him here for the second time this month, while his cedar-haired, ex-stepmother is inside and sullen, her fingers working at macramé wall hangings which resemble owls. She has been going to church lately I think, or somewhere else on Sunday mornings, with white stockings to match her white pumps, her little boy in a corduroy blazer, and her two girls Regan and Megan in matching yellow frocks. Happy swoops about in his winter-white hood until I can see his mind melt in rivulets behind his ears.

"Hey you, crazy fellow!" I call to him from behind the trees. "Why've you got that *thing* on your head?"

"Cause I'm a ghost," he calls back, swooping away behind the hedges.

Ten minutes later he comes back with a jar. A masking tape label on the side of the jar bears his stepsister's name, Regan, in black felt. There's a popsicle stick taped across the mouth of the jar with a string dangling inside. It's a science experiment from Regan's daycare. What begins as merely a jar of *very salty water* is transformed into an elegant string of crystals, like impatient diamonds which don't cost anything. Happy the ghost boy and I look at the crystals for a long time, all expanding time, sitting there on the green feathered grass. We put the crystals to our tongues to taste them, and he laughs at tasting salt. He *laughs* just because he *tastes* something.

"It's good that your sister is learning things like this at her school," I say, lying back in the grass, my eyes melting warm rivulets behind my ears.

"She's *not* my *sister*," he says crossly.

"Okay," I say, "forget her and let's talk about *salt*. It's important to know about how things are formed and how they change form, and how they do these things all by themselves. It's important to pay close attention to things, Happy," I keep rambling.

Now I turn my head and look back toward the housing unit to see Mister Mister the neighbour across the way with his perma-sprinkler fanning back and forth across his lawn forever. He is out today with a big box of salt, petrifying slugs in his rhubarb patch. They shrink like sore eyes, I've seen them, they die of dehydration. But if he lets them live, they eat his rhubarb.

39

WHITE ELEPHANT

> A gnat had settled on an elephant's tusk. After he had been there for a while and was about to fly off, he asked the elephant whether he would, after all, like him to go away.
>
> The elephant replied: "When you came, I didn't feel you. And when you go I won't feel you either."
>
> — Aesop's fable of the Gnat and the Elephant

When the mailman comes to Salmon Court, Dr. Spektor leans pale like a pine crutch in the frame of the door, shuffling through my mother's bills and paraphernalia from the clearing-house sweepstakes she may-already-have-won. He's looking for letters from suspected secret admirers, construction workers from the pagoda she supposedly helped design, patients whose teeth she particularly liked to polish. Now and then he comes across mail addressed to the old house on Dormier Street, or sometimes even mail for my father. Someone in the postal labyrinth will have struck through the old address with a grease pencil as though it were a spelling error, and a dot matrix sticker with my mother's forwarding address at Salmon Court would be plastered half-effacing it. *Palimpsest.*

"Here's one for your *ehx*," Dr. Spektor would drawl from the doorway in his reedy, bored voice. He's about six-foot-eight and weighs less than what a balsawood model of himself would weigh so he should just shut up about my father, who's not my mother's ex-husband but still her current one, which is why he only says *ex*. Meanwhile my mother seems to have *mislaid* all photographs of my dad during the move to Salmon Court, and daily seems to discover the absence of yet another item which hadn't survived the move.

Today it's not a letter addressed to Dormier Street but a letter addressed to me, and Dr. Spektor thinks it's funny to play a game of

Keep Away with it. He looks like a bastard aristocratic cowboy when he chuckles like he's doing now, holding the letter high over his head while I snatch at it from below.

"Just give me the goddamn letter," I hiss at him, balancing you on one hip, Rose, as though you are a jug of water. Still as quiet as a jug of water, as is constantly remarked upon, seeming only to burble when sloshed about. You watch my moving mouth if your head is positioned to see it, but otherwise you usually look around with your large aqueous eyes at other things. You look at things but don't seem to listen to them so much. I speak to you anyway, incessantly, at night. You look up at the fluttering envelope the same way you look up at a moth, an expression like indignant rapture. When the doctor finally lets the envelope fall, your eyes follow its swoop until it lands safely under a chair, then you stick your whole fist in your mouth and look the other way.

The other day you were fitted with a small pink device inside your right ear. It is exactly that shade of dusky electric peach which used to be referred to as flesh tone, though nobody's flesh is that colour. The same colour as that giant doll head I used to dance around the room with, to music in my head which no one else could hear. "Here we go, sweetheart," I say when I insert the device. "Let's put your shrimp in your ear. Are you ready to wear your shrimp?"

After feeding you new vitamin formula from a bottle, I go out to the swing set where I occasionally read letters, or more frequently write letters I'll never send to Buffalo man or my father, leaving you cocooned with my mother in the hanging basket chair.

My letter is still unopened. I had snatched it up from the floor immediately and tucked it in the ugly nursing brassiere I now wear, not realizing until that moment how accustomed to wearing it I must've become. To instinctively tuck something in one's brassiere implies a familiarity with wearing brassieres, which I wouldn't have said I had previously, tending to ignore undergarments in general. But since I have only recently stopped breastfeeding I am obliged to be keenly aware of my breasts twenty-four hours a day, as though sense of self resided in them, or at least sense of continuance.

Taking out the letter now I notice two things. That it's been darkened with a round damp stain smelling vaguely of caramel, and that it isn't my father's handwriting on the front. I hadn't really expected it to be. This letter is from my Great Aunt Hilda. That much is obvious in the bird-footed script pacing out my name in tiny prints. Also in the fact that the stamp is a default stamp, the strictly functional kind they give you unless you ask for one of the fancy ones with exotic birds or famous paintings. The stamp is a simple red maple leaf on a white background, and would suffice to get the letter to its destination, which it had. Great Aunt Hilda would never make a point of peering through the glass countertop at the Soapspit Bluff post office and picking the most exotic stamps. Not because she had anything against birds and paintings, but because her eyesight was failing.

Stamps licked and stuck by my father would've been more carefully chosen, like every strange communication he'd ever offered. I was sure every detail would have to *mean* something. Finding meaning in small details was similar to inventing a personal cult of tiny rituals to simulate the faith I couldn't always summon. Small details were all I had to go on, unable to read him very clearly between the lines. I was unable to recall the particular size and shape of him, as though he were the man behind the green curtain to whom I was supposed to pay no attention, as he threw switches and pulled levers and conjured fearful apparitions of himself. It had been a very long time since I'd received a letter from him.

Pinning the letter from Great Aunt Hilda to the lawn with a stone, I take a candle from my pocket and dig it into the grass like a tent peg. I light the candle and watch the flame, like an animal watching a flame, the flame itself an animal. The red-blue-yellow metal swing set creaks quietly, the seats shifting like listless children. Breeze, though soft to the ears, blows brittle red wax spittle across Great Aunt Hilda's page. In her hand the letters were spidery and tangled as ampersands.

> Dear Niece,
>
> You'll never guess. An antique dealer from the city came by the other day and offered me forty-five dollars for that old world globe which used to sit up on the

piano. Forty-five dollars! Maybe not much by today's standards, but for an old piece of ticky-tacky I don't know what-all else to do with....

Of course I remembered the globe. It always used to sit on top of the piano when Great Aunt Hilda played. Depending on what piece she selected and how passionately she performed it, from time to time the earth would quake. I couldn't believe she'd sold it.

> Well, my dear, what I've been thinking is this. Time is trickling pretty fast, and I've got a whole houseful of knick-knacks which'll have to wind up somewhere or tother. May as well go to folks as could use them, especially them as are willing to pay a bit. So I've been thinking of having a White Elephant Sale. You used to have a good strong back, as I recall, though I know soon as I say it your back may be a bit tired these days with a baby to cart around. But you come here and help set up my things and I'll pay for your fare. There's forty-five dollars in my hand to put to it.
>
> Love, Great Aunt Hilda
>
> P.S. You can bring your little Rose if you like, she's quite welcome.

40

Arachne

Dear Mum,

How was your architecture meeting? Dr. Spektor left around 7 and asked you to give him a call when you get in. I'm sorry I couldn't be here when you got home — but I just received a letter from Great Aunt Hilda today so I thought I'd go visit her for a bit. She sounds right as rain, sends her love and asks you to call her sometime soon. I can hardly wait for her to meet Rose! Few weeks in the country might do me some good as well. So I'm taking the night bus to Pink Mountain then that small bus to Soapspit Bluff. So you know where to reach me. Take care, and don't worry about Rose, she'll be in good hands!

Love, Agnes

It is suddenly mid-summer again when I step off the small bus with you in a Guatemalan sling, at the only gas station in the town of Soapspit Bluff, at the cross roads of the two paved streets Great Aunt Hilda referred to as *downtown*. Downtown there's a bank and a chemist's shop, still known as *the chemist's* instead of the pharmacy or the drug store. It is not one of the franchise types with the bright red signs, and still bears the original chemist's name, *Baird's*, in moss-green wooden letters on a white picket background. There's a very small grocery store which always smells of boiled ham bones. There's an Anglican church, a Presbyterian church and a Catholic church. The Catholic church is the most beautiful of the three sisters, with its stained glass windows like jars of Christmas candy. But my Great Aunt Hilda used to advise my brother and I never to step inside it because she felt that Catholics were too passionate about things they wanted to avoid.

"Seems to me a body couldn't spend so much time confessing sins," she'd say, "unless there's plenty of sins to confess. Too much time thinking about the devil, you're bound to summon him up, seems to me."

I could go inside the gas station and ask the guy in the green greasy overalls to borrow the phone, to call up my Great Aunt Hilda about arranging a ride. The route to her house is about five or six miles of gravel road on a steady incline in the heat of the afternoon. That gas station attendant is lean as a plank, with tanned-leather skin and a beakish nose, small eyes. He slouches about with chunks of black iron in his simian hands, then stops to wipe the grease on his overalls when he sees me standing there. But then Great Aunt Hilda would have to phone up one of the Boucher boys, who are long past being boys, and have one of them drive his truck into town to pick up me and my daughter, and I'd rather not.

It is impossible to do things in the town of Soapspit Bluff without somehow involving everyone else in town. Everybody is involved in everybody else's life because they need to be, even when they don't want to be. Even now, two ladies on their way home from a Ladies Auxiliary meeting are watching me from the steps of the Presbyterian church, leaning into one another.

"That would be Hilda's niece," the larger pillbox hat lady might be saying to the more nervous-looking one in the pale blue suit. "You know, the one with the baby girl."

"Well, what's she done with the *baby*?" the pale blue one might say. "You don't suppose she's got the poor thing in that sac?"

"Mercy," cries the hat-lady, "I should hope not. But these days you never know, do you?"

"No, you never do," sighs the blue lady ruefully.

"I understand there's no particular *man* in the picture either," whispers the hat-lady, "though it's none of my business."

I've arrived in Soapspit without any other baggage besides you, Rose, having woken up on a bench at the Pink Mountain bus stop to a snap decision between fetching my baggage from a locker and missing the bus, or catching the bus but leaving my bags locked up at the station. So I'd left my father's old typewriter in Pink Mountain, along with some biology texts I'd smuggled from Salmon Court. At Great Aunt Hilda's house, I could devour a certain set of Victorian novels by one

Mrs. L.T. Meade, dedicated to improving the minds of young girls, published by Grosset & Dunlap in 1892 and bearing such intriguing titles as *The Manor School* and *A Ring of Rubies*. If not, I still have a paperback about arthropods tucked inside the Guatemalan sling, and I still have you. The dusty walk from town would be easier with only a paperback and a baby to carry. *She ain't heavy, she's my Rosie.*

You cling to the sling like a chimpanzee and look around, sucking on your free hand. We pass the Soapspit Bluff post office then the Soapspit Bluff cemetery, where we stop for only a short stay. Then we walk on past green pastures leaping with young white goats. Great Aunt Hilda would tell me later how many people phoned her meanwhile, to ask if that wasn't her niece from Vancouver they'd seen walking up the hill from town, carrying her baby in a sack with no other personal belongings, stopping to wander about the cemetery for at least three-quarters of an hour in the blazing sun without even a hat on for heaven's sakes. Great Aunt Hilda told them she was certain little Rosie was fine, she evidently sleeps like a log, and that we'd only stopped in the cemetery because I'm writing an article on the first families to settle the town of Soapspit Bluff, way back when it was still an important mining town instead of an elderly and dwindling community of about four hundred citizens. Great Aunt Hilda wouldn't have put it quite that way, but she knew it as well as anyone did.

"Considering how few of our children chose to stay here, Enid," my Great Aunt Hilda said to the pillbox hat lady over the phone, "I hope you're not insinuating any scandal over such a blessing as a *baby*." The hat-lady's son had long ago moved to Calgary, and wasn't particularly good at keeping in touch. Poor Enid saw very little of her own granddaughter except in photographs.

In the cemetery I mostly look around for the stones of women who died very young, and for the smaller stones of those who'd died in infancy. The graves of babies are often marked by a white statuette of a little lamb, worn down earless and featureless by time and the elements. One baby stone bears the eerie nursery verse, *Sleep on, sweet babe, and take thy rest. God called thee home, He thought it best.*

I can remember being called home, when I was six or seven, from the vast empty lot across from the old house on Dormier Street. After dark, every clump of matted grass in the empty lot became a crouching sphinx, and every bottle cap an ancient Roman coin. Being *called home* by the voice from the lighted doorway across the street was a moment to be dreaded, it meant returning to the rooms where we couldn't see our breath. Where breathable air was rudely pushed up against the walls, crowded out by an invisible elephant which the grown-ups were pretending wasn't there. But out in the empty lot, we could make up our own rules, our own rewards and punishments, and we could breathe the sharp clear air so deeply that our lungs ached.

The stones of the Soapspit Bluff cemetery are tabs of an ancient filing system, recording the names of the ones who'd been called home, not the names of those who were still outside frolicking on the green. The ones who were trying not to think about the call of the voice, maybe consciously dreading it, or even looking forward to it in some weird way. The stones in the Soapspit Bluff cemetery recorded the names of those who'd reluctantly mounted the steps through the lighted door, not those who still crouched and pounced like lions, making dungeons out of blackberry brambles, tasting the air like copper pennies in the mouth.

Many of the inscriptions here are unreadable. They are overgrown with deranged vines, or occasionally a clump of hydrangeas, with its bluish-purple blossoms peeking out like the hats of elderly ladies hiding in the bushes. A few of the stones have personal shrines built in front of them, candle jars collecting rainwater, smudgy plastic flowers blooming greyer all year round. Ukrainian families have stuck tiny colour portraits to the front of their headstones, oval tiles bearing likenesses of the deceased in pointillism. The portraits themselves seem to age, as the dead do not. The tiles of the recently departed still appear rosy-cheeked and wholesome, while those of the longer deceased look yellow and hepatic. One of the very oldest tiles shows a frightening child who stares like a bulldog and has no hair.

I wander up and down the rows of stones as though they were a library, trying to remember where I left my sandals, while you burble softly to yourself. My feet have already grown blisters from the walk, and it feels so delicious to tread barefoot on the rich damp cemetery grass. But although I can remember the *name* on the stone where I've stashed my shoes, I can't remember its *location* at all. I imagine the thin bony hands of Miss Lillian Lure, who passed away in 1876 at age twenty-two, reaching out of the ground and grabbing my sandals, pulling them beneath the earth, trying them on.

The big country sky is beginning to turn purple and carnelian when I arrive, barefoot, out of breath and bearing a baby at the three slate steps which lead into Great Aunt Hilda's hog shed. The earlier heat of the day is still held in the stone of the steps, upon which, of a summer afternoon, it's said you can cook an egg. You once could also have cooked an egg on the bonnet of the old blue sedan, which had grazed the front lawn for years when it wasn't hibernating in the vacated hog shed. But the car had been sold eons ago to Ed Sullivan, who could still be seen tooling around in the old blue sedan, driving Great Aunt Hilda into town twice a week for groceries, and once a week to the Anglican church.

The proper front door of Great Aunt Hilda's house opened into the porch, which then adjoined the parlour, but no one ever entered the house this way. The porch door was winter-sealed with plastic wrap and caulking all year round. It wasn't worth the effort to have Vernie take it down when the winter came so fast and stayed so long. Instead, visitors to the house mounted the three slate steps into the cool and cobwebbed hog shed, then in through a side screen door into the kitchen. Great Aunt Hilda's house, like all our familial interiors, has to be approached obliquely. But I haven't even cleared the three stone steps, when there comes a gentle rapping on the parlour window. *Tap-tappity-tap*.

Trap-door spider. They can feel the vibrating footfall of insects drawing near, know instinctively the exact moment to throw open the door and usher their guests inside. The parlour curtains of dusty gauze are drawn obliquely open, and I see Great Aunt Hilda's crooked finger tapping at the glass, then the round sheen of her thick spectacles gleaming from the shadows. She stretches out a smile and waves at me, then waggles a talking finger at you, a crinkling caterpillar bobbing up and down. She's been waiting for me, of course, because everyone in town has already phoned her, and because a schedule taped above the old black beetle telephone tells her exactly when the weekly buses arrive and when they will depart. Time will move more slowly here. The decision to stay or to go cannot be made on the spur of the moment, as the decision to come had been.

I cross the three warm stone steps into the hog shed. There haven't been any hogs in here for eons, but their smell is immutable, carried on the wooden beams, pounded into the dank soil of the floor. The hog shed now holds cords of wood, their round ends stacked up the wall like the bottoms of kegs. I can imagine the shed as a monkish wine cellar, centuries old, with Great Aunt Hilda in a jute-sashed burlap garment, transcribing illuminated verse with a quill, and the skull of Great Uncle Arthur, brown and theatrical on a weathered wooden table, tallow candle wax dripping into its eye sockets. I wonder again if it is true that Great Uncle Arthur is buried beneath the crabapple tree out back of the house, as Uncle Vernie always said. Why wouldn't he be filed away in the Soapspit Bluff cemetery like everybody else? I had looked for his name among the stones, but like my sandals, hadn't found it.

Yet in the hog shed I see his name everywhere, the unwriteable name of a person inhabiting the objects they leave behind. The spindly fishing rods propped up like bulrushes along the wooden wall, which is shingled like fish scales. Shelves stacked with Chock Full o' Nuts coffee tins, holding nuts, bolts, nails, and screws. On the wall by the door are iron logging hooks, where Great Uncle Arthur's rubber mackintosh and overalls still hang. After dark, they would leap from the hooks and foot a mournful dance over the floorboards.

I step inside the house and my eyes adjust to the cool dim space of early evening in Great Aunt Hilda's parlour, which is a windowed vestibule between her kitchen and the living room. Her chair is turned to face the window so she can watch the road for visitors. I see her first in the darkening cameo of the window frame, the last of the daylight falling weirdly on her hands, which lie folded on her lap like the grey-blue wings of herons.

Also on her lap is the card of lace she's been working on, a baroque cribbage board with pegs sticking up from it. It is difficult to imagine how such a pair of hands as Great Aunt Hilda's could manoeuvre the finer points of making lace, unless one were personally acquainted with the woman who manoeuvred the hands. They were marvelous hands, though her relationship to them was turbulent. At times they betrayed her own sense of outer propriety, flying about the room when she spoke or again when they ran up and down the ivory keys like spiders, netting every single note. Other times she seemed to regard her hands with the downcast scrutiny of a disappointed puppeteer. Their bones were visible through translucent skin, their knuckles knotted pine, their veins like those on the udders of cows. But now Great Aunt Hilda's hands snatch up the card of lace and slide it quietly into the knitting bag at the side of her chair, before I am able go up and look more closely at the work they've been doing there.

"Come over here so I can take a proper look at you," Great Aunt Hilda rasps, and I do so. She studies my baggy black denim legs for an instant, and briefly my face, then holds out her arms. "I don't believe I've met *this* little bundle," she coos, "who might this little bundle be?"

I unwrap the baby sling from my shoulder and arrange you wide-eyed and curious on Great Aunt Hilda's knee, wondering how long it's been since Great Aunt Hilda held a baby.

You lie cocooned and squirming on Great Aunt Hilda's lap, while the elderly woman twitches a finger before your wide and baffled eyes. Great Aunt Hilda's long-sleeved black dress makes her arms look very thin and pointy-elbowed. It is the same dress she's worn for countless special occasions since its first appearance at Great Uncle Arthur's funeral, before I was even born. She wore the same black dress to baptisms and even weddings, also at Christmas time, adding accessories to befit the occasion. And always she wore it when she played piano. This evening, she's added a red silk scarf to the black dress.

"Who's got you?" she coos. "Who's got little Rosie?" The pink buds of your fists swing at the red scarf-tails, fingers unfurling.

⚜

When I was nine or ten, my Great Aunt Hilda's hands were a rain forest. They were thin-skinned and spotted like the backs of tropical frogs, her veins like vines. The dull gold of her wedding band hung loosely on the third finger of her left hand, where it spun round and round in circles, like the water wheel at the sawmill down the road. I could never comprehend how she'd slipped the ring past her knotty knuckle in the first place, or having slipped it on, how she'd ever get it off again. If Great Aunt Hilda ever died they'd have to bury her with it.

The seat of Great Aunt Hilda's piano bench folded back like the shell of a mollusk. After breakfast of Christmas bread flecked with red and green citrus peel, she pulled out her tattered sheet music and sat down. She folded back the wooden lid covering the keys, and suddenly there was a piano in the room. The piano seemed invisible much of the time, functioning mostly as a display stand for framed photographs, glass animals, and the old globe.

Resting hemispheric spectacles on the bridge of her nose, Great Aunt Hilda peered at the parade of black ants dashing up and down the musical staff. She positioned her fingers carefully to catch every ant, every single one. Her hands flexed tentatively over the keys, padding down lightly once or twice before striking. The first few chords croaked thin and hollow, like her own voice in the morning before she put her teeth in and washed down her handful of pills with a glass of prune juice. She played a few familiar chords, then called to me.

Hither Agnes, stand by me. You shall be my faithful page turner. The picture was vivid as emeralds in memory, of the large and regal man in the green velvet cape, breaking the crust of snow with his great fur-lined boots, forging a footpath for his faithful page to follow. A picture of Wenceslaus and his page was on the card which my father sent me that year, with a rhyme inside written by Luther Underhill himself, which ran this way:

> Those who faithfully repeat
> The path of someone else's feet
> Are more apt to make it home again
> than those who forge a new one.
> Wherever hidden gorges yawn,
> It's the forger who first finds them
> And by his warning or his fall
> Saves the souls of those behind him.

I should have loved to follow, if there had been such a man and such a path. No one could expect a blank page to know where on earth she was going in a snowstorm. My feet would fit easily in the boot tracks of the King, with plenty of room to spare, so other tiny feet might see the holes and follow there. At times a body longed for this sort of guidance. But other times a pair of boots might want to dash off and stamp their mad little feet in every direction *other* than the one prescribed, leaving boot prints behind which no other soles could follow, stamping out notes which no one could read, so no one could play.

"I can't read those notes," I said to my Great Aunt Hilda.

"You don't have to read them, dear, just follow along by counting them. You know how to count, don't you? *1-2-3-4, 1-2-3-4.* I'll nod like this when I want you to turn the page."

We staggered through *Good King Wenceslaus*, then moved on to *We Three Kings*. My father's Christmas card had predicted this second number also, in another verse scribbled on the back.

> Ye'll sing of three *more* Kings who've things in common with the first.
> Like his, their cause is philanthropic, and like him, they'll speak in verse.
> But unlike He whom others follow in the footsteps He hath tread,
> These three will know they *also* serve who let themselves be *lead*.
>
> Convergent on a single path they'll travel from afar,
> Hailing from exotic lands, rich in 'orey and in tar.
> Whatever 'orey is I canna' say, I dinna' know
> But I know that tar is glossy black, the shadow-twin o' snow.

And that the writer of the carol would know little of the Kings
Being from another century, his concern was other things.

His song does make one King sound like a harbinger of doom
With his sighing, bleeding, dying mummy-casket of perfume.
Your own mum would not have found *him* a particularly jovial guest;
She'd thank him kindly for his gift if he'd take leave at her request.

Yet wise Kings they were, to set their sights on a thing so far away,
For a star won't crumble from your blaming it for leading you astray
Since stars are deaf and dumb, they canna' hear a word you say.

I did admire the three kings, their mournful caravans in silhouette against the sands, at least they seemed to know where they were going. With my eyes I followed the disorderly army of ants across the page of sheet music, while Great Aunt Hilda's hooked fingers picked them out one by one, pressing the keys to extinguish them. Now her hands were spiders, crooked and jointed, spinning webs to catch the noisy notes as they came marching in. As she struck the keys each sang its single name then nothing more. I counted them, then once they were all accounted for, I turned the page.

I did not want to be this person. I was becoming conscious of it then, that I didn't want to be the one who stands and turns the pages of what someone else had written, the one who follows in the footsteps someone else had trod. It seemed that they who followed yonder star had done better for themselves in the end, they were kings after all, and not pages. Sense of direction seemed a sort of private club. And only *here*, in the big sky above Great Aunt's Hilda's house, were there ever stars to follow. At home in the city, they were buffed away by the scouring wool of city lights and traffic, they were wired to the ground like the yellow eyes of streetlamps and the windows of skyscrapers, they were blinded by smog.

If I could find something like *this* to have faith in I'd follow it. I'd memorize the whole book, to recite chapter and verse at family gatherings. I'd play every single note, not minding that I hadn't written them myself. To be their instrument would be enough. But my hands were dumb and clumsy like my father's, not graceful like my mother's hands, nor gnarled and eloquent like Great Aunt Hilda's. My hands were lumps of stubborn clay, and for now I wanted them that way, there was still plenty of time to learn grown-up ways of killing the time on my hands.

"Let's sing the *Twelve Days of Christmas*," piped in my mother once the *Three Kings* had departed in solemn chord. My mother loved the many gifts, and loved the true love whose devotion was matched only by his seemingly endless resources. The doves and the geese and the swans and the French hens, the hired musicians and dancers, especially the five golden rings every time a new verse rolled around.

"*Imagine!*" said my mother, sipping eggnog from an amber goblet. "That would be *five* golden rings a day, times *twelve*, which comes to a new ring for each finger and thumb every couple of days! *Sixty* golden rings by the end of the song, if you read that way, which you might as well. *Imagine!* The poor fellow would have to buy a whole new *house* by the end of it, just to hold everything, with an ornamental pond for those eighty-four swans-a-swimming."

"Don't forget the geese-a-laying," said my Uncle Vernie slowly. "Maybe the eggs they lay are golden, too."

"Let's hope so, God love 'em," said my mother, "or they'd end up golden themselves, with cranberry sauce."

I thought of my father, hundreds of miles away, mumbling prayers in his basement room or banging tools at his hapless workbench on Boxing Day. Perhaps he'd say he had something to follow, or perhaps not, but it was certain none of us could follow *him*. His name was not written in the sky but scratched onto the undersides of things, like the names of bone-china purveyors on the undersides of cups and plates. It was impossible to follow him without being drawn into an underworld of half-vision, half-hearing, half-statements and questions only half-understood. He never came with us to Great Aunt Hilda's house at Christmas, the season passed without him, despite that so many things we said and sang about had to do with fathers, and men who were like fathers. About being grateful to them, singing praises to them, following them and placing our small and mortal faith in their hands.

41

ECDYSIS

Arthropods periodically undergo ecdysis, until they are mature. When they outgrow their exoskeletons, they form a new one underneath the old one. This process is controlled by hormones. When the new exoskeleton is complete, it becomes separated from the old one by fluid, which increases in volume. Finally, the original exoskeleton cracks open, usually along the back, and is shed. The arthropod emerges, clothed in a new, pale, and still somewhat soft exoskeleton. The exoskeleton subsequently hardens after exposure to the air or water in which the animal lives. When the exoskeleton is soft, however, the animal is especially vulnerable.

— from *Biology*, Raven & Johnson

"His back's split from head to tail, for heaven's sakes," Great Aunt Hilda says. "Well, there's what a dozen years of cuddling will do to a feller." I am lying on my back on Great Aunt Hilda's living room rug, which is made of tweedy braided snakes stitched together in a coil. I am doing pelvic tilts for my lumbar region. You are lying on your stomach Rose, learning how to support your small wobbly body on splayed hands, cobra position.

From my vantage point on the rug, I can see two stockinged feet poking out over the footrest of Great Aunt Hilda's chair like the feet of a witch upon whom a house has fallen. Not my mother's feet, her thin tapered toes, her Cinderella slippers of blue rabbit fur with toenails smelling of cuticle lotion. These are Great Aunt Hilda's feet, ascending in beige knee-high stockings with reinforced toes, thick ankles, her toenails ribbed like the hooves of a goat. They have a faintly sweet dry-skin smell, mingled with lavender powder.

"A *dozen* years?" I ask. "Really?"

"From the time you were no bigger than Rose until your early teens, as I recall," answers Great Aunt Hilda.

The split body upon whom her hands work is Koko, the legendary stuffed bear of my childhood, rediscovered in a box upstairs in my mother's old room. Koko is a koala bear about the size of a lemon loaf, with a key in his belly which plays *Waltzing Matilda* when you wind him up. I'd hardly ever wound him up, all those years, only because I hated to hear him wind down again. The slow slurring of the tune to spindly drunkenness, the tiny heartbreak with its final *click* to silence. But I'd slept with him a thousand nights, there'd been a perfect chin rest between his tufted ears, my square sweaty hand cradled his back for a dozen years until his fur was worn. The fur was real, probably not real *koala* bear fur, rather it looked like a goat. He looks so different now that I know he's not even a bear but a marsupial, although I'll never stop calling him Koko koala bear because that's been his name since I was less-than-one. And now my bear's back is bald, the skin brittle with visible follicles where possible goat hairs used to be. Over time the seam had split, right up the spine, with cotton stuffing emerging.

I couldn't hear him play right now without dissolving in torrents, I know it. It's what happened another time at Buffalo man's place, the last night I spent with him, when he'd flipped *Small Change* into the tape deck and suddenly here was this barnacle voice growling out Koko's song, as though the tiny marsupial had become a jolly swagman since the last dozen years, stowed many a jumbuck and was coming home to tell me about it. I had one of those time collapses, as though a time capsule bursts open within you, and any conventional measure of time and space evaporates, recondensing as torrents of something like laughter and something like tears. I do not know what they are, these episodes, but they don't seem pathological so much as blessed.

"We'll have him good as new in no time," says Great Aunt Hilda, smiling to herself.

We'd been talking a bit about sex, as graphically as was possible considering our very different stations in life. I'd been trying to sound angry at Buffalo man, even though it isn't much like anger that I feel. It's more like being divided from yourself at some level, and leaving a big chunk of you with the other person.

"Well, your Great Uncle Arthur didn't think using anything was natural either," says Great Aunt Hilda, "not that it made any much difference. Arthur never heard the patter of little feet in *his* lifetime, he didn't. Vernie was more of a clomper. Any rate your uncle Vernie never had the privilege of meeting dear Arthur, God rest him, and too bad he didn't. That boy would've been much better off with a good strong man to look up to, it's plain."

Great Aunt Hilda makes a few tiny stitches and takes out a pin. Then a few more tiny stitches and another pin. Koko's back is stitched up like a mummied mouth, stitch by stitch, Great Aunt Hilda's fingers tucking in the stuffing as they creep up the spine, pin by pin. Then she draws out a couple more pins and sticks them sharply into her right breast.

I never got used to her doing that. I wince every single time. Though the breast hasn't been there for years, I still never got used to it. Her *pin cushion* she calls it, the foam-rubber cup which replaces the missing breast. At night it sits on her dresser like a sea peach, porous and salmon-coloured, while during the day it nestles under her black dress, sometimes with pins stuck in it like the insensitive region which exposes a witch. Sometimes the pins secured little slips of paper, reminding Great Aunt Hilda to whom she must send golden anniversary cards or octogenarian birthday cards, or sympathy cards.

"Do you really have to do it like that?" I say mildly, meaning the sticking pins. But Great Aunt Hilda thinks I meant the bear repair.

"Well, dear, just thought one of these days you'll appreciate it," she sighs, a bit hurt. "Thought you'd want to see your own Rose with the same old bear you had when you were so tiny."

"I totally do," I say, "this is great, Aunt Hilda. I didn't mean that, I meant the other thing."

She doesn't notice the sticking pins at all, as though the action were quite natural, which I guess it is. Although for most of her life there had been a living breast there, now there was not, and what was natural was Great Aunt Hilda's adaptation to the fact. The part still had a function, clearly. Just now it was holding half a dozen stick pins, arranged in a cluster like the six of swords in Tarot.

Great Aunt Hilda holds the bear away from herself at reading distance and sighs at her stitches. Koko's spine is a now a bit crooked but it can't be helped. The stitches can't be undone, unless she rips them all out again with her stitch ripper, but the skin is far too fragile for that. The stitch ripper lies capless on the doilied wooden lamp table by her chair, curved and glinting like a dental instrument.

"Well," says Great Aunt Hilda, that's as straight as he's going to get, at his age." She turns Koko's face to her lap and picks up her needle again.

"It wasn't that he didn't believe in using anything," I say. "He never actually mentioned using anything, and neither did I. So we were both stupid, we had that in common anyhow, but especially me. If he ever talked about what was natural he was probably thinking about things humans beings have in common with other primates, you know, eating and scratching and rolling around. We're the only ones who use birth control, all the other animals can just trust us to curb their populations for them."

"So he thinks we should all run around and just have babies wherever it happens?" asks Great Aunt Hilda. "I hope not."

"No, he doesn't think that at all," I say. "I'm trying to explain what Buff— what Noah thought about human beings, he didn't have much faith in them. He thought the human brain was great for certain specialized tasks, like snaring things and making parachutes, but it still can't save us from being squashed by something *bigger* than the human brain. Like a flood or a war or a landslide or its own ego. He thinks that human nature is quite simple. All animals, including us, are attracted to things which are pleasant, like food and sleep and physical activity and enlightenment, and try to avoid things which are unpleasant. Then he told me I was being unpleasant. Or at least that I had no knack for *avoiding* unpleasantness. Which is completely true. Plus I'd been having weird dreams and missing all my classes, bitching all the time... complaining, rather, excuse me."

I'd heard Great Aunt Hilda say *shit* only a couple of times in reference to the white streaks on the windscreen of the old blue sedan when it finally emerged from the hog shed after an early spring of resident sparrows. And though I'd heard her say *bitch* dozens of times, it was only in reference to female dogs, those hapless creatures who limped around the barn with hanging teats and endless puppies. I was more concerned that the *b*-word might conjure images of me and Buffalo man down on all fours in a barn, than I was really worried about mild cursing.

"Sometimes a man has to put up with a little unpleasantness," says Great Aunt Hilda. "Just like a woman does," she says, pulling the final stitch taut and cutting the thread with her stitch ripper. Then she leans back in her chair, and begins to travel backward through time. It is possible to read it on her face when she does this, the face of a younger woman rises up and smoothes away lines, then recedes again when the reverie is broken. Her bifocals catch divided light as she turns her face to the lace curtain, out to the yard where the old stone well is, then beyond, across the hayfield to the woodpile. Perhaps she could still see him out there, Arthur, her strong determined husband. He would inevitably return, at the end of the day, with clomping boots smelling sweet of hay and manure.

Great Aunt Hilda blinks and arranges a bouquet of hands on her lap, gently tapping one against the other. "A sensitive man needs something to do with his *hands*," she says. "Idle hands are the devil's workshop, Agnes, that's the truth of it." She leans forward and waggles her finger like a cautionary fairy tale witch. "A man with only time on his hands finds all sorts of mischief to fill it up with. You be careful of men like *those*," she says, leaning back again, reposed. "Your Great Uncle Arthur never had a day of illness in his life."

Perhaps Great Aunt Hilda was right, that I'd be happier with a man who was so busy pitching manure that he'd have no time to spend with me at all.

Suddenly you start sputtering Rose. I spring up automatically to pick you up and pace circles round the braided rug as though it were a Lilliputian hippodrome. I pat your back and make *sh-sh-sh-shhh* sounds. It seems to me that I can *hear* things better out here, at Great Aunt Hilda's place. I can hear you coughing and I can hear crickets at night, the slow creaking of the house itself like the turning of a great wheel. Ever since the question of your hearing had arisen, my mother'd been convinced that there must be something wrong with *my* hearing as well, as though you must've caught deafness from *me*.

There'd been at least a couple of mornings when my mother greeted me sternly as I shuffled bleary into the kitchen. "Rosie was coughing her lungs out last night, kitten," she'd say. "I don't know how you managed not to hear her. I finally had to get up and see to her myself." Then my mother would disappear up the stairs into the bathroom, trailing her voice like a feather boa as she went. "Good thing I was there, too, pet, or who knows what might've happened. You'd've slept through it all, kitten." So then I'd be left to imagine the *it all* which I *would've slept right through*, the shadow-image slinking behind my mother's words.

Yet out here at the old house, I can hear more clearly those hushed internal voices which tell me she may be mistaken. Out here at Great Aunt Hilda's, my hearing seems fine and so does my head. I can hear crickets and creaking floorboards, and the hanging silence of the hayfields outside. And I can hear you Rose when you cough. I pick you up and pace around the living room rug, loving all your fidgeting limbs, your determination. *Sh-sh-sh-shhh.*

42

Hen's teeth

Blessed are they that have not seen, and yet have believed.

— St. John, XXI. 29

Don't go inside yet, Agnes. Uncle Vernie was calling my name, while my feet in blue sneakers had already crossed the darkening lawn to the back porch of Great Aunt Hilda's house. The kitchen would smell of bleach and peach cobbler, if I did go inside. My mother would be stripping stains from underthings, and Great Aunt Hilda would be slicing fruit in crescent moons, then baking the expression of juice out of them. Bake until golden brown, or until peaches express their juice.

The back porch was a small wooden platform where Great Aunt Hilda always stood to hang laundry. There were pullied ropes, swooping like trolley cables, to a tree at the end of the yard. Sometimes underthings would leap from the line and get stuck in the tree like kites.

I stopped still on the platform. My blue sneakers on grey sun-bleached wood, pitted rusty nail heads, the trace stains of fish blood from the first and only speckled trout I ever gutted here, two summers ago when I was nine.

"Don't go inside yet, Agnes," called Uncle Vernie. "Come play ball with me, for once."

I was now eleven. For sure I was eleven, since my father left on my last birthday. I now wore braces, which Dr. Spektor gave me for Christmas last year because the caps on my broken front teeth wouldn't stay put until the real ones were straighter. My back teeth were growing in all crooked. Four crooked wisdoms pushing up from behind, forcing all the front ones out of line. This made my caps keep popping off, whenever I tore shreds of chewy bread or gnawed the lids of pens, or whenever I committed nocturnal bruxism in my sleep, which Dr. Spektor accused me of doing routinely.

Sleep, that sand which appears in your eyes in the morning, may be the gravel of pulverized tooth enamel. Night, like the crop of a hen, grinds us to sleep. Cows sleep on the ground and dream clouds, then awaken to move like clouds, under patchy cover of their shade.

"Stay out *here* and play *ball* with me, Agnes," called Uncle Vernie.

Uncle Vernie always looked me in the mouth, instead of in the eyes, when he spoke to me. So I started covering my mouth with my hand, as though it were a hole in my T-shirt. I was eleven, flat as a plank with glasses and braces and not one single pair of authentic denim jeans. I had the polyester flood pants in a *faux* denim pattern, with an elastic waistband. I couldn't really walk into town and hang out in front of the Soapspit Bowl, where older farm kids slouched in jeans and smoked. But I could stay out here in the yard and play ball with slow Uncle Vernie until the mosquitoes sent us to bed, or go back inside the bleach-peach house and then up inside my adolescent head.

"The lights are on, but nobody's home," my mother would mutter, whenever Uncle Vernie didn't appear to understand something she said, or stood too long in a place she was silently willing him to move from, so she could pass by to the sink or the liquor cabinet.

"You'd *think* some things would seem *obvious*," she'd say, when he finally got out of her way.

Maybe the lights are on *because* nobody's home. It's what you do, when you go out, you leave the lights on so people will think you're at home, and won't break in and take things. If I were to cover my eyes with a curtain, or with one of those blue gelatinous masks my mother uses to sooth and rest her eyes, would I seem any more at home?

I chose to stay out in damp rural dark, and to finally let my weird Uncle Vernie teach me how to catch. I had been coming to Soapspit Bluff every summer since I was two, and every year he'd been trying to teach me how to catch. I'd always refused, first timidly at three, then defiantly at nine, sarcastically now that I was eleven. It was something in the manner of his invitation. Not simply an offer of instruction, but a challenge he suspected I wouldn't want to meet, as though he *knew* my reasons for not wanting to catch a ball, even if I didn't.

Ag-gie ca-an't ca-atch, Ag-gie ca-an't ca-atch, he'd sing, all grizzle-faced and blue-eyed like a cataract border collie. "Can Agnes catch a ball? *Can't* Agnes catch a ball? Here, Aggie — catch a *ball*!" Then suddenly there'd be something flying at me, a roll of socks or a Christmas ornament or a tomato or even an egg. No one ever feels completely prepared to see an egg smash on the floor unless they deliberately throw it there. Yet my hands would dart out more like they were pushing somebody away on a swing, not the hands of someone preparing to receive a flying object. I was never able to envision the egg landing safely in my hands, I always saw it hitting the floor and smashing before it even happened. Was this a premonition or a secret wish?

"Just *hold* the ball, Agnes," said Uncle Vernie. He handed me a red rubber ball the size of my head, dark and empty like my head when I was at home. The ball was one of those maroon rubber balls from the gymnasium of an elementary school so I wondered how he got it, we had to sign out for those.

There was that story of Uncle Vernie being kicked in the head by a horse when he was just little. That he survived, but that surviving was a slower sort of state for him. I never believed it, like I never believed that other story about his father, my Great Uncle Arthur, being buried under the crabapple tree. I also never believed the story about pigs being unable to swim, because they'd slit their own throats with their front trotters if they tried, even though Uncle Vernie told me he'd even seen it with his own eyes, one time when the river overflowed and flooded the barn, and all the animals were frantically trying to swim out. One or two of the horses burst down the door and escaped, but the cows were all chained to their stalls when the water came up so they drowned, then floated up like bloated carnival dirigibles on tethers.

It was hard to believe that my Uncle Vernie ever got kicked in the head by any horse, because this didn't seem to fit his particular quality of strangeness. It would happen so fast, a kick in the head by a horse. It would probably come from behind and out of nowhere like an act of

God. I would have expected this to make a man pathologically baffled, or at least edgy. Yet Uncle Vernie's manner was nothing like this, none of this wariness. He was like the man who knew *exactly* where the hoof had come from, he'd even seen its face. He was the twisted-grin man who'd seen it all, aware and awake and looking straight into the eyes of whatever-it-was that got him. He seemed to be half-grinning at it constantly, as though *whatever-it-was* were a demon floating in the air just to the left of everyone else's head.

"Okay, I'll play catch with you," I said, shrugging my reply like a jacket off my shoulders like the girls who pick fights. *I don't even believe you*, I was thinking, I have never seen the scar. There would have to be a crescent-shaped *dent*, I'd imagine, like the ones in the gravel at the side of the road heading out of here. There'd be the hoof print of a horse somewhere on Uncle Vernie's *head*, if it were true. There's always a place on the body which tells the whole story.

Uncle Vernie handed me the red rubber ball. I let it fall right away to the ground, landing in the wet grass at our feet. I wanted just to talk for a while first.

"Agnes can't even *hold* a ball, never mind *catch* one," said Uncle Vernie with a crocodile grin. "Hold the ball, Agnes. At least *hold* it."

Uncle Vernie picked up the ball and placed it in my hands and again I let it fall.

"I don't really *want* the ball," I said. "Why don't you just throw it up in the air and catch it *yourself*, if you want to play catch so much?"

"If Agnes can't hold a ball, Agnes won't be able to catch a ball, or even throw one," said my Uncle Vernie slowly. "Me, I can throw a ball, and I can catch a ball. It took me a lot of years to get it right, but I can catch a goddamn ball."

I hadn't known the part about it taking years. It never occurred to me all that time he was trying to teach me to catch, maybe he was also trying to learn how. I just assumed he was another strange old guy trying to get me to do something, and that I wasn't supposed to listen to what he said because he smelled like bottles. My mother smelled like mouthwash, which was different. She had less of a problem with *being* drunk than *smelling* like it. It didn't make much difference to me either way, it wasn't as though no one knew, things don't need to be said. Anyone who takes out the garbage isn't stupid. The silence inside an empty bottle defines what its function was, the label only says where it came from.

"I can too catch a ball," I said.

"You can't even catch a *cold*," said Uncle Vernie. "You can't even *hold* a ball. You can't hold *anything*, never seen you, never. Why'd you think your Great Aunt Hilda doesn't let you put away the fancy bone-china when it's clean?"

"Maybe because I don't *want* to?"

"Maybe because you'd drop the plates all over the floor. You have too much gravity, causes accidents."

"I should tell my father on you," I said. "He can bend soup spoons with his mind, you know."

"You can't even hold onto your father," said Uncle Vernie. "Where is he now, Aggie?"

"*All right*," I said, "I'm going go to stand way over *here*. Throw me the stupid-ass *ball*."

"Your *father*?" said my uncle, "You think he's got *jack* to say? Chances he'll ever come back'd be about as scarce as hen's teeth." He threw the ball on *chances* and I caught it on *teeth*, actually caught it, and held it for a while, my empty head.

Well, I wish I'd known when I was eleven years old that what my Uncle Vernie called *as scarce as hen's teeth* were those phenomena which occurred *not at all* in nature. I wish he'd just said what he meant. I wouldn't have got down on my hands and knees in the middle of the night, in the chicken-shitty grass around the coop, holding a handkerchief over my mouth and nose but still practically gagging from the smell, searching with a flashlight, if only he'd said what he meant. Why do grown-ups so seldom say what they actually mean? If hen's teeth were only scarce, as opposed to definitively impossible, then there had to be a few of them around, somewhere. Hens pick up small bits of gravel along with the corn kernels, they must break a tooth now and then. Somewhere in the general compost of seasons there *had* to be a hen's tooth. People had found the bones of whole dinosaurs and rebuilt models of what they might've looked like, so surely I could come up with one single hen's tooth. But holding the handkerchief over my face with one hand, and focusing the flashlight in the other, made it difficult to crawl. It had been so long since I'd really crawled, so instead I sort of waddled on my back legs, to be very close to the ground, to think like a hen. If I were a hen, where would I leave my teeth?

There is reason to hope, my father used to say of those phenomena which were at least slightly possible, such as going to the zoo, or his employment. We never went to the zoo either, but there was reason to *hope* we would go, and this in itself had some worth. But that night in the grass by the chicken coop, I wished Uncle Vernie had just admitted there was *no hope* I'd find a hen's tooth because they didn't bloody *exist*. Instead, I had to find out years later from my biology textbook.

I hadn't touched that chicken-shitty memory in years, there remained some cells in my brain which still had faith in hen's teeth, until I read: *Most vertebrates have teeth. Exceptions are the MONOTREMES, such as the duck-billed platypus, whose mouth is specialized for eating insects, worms, and small crustaceans. Other exceptions are THE BIRDS.*

It would have changed my whole approach to the rest of my childhood had I known. I would not have persisted in the dark with a flashlight, searching for a thing which didn't exist, I wasn't quite that stupid. I wouldn't have bothered conjuring in my mother's face an underlying faith that everything was well, despite how it seemed. I understood that my parents did not particularly want to live with each other anymore, nor talk to each other, really, but had faith that there were reasons for this, and that I shouldn't be alarmed. It was understood that some things were not to be spoken about, but I had faith that this was for the common good. The common good appeared to be something similar to Great Aunt Hilda's tin canisters for storing Flour,

Sugar, Salt, and Oatmeal. It involved that each of us conspire to be as self-contained as possible, labeling ourselves legibly and be bordered with daisies.

What I hadn't understood was the part about the chances that my father would ever return to the house on Dormier Street, the slim incisive chance that he might be asked to come back. I had not understood that, according to the dark and lucid vision through which my Uncle Vernie saw the world, these chances existed not at all. The chances would not adapt themselves to the needs of an evolving species, they would not mutate any anomalous miracles, they simply didn't exist.

43

METAPHORMOSIS IV: ANT HEAP

> In certain species of frog, the male gives birth to tadpoles through his mouth. After the female has laid the eggs, the male collects them in his mouth and stores them in the expandable sac beneath his jaw, which is very wide. He keeps the eggs safe from predators [who include his own species], without swallowing them, until the tadpoles hatch, when they are born live from his mouth. The father will continue to gather his brood into his mouth when there are predators nearby, until at a certain point in their development when he finally abandons them to their lives.
>
> — Torn by Luther Underhill from a textbook in 1967. Rediscovered by Agnes in Great Aunt Hilda's granary

I ask my Great Aunt Hilda whether she'd ever heard from my father all these years, since I officially hadn't. These days I tended to imagine him living in a trailer somewhere up the Sunshine Coast with a typewriter and an African Grey parrot, whom he's taught to speak. Other times I figured he must've either passed away or become a monk, given up the worldly stuff which allows a person to be traced. Maybe he jumped a boat to Burma to assist the tribal resistance, or became a back-packing journalist in war-torn Nicaragua. These were things people my own age were doing, but not girls with babies. Maybe they weren't very smart things to do anyway. Or possibly he was living right under my nose in a rented room on the Downtown East Side. You'd think I'd know. Maybe he played chess at the Carnegie every day, and all I'd have to do is walk in and sit right across from him. You'd think I'd know how to play chess.

"Well, Agnes, if you'll kindly recall," says Great Aunt Hilda slowly, "you didn't want to have much to *do* with your father, not since the day he struck off on his own. And not for quite some time before that, from what I gather. You're certain you didn't tell him *yourself*, not to write to you? Folks say some foolish things when they're upset."

"I don't think I'd say that," I say.

"Maybe he found it easier to write to other people," says Great Aunt Hilda. "Any letters I got from him were perfectly cordial, never going into matters much. He always asked after you. He even offered to come live in Soapspit Bluff at one point, to stay here at the house and help take care of things. Course I still had Vernie here for that, though his help's more valuable when it's declined. Truly I didn't see what your father'd be able to add. Didn't tell him so, though. When a man's believed the worst of himself his whole life. Well, that was quite some time ago now."

"Why do you say he believed the worst of himself?"

"Well, does it really surprise you?"

"No. But I'd never say it. Wasn't there any *forwarding* address? Where are the letters *now*?"

"No, dear, there *wasn't* any forwarding address," Great Aunt Hilda says. "He was travelling a lot. He wrote to *you*, too, Agnes, I'm sure he wouldn't make up something like that. Don't suppose you kept his letters. It's too bad. Any he sent here would still be in the house somewhere, if you care to look. Course, that was quite some time ago now."

"I don't remember getting any letters," I said. "I remember *not* getting any letters. I don't have many memories of my dad at all, because he was always in the basement. I had the impression he was trying to seem more mysterious but really it just made him seem more creepy, like I didn't know him."

"Creepy indeed, Miss," scolds Great Aunt Hilda. "If you were *my* daughter, I'd box your ears. You complain about never hearing from your dad but you can barely remember the words he *did* write to you. I'd caution you not to mistake your father's side of things without knowing the whole story, Agnes Joan. While I never knew the man well I'd say this on general principle. No good comes from speaking ill of your family, I've seen the damage enough. If you're going to pin blame on a person you have to make certain you're justified, or else better hold your tongue. That much I *would* say."

"Well, on a positive note," Great Aunt Hilda continued, "and what I gathered from his letters, he was an intelligent young man, if too sensitive. Too variable a character, Arthur would've said. He should've tried being a farmer for a while, your dad. It would've done him a world of good, it would."

I stand up wobbily in the middle of the braided rug as Great Aunt Hilda reaches out to hug me, her arms thin and light as wings.

"Oh look," I whisper. "Rose's fast asleep now. Good, good... I'll move her upstairs in an hour or so. Are you staying up for a while?... I think she likes it here.... Can you remember even what *room* those letters might be in? Oh geez, never mind that tonight... g'night, night-night."

"Agnes?"

"Yes?"

"I was just planning to sit here in my chair and do a puzzle, dear, it'd be fine with me for Rose to stay put, as long as she's happy sleeping where she is. I'm as comfortable here in my chair as I can expect to be. Would it be all right if she just stayed down here tonight? I know how to bottle feed, I've done it before. Baby people and baby cows, too."

"That would be nice, thanks. If you need me just knock," I say, pointing at the ceiling. Great Aunt Hilda has an umbrella beside her chair, with which she can tap the grate on the ceiling. The grate leads directly to my mother's old bedroom, where I'll be sleeping. If you kneel on the floor of my mother's old room, you peer down on people in the living room, through the grate, or open it up and reach your whole arm through the ceiling of the floor below.

I mount the stairs to my mother's old room and find my book about arthropods. The floor whines like a lost child, in these upper rooms where I've never been able to stop my heart from pounding. The house is alive but this alone is not frightening. You can see parts of it moving, the mice and the dust mites and the spiders and flies who are born and die here. Those aren't frightening either. It's what an old house knows which is frightening, also magical. Every life which passes through these walls leaves its animate shadow behind, why should these be any threat to anyone? There's that portrait on the wall, the girl with the tapioca teeth. A portrait of my mother as a young girl, that's obvious now, why had I been so scared of it?

And there's that odd little lamp above the headboard, a brass pony in a prancing pose. If I jump into the centre of the old iron bed, the patchwork down quilts will billow up around me like lemon snow, and the springs will creak like frogs. I remember very well. Ribbons and bows collected and pinned to the armoire by Berenice in the 1950s are still here, and that old doll with the cracked repainted face as well. And there's that chamber pot under the bed with handles that resemble bunches of plums.

I let all my baggy black clothing drop to the floor and creep carefully beneath the colourful quilts, then open my book to devour an article about ants. I curl my tongue round marching rows of print and drag them in like they're candy-coated. I read about certain worker ants, who must be constantly occupied with carrying grains of foundational sediment from the lower chambers of the ant heap up to the roof, to air and dry in the sun. This work must be continual, grain by grain, strata by strata. Eventually the original *roof* of the ant heap sinks down to the *basement* while what had previously been the *basement* rises up to the *roof*. Entomologists measure this process by painting the roof of the ant heap with a blue pigment, then cutting open a cross-section to watch the blue layer descend, grain by grain, strata by strata. The work never ceases but the ants must keep doing it to prevent their basement storage chambers from rotting.

Metaphormosis IV: Ant heap
Hypothesis: That certain functions of memory are akin to the carrying of foundational sediment from the basement, up to the roof and into the sun. That the past rises to the present as the present sinks into the past, to prevent things from becoming malignant in the psyche.

Observations: The work of memory is constant, the priority of arrangement changing constantly. Centers become peripheral, while other peripheries become central, in cycles like psychic seasons. Often you don't come up with only one channel of the story, but several of them, dozens and dozens. Sometimes memory is spiral-shaped, circling from a central detail outward to a larger picture. Or circling inward, from a general circumference of time and feeling to a focal detail at the heart of things, becoming one of several hearts of things.

I'm scarcely bothered by the fat flies who've come to buzz against the lamp as I scan the next chapter about soldier ants who literally use their *heads* to plug up the communal sewage ducts, to prevent intruders from entering the ant heap through the plumbing. Certain soldier ants within the colony have evolved gigantic heads, to the exact circumference of the holes on the side of the ant heap through which the communal excreta is ejected. But despite their large heads, the brain ganglia of the latrine-patrol ants are no bigger than the average ant's. In fact, though the oversized head is perfectly evolved to its function, it's a bit of a handicap to the individual ant. It practically incapacitates her. She has to be fed and tended to by other ants, because her enormous head makes it impossible for her to care for herself. So, what's perfectly adapted to the welfare of the ant heap as a *unit* is not necessarily adapted to the welfare of every single ant. *An ant alone is no ant at all,* as the book says.

How many human beings would be willing to make such a sacrifice for the good of their neighbours, knowing that it would expand their scope of opportunity, their identity and prestige, not one *bit?* On the other hand, ants produce some pretty impressive-looking architecture. In my book there are photos of impregnable sun-baked façades with myriad labyrinths inside, like Egyptian pyramids.

One of the fat old flies falls on its back on the white linen pillowcase, and twiddles all its legs in the air. Crazy old fly. The legs kick and then it dies.

They say the more briefly a person's life story is told the more comic it is. To throw a sudden spotlight onto a person's life story might not be a revelation so much as a punch line. What if there are no ancient riddles to solve after all? A person's life is not aimed at any single revelation, even so she goes in search of one. And in the end, she finds that getting there was not only *half* the fun, but *all* of it. This is the part which is funny.

44

Biscuit tin

In the early morning Great Aunt Hilda again volunteers to give you your bottle while I go exploring up granary. The granary is an airy attic above Great Aunt Hilda's hog shed, requiring an ascent of thirteen wooden steps, steep and bare as a ladder, through a wooden trap door at the top. Along the walls of the granary are wooden stalls as still as cattle, where oats, peas, corn, and barley used to be kept. The shape of a cross is cast over the knotted floor by the shadow of the window pane, and a million dust motes float in amber gyres of early light. Beneath the window there's a wooden work bench with a herd of prehistoric butternuts scattered across it, their eye-shaped shells spined with short bristles. The butternuts resemble hedgehogs. Attached to the bench is a rusty iron vice, to crack them open.

It takes a long time to take in the whole room. I see the iron-girded steamer trunk which my father had brought from Scotland in 1957, the wooden sled I've seen in pictures from my mother's childhood, a coffee tin from the Chicago World's Fair in 1893. There's a framed print hanging at a slant from a nail, of a young girl weeping and clinging to the neck of her chestnut colt who's just been sold at the county fair. My mother told me once that she'd sent away for that poster herself, using three oatmeal labels and a dime. It was just after Uncle Arthur sold all his horses, and she'd cried about it for days.

In the corner of the granary are three hanging wardrobe bags, quilted and zipped-up like huge pink cocoons. Rusty farming implements hang from the rafters above, a scythe, a bridle, a pitch fork, tractor parts.

Other presences are here in the granary as well. Ghostly ones, in which my cloven mind does not believe while knowing perfectly well they're there. I walk over to the bench and crack open a butternut in the vice. This seems to be the only way to get inside a butternut because they are as hard as bullets. But inside are slender sheaves, like those helicopters which spiral from oak trees. The butternuts look about two hundred years old but don't taste half bad. I remember reading about two-thousand-year-old honey which archeologists found in a tomb, and actually tasted. Imagine. Perhaps there is a kind of hunger and accountability which overtakes an archeologist, when she finally comes face to face with the thing she most desired.

I feel watched by the beady eyes of rats. It's uncanny how discovering things can feel more like being willing to remember them, especially if one feels watched by rats. I find a biscuit tin full of letters, in the very first place I look. It has been stashed at the very bottom of one of those creepy hanging wardrobe cocoons, with a tartan blanket wrapped around it. There is no one who could have put it there except me, or no one else who would have. I gather up the whole package and step backwards down the wooden steps, lowering the trap door behind me as I go. The most unnerving thing about the granary, even more than the rats and ghosts, is the probably irrational fear of getting locked up there.

Sitting on the cool linoleum in my mother's old room, the yellow room with the grate on the floor and the slanted ceiling, I settle you on my lap with the biscuit tin in front of us. *Smooth runs the water where the brook is deep*, reads the tin, with a picture of a mill by a brook. There's a tartan pattern around the border of the tin, garnished with thistles. I pry off the lid and empty the contents onto the floor. Scraps of paper, dozens of them, fall more-or-less in a clump like raked leaves. Two or three late leaves sail more slowly, violin notes settling down.

At no previous point in my life would I have felt prepared to discover a dusty biscuit tin with the voice of my father inside it. The real voice, not the speaking-in-tongues voice which seemed to seep in everywhere. At no point would I have been ready to read the hand of a human man, and see that he crossed his t's the same way I did, and notice again that we'd both evolved a habit of writing our capitals too large, then turning them into animals. The *Q* in his *Question*, for instance, as in *Please permit me, Miss Agnes, to ask you one very important Question*, was a bristling mome rath, which is a sort of green pig. Some of the papers had transcriptions of animal facts which he thought I'd want to know, or peculiar Bible quotations, or trollish rhymes meant to *sound* like peculiar Bible quotations. Some of the letters are typed and some are handwritten, some gracefully, some shakily. The biscuit tin is like a window through which light comes streaming, contours and features are more cleanly highlighted, the features of a human face. A man's hand holding a pen to write a letter. A man who is my father sitting down to his old black typewriter.

There are a few photographs in the box as well. The first was taken in Great Aunt Hilda's kitchen, an expanse of red and white gingham tablecloth with my head and shoulders perched like an elf at the far corner. That pink frothy angel food cake must be for me, since I am the only person at the table. There are three lit candles stuck in it. But the direction of my eyes skims right over the candles, to a tape recorder in the foreground of the picture, with a small microphone attached to it.

This would've been one of those birthdays my father was absent from, when my mother took Gavin and me to Great Aunt Hilda's while he stayed home on account of his punctured eardrum. The tape recorder was to record my voice, which would then be wrapped up and mailed to my father. He must've received dozens of these tapes, of me rattling on about Uncle Vernie trying to teach me how to milk a goat, or Gavin and I getting pin worms. Recordings of me thanking him effusively for his gift of a rubber frog or pom pom socks, which he'd had my mother bring with her to Soapspit Bluff in her suitcase. It had seemed especially significant that the frog or socks had travelled *all that way*, as my father would've done himself if he'd had better ears.

The second photograph is of the wooden platform at the side of Great Aunt Hilda's house, where she used to stand to hang up the wash. My mother, my brother and I are crouching on the platform as though it were a tiny raft. Instead of a steering pole, my hands are wrapped around a broom handle, with an upside-down ice cream pail balanced on top of it. A hooded jacket has been draped over the tilting pail, to represent a tall thin person with no face.

"Oh, that's supposed to be your *father*," Great Aunt Hilda laughs, when I show her the picture later. "I had so few pictures with you all in it, we just stuck in that broom handle fellow to complete the family. It was your idea, as I remember."

It was quite obvious from the picture that the broomstick man had been my idea. My knuckles are clenched around its middle, my head tilted to rest where its hipbone would have been. I'm smiling with pink eyes and waving at the camera.

Dear Agnes,

A cartoon I saw today made me think of you. It's not a very funny cartoon, more notable for its drawings than its comic merit. But it had to do with animals, so of course you came to mind.

There are two frames, the first showing a reconstructed dinosaur skeleton in a museum. The skeleton is of a prehistoric animal with four pointed spines protruding from its tail, bony plates of armour on its back, and two horns growing from its head.

The second frame travels back in time several million years to the age of dinosaurs, where we see one of these animals grazing on leaves in a field. It has four pointed spines protruding from its *back*, bony plates arranged like petals round its *head*, and two horns growing out of its *tail*.

Unlikely that our ability to reconstruct prehistory is so remiss as this, since there's only so many ways you can put the thing together! What do you think?

Love, Dad

Like many of the letters in the biscuit tin, this didn't appear to be one I ever received, but in another corner of my mind I was not surprised by any of it. As soon as I started reading I knew I'd read them before, but not since that horrible summer when I'd searched for hen's teeth and couldn't find any. I had then gathered up all my father's letters and buried them in a biscuit tin in the wardrobe. At the very bottom of the heap, I find the story I've always been half-looking for.

Tale of the Horse Leech written for Agnes on the occasion of her 11th Birthday by her father Luther Underhill

The horse leech has two daughters,
Give & Give.
There are three things that will not be satisfied,
Four that will not say, *Enough*:
Shoel, and the barren womb,
Earth that is never satisfied with
water, and fire that never says,
Enough.
The eye that mocks a father,
And scorns a mother,
The ravens of the valley will pick it out,
And the young eagles will eat it.

— Proverbs 30: 15-17

Once upon a time at the bottom of a pond lived a leech of peculiar size. It had two fine suckers, one at each end of itself, with which it was able to move along the muddy floor like a Slinky, endlessly, endoverendoverend. Just as certain flies of peculiar size were known as *horse flies* because they are as large as a *horse*, this leech was known as the *horse leech* because it was large as a *house*, or at least had once been large as a house. But after many lean years in the absence of those to whom the leech could really feel *attached*, it had shrunk to the size of a *horse*. The *U* was lost in the translation, as it were, and its absence soberly noted: *U was lost*.

Are lost, corrected a little girl named Agnes who was hearing the story for the first time.

R was lost? asked the leech, slinking round her little finger and attaching himself to a benign mole on the palm of her hand, which was a part of herself the girl knew very well, like the back of her hand. The girl also knew that sometimes her hands were so large she'd find stray horses grazing on the palms, or other times they shrank as small as a flea in the ear of the horse, and she'd have to speak gently to her hands, and listen carefully, to hear all they heard.

But no, insisted Agnes, *R was not lost. You are lost*.

So then *U* became lost, and *R* took its place, and the leech shrank to the size of a *horse*, which was smaller than a *house*, but still quite large for a leech. He sadly took a stick and wrote a poem about himself, scraped wetly in the sand along the beach…

When the leech reached his nadir of diminishing size,
He felt ashamed to have become so *lost*, in his daughter's eyes
So he sulkily slunk way down in the mud,
'Til he'd sunk just as far as a leech could sink.
There, he felt things that all leeches feel in their blood,
Which primarily concerns finding something to drink.

Whenever sanguinary drinking partners popped by for a chat,
The leech would drink them under the table, or on the doorstep welcome mat.
He sucked up all the fishes, and the ducks and geeses too,
whose feet dangled like lures to his all-sucking view.
He sucked up the willows who wept on the bank,
like widows who weep for a ship that has sank.
He sucked up the bulrushes brushing the shore,
seduced a dozen swooping swallows in for tea.
He swallowed every swallow 'til there weren't any more,
And chortled at how *mouthy* he could be.

Any V-shaped flock of geese bound for destinations south,
Was rerouted with a road sign to his great all-sucking *mouth*.
And though by his own estimation the leech's stature grew,
It conversely shrank in the eyes of others, of whom there now were few.
(I believe at this point there's one thing I should say
Regarding the sex of the leech, by the way:
Although up to this point we've been calling him *he*,
It is equally true that each leech is a *she*.
For leeches, you know, possess parts of both types
In the folds of their annuli, which are their stripes.

Yet despite this, the leech, in its mud bed embedded,
Won't do well if to only itself it is wedded.
If its species is destined to stay in the game
It must find itself mirrored
in those of the same, as well as the opposite, sex.
For clearly it's proven, when leeches are mated,
that sexes aren't opposite, just inversely placated.)

But that night in his mud bed, as the leech lay
digesting the various events of the day,
Each creature grumbled in his belly
In whatever voice it knew
and each one told the leech its *story*,
Which was now *his-story*, too.

"I'll hear your dreary tales if you must tell them," yawned the leech,
"But do omit the parts which suck, is all I would beseech.
And I hope you'll be so kind as not to curse me for your fate...
You'd've all had to go some time, I only helped firm up the date."

But the fish rebuked his theory that they'd someday have grown limbs,
they'd booked the next few hundred million years to finish up their swims.
And though the swallows flirted with the earth, they'd no intention of embrace,
Since to swallows such a union would be death in any case.
And the willows only wept because it suited them to do so,
Their limbs drooped not from sorrow, but because they simply grew so.

As for those who paddled on the water when not waddling on the land,
No screw loose in their bird brains made them loath to take a stand
Upon one firmament over to the other. They swung both ways
because they had the proper appendages to do it —
Given chance to try both sea and sky
Shouldn't one at least review it?

"But I suck," wailed the leech, "So what else can I do?
And sucking can scarcely be said to exist
In the same way that paddling does for a duck.
For a duck can fly south when long winters persist,
But if one is a leech, one needs something to suck.

If a willow needs no reason to weep,
What cruel design makes me so needy?
If a swallow loves but does not take,
What divine mistake makes me so greedy?

The rump of a horse takes nothing from me
How came I, then, to so miserable a course?
By what unkind Divine or else Darwinian decree
Am worse than a scourge on the arse of a horse?"

The leech buried himself in the cool dark mud
Then covered his ears, did the leech.
He stood like a man on the bridge of his fears
and split the night air with a *screech*...

"When I think of the life I've sucked away it makes my belly ache,
And I long to reverse the natural course which I've been forced to take.
The memory of willows makes but mournful company
When, aside from the mud at the bottom of this pond,
There is no one left but *ME*."

The story ends there. *Happy Birthday Agnes* is garishly scripted in purple felt underneath, along with a small depressing drawing of a party hat and some confetti. This is what he left me on my birthday when he left for good, along with this disclaimer:

Dear Agnes,
Here I meant to write you a funny story about a very greedy creature, hoping to end with a moral about not eating too much birthday cake, and what I end up with is a somewhat gloomy story about a very lonely creature. I fear I have written myself into a corner, here, because the creature clearly isn't you. There's only a few other people whom this leech could be, and one of them, certainly, must be me.

When I was a youngster, I closed my hands around the bars of the iron fence which divided our small yard from the street, where other boys played and skinned their knees and did things which they'd never tell their fathers. I only watched them. My father was proud and forbade me the company of rougher boys who'd steer me from the path God had laid for me. I tried to accept this as true, that I was superior to other boys, in ways which were otherwise invisible, and that they would someday turn to me for help, those who had shunned me. But I'd have still given my eye-teeth to be out there running and shouting and skinning my knees, right along with them.

What I'm trying to say, my dear girl, is there really is no point in my continuing to live here with you all. I take up more space and groceries than I'm able to replace, and your mother doesn't feel about me the way she used to. I have all the proof of that I need and then some. I'd be better off seeing if I can't make my fortune some other way, without taking from your mother who's just trying to build a home for you and Gavin. I don't see a place for myself in that picture at the present time. Maybe someday your mother can explain this to you, but right now I'm lonelier there with you than I would be without you.

I wish it didn't have to be on your birthday, little soul, it would have made me happier to stay and celebrate with you. I'm hoping my poem has at least a few funny bits, even if the ending is a bit of a disappointment. Maybe it's a sad Happy Birthday, this year, but the wish to you is still the happiest one possible. I hope you'll understand this someday.

Well, I'm rattling on. Just to say I'll be dropping by the house in a week or so to pick up some of my things, we can talk about it then if you like, just say the word. Maybe you could suggest another animal whose luck turns out a little better than the leech's. Let me know, if you want to change the story, and I'll write you a better poem.
Much love, Dad

P.S. The doughnut is for you. It's an old-fashioned sour cream glazed, if anyone asks. They're the best ones. I could not find any candles.

45

Pin cushion

Today I begin the reluctant task of packing things in boxes for Great Aunt Hilda's White Elephant Sale. Despite my heart-felt protests, she absolutely will not be dissuaded from conducting it. She wants to make some extra money to buy some presents for her great-grand-niece. She's been looking at car seats in the Sears catalogue.

"But Great Aunt Hilda," I say, "I don't even have a car."

"Well, I certainly can't buy you a whole *car*," she says, "but the baby seat might be a step in the right direction. This one here has detachable wheels. Pretty soon Rose will be too big to carry around in that sac."

Almost nothing in my Great Aunt Hilda's house has been thrown away in almost two hundred years, most of it hasn't even moved in over a century. Suddenly she doesn't want the house to suffocate, she tells me, after all the life that's gone on inside it. She's already borrowed two long pine tables with folding green legs, from the Anglican church. She even had me set them up outside on the lawn, to estimate how many items could be liquidated upon them. Through the small window of the room with the slanted ceiling, I can see the two tables, leggy and unwelcome like giant mantises on the lawn. I return to packing the things in boxes, one by one.

The porcelain chamber pot, with purple clusters of plums swelling into side handles. When I was little, I'd always been grateful for that pot. It rescued me from having to descend the creaking wooden stairs in the middle of the night, across the chilly linoleum to the newly installed bathroom, which never ceased to feel like going outdoors. It was always freezing in there. The skeletal hands of the crabapple tree scraped at the window, and a hundred mummified flies were scattered moon luminous on the sill.

Instead of all of this, I only had to creep from the bed and crouch down on the floor. Then reach into the dark beneath the old iron bed, and feel around until my hand touched the chamber pot. Most times it would, although once or twice it had been a human face. Those times the whole house was awakened by hysterics, while my little brother Gavin was coaxed from beneath the bed and sent back to his cot at the foot of my mother's bed in the next room. I'd climb back trembling beneath the covers, having completely forgotten to pee, now worrying that if there'd been *one* body hiding under the bed, then possibly there could be *two* or *three*, and who *were* those people, exactly.

I pack the chamber pot in the bottom of the box.

An old alarm clock, in the shape of a horseshoe. The face of the clock is set inside the crescent of the shoe, with the horns pointing downward, which Great Aunt Hilda says defeats the purpose of a lucky horseshoe, which was why she never used the clock. The horseshoe hanging above the door in the hog shed had its horns pointing upward, so that luck would not run out like time, but be gathered up like rainwater. Or so that luck would not run out like rainwater, but be gathered up like time. A body positions itself, precariously, on a beam between past and present. It tries to remember how to breathe, how to balance. Guided by some vague recollection of what it feels like to fall, it does not fall.

I set the clock at the bottom of the box, *clink* inside the chamber pot.

A rectangular wooden box from China, with an inlaid design of a red pagoda on a hill. The Chinese box slides open sideways like a box of lozenges, and is magic. If you stick a penny in the round interior compartment, then close the box and tap it in a certain way, the penny will disappear, evidently, but I've never been able to work the thing. Shaking it now, I can hear a coin trapped inside it somewhere, but still can't make it reappear.

I stash the Chinese box in the front pocket of my red kangaroo jacket, after taking out the bunch of crumpled papers I've been carrying around for months. Most of them are bus transfers and dried Kleenexes, flyers I'd accepted for gigs I'd never go to, grocery receipts and wrappers from Atomic Fire Balls. One scrap of paper has bits of conversation scribbled on it, in two different handwritings, mine and

Buffalo man's. I've been compulsively transferring this scrap from pocket to pocket for months.

Why don't you just tell her? he'd written on the scrap.

Because, I'd written back.

??? was the next line.

She doesn't even know who you are, I wrote back. *She'd freak.* Below this last line, I had doodled a hieroglyph of my mother freaking. Her eyes were like cartoon breasts, simple circles with dots in the middle of them, while her hair was three spirals standing up on her head. I'd also given her about two dozen sharp teeth to grind together. *Gnash, gnash* was written on either side of her jaws.

"Agnes?"

I crumple up the paper like a dried corsage. I hadn't even heard Great Aunt Hilda padding up the stairs, shuffling across the smooth old floor in knitted slippers.

"You nearly gave me a heart attack," I mutter to Great Aunt Hilda.

"It was taking you a donkey's age up here," she says. "I figured you'd fallen asleep."

Just then the yellow gingham curtains billow at the window, and briefly we can see Uncle Vernie's orange tractor pulling up onto the lawn. Uncle Vernie is yelling something we can't hear over the tractor.

"*Mercy*! What a racket," says Great Aunt Hilda, pushing away the sound. "Heaven forbid anyone fails to notice your Uncle Vernie, when he pleases to come home."

"I heard him crashing around downstairs earlier, hammering pipes or something," I say. "I thought he'd been here all day."

Great Aunt Hilda shuffles out of the room evasively, and I follow.

"Well, he *was* here, earlier on," she says vaguely. "He had to go downtown to see about an appliance truck or other...."

The descent of the stairs is painfully slow, Great Aunt Hilda having insisted on going first. I watch the top of her silvery head bob slowly down the stairs, her hand clasping the wooden banister.

"There *is* something I've been meaning to mention," she sighs, but doesn't say what it is.

When we reach the bottom of the stairs, I see the thing. A tiny spasm constricts in my throat. There in the middle of the room is a large object draped in a canvas tarpaulin. Lying close to the mammoth shape is an old-fashioned hair dryer, its segmented hose and wrinkled cap completing the illusion. For the span of three pulses I see it with absolute clarity, the elephant in the room. You just go back to the oldest place you know and there it is.

I turn toward the bare corner where the piano had stood, and can see four round hollows where its feet had borne its weight since the beginning of time. The ornaments and pictures which had always decorated its back are now arranged in baking pans on the floor, like organs. Conspicuously absent is the old world globe which Great Aunt Hilda sold to pay for my ticket up here.

In the next instant, Uncle Vernie in gumboots and overalls charges into the kitchen and braces his bullish shoulder against the hind-end of the elephant. He gives her a shove. The elephant sighs a low soft chord.

"She's not rolling very good, her wheels are busted," Uncle Vernie announces. "We're going to need a coupla other guys to move 'er out. I went over to ask at Boucher's there but a few of the boys were over and we got to talking and having a beer. They said they could come and help out tomorrow, if you still needed it."

Having said this, Uncle Vernie stands awkwardly for a moment, as though waiting to be dismissed. Then he turns and marches back out the door in his gumboots, remounts his tractor, and thunders away again.

"I don't suppose we'll hear from him anytime soon," sighs Great Aunt Hilda, turning and heading for her chair.

"D'you want to tell me what you're doing selling the *piano*?" I ask.

That evening Uncle Vernie does not come home at all. Great Aunt Hilda grumbles about having to postpone her White Elephant Sale another day, and decides to wash her hair. She has me help her put her hair up in green prickly curlers. Then she retrieves the old hair dryer from the items for sale. She now fumbles with the cable of it, trying to reach the socket behind her chair.

"You're not going to help me?" she says, exasperated.

"I see you've changed your mind about selling the hair dryer, but not the piano," I say. "In years to come, may you be remembered for how dry your hair was."

"Wretched girl!" sputters Great Aunt Hilda. "If that's the sort of jaw you give your mother it's no wonder she's at wit's end with you, Agnes. You'd try the patience of a saint, you would, and heaven knows your mother is no saint."

In fact, I seldom spoke that way to my mother, all it would likely get me is more painful and possibly unnecessary dental work. But Great Aunt Hilda was an artist, in my eyes, she was the only artist in my family that I knew of. If there was *anyone* who might understand the silent shape at the centre of things, it would have to be my Great Aunt Hilda. She had been here the longest, an elephant's age, and like an elephant she would carry old stories in her bones. She would feel them, the way she could feel a drought coming or a storm brewing, in her bones.

Great Aunt Hilda now settles stiffly into her chair and pulls the lumpy dryer cap over her curlers. Despite fiddling with it for some time she has not succeeded in plugging in the cord, so she simply sits in disconnected silence with the cap on her head like a mushroom. I go over and crouch at her footrest, as I used to do when I was little. Now Great Aunt Hilda closes her eyes, and begins to murmur a familiar hymn to herself, her favourite hymn. *When other helpers fail, and comforts flee, Oh Lord, who faileth not, Abide with me....*

"I'm sorry for being so rude to you," I say. "Actually, I'd like to talk to you about a couple of things. You must be the only one who knows certain things."

Great Aunt Hilda stops murmuring and appears to be patiently waiting for me to continue, her eyes closed like a clairvoyant. Then I hear the gravelly rumble in her throat. She has fallen quite asleep. I carefully detach the flexible tube from the hair dryer and whisper softly into it, *Great Aunt Hilda*....

She wakes up instantly.

"*Wha... who?* Well, what *is* it, for pity's sake?" she stammers, reaching for her glasses. "Between you and that brother of yours, you're enough to wake the dead."

"My brother is off in Turkey somewhere," I say. Great Aunt Hilda sits blinking at me for a moment. She rubs her eyelids and puts her glasses back on the side table.

"Oh, bless me, Agnes, it's only you," she says, settling back. "For a moment, I thought you were Berenice, dear. I took you for your mother."

"My mother doesn't *have* a brother," I say, cautiously. As soon as I say it, I know it's not quite true.

Great Aunt Hilda shakes her head then strikes the arm of her chair.

"Oh, my dear, she does," she says. "Your Uncle Vernie, truthfully, is not my son, and he's not Arthur's. If you want to know about Vernie, you go ask your own mother about it."

Then she slumps back in her chair. The phantoms of several people seem to leave her body now, and Great Aunt Hilda is just herself, a woman in her late eighties, a country girl, a farmer's wife. This was more than enough for one day.

But as soon as the sun slides like syrup over the hayfield, the parlour begins to glow, and I watch Great Aunt Hilda's face as though she and I are cowgirls sitting around a campfire, fading into silhouette, casting our shadows on the walls like ambered damsel flies. Story carriers.

46

ANIMAL HUSBANDRY

Dear Agnes, my water-bug, my jellyfish, my sea peach,

Wow. In truth I'm no more certain than I ever was where you and I are supposed to go with this, but I understand more about choices than I did before. I feel like a father saying that, and now I am one. Would you look at that.

I also figure that in order to draw any wisdom at all from an experience, it's necessary to sit with it for a while. Some people take naps after dinner. Some people garden, or set pies out on the porch to cool so they don't burn their mouths. You have to let things sit for a while, you have catch your breath. Passions get triggered all the time and you can't chase after all of them. A man can run after a passion for years, until he's so hot and bothered that even if he catches up with his object of desire, his words wind up coming out in a desperate scramble. Then there's the constant fear that the desired object will run off again. When love is a chase it doesn't feel like a choice.

I oscillated back and forth every day, Agnes, over whether I never wanted to see you again, or wanted to see you every day of my life. I can't believe I'm saying so but it's true. When you were here I could see no end to wanting you, sometimes, but other times I thought I better find a way out as quickly and painlessly as possible. Bouncing back and forth like that was terrible.

So that's what I mean about sitting with things being a matter of choice. You can wait forever for the right answer to show up, but eventually you just have to say Yes or No, or it's all pisswater. Neither of us was exactly in the position to admit to anything long term, so everything we did felt like either a Stop or a Go, or a slap in the face. As though we couldn't just be the whole street, with both kinds of signs. Stops and goes and pies and naps after dinner and passion, and now a baby, too. How could we run out of things to do?

Probably been in love a dozen times but never was ready to do that, sit with it. With Agatha I was a dog and I know it, she could scarcely keep me tied in the yard more than a month at a time. I kept thinking about how moving targets are so much harder to hit, and I didn't feel like getting hit anymore.

But I've been thinking of what you said about always knowing where the nearest exits are. Once you figure out where they are, Agnes, do you need to keep checking? Mark them with a red X if it makes you feel better, then forget about them, or you're gonna look shifty and paranoid, always looking for the escape hatch. Don't know if I'm describing you or me.

I do understand that the reason a person might keep checking for the door is so she can feel safe where she's at. The actual feeling of safety, though, seems about the opposite of that. Feeling safe is the opposite of sending all your focus into exile every time you see a red exit sign. Remember it's a taxidermist saying this, but lately I've been thinking that safety is more about being comfortable to sit completely still, where you are. On your butt on a seat in the dark, not only watching the film but being the film, and the seats, and the popcorn, and the salt on your fingers.

Love to see you soon, see you to love you soon, it's pretty much settled.

Noah, your Buffalo guy

P.S. I got your letter, obviously, and haven't asked any questions about this mysterious rendez-vous, you ridiculous woman. I have a ticket to Bridal Veil Falls on the date you said, and I'll try to find someone to babysit Mae West, okay? It wasn't easy to follow your instructions to not ask anything about Rose, but on the other hand what could I possibly ask? I'm terrified out of my mind and more excited than I've ever been about meeting a stranger. That's both Rose and you too, stranger.

47

Bridal Veil Falls

I am sitting on the Astroturf steps of Cabin 3 at the Thunderbird Motel when the red Gremlin growls over the gravel and comes to a stop out front. My heart leaps up and sinks at once, he has brought Mae West with him after all. I watch from the steps as he persuades her to stay in the car. She is wearing my salmon-coloured toque and does not fight him, she seems quiet. When he turns to walk toward me, a watery figure in parking lot heat, I pull your red visor with the lady bugs over your eyes, and adjust the Guatemalan sling at my shoulder.

His face is a surface of stone and black moss, unshaven for weeks. I am unable to see his eyes yet, though I seek them beneath his oil-puddle sunglasses. I try to look past my own face reflected twice but still I don't see them. Zooming out to his body instead, perhaps as he does the same to mine, I see a blue denim animal with copper rivets and double stitching along every limb, the rubbing places where the blue cloth has faded to clouds. His oversized head is still a cliff to tumble from, the dark cleave of his forehead. I look for parts of him which aren't visible, the small of his back, the back of his neck where two muscular cords turn his head this way or that like reins.

For a long time we have nothing much to say to one another, only monosyllabic words like *Wow* and *Well* and *Rose*. You don't cry when he holds you, you sniffle a bit and look into his face with stern interest turning to amusement. When he notices the ear with your shrimp curled inside, he only looks at me once then back at you. He doesn't try to tell you that he's your daddy. He only tells you in soft tones that you are miraculous.

"She looks just like you, Agnes."

"Oh don't say it, please." I am shy to receive what feels like the deepest compliment I have ever received, and surprised it feels that way.

"I think she's going to have your nose," I say.

"Poor kid. She won't have trouble sniffing out who her friends are, anyway."

You fall asleep amid clean motel laundry, between the crisp down pillows of the double bed. Your father goes out to the Gremlin to check on Mae, and comes back hand-in-hand with the chimp shambling along beside him. I position my body between you and Mae instinctively, and keep my eye on her as she finds a spot under the TV table and shyly looks around the room. That salmon-coloured toque, I had wondered where it got to. Now she looks just like me if I were a chimpanzee.

But I am firstly your mother. We need each other, and there's no way the four of us are going to happily fit into that crappy car and drive off into the sunset. I have to wonder where his head is at, and what part of my own plan I had smudged a bit, not even admitting to myself what I had come here to do. Did I leave a trail of breadcrumbs behind? Would local authorities close in on me like in a courtroom drama, and take you away from me? They'll say, *What was she thinking? Not only running away with a much older man, but also a volatile chimpanzee? And she's got a baby? You've got to be kidding me. How could she think it's okay to keep running away instead of creating some kind of stability?*

The imp of the perverse still present in me. I sense that things could go from weird to worse unless I pay careful attention to something I already know by heart, chapter and verse. I sense that now, for the first time, my life can go on unrehearsed.

"There's some things I need to give to you for safe-keeping," I say, "but you have to promise not to open the box, okay? You need to take Rose out for lunch on her eleventh birthday, somewhere in Chinatown, and give her this box. It's mostly letters and stuff I've written down for her. Promise?"

"That's a hell of a lot of letters. Why don't you give them to her yourself?"

"Because I want her *father* to give them to her," I say. "You of *all* people should understand the significance."

"Okay, then, but why give them to me *now*? Won't there be plenty of time in the next eleven years to pass them along? Unless it's a question of not wanting her to have much to *do* with me for the next eleven years...."

"I want to make sure she *does* have something to do with you."

"Well, crap, thanks for *that*, because it was kind of the impression I got from your letter... didn't you read what I wrote back to you? I thought I was coming up here because you wanted to make another go of things. And I, for the first time in my life, am ready to step up to the plate. But you're not acting like this is a happy reunion. You'd tell me if there was any information you're deliberately omitting, wouldn't you?"

"I'm not seeing someone *else*, if that's what you mean."

"*This* is just fucking *not* what I expected! What it looks like to *me*, is like you've already *made* your decision that our future contact is going to be pretty *remote*."

"If that's true, then I'm not the *only* one making that decision. You're making it, too. I'm calling your bluff, here, and I know what I'm talking about."

"Why is this so hard for you to *understand?* I'm *telling* you that the reason I drove all the way up here, is because I want to be with you."

"Well, then what the heck were you *thinking*, bringing Mae West with you? Didn't it occur to you there might be anything *incongruent* in that travel arrangement? It should be obvious, that Rose and I will have to *leave* Bridal Veil Falls the same way we came, by bus, because you couldn't foresee that Mae West and Rose in the Gremlin at the same time is completely asinine."

"Mae in the front seat with me, you and Rose in the back."

"No."

"I'm being *set up*! What *was* this, some kind of nasty *test* you devised? Are you trying to corner me into dumping you instead of hearing me say that I want to *be* with you? What, so you can hit me up for child support next month?"

"Sh-hh!" I whisper, waving my hand toward the bathroom door. "We should take this discussion into the loo unless we want to wake up our daughter."

"What about *Mae*?" asks Buffalo man.

"You tell *me*!" I say.

"I'm taking her out to the car."

"Good idea. Are you coming right back?"

"Yeah, yeah. I'll be right back."

I check to see that you are sleeping peacefully, then sneak down the green Astroturf steps of Cabin 3 and quickly round the back, to the gravelled area behind the cabins. I tiptoe over the gravel, like small teeth beneath my feet, then halfway across the highway to stand on the cool painted lines like yellow skis. Before me are the black serrated trees, and the mountains, moony-blue and eternal. I finish crossing the road and leave it up to riddles why I did it.

I climb an embankment to find the falls, a constant bolt of lightning travelling in slow motion. Travelling quick and flickering, the bounce of water on slippery rocks, cutting them clean with its silver sheen. It falls and pools and froths, but when I try to see it all at once, it altogether seems to stop. I hold my breath and jump into the water.

A shape, a shaft, a cord of fibre optic cables, light caught and carried like minnows through rushing current. The water sprays forth in little fans, where potential stony footholds are, if a person were looking for footholds in a waterfall. Who have been my teachers? "So you think you are changed, do you?" *say my father's eyes through the bubbling surface.* "Take another look...."

Rose. Sometimes I think the most powerful bull pulling my life has been the need for a single conversation. The conversation which makes things right, the one which gets more moth-eaten and full of awkward silences the longer it is postponed.

But at some point emphasis has to switch from what has been lost to what is still there. Things suddenly take on a new quality of light, and are known at once to be valuable, because they are not lost, because they are still there.

Today I remembered what it felt like not to love you, or rather I remembered that this had never, ever been the case. You will read the shadow of ambivalence in my early letters, Rose, and I will have trouble explaining it. But the decision to tell a story is an iteration of a formula set in motion long ago. The pivotal iteration, when the pattern must break or evolve. There is a leap of faith, and there is a tunnel with a light at the end of it. This is the transport of imagination. A generator within calls for light, and eventually there it is.

There had been a long highway tunnel outside of Soapspit Bluff, my mother always drove through it when she took us away to Great Aunt Hilda's for a while. The tunnel was tarry and dark along the walls, but striped with episodic yellow lights like the clicky legs of centipedes. Gavin and I used to try to hold our breath for the entire length of the tunnel, gulping our last mouthfuls of air just before the trees and the sky disappeared and we were *inside*. The tunnel sped by like an amusement park ride, strobe-lighting our puffed faces as we tried not to laugh. You can spend a lot of oxygen trying not to laugh.

By the time we reached the end of the tunnel we'd be blue, banging the vinyl seats with our fists, stomping our feet for air. Then suddenly light would appear again from above and pick the car straight up into the sky, and we would let go of our breath, gasping and laughing and turning from blue to red. It had always seemed strange to me, that even after holding your breath for a long long time, the first thing you do when you let go is exhale. Even before you start pulling oxygen back into your lungs, you spend the last bit of what you swore you had none of left.

"This your suicide note?" Noah flags some papers at me when I come back inside number 3 at the Thunderbird. I am drenched from head-to-toe, but quite alive.

"It's obviously not my suicide note," I say. "Why, were you reading it? I asked you not to!"

Noah tears the blotchy purple coverlet from the bed, and wraps it around my shoulders. Then he goes back and sits down on the bed. He laces his fingers on his lap. When he inhales it takes a long time, yet when he exhales he does so very quickly. Drops of water from my hair fall in dark stains on the flat blue carpet.

"Please tell me you didn't drag me out here to bear witness to some adolescent phony suicide attempt. You better have some explanation, young lady, because I thought I knew you better than this."

"Lookit, Noah, do I look dead to you? I haven't killed myself, nor do I have any *intention* of killing myself."

"Oh, no?" says Noah. "Then what's this hysterical *phone call* forwarded to Cabin 3, this lady practically *yelling* at me as though I were a bloody *murderer*..."

"My mother?"

"Who do you think?"

"Her. Except the hysterical part doesn't sound like her. She'd normally never yell at someone she's never met, especially... since she'd know that you're Rose's father."

"Let's assume she'd know that."

"Stop it! I can't believe you thought I was going to kill myself."

"Well, frankly my dear, the more your charming mother *screeched* at me, in salty language, may I add, the more it made sense that you *both* could be unstable. Why else would you have lured me all the way up here, like it's some kind of hoop I have to jump through, knowing full well I'd never be able to find a babysitter for Mae, because I don't have any friends anymore, except you and Mae, and *you* appear to hate me."

"Why don't you read the letter, then?" I say. "Read it, then take Mae West and go home."

"Really, though, I probably should just go home."

"You probably should."

Dear Rose,
Here is another piece of advice from an irresponsible woman, who is responsible for you. If a voice in your head tells you something, listen to it. Listen to it, whether the voice is in your head or caught in your throat or

muttering to itself in the visceral labyrinth. If what the voice says involves personal injury, take it as a metaphor.

Sometimes it is necessary for a person to go through a sort of death, and your body will tell you when this is happening. But it is taking things too literally if you actually throw yourself from a bridge. If the image of the bridge keeps coming up, more likely you are meant to cross one. You might go to the bridge, and drop a stone from it, instead, or a box of letters, or any other weight equal to the part of you which desires to cast itself off. If you can't stop thinking about knives, there's probably a connection you need to cut through, some mental carpentry to do, or a call to create sculpture. If a red muddy bank in your abdomen ever says, "I cannot bear a child right now, I could not bear it," then don't erase this message either, but take the time to trace the call to source. Fearing something can often invite it into your life, because holding something at bay actually means holding it pretty close.

Perhaps it is necessary to undergo a kind of metaphorical death every few years, some magical number of years. Perhaps you choose the number, or perhaps it is decided by some larger pattern. The regeneration of cells every seven years. The watery pull of stars and planets. The distillment of memory, in kegs in the cellar, ready for consumption only when bubbles minnow toward the surface. Some force decides, those points in a life where many strands converge at once. Those points when the only solution is to cut through the pattern and break it, though it cost nothing less than everything to do it.

The people who actually kill themselves have got it wrong, taking too literally what was supposed to be an opportunity for change. It would not be difficult for certain types of intelligence to make this mistake, since the metaphor is a very deep one, almost indistinguishable from the change it represents. Not literally to die, but to be prepared for transitions which no current knowledge can predict. The death of the little self, the self who does not know but fears.

But here's why actually killing yourself makes no sense, in practical terms. If voices or forces seem to be urging a person to let go of life, and one decides to trust these voices and forces as instructive, then it works cross-purpose to cancel out the possibility of being instructed by them. Voices or forces who had any authority at all, would not address a personal message to an agent who could make no further constructive use of the message. The trick is to go to the darkest place, but to come back and tell of it in a different tongue, and a voice you have never heard before.

And so a body defenestrates itself from the turret of current engagement, and into a dimension whose parameters are not yet defined. This is the choice to change one's life. Falling becomes no different from flying.

Love, Agnes, your Mum

Noah holds the back of his hand to his mouth as he reads, as though he were grazing on it, digesting the letter slowly, eyes damp. Then he

folds it up again, shyly, as though it were a lady's undergarment.

"And I'm part of the old pattern you have to break, is that it? In a nutshell?"

"I wouldn't put it like that. But, look, I'm not even sure what we have in common, we were substitutes for other things the whole time. Rose is the first real connection we ever made."

"You think that?"

"I'm sorry."

"I couldn't agree with you more."

Noah hesitates a moment as he stoops to pick up his jean jacket from the bed, because the position brings him face to face with his sleeping daughter, silver in the moonlight.

"I love her," he says, half under his breath, then walks over and kisses me on the forehead, lingering there. Then he opens the door of Cabin 3 and walks out leaving this box of letters behind. I hear the echo of his crunching footfall, then the slam of the Gremlin's door. The engine starts up and he drives away. I listen to the departing car until it becomes indistinguishable from the rush of the falls.

48

Crossing Guard

*One must at least pretend that Something anchors thought,
in order to think at all.* History is a chain-link of substitutions,
one centre for another centre. No matter how large
a circumference any thought attempts to draw,
and no matter how it names its centre,
the area of its scope will always have an inside
and an outside. In order to have Sense, there
must be Non-sense.

Such a person as the godless, the ceilingless
would be compelled to invent other things,
to compensate for the oppression of space.
But such a person would learn that anything
one could build is only free-floating,
like a flower whose petals are continually
pulled downward to act as stems,
whose stems are constantly drawn
upward again to act as petals.

— from a chapbook anthology of West Coast poetry, signed with the
initials L.U.

I see the children first, a row of them linked like charms on a bracelet by a strip of yellow nylon with hand-holds to hold on to. They are crossing the street at an adjacent crosswalk, when my mother's old green Torino stops at an intersection heading out of Bridal Veil Falls. We'll be back at Great Aunt Hilda's house before it gets dark, even making a stop at the Pink Mountain bus station to pick up my father's old typewriter.

It is then that I see him, a tallish baldish man with his back turned. He is holding up a stop sign, wearing a neon orange smock with a large X in silver reflective tape. X, for the unsolved quantity, the face I've never been able to place. I am certain, absolutely certain, it is him.

I know this man, although I can only see the back of him. He steps into a pre-existent shape and fits exactly. Except his shoulders seem more stooped than I remember, unless perhaps they are broader. There are always the visible physical changes which time brings but these are the gentlest of all deaths. As the light changes I crane my neck to see his face, but with a baby on my lap I can't look over my shoulder and anyway it doesn't matter just now. By the time I have considered saying something he is behind us, and we're not going to turn back now.

49

Horse mother

The family wishes to thank those who sent flowers and offered their sympathy in memory of Mrs. Hilda Pallace [neé Porter, widow of Arthur Pallace] who passed away peacefully in her home this Friday morning at the age of eighty-nine, with family present. Mrs. Pallace is survived by her nephew Vernie [Bernard] Porter and her niece Berenice Underhill [neé Porter]; also by grand-niece Agnes and infant great-grand niece Rose. The memorial service is to be held this Sunday at the Soapspit Bluff Anglican church; visitors will be received between two and five in the afternoon. The interment will take place this coming Tuesday in Soapspit Bluff.

"We should turn *here*," my mother says, gliding the Torino onto a smooth road of new blacktop, with green fields and Holstein cattle on either side. Yellow grasses in the ditch whizz by like static in the foreground, while cows pass slowly like grazing clouds. The ruminant scent of manure diffuses and softens the more pungent smell of the diaper bag, which is getting warmer no matter where I try to stash it.

My mother's sunglasses have no arms. Instead they have metallic clips like butterfly antennae, between two smoky lenses. She could attach them to her prescription glasses at the bridge of the nose, then flip them up or down like a visor. Just now she wears her visor down, and is singing that same hymn Great Aunt Hilda used to sing, *Abide with me, fast falls the eventide....*

Sheets of cool breeze fly in through the side windows and flutter the map on the seat beside her. I am sitting in the back with Rose, whose face is fidgeting with a sunbeam to avoid its sharp edge. I dig through my bag for her hat with ladybugs on it, which has a window of shiny ruby plastic stitched into the brim. It can be pulled down over Rose's eyes to tint her vision the colour of her name. She laughs and stares astonished at the changing colours of the world, and shakes her small fists.

"Hey, that looks like a fry stand," I say of the tidy white bungalow with two picnic tables and a trashcan out front, a quarter mile up the road. My mother continues to sing with her lips almost closed. *The darkness deepens, Lord with me abide....*

"Hey," I say again, resting my chin on the back of the front seat.

"Hay is for horses," she says. Then, "Did you want to stop for a *slush* or something?"

"I want to turf these smelly baby things at least," I say, "and a slush would be nice."

An impotent panic crosses Rose's face as the car swerves off the soft blacktop and onto the crackling gravel of the fry stand parking lot. She punches the air and begins to cry, then seems to think better of it and stops. Better not to cry wolf, in case there are worse things ahead, such as being cooed at by strangers or spoon-fed something strained and unfamiliar.

The air smells of heat and hay and exhausted frying oil, and *horses*. While I'm adjusting Rose and turfing the baby things, my mother gets out of the car and crosses immediately to the corral where the horses are. She's digging through her purse for something.

"How about you run inside and grab some packets of sugar for him, kitten?" she calls to me. "Thought I *had* some, but looks like I don't. I'll watch Rosie for you. Just bring her over here."

So I go inside the fry stand and order two cherry-lime slushes and some sugar packets. I have to request the packets, because the sugar on the tables is in bowls. Through the window I can see the sun glinting off the chestnut-brown, glossy as oil on his back. Chestnuts are exactly that colour. I remember peeling away the spiny green rind of horse chestnuts and finding the shiny seed inside, which was exactly the same colour as that horse.

When I come back with the sugar packets, my mother is already feeding a handful of clover to the chestnut-brown.

"He has terrible *teeth*, unfortunately," she says to me, "the clover's much better for him." Then to the horse, she says, "Someone's *already* been spoiling you, *haven't* they? Yes, I bet they *have*, you handsome beast."

"You two know each other?" I say, handing her the sugar.

"We're just getting *acquainted*, aren't we?" she says to the horse, scratching his whiskers and tucking the sugar packets in her purse.

"I'm *melting*!" she says finally, adjusting the broad brim of her black straw hat and heading toward the shade beside the fry stand. As its shadow falls over her, she becomes cool and still again. She makes a personal picnic blanket of a paper napkin and sits down on it, on the white wooden steps. I wonder whether my mother and her young groom from the riding stable ever stopped for cherry-lime slushes on hot afternoon drives through the country, and whether they ever went horseback riding together. I'd never even seen my mother on a horse.

Now I'm sitting in the sun on the grass with Rose on my lap, warming cherry-lime slush in my mouth before letting it fall back through the straw into Rose's mouth. I'd been thinking of the tongues of butterflies, their surprising length dipping into flower nectar. In the shade, my mother flips her visor up.

"I wouldn't think you'd want to *do* that, pet," she calls. "You never know what-all germs you might be passing on to little Rosie."

"But look, she's smiling," I say, as though only Rose would know for sure whether or not I'm passing her any bad germs. My mother smiles stiffly and lets that one go, looking past me toward the wooden fence with the two horses on the other side of it, a grey mare and the chestnut-brown. Instead, I follow the worried furrow of Rose's eyebrows to a nearby grasshopper, wound up tight as a top, ready to spring.

Probably I'd been such a lousy biology student because I never understood how anyone could really have much clue what a grasshopper was capable of seeing or comprehending. The same for baby humans. Maybe for Rose, it's most useful to assume that if something is *moving*, then it is alive, and if it *isn't* moving, it is asleep.

I lift my hand and slowly move it over the grasshopper until my fingers shadow its relative sky, just as skies were said to darken under swarms of them. The creature tenses itself to leap. I quickly let my hand fall and scoop the grasshopper into my palm. Its texture is scritchy like a whiskered muzzle, bucking against my hand with disproportionate force. I wait, then at last I open my fingers, and we look at it, my daughter and I.

The grasshopper sits very still for a moment, its hind legs thick like turkey drumsticks, its mouth parts muttering silently to themselves. Rose stares mesmerized. The mouth parts expel an acrid droplet of orange fluid onto my palm, then the grasshopper leaps away in a flurry of leafy wings, yellow and black, straight into the sun where no one's eyes could follow it.

Once back in my mother's car, we drive along in comfortable silence for several minutes, listening to a phone-in show about the best gifts listeners had ever received. Breakfast-in-bed with a diamond ring in the mimosa, nearly swallowed. Flying lessons. Fifty pounds of lunch meat. A monogrammed snow shovel. A new kidney.

"What *I* always wanted was a *pony*," my mother blurts out suddenly, her voice tremulous and peculiar. She pulls the car to the gravel shoulder and stops. "*Look* at them running around down there, without even a saddle on their backs. It always brings a lump to my throat when I see horses running in a field."

"Why don't you tell me some things about your mother, Mum?" I ask. I want to know whether she'll ever talk about Uncle Vernie being her brother, especially now that it was in the paper, or whether she still half-believed he was not. It seems to be possible for a person to rewrite her own history however she feels compelled to. It's like installing a new bathroom, you're still drawing from the same well but the way you access it has changed. Still, there has to be a reason why a person feels compelled to choose one version of the story over another, and often these reasons are uniquely complicated.

"Well, if you *must* know, kitten," says my mother, "all I can remember about your grandmother is that she was a thin pale beautiful woman who was nervous all the time, and that she was hardly ever *there* even when she was. Uncle Arthur and Aunt Hilda were there, and sometimes this sick woman who was my mother, who only dropped in at odd times for odd reasons."

My mother's voice is hurried but reasoned, her head nodding as she speaks.

"Most of the time my mother was kept in a sort of home. *Imagine*! In *that* day! The poor woman mustn't've had a friend in the world. All I knew was that she lived in this home which I wasn't allowed to go to. 'No, Berenice, Mummy doesn't *want* you to go to the home,' Aunt Hilda would tell me for the umpteenth time, meanwhile Judy Garland was telling me there was no place *like* it.

"I remember being very young, one time when my mother came to visit. She picked me up and put me in a room and closed the door. She kissed me on the forehead and *left*, and left me with something-or-other to play with. I think it was a ribbon and a button. Then there was a lot of *splashing* downstairs, in the kitchen. We used to bathe in tin tubs on the kitchen floor before the new bathroom was installed.

"And all I could hear was splashing and muffled sounds," my mother says, miming with her fingers the waves of sound going into her ears. "Well, I started to cry. I was frightened out of my wits. When Uncle Arthur finally came home and heard me wailing, it must have been a few minutes but it felt like *hours*. He must've come upstairs, must've heard me before he registered anything *else*, because I heard him bounding up the stairs to find me. Then he was at the door, and I ran right to him. But then he heard the splashing, it was really loud now, and he almost *dropped* me. He set me back down on the floor and ordered me to stay *put*. Then he bounded down the stairs again, and I waited for the count of ten. Then I followed him."

"How old were you?" I ask. I hadn't seen many pictures of my mother as a child, other than that old portrait.

"I don't know how *old* I was, kitten, it doesn't matter. What I *saw* was..."

My mother claps her hand over her mouth and holds it there. When she draws it away again, she waves her fingers like a whisk, as though sweeping away something. She keeps doing this as she speaks.

"What I *saw* was my mother, sitting in wet clothes on the floor, with her eyes staring at nothing, literally *nothing*, even though I was standing right there. She was gasping and her hair was all wet and tangled. And there was Uncle Arthur, leaning over the tin tub with his back to me. There was water everywhere, all over the floor.

"Uncle Arthur was helping Vernie, pressing him and thumping his back. I could hear him coughing like he had a terrible cold, sniffling and coughing on and on. I didn't completely understand what I was looking at. I knew it was something very bad, and that if my mother touched me I would scream."

My mother turns off the engine. The car is very quiet. I hear Rose stir sleepily in her new car seat. Our voices hadn't disturbed her a bit, but she doesn't like stopping suddenly so she starts to cry. I unfasten her and lift her onto my lap.

"They never let my mother out of the home again after that," my mother says. "I never even *saw* her again. Vernie was in the hospital for quite a while but in the end he was fine. He lived. He was never the same after that, he'd been underwater for quite some time, but then who *knows* what kind of person he'd otherwise have grown up to be? As it was, he was angry all the time. Picked on other kids and animals and whatever he could get his hands on. Your Aunt Hilda was the only person who could deal with him, so he ended up staying with her in the end, wearing Uncle Arthur's clothes when he grew to fit them. Aunt Hilda steeled up a bit. Uncle Arthur loved your Great Aunt Hilda to distraction, I knew that even as a very little girl. Aunt Hilda used to actually *giggle* and tell him to mind himself, when other folks were around, he was always pestering her."

My mother's face is almost trance-like now, and glowing, like Great Aunt Hilda's face that night in the amber sitting room. Like Rose's face glows when some caterpillar or soap bubble has her transfixed, her eyes widening like lanterns lighting up her whole face. *My theory is this, Rose.* That when human beings deeply learn something, it makes them bioluminescent. There's probably some neurological reason for this, or something vascular-related, I don't know. I just mention it because it appears to be true.

"There are *some* things I still could never tell a *soul*," my mother says. She looks about ten years old now, tilting her chin upward to gaze brightly through the windscreen at the sky, clasping hands on the steering wheel as though she were flying a kite up there.

"Am I allowed to ask?" I ask.

"No," she smiles, "but I can tell you, I suppose. I think my mother was the sort of woman I never wanted to *be*, not what you'd call a *good* woman. She went around with so many men I guess because she thought she was good at it, so she set it up as a *game* for herself." My mother laughs. "Some *game*! Imagine a game where you take all the tricks together, then your partner trumps your ace. You end up losing in the suit you thought you were strongest in. Anyway, I'm getting away from my story and I don't even *play* bridge yet, thank goodness.

"My mother apparently never liked Aunt Hilda very much, and neither was Hilda much for her sister. Uncle Arthur was kind and polite to her, of course, but a little wary too, on account of her *state*. Uncle Arthur regarded mental illness with the same gracious, blind eye he regarded all female trouble. He had no appreciation of hysteria, which is why he married your Aunt Hilda, who was never hysterical in her whole life. Not even when Arthur died so suddenly. She just clamped shut after that."

My mother sits back and lifts her gloved hand to her neck, where it remains for a moment, resting like a black lace rabbit between her collar bones. Usually this is the familiar sign that she doesn't wish to speak anymore, her fingers pressing the mute button at her throat, but here it seems to serve a different function. *Rewind*. Somewhere in the junction, my mother's train of thought derails and goes off in another direction. She follows its faraway course with her eyes until it disappears, then she speaks.

"When I was a little girl, there was a storybook my mumma gave me. Or *left* me, really. Aunt Hilda gave it to me just before telling me that my mother would probably not come back. It was a grade three reader. I was only going into grade two at the end of the summer. It *did* seem a frightening book to give a young child, quite frankly. I don't remember any of the stories except one of them, about a horse. A white horse, and these terrible bullfrogs. I can only remember the picture, it was a *beautiful* horse, pure white in mane and tail and everything. I remember the picture better than the story. It was running wildly through the forest, trying to escape some men with ropes I think. There were some men who were trying to *capture* it with ropes and bridle it.

"Anyway," my mother continues, "the *next* page was a picture of a swamp, with terrible croaking *bullfrogs*. The horse had been running so wildly she wasn't even looking where she was going, the little fool. She ran straight into the marsh and got *stuck* there."

My mother's hand flies away from her throat and flutters at her mouth again, stifling a strange laugh.

"I know it's not funny," she says. "I don't know why I'm laughing. I remember that picture as clear as if I had it in front of me. Legs thrashing about, and her neck twisted round like that, her big horse-eyes bulging."

"That's terrible," I say. I could tell it was terrible.

"It *was* terrible," my mother insisted. "And I haven't even told you about the *bullfrogs*. They were lined up like fat trolls, all along the marsh, with their glazed eyes, croaking, *Too late to leap. Too deep, too deep.* Doesn't that *sound* like a bullfrog, too? *Too late to leap. Too deep, too deep.*"

My mother starts rubbing an area at the centre of her sternum with her thumb. She continues to do this silently for a few minutes, until eventually more of the story comes.

"It's a bit peculiar that I remember *that* story and not any of the *other* ones, when I couldn't possibly have understood the significance of it, at the time. Though it seems to mean plenty now."

She chuckles softly and shakes her head, as though in disbelief.

"Anyway, I forgot to say it turns out all right, in the end. The white horse gets rescued, of that I'm quite sure. Some men come and pull her out with ropes." Her eyes freeze at this hitch in the storyline. "Now, you know, kitten, I can't even remember if the men with the ropes were trying to *capture* the horse, in the first place, or whether they were the ones who *rescued* her in the end. I honestly can't remember." The caboose in my mother's train of thought comes late, and by itself, towed by a piano cable thirty years long. "I didn't know how it would *be,*" she says quietly. "How *could* I know how it would be?"

50

Milk

Now it is long past dark but I can see the shapes of cows standing like huts on stilts, scattered over the calm of Great Aunt Hilda's hayfield. The cows all have one ear pierced, and wear red plastic eartags with numbers. From wandering black and white cows, I gather strength and slow curiosity. I slide down the muddy embankment between the road and the field and stand outside the fence, watching them, for a long time. The moon is a luminous hoof print, the place where night mares touch down before galloping elsewhere. There is such stillness here.

Eventually cow *23* approaches me. I have to bow quite low to reach her nose without touching the electrical fence. Her strong neck strains toward me but she bucks her head away, and will not let me touch her until she tastes me first. *Cow tongue.*

She does not use her teeth to pick up the hemispheres of apples I've brought but curls her long tongue around them, dragging them into her mouth that way. The apples are waxy and smooth, so her tongue can't slither around them as well as it can with clumps of grass, unless I feed her the apples by hand. She wraps her tongue around my fingers, then my whole hand. Her tongue is as rough as sand inside a wet bathing suit, then the grainy slither of cow spit. When she licks the sleeve of my green nylon shell it makes a sound like a sleeping bag. I catch the zipper of the jacket just in time before it touches the electric fence. I don't know what would have happened if it had, sometimes the fence is on and sometimes it's off. You can't tell what kind of shock you're in for unless you touch it.

By the time cow *23* lets me touch her forehead I'm a slimy mess of cow spit up to my elbow, but I warmly scratch her forehead and behind her ears, this big and gentle animal. Cow *23* has a crest on her forehead the shape of home plate, a white pentagon perfectly centered. *Home. Free.*

Metaphormosis. The process of seeking and finding those luminous objects and persons who offer themselves as keys, doors, or windows onto the expanding green. There are lighthouses, as tiny as pores, on the surface of the mundane. Cows in a field may carry keys to things like simple contentment and how to *see* the world for the first time again.

Now my mother stands at the window in Great Aunt Hilda's kitchen, sipping milk from a martini glass. Her pink nails tinkle like enamel cat bells at the rim, in time to something which makes her smile and nod. Such as an aeroplane departure, or a walking man who tips his hat, or the woman who raised her waving good-bye. The warm rusty light of the room turns to blue at the window sill, my mother is lit both cool and warm, like those fancy two-tone bars of soap. She sees something in a lazy glance, then quickly turns back to the something, pointing at it gently with her pinkie, *Agnes, come look!*

A shadow clings to the outer window, as large as a hand pressed there. When I come closer I see it, the largest moth I have ever seen in my life. Its markings resemble an Appaloosa pony, with patchy spots of black, white, and grey on the wings and thick furry legs. The eyes are beads of tar, and the spiral tongue like the inner workings of a pocket-watch.

"Do you know what it is?" I ask my mother.

Mm-hm, she nods. "I used to see them around here all the time, when I was a little girl." She draws her blue bathrobe closer around her body. "It's a night moth... it's called a *False Hemlock* moth, I think."

"I'm not sure that *is* a False Hemlock, Mum, they're more *stripey* than spotty..."

"Oh, Agnes, dear, the *point* is I used to be *terrified* of them," she continues. "Their cocoons were the size of cuttlefish bones. That's what I used to think they *were,* those things in budgie cages, when I was a little girl. I thought they were night moth cocoons. Isn't *that* horrible? I thought that if the budgie didn't manage to chew through the cocoon and *destroy* it before it hatched, then one of these *giant moths* would come out and eat the budgie, before anyone was even awake. That's what I thought. There was no doubt in my mind who would win, either. The night moth would win. If it survived, I mean. Imagine. What a silly thing to think."

My mother stops and sips milk from her martini glass. The glass has a decoratively crooked stem, like a bonsai tree. My mother's mouth still makes a liquor grimace unconsciously when she swallows, no matter what it is she's drinking. She touches her pink frosted fingertips to her throat as though to cool the place.

"Looking at it *now*, I can't really understand what I was so *nervous* about," my mother says. "Look at this big ol' moth, for petesakes. It's just as leggy and furry as I remember, but *this* one looks kind of sweet. Looks a bit like a little colt, like a pony, rather. Don't you think so? The expression in her eyes, and the fur around the hooves?"

With great thanks to the many people who encouraged and supported this book in its various forms: Robert Allen, Patrick Crean, Katja Pantzar, Jack 'Beets' Biswell, Francesca LoDico, Ian Ferrier, Patrick McDonagh, Michael Patterson, Richard Medrington, Mitch Albert, Anna Wilson, Geoffrey Agombar, Andy Brown.